Acclaim for
THE LAST WAYFINDER

"An atmospheric tale of love, sacrifice, and unbreakable bonds that will leave you guessing until the very end!"
  MELISSA POETT, author of *The Enemy's Daughter*

"*The Last Wayfinder* takes us on an unforgettable journey of discovering our true power and what we'd do for love. Infused with magic, danger, and sacrifice, you'll find yourselves turning pages and longing for more!"
  NOVA McBEE, award-winning author of the Calculated Series

"An immersive and rich world that combines fantasy, folklore, and historical Japan, tickling any fantasy-lovers imagination!"
  JUDY LIU, award-winning author of *The Vending Portal*

"With poignant beauty and heart wrenching scenes, *The Last Wayfinder* takes readers on a journey of discovering how the monsters we fight inside of us do not have to be the ones we become."
  CAITLIN MILLER, award-winning author of *The Memories We Painted*

THE
LAST
WAYFINDER

THE LAST WAYFINDER

ELLEN McGINTY

The Last Wayfinder
Copyright © 2024 by Ellen McGinty
Published by Ellen McGinty

All rights reserved. No part of this publication may be reproduced, digitally, stored, or transmitted in any form without written permission from the publisher, except as permitted by U.S. copyright law.

This is a work of fiction. Names, characters, and incidents are products of the author's imagination or are used fictitiously. Any similarity to actual people, living or dead, organizations, business establishments, and/or events is purely coincidental.

NO AI TRAINING: Without any limitation on the author's exclusive copyright rights, any use of this publication to train generative artificial intelligence is expressly prohibited.

ISBN: 979-8-9920301-2-9 (hardcover)
ISBN: 979-8-9920301-1-2 (paperback)

Cover design by Damonza
Case Laminate design by Sonia Wong
Typesetting by Jamie Foley, www.JamieFoley.com

To Kai,
Hope is always closer than stars

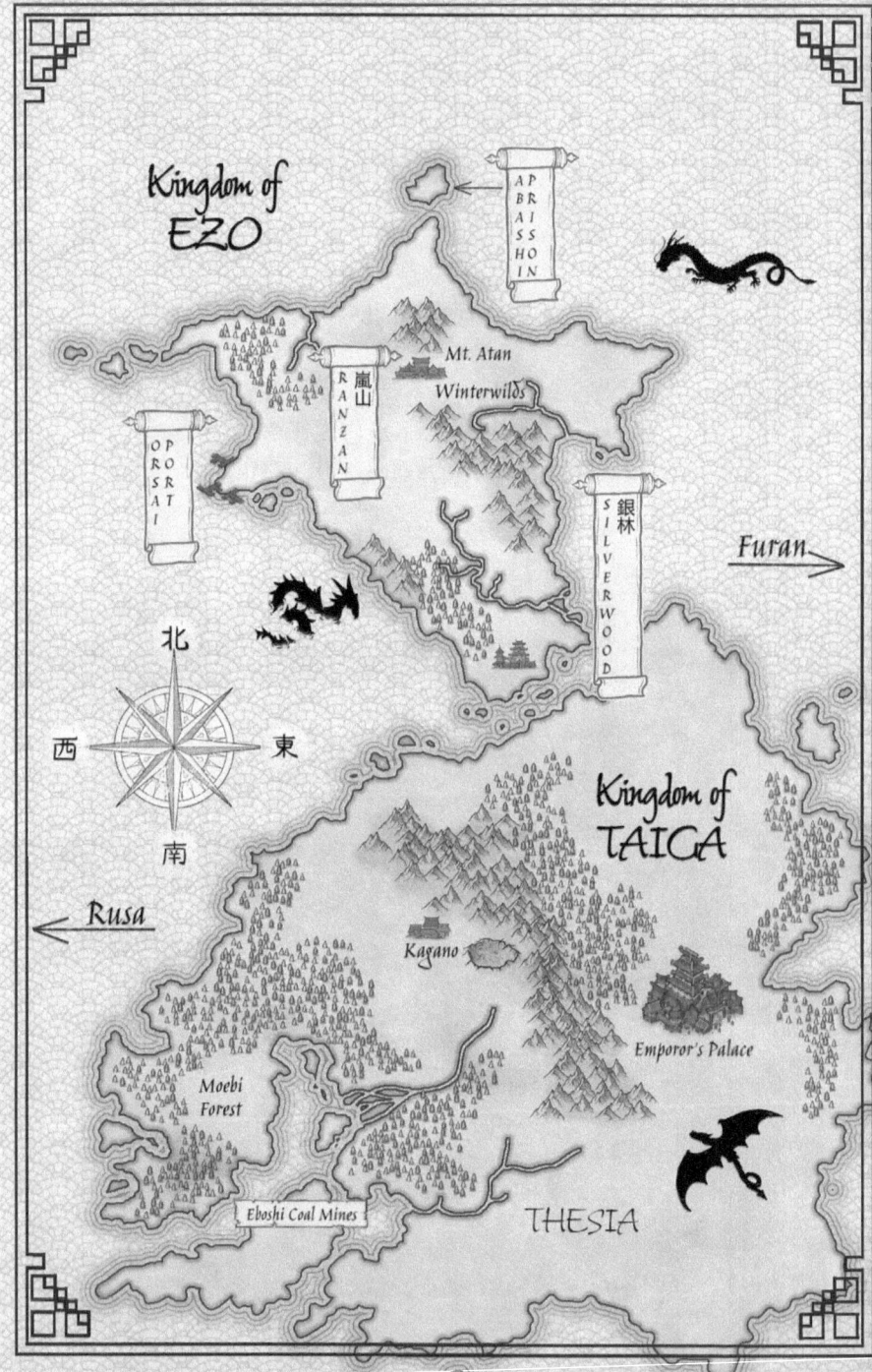

PROLOGUE

I WAS BORN BLUE IN THE SNOW.

My mother refused to give birth inside a cell. On a cold night blanketed with stars, she planned her escape into the ice-strewn forest outside the prison gates.

Be free! the stars whispered.

My mother hurried, the wind of the forbidding ocean at her back and the bite of white water at her heels. The prison beacon glared from the watchtower followed by frantic shouts. Hope was far off. But just because a thing is far off doesn't make it insignificant. Even the pinpricks of stars are large raging fires.

That's the only part of my story Mother will tell me. Storing secrets is her recipe for brewing hope—for keeping my sister and me alive.

I scurry down the icy prison corridor, hurrying to keep up with Mother's brisk steps. My bare feet tangle with a wooden broom, and I catch myself against one of the center posts in the hallway. Naven laughs from his cell, spittle falling from his tattooed lips. The laughter echoes in the cramped hall and my chest goes tight. Heat rises to my cheeks, but it doesn't warm—nothing does.

A few other prisoners chuckle, but Sasa bangs his fist against the wall commanding silence. I nod in thanks to the one-eyed pirate. He waves as if batting away my gratitude, but I don't miss the smile lifting his heavy beard. My eyes flit to the other prisoners in our wing, all serving life sentences—*like me.*

Ten years and I've never known the outside world.

Mother snags my hand and pulls me after her. Before we reach our cell, I count fourteen iron chambers, one hundred and thirty-seven dirty fingers. The calloused hands draped over iron bars taught me to count. Not a fancy way to grow up, but it's all I know.

Except from the stories.

Mother drops my hand, her eyes already on the guard leaving his heated booth at the end of the corridor to lock us in for the night.

We could escape them. But not the island.

The walls of Abashi Prison close around me like a grave. We work the compound, scrubbing floors, building parts for the emperor's railroad, and shoveling snow in exchange for shelter and food. There are no chains, only vast sheets of ice and the promise of a slow, agonizing death if we try to escape.

My sister and I are given leeway, a few extra minutes outside our cell and lighter chores, since neither of us broke the law. Mother had begged for our freedom, her forehead pressed against the cold ground, but the warden refused.

"No one leaves the island," he'd said. "A man's birth is his sentence. A peasant is born to the dirt. Your daughters were born criminals—they'll die in Abashi."

His heartless words seared into my mind, but Mother took it like a spark to a parched forest. Each night she trained us while nestled together on the cold floor.

"But Mama, we'll never leave," my older sister, Yuki, would complain.

"Nonsense," she'd say. "Hope is closer than the stars and stronger than ice. The best way to fight despair is with our choices—the stories we tell others with our lives."

In whispers, she'd share stories of the outside world, drill us on mathematics, geography, and writing. But Mother never told us *why* we were in prison. The question burrowed deep inside me, needling like the mice in our walls. So, Mother made a deal with me. She'd answer my question, but only after I'd asked it of all the other inmates.

What is your story?

Day after day, I'd sit with bartered notebook in hand and beckon prisoners to the bars to tell me their secrets.

Sasa hadn't cried when he mumbled his story through the bars, but he'd trembled. His story tumbled out in waves like the changing colors of the sea—a hungry boy who'd wanted more, a ruthless pirate who'd silenced with the katana, and an old man now full of regret and kindness. In the margins of his story, I drew a black ribbon reaching to the stars.

But not everyone liked questions.

Naven had grabbed me by the collar and smashed my face into the bars, breaking my nose. His story hadn't been easy to get. But I persisted and eventually filled a whole notebook with the prisoners' stories: dirty secrets and tales so tragic they'd bleed the life from the stoutest heart.

A guard locks the door behind us, rattling me from my thoughts. Today, I finish the deal. My stomach churns, gurgling louder than usual. Mother casts me a sideways glance as she sweeps the room with a handmade duster before settling onto her moldy rush mat.

"Guess there's no meal tonight," I say. My stomach pinches, punishing me for the mention of food.

"Your mind is the highest point in your body," Mother says, "and your gut is down here. Listen to what is higher, and you'll live."

"I'm tired of that," I groan. "I'm *hungry*."

"Then let me tell you a story." She collects a pile of spun elm bark and sets to work with her fingers while she talks. She weaves a tale I've heard often. "Once upon a time, there was a dragon with silver scales that glimmered beneath the moonlight. He drank from the stars in the north and his heart magic guided the spirits of the great bears before they were hunted to extinction. Those spirits are forever searching for a home . . ."

I stop listening.

Another Ainur myth, legends from our ancestors. The story I yearn to hear—the one I *need*—never crosses Mother's lips.

WHY AM I HERE? Why do we live in a prison?

My fingers work their way beneath the rush mat, finding the frayed edge of my notebook. I pull it into my lap and try not to think about the pages splattered with grief-laden secrets that belong to my fellow prisoners and, dare I say, friends, like Sasa. Hope claws at my ribs, hurting more than the empty stomach.

Mother will finally tell me the truth.

I know she's trying to protect me, but the truth locked away is like poison. I fist the worn notebook and scoot across the cold floor to huddle beside her.

"I did it." I summon my flickering courage. "I questioned everyone—thieves, insurgents, murderers, even *Naven*."

Mother looks up from weaving threads of elm bark into a new winter coat for me. Her blue eyes, like the sky on a clear day, appraise me with warmth. Still, the question clumps in my throat.

What did you do to be thrown in prison? With murderers! Why are my sister and I punished too?

I glance at my half sister's starved form curled like a sleeping rat in the corner. Yuki should've had answers. She was born *before* Mother arrived at Abashi Prison twelve years ago. Mama never told us why Yuki came with her. Was it to keep her from being a foundling? Did the warden consider it a mercy? Yuki doesn't ask; she's accepted being kept in the dark—but not me.

I swallow hard. "Mama, what's *your* story?"

She sets aside the elm bark coat and eyes the notebook. "How did you get stories out of the men here with questions like that?"

I shrug. "Most people just want someone to talk to."

"Most don't have children." Mother hides a smile, her chafed hand cupping my cheek. "Who can resist this face?"

"You," I grumble.

She holds her arms out to me, and I climb into her lap. "Have I told you of the time I got lost at Silverwood Market and took your uncle's rifle?"

I shake my head.

"You better listen, because I'll only answer your question once. My story begins with a rifle and a cherry tree."

"Not that kind of story," I interrupt. "I want to know how you got here . . . to the northernmost prison in the world."

"With a rifle and a cherry tree," Mother insists. "It was the first time I broke the law."

"The first?" I raise a brow.

"Shh, listen!" Mother needles me in the ribs, forcing a laugh. "They said firearms were for boys at the School for Ancient Hearts, and girls must use the long spear. Your uncle knew I wouldn't be happy until I'd tried all the weapons at the school. So we planned it together. Only I hadn't anticipated the prince setting loose a muster of peacocks . . ."

As Mother's words string on, I imagine her not in a grimy prison shift, but in the flowing robes of a wayfinder as she scaled a tree during a royal parade.

"What's a peacock?" I interrupt.

Mother snatches my notebook and draws a long-feathered bird in the margins. "Each feather holds a rainbow," she whispers, "shaped like teardrops, and just as shimmering."

I lean closer, aching to hear more.

"The school had a shooting practice scheduled for Prince Bastian," she continues. "It was right before the rebellion, when the Taigan Empire attacked our homeland. I made the shot instead of my brother. I had to focus a great deal since I was farther than the other marksmen. No one would have noticed since my brother pretended to shoot from below the tree, but a stray peacock flapped to my branch." She pauses, a wry smile crossing her face. "I fell and startled the prince's stallion. Threw him from his horse. So, here I am."

Tales from other prisoners bubble to the surface in my

mind—the rebellion against Taiga, a legion of female soldiers who fought on the Barbary Ice coast, and the battle of Mt. Atan, when a whole side of the mountain burst lava for days. Yet still they fought on. I'd gleaned enough to know that Mother was a general in the rebellion—but this wasn't enough reason to cast her into prison, nor was a mishap in a cherry tree, prince or not. The emperor had pardoned the rebellion, asked them to join him in uniting the eight kingdoms.

"What's the real reason?" I attempt to copy Mother's stern eye and squint but fail miserably.

"I broke the law, dear heart."

"Yes, but how? Why are Yuki and I prisoners? Where's my father?"

"Speaking about your father wasn't part of the deal." Mother's voice turns to ice.

"That's not fair. At least tell me why *I'm* a prisoner!"

Mother takes me by the chin, her fingertips digging into the soft underside of my jaw. Startled, I meet her clear-blue eyes. We have the same eyes, but mine are dull in comparison to the cerulean fire that rages in her gaze.

"You are *not* a prisoner." She lets go of my chin and shoves a bony thumb at my forehead. "Not up here."

I nod. I've heard it all before.

"I know you're hiding something," I mutter. "We're tucked away on an island of ice. I need to know why!"

"You think too much. You're so eager to stuff your head with knowledge and escape. But it won't do you any good if you don't know your place in this world."

"Behind bars?" I snort a laugh.

"No, dear heart. Your place in this world is not a location. Your name is not what others think of you. It's your choices that define you. That is your freedom."

I sigh. "Yes, General."

"Kirarin." Mother calls my full name, her voice warm.

My eyes dart to hers, expecting another lesson to be drilled into my overthinking brain. No matter how much my mother tells me what I should believe—I can't. The gap between my head and my heart is a ravenous cavern.

I want more. To be free. To be out *there*.

She wraps her arms around me. "You'll be free of this place soon. Just promise me one thing."

"What?"

Her voice is a hush against my ear. "When the time comes, and you run—keep your sister safe. Guard her above your own life. She's not as strong as you."

"But Mama—"

"Keep her safe." Mother folds me into her arms, squeezing so tight that I'd have lost my rice gruel had I been given any. "Promise me."

A rare tear slips down her chapped cheek as she lets me go. I lift a finger to smooth it away.

Above your own life.

The words settle in my chest like stone, pressing old bruises. She doesn't love Yuki more—I know this, bone-deep. And yet, the difference in our fathers drifts over me like a cloud. My hollow chest aches, then lifts as I wrap myself in the truth.

She trusts me.

Believes I'm strong.

I can carry this.

"I promise," I whisper.

Mother's eyes shine in the darkness of our cell like twin stars, beacons of light and love. More tears slip down her face, carving smooth paths along frostbitten skin.

She avoids crying while we're awake. Tries not to show us love so the guards won't use it against us. A cloak of strength and coldness to insulate the warm, fragile heart inside. I wrap my arms around her, wishing all my body's warmth into her own.

"I'll keep you both safe," I say. "I promise."

CHAPTER 1

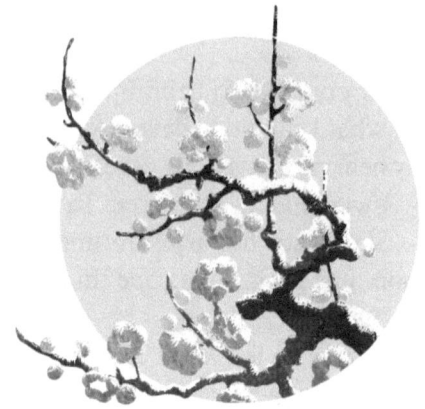

Seven Years Later
ABASHI PRISON

THE FLOW OF DRIFT ICE NEVER

sounded so much like cracking bones. I slump against the wooden dock, my body contorting against the cold as I steal a glimpse of frozen sea. Great mountains of frigid jewels fight to come ashore, burying each other in the process with a biting crush. Nothing wants to claim Abashi Island as home—except the ice.

"Kira, fetch me that shovel," Mother calls.

I cast one last look out to sea and savor the salty tang of the wind. My eyes devour the morning horizon for a glimpse of silver sails. *Please bring more food.* We haven't had a food shipment in a year, living off scarce fish and the depleted prison storehouse. This week we'd only eaten boiled bone soup with a single grain of rice swimming in it.

"Watching won't make the supply ship come any faster," Mother says. "And it won't do any good if this path isn't finished when it arrives." Early wrinkles cup my mother's mouth as she leans against a winter flagpole, freshly uncovered by her own calloused hands.

Our smiles come easier on the morning of Winterfest, even with a dozen more faded flags to dig out of the snow ahead. The tattered orange cloth marks the buried road to our prison home for the last seventeen years.

I glower at the wooden parapets where the guards stand with warm trench coats and faintly glowing cigarettes, watching us slave in the shoulder-high snow. Steeling myself, I drag the shovel to Mother. It takes two to break a path through Ezo snow, deep as the blue lake, heavy as a bear, and white as the moon at rice pounding. I give Mother my scarf. It's freezing, and even though I know the thin cloth won't make her feel any warmer, I must try. Unlike her, I was born here. Cold runs in my veins.

I furrow my brow, staring at a crimson crane flying overhead. The birds make freedom look so easy. A hop with outstretched wings—not even a run—and then soaring. The crane glides over the ice, white wings carrying him to places I've never seen.

Whatever it takes, I'll escape—or end up just another body in the ice.

"Do you think the ship will bring cakes?" I turn my attention back to the empty dock. "Or sugared persimmons, egg custard, or sweet red beans?"

Mother laughs. "Not likely. But I'd rather have pickled vegetables."

I suppose she's right. I'd settle for anything. My stomach doesn't even growl anymore. It claws at my sides like a drowning wolf. But whenever the ship comes to port, I begin to hope again.

Someday I'll stow away and travel to Silverwood, where Mother grew up. I'll build us a real home with a warm hearth, open doors, and a wide field of lavender. I'd held some once— just a handful—and licked my palms for days after, chasing the sweet floral taste and the salt of my own skin. Prisoners say salt keeps you sharp when you're fading. Maybe that's why I couldn't stop.

A shout rings out from the guard tower, followed by booming drums. "Ship sighted!"

I spin toward the dock, my breath catching as skeletal rigging and a plume of smoke appear on the stretch of blue sea not yet smothered in ice. A flare bursts from the watchtower, racing toward the clouds until it splits into a spiderweb of light. Guards stomp down the path and snow topples over where we'd just shoveled. My numb fingers curl over the handle.

"Get back to work," the guard hollers at the prisoners gathering round the dock for a better view.

I understand their excitement, but we won't get our share of food until tonight. If patience is a virtue in the outside world, it's a necessity in Abashi. Of course, the festival shipment is mostly for the warden and the guards, but even we get a cup of hot cider and grilled rice cakes.

"Fools," Mother says in a censuring tone. "That ship brings more than food."

"Sure, like gossip and drunk soldiers we can pinch food from."

Mother dumps another load of snow, her eyes narrowing on the distant sails. "Ships bring *change*. They bring the yearly inspection and new guards from Taiga. We should be ready."

I take a deep, cold breath. *Ready.* Our code word for escape.

We've whispered about leaving on that boat, made subtle plans, but it's never been the right time. Yuki's always been too sick. The prison inspector too thorough.

Could it be this year? Curiosity flutters in my chest like an ice moth to luprite, the rocky substance that illuminates our shores with glowing yellowish veins at night.

I tear my gaze from the boat and drive my shovel forward. Sheets of snow fold over and collapse. Mother works harder than I do, sweat pooling on her brow beneath the twin scarves she wears to cover her ears and nose from the cold.

Her scarf was once the brightest red I'd ever seen, stitched in white with a dozen stars that seemed to dance and twirl. I've asked her about it many times, and the story changes like the wind but always with a wink of magic.

"The stars are eternal warmth, the sons of the bear-god."
"The silk scarf of a nobleman I once loved and lost."

"A gift made from the needlepoint silk of an ice moth."
"Get back to work!" a guard yells.

I snap my head toward him and try not to envy his warm coat and gloves. But he isn't speaking to me. Yuki stands on the short five-meter path we'd carved out that morning. She's a tall wisp of a girl. I can't help but feel sorry for her as she lifts her pale face to the sky, red-splotched from the glaring sun and subzero cold.

"Yuki," I hiss.

I must get her attention before the guard reminds her without words. I'd seen a guard's baton do worse than shatter bones. Old Sasa's brain was knocked from his spine a few years back. It wasn't the first time I'd seen a prisoner die, but it was the first—and last—I'd cried.

My jaw tightens as my older sister does not move. Yuki studies the sky with her sharp brown eyes and delicate chin jutting upward.

"Get moving," the guard barks, stomping through the labyrinth of snow tunnels we'd carved to reach the dock.

Mother nudges my shoulder, and I pass her my share of the handle. It's nearly impossible to push alone along the compacted snow wall, but she does it, her tattered salmon leather gripping the ice.

I rush to Yuki. The guard's already marching toward her, frustration pulling at his brow beneath a wool cap. I gulp. It's Beetle. I'd adopted all Yuki's nicknames for the guards: Storklegs, Wraith, Blubber, and my least favorite, Beetle.

I grab Yuki's elbow. "You need to move."

She sets down her salt bucket and finally looks at me. Her job is to scatter salt behind us so the ship can unload safely.

"Did you see the crane, Kira?" Yuki's voice is a murmur in the wind. There's a fevered warmth to her, even in the biting cold. "It's like one in Mama's fairytale, the prince who swallowed a dark heart and became a bird. Look him in the eye and fortune's on your side. But if his eyes close, ruin awaits."

"Superstitions," I say. "Come on, the guards are watching."

Yuki glances behind her and rolls a shoulder. "They're *always* watching. It's their job, Kirarin," she says. "Old Beetle doesn't bother me, but the crane closed his eyes." She tilts her head and studies me with those smart brown eyes I can't quite read.

"So what? If I had a bow and arrow, it'd be bird soup." I reach my arm to the sky as if drawing an invisible string. "Forget the stories."

"Never," she says playfully and chucks a handful of salt in my hair. "Unlike you, I prefer stories to soup."

Beetle waddles over to us like the creature he's named after—stout, proud, and hairy in the worst places. His beady eyes pin me where I stand. "What's this? Taking a break?"

"Ugh, that smell," Yuki whispers, pretending to gag. "Does he ever bathe?"

I swallow my laugh, wondering if the rumors are true that the other guards won't let him into the communal hot spring for fear he might pollute it.

Beetle smacks his baton into his gloved palm. "The supplies will be unloaded soon, and the inspector better not slip on the path, or you'll be losing more than your dinner. I'll bar you from Winterfest entirely!"

Yuki's eyes narrow. "You think our mother will track your precious game if you do?"

The warden always sends Mother to track fresh game for Winterfest. The guards think she uses Ainur hunting techniques to locate deer and boar in the mountains, but Yuki and I know better.

I've seen magic woven in blue threads, witnessed Mother predict the future one too many times. She told us that a wayfinder has mastery over nature—finding a path to every living thing. A gift from the dragons who once roamed the sea, one of eight that had been given to mankind before the emperor murdered the dragons and turned the gift into a curse.

But wayfinding, like the other ancient hearts, is dangerous—a rich commodity in the eyes of the empire. It must stay our secret. A shimmer tingles down my spine, knowing that I've felt the path before, even if only a drop.

"Yuki..." I pull her back by the elbow before she says more.

She tries to stand tall but is crooked since her hip broke last year. With Yuki, something is always breaking, popping, snapping.

"The warden can always send one of you in her place," Beetle barks. "Now, back to work!"

"No." Yuki's mouth pinches in defiance.

I close my eyes, sucking in a breath. Yuki has the worst timing to flaunt her sense of independence. Unlike me, she's taken Mother's 'not a prisoner' speech to heart. Some guards might ignore it or hit her across the arms or back with a wooden bludgeon. But Beetle...

"Forgive us," I say, stepping between them with a bow. "My sister's had too much sun today. I'll finish the path, sir."

He laughs, cool and quiet, cupping his baton in one hand like a beloved pet. "She finishes the path—alone. Swap now."

I feel the blood drain from my face. Yuki's eyes flicker with a lingering defiance before she relents and hands me the salt bucket. She can't push the shovel a few steps, much less make it to the storage shed. A deep cough rattles her lungs, and she hides it with the back of a hand.

"She can't," I say. "She's sick—"

He lifts his baton in answer.

Yuki obeys and shuffles, running as best as she can on the ice-packed trail. Mother pauses, waiting for her so they can work together.

"I said she works alone!" Beetle yells, following on her heels.

Mother turns. "No one works alone on the ice."

The baton crashes against Mother's chest with an audible crack and sends her tumbling into the snow. I dart forward, but she lifts a hand for me to stop.

Beetle grabs Yuki by the collar of her faded orange prison

shift and shoves her toward the unfinished path. She stumbles and catches herself, shins bruising against the ice.

Mother calms her breath before steadying any other part of her body. Then she rises to one knee and stands. Even in weakness, she is calculating.

A spark of pride flickers in my chest as she steps toward the guard. But then she trudges past him, making her way back to our cell in the fifth wing.

Beetle snorts.

I stare at the snow, a hole opening inside of me with each of Mother's retreating steps. She left me to deal with this. Alone. But Mother's told me again and again, she's not leaving us. She's teaching me to protect my sister on my own, because someday I'll have to.

I fist my hands and will the hole in my heart to ice over. A wayfinder's daughter keeps moving. Always finds a way. Only Mother hasn't taught me the skill yet. I'd gleaned bits and pieces, usually when she was too exhausted to protest.

Keep your mind calm, she'd instructed. *Eyes open. Breathe. Feel the life around you. You must first master this before you can see the path through any forest, ocean, or inside the heart of man. But you must never use it. Never let anyone know you carry the gift of a dragon heart.*

"Don't worry about me, Kira." Yuki throws her weight behind the shovel. "I'm made of stronger things than ice."

"Of course you are." I smile at my sister's pluck. "You're sharper than it too."

Yuki's shoulder audibly pops as she fights against the wall of snow. We're both like Mother in that stubborn way. We've had to be. Sometimes I forget that we're half sisters. Her father was someone Mother had married before the war, and mine . . . was someone she won't talk about.

Beetle cuts into my thoughts, throwing his head back with a laugh. When he speaks, sour fish breath hits me in the face.

"You'd like to escape, wouldn't you?" He tucks the baton in his belt and opens his arms wide as if to say, *I won't stop you.*

I turn away and stare at the expanse of glistening ice that stretches to the far coast off the Ezo mainland. Beetle's hot breath rolls off the back of my neck, and I stiffen.

"Freedom's just on the other side of that sheet of ice and the mountains beyond that. You have my word, no one will hunt you down for the first hour. Of course, the Northern Watchmen might catch you with that savage captain of theirs. Still, a gracious head start, no?"

"At least *he's* handsome," Yuki shouts over the snow, earning a scowl from Beetle.

Blizzards, Yuki.

"How would you know?" Beetle sneers. "Lot good a handsome face will do if he cuts you down and leaves you for the wild beasts. But Kira's smarter than that."

I make a show of rolling my eyes. Beetle did this yearly, made me hope, promised me time—a mere hour. He wasn't serious enough to let me go at dusk, never gave me the three hours, rations, and warm clothes necessary to cross the ice and arctic mountains on a good day. Does he really think I'll fall for his death march dressed in hope?

My hands knot, resisting the urge to hit him with the salt bucket and steal his warm coat and his offer. "You'll have to do better than that," I say. "I don't go anywhere without my family."

He jerks my arm, an amused gleam in his eye. "Then take your sister. I'll even give you an extra hour," he whispers, waggling a brow. "With Winterfest tonight, no one will notice you're missing until it's too late."

He can't be serious. No one has *ever* escaped Abashi Island, and those who tried usually didn't survive the punishment. The marks on Mother's back from when she tried to escape while pregnant with me are warning enough.

Dare I escape, now, in the middle of winter?

A dangerous hope stirs within me and, for a moment, I

consider his words. It's the best opportunity he's offered. But he's only tempting me for his own entertainment. It'd be foolish to think Yuki could make the journey.

I yank my arm away.

He laughs. "Coward. Even given a chance, you won't leave. Are you afraid of hypothermia? The law chasing you? Or maybe it's the monsters in the mountain waiting for a bite to eat?"

"I'm not afraid," I say, hating how my teeth chatter.

"You were born afraid," he says. "No one comes into this world laughing. We come in tears."

Snow plops onto the path as Yuki struggles to lift the shovel high enough. I turn my back to Beetle and take the shovel from Yuki.

"Feel free to run away," Beetle says, not trying to stop me. "It won't be as easy on the Prisoners Road. The order came this morning by seahawk. There's a new prison inspector this year. He's ordered all prisoners in the fifth wing to be shipped out come morning."

Shivers rack my spine. *The Prisoners Road.*

Rumor says hundreds are missing from working the railroad between Abashi and Silverwood. The Taigan Empire wants a direct line crossing Ezo so they can control its borders and leverage it as a buffer against Rusa. Whoever controls the trade route has power, and those who get in the way are just fuel for the fire.

"You're lying," I say. "The fifth wing has the oldest—"

"That's the trouble with a life-sentence prison. Gotta make room for new prisoners. Forcing a dozen old men—and three girls—to build a railroad is easier than executing the lot. But I won't say anything if you and your sister run off before then." He winks as if handing me a favor. Then he turns and walks away.

My jaw clenches so tight it aches. Escape? It's a cruel joke. Yuki can barely stumble back to the prison compound, let alone cross a mountain. In the dead of winter, food is scarce, warmth even scarcer, and while I don't believe in monsters, there are hungry wolves and bears.

But one thing is certain: we have to get off this island.

My sister won't make it on the Prisoners Road. I'm not even sure I can. It's heavy labor in the coldest mountains of Ezo. Call it what it is—an execution.

Mother had said to be ready. Did she know it would be today?

A path blinks before me, a dim trail of blue drifting out the prison gates and over the ice floes. It's grown stronger the last few weeks, even as my sister grows weaker.

"Kira." Yuki leans against the snow, her breath a ghost of white.

"Hmm?" I stare at the icy strait separating our Island from the Ezo mainland. It glistens in the sun like a welcome invitation.

When I don't turn, she reaches over and pats my head, mussing my hair into a crow's nest. "Kira," she says, stronger this time. "Maybe he's right. You could do it, you know . . . escape. Mama and I will be fine."

I startle, eyes glued to where the words spill out of her pale, blistered lips. "Forget it." I duck out of her hand. "Not on his terms. We'll find our way. A safe way. But first, I'm finishing this path and getting you to the bath before you freeze."

"Don't worry about me, Kirarin. This is my home." She twirls her wrist in some grand gesture to the prison, the mountains, and the sea.

"If Mother heard you say that—"

"I'd be a deserter, wouldn't I?"

"They don't call her general for nothing."

Yuki smiles, but I see the truth on her face. She's given up on escape for herself. She's determined to make the best of life here with her sewing and sculpting wooden figures for the guards' game of King's Crag.

My fists clench with effort as I try to imagine a world without ice—without cruelty. A place where Yuki could see real gowns, where Mama could laugh without fear. It's a fairytale, but I swallow hard and hold on to it.

I wrap my elmwood coat around Yuki. Survival might be second nature, but protecting family is first.

Yuki catches my intention and straightens. "Kira, if you insist on staying, I won't let you treat me like an invalid."

Together, we push against the walls of snow, forcing them to the left and right, clearing a path for the new inspector.

I will escape this prison.

I will find my family a home, a real home like Mother told us about so we wouldn't forget. A home where children curl in warm beds after a meal by firelight. Where fields are ripe with wildflowers and the town comes to play at the harvest. A place where winter is a passing thing and spring brings the warmth of the sun.

There's another world out there.

And I will find it.

CHAPTER 2

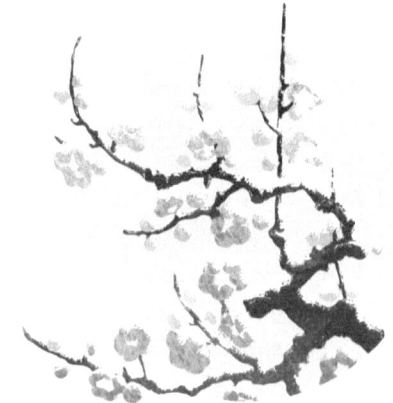

SUNLIGHT SKATES ACROSS THE ICE as I trudge up the dock for the yearly hunting detail. It should've been Mother's job, not mine. She tried, but Beetle stopped her with a single prod to the ribs, where his baton had struck earlier. Then his eyes slid to me.

Now, I stare up at the black steamship with its iron beak and bare rigging, new recruits working the deck. Panic storms in my ears.

I've never set foot off the island.

I should be excited, but something locks inside my chest.

"Can she hunt, or is she just bait?" Storklegs bellows from behind and pushes me onto the Ice Crusher.

My feet move begrudgingly, heels torn from the snow-crusted ground and replanted on steel planks. I've always dreamed of riding this ship, but with my family, not with two men I'd rather drown below the ice.

"If she's anything like her mother, she can track," Beetle says.

I swallow hard. *Can I?* The rats in our cell probably don't count for tracking practice.

Storklegs gives me the rules as a crew prepares the ship. "Do exactly what we say. Two guards"—he gestures to the Beetle and himself—"will be with you at all times. Run, and we shoot. Fail to bring back game, and we feed you to the wolves. Escape, and your family pays the price. You have one hour to find game, understand?"

"Yes, sir."

He keeps talking, but I'm not paying attention. I analyze the vessel and how many men it takes to sail it. Could Mother, Yuki, and I escape on this craft? It won't sail without at least eight hands, and this crew is double that. But maybe, just maybe, I could find a safe place to hide in the mountains if we escape en route to the Prisoners Road. That is, if I can find game for the guards in one hour.

"Scheming little demon." Storklegs raps my head with his baton, causing me to wince. "The arctic hasn't broken you yet."

"I was born in it," I mumble, glaring at him.

"You'll stay in it too," he says and opens the cargo hatch.

I step back, but Storklegs shoves me inside. A whoosh of cold air, and I'm airborne for one painstaking breath before landing in a thick, wet net. I scramble out of the tangled fishing net, my legs shaking uncontrollably as I straighten.

Storklegs laughs overhead. "Enjoy the ride," he crows and drops the slatted door with a bang.

Faint light filters through a cloud of dust from the hole above. My eyes adjust as I survey the cargo hold. Storklegs can laugh all he wants. He's just given me a chance to make escape tonight real.

For what seems like an hour, I scour crates in search of supplies to smuggle. Nothing but barrels of coal and a few luprite stones, which I pocket in haste. The prisoners say the island exports them for mining tunnels along the Prisoners Road, so it must be good for something. When I pry open the next crate, a hysterical cackle escapes my lips. A boon of dead fish and dried seaweed!

As I finish my second salted mackerel, the Ice Crusher halts, pitching me forward. A tremor vibrates through the metal hull and into my bones.

"We're here." Beetle's voice booms overhead, and a ladder drops into the hold.

I climb the rungs, tilting my weight to keep from falling. As I surface, cold wind stings my eyes and black hair springs from my long braid to lash my face. I pull my elmwood coat tight, nestling my chin into the worn fabric threaded by Mother's hands.

Beetle hauls me by the elbow to the bow of the ship.

I'm riveted by the largest—and only—cliff I've ever seen. The Ice Crusher's sharp metal nose wedges into a hefty block of ice a half kilometer from shore. Ice dots the rocky beach like a handful of frosted coal, beautiful and frigid. Crisp scents crowd for attention: northern pine, fresh snow, damp earth. But it's the things I can't smell that cause my throat to go dry.

There's a reason the guards rarely send anyone to the woods for food. The same reason no one returns from the Prisoners Road—this is the edge of the Winterwilds. A forest of deadly beasts and dark thickets that turns the kindest of souls into madmen, except the Northern Watchmen who govern it.

"Last chance," Beetle whispers. "Just like I promised. Even free passage to the mainland."

"Nothing's free," I say.

I study the bay and the wall of skeletal trees standing like sentinels. Land and life hum around me. I sense the forest is alive with creatures vanishing into the trees and burrowing beneath the ground. The wind carries their breath, their life, in a swirl of strange colors. Curiosity dares me to test out the paths. It feels stronger here, away from the island. I cross my arms against the biting wind and shut my eyes to the blue threads. Everywhere eyes watch me, waiting.

Waiting for me to make up my mind. *Can I escape tonight? Can Yuki survive the winter? Even if we make it into the woods, what if the monster stories are true?*

I set my shoulders, closing my ears to the cold answers. *No. No. And no.*

Still, it's better odds than the Prisoners Road.

Two guards haul me off the ship, onto a tethering boat, and toward the edge of the forest. Mt. Atan looms above us, guarded by colossal foothills, each tall and dark enough to cost a man a day's worth of travel.

"What are you waiting for?" Storklegs shoves me forward.

I glower, but I know better than to give him a piece of my mind.

Obediently, I stagger toward the snowcapped woods. Beetle and Storklegs, both fully outfitted with new repeating rifles from Taiga and water-repellent wool uniforms, trudge behind me. I'm live bait walking out into the woods before them. Freezing wind slices through my elmwood coat and the faded orange prison shift beneath. I pause a few times as my braid catches in a tangle of dense branches along the trail.

I'd asked Mother for advice on how to find wild game quickly. Her words stick in my mind like frost to glass.

"When you get the chance, run." Mother's words came in a whisper as she nursed her bruised ribs. "Look for the rabbit in the talons, Kirarin, and don't look back. You're not a prisoner. You're stronger than you think."

Kirarin—sparkling one. My heart skipped at the nickname. Mother named me after the ice. The sound when it crackles and shines in the sun. The sound of cold melting. Because no matter the suffering, having a caring heart is worth the cost.

"Mama, please. Tell me how to be a wayfinder."

"You're not ready, dear heart."

"But why?" I begged.

"Magic attracts other magic." Mother winced as she sat upright. "It's too dangerous."

"So is escaping!"

"You *are* a wayfinder," she'd said, voice clipped with pain. "It's an ancient gift passed down from the dragons, a way to foresee the right path. There are colors in the sky, in rocks, in rivers that men are blind to. If you keep your eyes open, you'll see them. We are connected to the path, Kira. It always illuminates the way for those who seek it. It leads you to your heart's deepest need. But you must keep it hidden. In the wrong hands, it's a terrible power."

I grit my teeth and try to still the emotions roiling within. Mother had told me that wayfinders have a connectedness with all living things, but she hadn't told me *how* to use the ancient heart. She'd dropped hints here and there, instructed me in techniques for hunting and gathering. But there's an element I'm missing.

"Your mother would have found something by now." Beetle checks his rifle and dusts a pinch of snow from his waterproof coat.

"I'm not my mother," I say, the words sticking in my throat.

Who would I have been if not raised in prison? If I'd had a normal life? My chest aches and it's more than the cold burning my lungs.

Icy air bites my fingers as I stretch out my hands and quiet my mind. I have to do this without relying on Mother. I need to forge a path—alone.

Please find a path.

I take a deep inhale and exhale, visualizing a way out of this wood, seeking, asking, listening. My eyes focus on the wind, watching my breath crystallize as it rolls out into the arctic mountains.

And then my breath splits into five faint paths, like tendrils of blue smoke reaching out into the dark wood—searching. The paths wend through fir trees, across frozen streams, and into hollow caves. I don't dare turn to Storklegs and Beetle for fear the trail will disappear like a vapor. A smile breaks from my lips. I don't believe my eyes. I'd seen faint paths before, like a string connecting me to another place, but never *on command.*

I sharpen my focus on a path leading to a cave that I can see in my mind. I could run for it, were it not for the guns trained on me. The cave would provide shelter until I could rescue Mother and Yuki on the transport vessel to the Prisoners Road. But as

I focus on the path, I can't see further. My head aches. It's all a cold haze. I shift my focus to the next path, a heavy, slithering trail. I shiver and step back, bumping into Beetle's solid chest.

"Find something?"

"I-I'll let you know when I do." Fear slicks my throat.

Does Beetle know that Ainurian hunting stretches beyond tracking into the realm of magic?

I reach out for the next path, but it disappears as suddenly as it arrived. Vanished. The magic I'd felt tapers out. My stomach sinks, and my hands fall in front of me with an audible clap. The only thing left is a lingering feeling that every path ends the same way.

Empty.

Suddenly, a large lifeform hums across my vision. I sense it down the next hill and beneath a thicket tucked into a rock outcropping. Thunder. A waterfall. I follow the sound of it like trailing a ball of twine winding through the forest. Along with the waterfall's roar comes the hum of my mother's words: *You're not ready, dear heart.*

But the path drums beneath my fingers, full of possibility if I'm brave enough to follow. I reach out, begging my latent magic to show me more.

This way, the path hums in a voice as brittle and clear as the ice crunching beneath my feet. *Follow.*

Roots bend beneath my thin salmon leather. The snow seeps into the edges, numbing my feet. Snow-speckled branches graze my face as I leap onto an outcropping, jutting over a deep white valley. The guards behind me curse, whacking at tree branches and sending a cascade of snow thumping down. I shoot them a silencing look.

How did Mother ever track game with these buffoons?

Finally, I home in on movement in the trees. North. Alive. Large. Its life force shimmers in the air as if I can see its soul, feel its intentions. *Is that the Ainur way?* I point in the direction of the sound.

The rock juts roughly against my thin boots as I crouch and peer into the valley. Not too deep, just high enough that I wouldn't risk jumping. Halfway down, a waterfall bursts from the stone, its top crusted in ice while hot water gushes beneath. Steam rises in delicate clouds, warming my face.

Below, glassy ice covers the surface of the blue pond. A spark prickles down my neck as I realize the lifeform I've been tracking is watching me. Energy pulses through my veins, warm and soft. Feeling comes back to my toes, and a quiet pull like an invisible current, tugs me in one direction. My eyes drift toward it and meet two black, bottomless eyes from the valley thicket.

A bear stares at me.

I nearly topple over the cliff.

The hulking black creature claws at the snow and snorts. It lumbers to the edge of the pond. Large and terrifying, the height of a man with claws that could eviscerate me in a single swipe, but those eyes . . . I can't explain the path that flickers out of them. It's full of regret, an emotion animals don't have—almost human.

It knows the men are going to kill it. I've told it with my body language that two guns are aimed straight at it. My stomach tightens with disgust and grief. Bears are sacred to the Ainur. I don't want them to kill this creature. Why couldn't it be a rabbit or a boar? But if I don't bring back meat, Mother and Yuki will be punished.

I close my eyes, trying to break the path I'd seen winding into the bear's eyes.

"Run," I whisper, a picture forming in my mind of that creature tucked into a cave, safe and warm. *Run away, you dumb beast!* To my surprise, I watch as the wind carries that word, *run*. It brushes the bear's fur, and the beast obeys.

The bear shakes its head and turns back to the wood. Too late. A pop rings out, dusting snow from the trees.

Silence.

No more birdsong, but a whisper I wish I couldn't hear drifts back to me. A hole opening inside the bear, the dull impact of the bullet sinking into its meat. The pain of the bear's growl rings inside my ears. It falls back, then it staggers into the forest at an awful lope, one side of its body dragging a trail through the snow.

"Follow it!" Storklegs yells.

"No." My voice comes out in a muffled cry.

"It's going to die either way," Beetle says. "Poisoned by a bullet or with a second one in its brain. The latter is faster. Merciful."

"Don't reason with her." Storklegs shoves me with the butt of his gun.

There's no point in arguing. I came here to track game. If I can't help hunt, we will never survive, even if we do escape. Mother killed dozens of animals. I must be strong if I'm going to escape tonight. Family is more important than a bear. I *have* to do this. What's more, I felt wayfinder magic. It's singing in me now.

Shaking, I point to the far thicket behind the frosted pond. The second shot comes closer than I'd expected. My heart twinges, sharp as a needle prick, as if a connection snaps, a light I wanted to hold onto slipping away.

"Go get it," Beetle says, lowering his gun and tossing me a heavy ball of rope. I catch the glint in Beetle's eye. The one that says, *Run, I'll cover you.* The deal I can't trust and resent. "Tie the beast, then we haul it back to the ship."

Storklegs raises a brow. "Does she even know how to tie it?"

"Let her try," Beetle says. "Give ourselves a break." He takes a swig from his insulated canteen as though I'm already forgotten.

I climb down the ravine and stalk around the half-frozen pond. When I reach the bear, a hole opens inside me, scratching at everything sacred. I rest my hand on the bear's head, the only way I know to show that I care.

Why did the path lead to this?

I stare at Beetle in the distance. He intentionally gave me space and time to make a run for it. *Why? For sport?*

No matter, I'm smarter than that.

My eyes turn to the bear fallen in the snow-dusted underbrush. Unwinding the rope, I tie it over the bear's head and paws, and loop it into a bowline knot for hauling. A deeper knot tightens in my stomach as I work.

If we try to escape, will we end up like this bear?

"Done yet?" Beetle calls, working his way down the cliff. "You know, last time we let a prisoner besides your mother do the tracking, they tried to run."

"As you said, I'm a smart girl." I lay my hand on the bear's head once more, thanking it for its sacrifice.

Beetle laughs and lifts the rope, handing the other end to Storklegs. But as we haul the bear back to the boat, I have an aching feeling that another pair of eyes watches us from the heart of Mt. Atan.

A feeling that we're not the only ones hunting.

Mother never fully explained the dangers of wayfinding. But I'm beginning to wonder if there's a price. After all, if Abashi Prison has taught me anything, it's that nothing is free.

CHAPTER 3

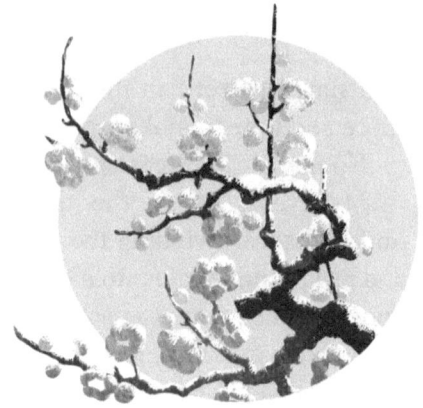

MY BATH IS INTERRUPTED by gunshots—not what you want on a night you're trying to escape. I lean over the edge of the long rectangular pool, arms crossed over the black-cedar ledge, and listen.

Ban . . . ban . . .

"You hear that?" Yuki whispers.

I shrug it off. "The guards are probably just celebrating after a hunt."

I draw my knees up to sit on the underwater bench, my dark thoughts returning. We've got bigger problems than the guards.

I glance at Mother. Out of the bath now, her wide feet plod over to a bench as she slides into her prison shift, wincing from her bruised ribs. Is she thinking about escape now that the Prisoners Road looms in our future? Will we be hauled off as soon as the sun rises? Will we cross the ice to the cave I'd found? If we don't, there is no running with a nine-pound shackle once we get to the Road.

Questions ricochet in my mind like the continuing gunshots. But I don't ask them, not in front of Yuki. She can't survive the cold. And while I'm grateful for the rare bath, tonight it just might save Yuki's life. She'll need the warmth for our plan to work.

Bitter water makes my skin feel slippery and smooth, almost like it's peeling off layer by layer like a wild onion. The natural hot spring scalds before we cool it with buckets of snow. I swirl the water with my finger, eyes staying on Mother.

She pulls off the red scarf around her head, and her long black hair falls like a curtain to her waist. She combs it out with her fingers, a song escaping her lips. "Fire fell on me like rain, but I didn't care at all. Where I ran, the earth glowed blue, and your fine lips I saw were true . . ."

The lyrics tingle my spine. "Is that song about the old magic?"

"It *is* old magic," Mother says with a sparkle in her eye. "I'm tracing a path with song. What you told me today requires some searching out."

"Fine lips?" Yuki chuckles. "Sign me up for that path, please."

Mother smiles, and her eyes twinkle as she continues her song in a hum so we can't hear the words.

I wish she would teach me more about wayfinding. There's something to Mother's ability to see the future—at least, glimpses of it—that goes beyond my understanding. Dangerous or not, I want more. And the power, the connection I felt in the forest, only whets my appetite. The path knows what lies beyond these walls.

But when I mentioned what happened in the forest to Mother, all she said was, "The right path too early leads to destruction."

She reties her hair and waits for us to finish our bath.

Dark iron-rich water ripples in concentric circles, piling against the side of the rusted pool like it, too, wants to escape. I plunge my hands into the depths, soaking in its stinging warmth. The hot spring is the one place where we can be truly warm. It heats the marrow in my bones. The light plays tricks on my skin beneath the surface, and thousands of tiny bubbles collect on my arms like goosebumps. I draw lines on my arms and watch the bubbles burst, thinking about that blue path in Mother's song.

Yuki leans beside me, her skin whiter, softer than mine. Her long grizzly-brown hair piled on top of her head escapes the handmade scarf holding it up in wispy strips.

Ban. Ban. More gunshots.

Mother stiffens, her face turned toward the bathhouse door. "That's not the guards shooting drunk," she says. "Bath time is over."

"But we still have time!" Yuki balks. She sinks down to her nose, her mouth making bubbles under the water.

Normally, I'd relish the smooth dragon steam that caresses my face and the warm water swaddling me like another layer of skin, but the look on Mother's face demands I obey.

"Come on, Yuki," I say.

Another gunshot. This time, the sound of it reverberates inside me.

I climb out of the bath and grab the towel Mother throws at me. I rub my body dry and then hold the towel out for Yuki. She scoots to the side of the pool like a water demon, only her chin above the simmering water, reluctant to leave. Shivering, she climbs out under the cover of the towel. It's so cold outside that a mere minute later, my body shakes.

Yuki and I pull on our prison shifts, robes for the top and wide-legged pants that skim our ankles. The thin yellow cotton used to be orange before years of snow and salt and tears. On the back, in faded black letters, are the words *Abashi Prison: Dangerous Criminal.*

Mother made each of us a thick coat from old bed quilts and elm bark. Traders from mountainous Atan sold practical wares to the guards once a year after the Great Melt—the eight weeks of the year we could actually see the ground instead of snow. Yuki had bartered to buy Mother two spools of colored yarn. My robe is a soft charcoal with white swirls and red stars. It's not enough, but the warmth of a second layer is lifesaving.

A gunshot rings hollow. Closer.

Yuki jumps then pulls on her leather shoes, made from salmon skin and bittersweet threads, just like mine.

"Back to the cell!" Storklegs shouts from outside, his fist pounding on the door. We obey and scurry onto the ice-packed trail that leads to our prison wing. Storklegs stalks behind us, rifle in hand, as Mother leads the way.

Snow piles to our ears, a trail that could easily cave in and bury us. But it's the base of the trail that's most dangerous. Black ice glistens in the fading light along a worn and trampled path. Abashi Island is so far north, the sun has yet to set this time of year. I squeeze Yuki's hand as we shuffle across the ice, using each other for balance.

Before we reach the center compound, the prison gong rings—an emergency. Had someone heard the news about the Prisoners Road and made a run for it?

"Hurry it up!" Storklegs growls. His eyes twitch, darting to the watchtowers.

Mother slows her pace, and Storklegs shoves us out of the way. He hurtles down the path as if he knows something we don't.

Clumps of snow fall around us as the gong is broken off by an earth-shattering roar. Yuki clutches my arm. "What was that?"

"My stomach." I force a smile and squeeze her hand.

Mother pulls us into a quick huddle. Our bodies coil with nervous tension, and warm puffs of breath collide in this small space. I've no idea what's happening, but there's a glow about Mama, a shifting in her eye.

"Kira, remember what I told you about getting off this island?" Her usually rough voice drops to a whisper. "Go to the storage room and get the supplies—don't leave anything. Yuki and I will wait back in the cell. If we get separated, look for the rabbit in the talons."

I pause, my hand fisted around Yuki's. "A rabbit? But—the gunshots—what's happening?"

Heat surges in my chest. I'm tired of being kept in the dark.

"Those gunshots are to *protect us* and the guards," Mother

says. "I'd bet my life on it. The prison is under attack. Now, do as I say. You're getting off this island."

I gulp. All warmth from the bath has vanished. My heart slams against my ribcage. Seventeen years I've waited to hear those words.

I want to ask more—what are they shooting at and why? But the urgency in her eyes tells me there's no time. Instead, I ask my most vital question. "Are we going to cross the ice?"

Mother nods. "Fetch the supplies and meet us outside the cell. Yuki and I will collect the bedding. We'll freeze without the extra warmth."

Worry needles across my brow. I don't want to be separated from my family if something goes wrong. And a rabbit in the talons—*whatever that is*—won't help me. Mother knows Yuki can't cross the mountains, not with her weak lungs and bones.

"Will it work?"

"Yes, dear heart." Mother's voice is a calm sea, ready for a voyage. "I saw a path."

My stomach twists. We're already out of our cell, we've had our measly dinner and our bath for warmth. There's nothing else we need except the rations I've been hoarding under a floorboard in the kitchen storehouse. The guards won't be looking for us if they're distracted by something . . . else.

A haunting image slips into my mind. A sense that something sacred has been slaughtered. Dark animal eyes flash in my memory, but I push it aside.

Another gunshot, followed by the shouts of men.

"Mama, what's out there?" Yuki takes hold of Mother's hands. "I-I don't want to leave. You know I can't make it. Go without me."

Ban. Ban.

"No." Mother kisses each of our cheeks, then she nudges me forward. "Kira, go! Meet us outside the fifth wing."

I nod shakily and then dart back toward the bathhouse, only

turning to see Yuki tilting her head at me and trudging behind Mother in the snow.

The kitchen storehouse is just behind the baths, next to the central guard cabin. A troop of guards emerges from one of the bunkhouses, all armed with new repeating rifles. They run down the trail in the same direction as Yuki and Mother.

I jerk my body against the outside wall, praying the snow doesn't cave in and bury me. But my steps are light, and a lifetime of prison food has made me even lighter. I am a wraith compared to the men here. As soon as they pass, I gather my courage and scurry to the storehouse door. It swings open. Empty.

I crouch to the familiar plank coated in soybean dust but with a distinctive burned strip of wood. My fingers pry numbly into the board. I kick at it until it loosens and then snaps up, nearly knocking me off balance. Dust flies into the air, thick with the scent of soy and salted seaweed. Inside the dark hole, a few blackened potatoes are wrapped in an old cloth. I stash the lot into my pockets, wishing I'd saved that bit of candied persimmon I'd pinched from the warden.

A roar, louder than before, shakes the rafters and riddles my clean hair with soot. I freeze, not bothering to secure the plank back into place. That wasn't thunder.

Whatever it was sounded angry . . . full of pain.

The metallic smell of blood taints the air from an open window. It's not like the bleeding red of a dying deer. No, this blood is a hungry, shining thing. Ravenous.

A chill skitters up my spine as a wintry gust slips through the only door. I force myself to turn.

A young guard stumbles into the storeroom, his hand slick with something dark. He slams his back against the wall, breath ragged, one fist locked around the hilt of a sword buried beneath his long coat.

I freeze, heart thudding against my ribs. *Just my luck.*

The guard's keen eyes flick toward the noise outside, his brow creased in something closer to annoyance than fear. The wool uniform hangs off him like mud on porcelain—wrong and ill-fitting.

I should slip away, pray he hasn't seen me. But my gaze snags on him.

Dark messy hair falls across his brow, his stance caught between boredom and readiness, as if the chaos outside is only a passing storm. There's a beauty to his calm, but winter has long taught me that beauty can be dangerous. A ripple of unease curls through my chest. *Who is he?*

No matter. Today, we escape.

Without a word, I edge to the side of the storehouse and reach behind me for a weapon to use in my defense. I grab a broomstick, but my elbow hits an iron pot. It clangs to the floor.

The young guard jumps and grabs his sword.

I swing the broom at him, but he blocks it easily with his scabbard. No one is taking me prisoner again. Falling back, I scramble for the countertop and hurl a crate of hardened mochi at him. The small white bricks rain down, clattering on wood.

"You idiot," he hisses, snatching a mochi bar midair. "There's a monster outside. It'll hear you."

His statement takes me by surprise. I straighten slowly, scrutinizing his smooth skin and stormy eyes. He's not from here.

Mochi, I decide, watching as he pockets the white brick like it's war rations. The nickname is softer than the other guards, but it fits.

"Spooked by the mountains and ghost stories already?" I say, raising a brow in jest. But I can't pretend I didn't hear it; the echo of the growl outside still snakes under my skin.

"Quiet," he whispers and replaces the scabbard at his side.

I reach for a few more mochi projectiles, but the guard is quick and jerks my hand behind my back in a way that makes my knees buckle.

"Let me go!" I cry, attempting to get out of the hold.

He pushes me outside into the snow, my back close against his body like a reluctant shield. Beneath his stench of sweat and forest, the faintest trace of lavender clings to him, a scent that normally dies in the cold. He must be from further mainland, maybe even Taiga.

I struggle against him, our feet tangling, and together we fall on black ice. Instantly, his arms wrap around me, solid muscle shielding the fall. His shoulder hits the frozen earth with a swear that certainly sounds like the other guards. He controls the fall with a roll and nearly lands on me, one arm pinned beneath my back and the other holding space between us.

"I'm trying to save your life," he says. "That *monster* is coming back, and anyone outside a cell isn't going to make it. I need you to live."

Those words shouldn't be a gut punch, but they are. My eyes widen, searching his to root out the lie. "You're trying to trick me."

"I'm trying to save you, but you're making it very difficult." He pushes up and extends a hand to me. No guard's ever done *that*.

My eyes snap to his, pointedly ignoring the offer. I stand and dust the snow from my coat. For the first time, I notice his sleeve shredded into strips and a bandage around the muscles there.

"How . . . did you get that?" I gulp, biting back any pity for Mochi. A small part of me wonders what his story is. The air is so tight, I can almost hear his heart pounding in answer.

"A bear," he says, his voice grave. "I heard stories how primitive this prison island is, uncivilized. The Taigan Empire thinks they can tame the north but even I've never seen a bear so big. Size of a small ship. It's against the rules to use a blade in Taigan territory, so . . ." He holds up his arm as if it explains everything.

A bear.

My body goes slack.

"A bear can't cross the ice," I say. "It wouldn't be big enough to get past the rifles. I know the inspector's sending us off—"

"I don't care if you believe me," he says. "I'm asking you

to be quiet so we don't get killed." His dark eyes swim with raw emotion, like the sea beneath ice-capped waves. "I'm here to help."

Never trust a guard. That saying kept me alive for seventeen years. But his grip is firm without bruising. His words . . . too caring for this place.

Mother's ballads come back to me. Her songs of ancient lore, of dragons and saints, of fiery kisses, of the path that shaped her people, the Ainur—and of monsters. *Don't venture too far into the mountains, or the creatures born of dark hearts will come and carry you away.*

Inmates say the monsters are just fairytales meant to keep us out of the woods. But what if they're true? What if the world outside Abashi Prison is more dangerous than the island itself? What if he knows what's out there?

"We don't have time." Mochi grabs my wrist and pulls me along the path.

A small brick building protrudes from the snow, barely visible in the mounds of white. My knees lock.

Solitary confinement.

Someone hollers from within.

"No! How is that supposed to keep me safe?" I dig my heels into the snow. "I've got to find my family."

He pulls the keys from his pocket and shoves me inside. I grab the iron bars and shake them. "You tricked me!"

The view is blocked by a bamboo shutter tied to the bars. Thin stabs of light cut through the edges, but the rest is a dusky haze. I'm in the dark, again.

"It's coming," he says, his voice close to the bars. "Don't worry, it can't get you now. *Blizzards*, Zenri should be here already."

"Please, let me out. My family—"

"Not enough time," he says. Two fingers slip through the side of the bamboo shutter, passing me the key. *"Don't* leave until it's gone. I can't save you now, it'd be against the law. Meet me on the Road."

The ground shakes. I stop rattling the bars, and my hand drifts to his, taking the key and brushing the smooth skin. Then suddenly, his fingers whip away. A body thuds against the chamber as though he'd been punched. No . . . rammed by something. Outside, a clash of steel and bone rings then goes silent.

Warmth prickles my skin where his fingers had touched mine. I stifle a scream.

What. Was. That?

Fear holds me in a silent chokehold.

"I knew it would come," a voice says behind me, unnatural and high-pitched as though speaking with a continual hiccup.

I jump and turn to notice an old man curled in the corner of the tiny space, shivering, knees to his chin.

"The monster," he hiccups. "I saw it on the Prisoners Road. Eyes like black mother-of-pearl, fast as the wind in the pines, teeth like razors."

"Naven?" I recognize his eyes behind the overgrown white hair and beard. A former prisoner in our wing who'd made life even more miserable for me.

Naven wipes his lips with a sore-speckled arm. The tattoo is still there, circling blackened teeth—a few missing. "Kira?"

I nod.

"Can't forget you. Poisoned my millet for breaking your nose, you did." Naven chuckles, but it twists into a ragged cough. "Where's your mother? Sent to the Road already? They all died building it. Just put the bodies under the tracks they did. That boy was right putting you here. It's safe, safe, safe . . ."

"Mother's *out there*," I say and hold up the key. "We're escaping."

My fingers still tingle with warmth where Mochi had touched them. Why had he saved me?

Naven scratches his head and a shiver runs through him. "Go," he says. "I'm staying. It's not worth facing a monster."

"Bear and monster are two very different things." I reach through the bars with the key. "Either way—I'll take my chances."

Pity pricks my heart, and I fight against the urge to help the man that'd made my life miserable as a child. *Caring only causes pain.* My stomach pulls taut as I open the door.

Outside, Mochi is nowhere to be seen, only a thin trail of footprints in the snow. I sigh in relief that he's escaped, or at least I hope he has. Smoke plumes like great black horses running pell-mell to the sky. Fire, coming from our prison barracks. My heart lurches.

Yuki.

Mother.

My feet hit the snow at a run.

CHAPTER 4

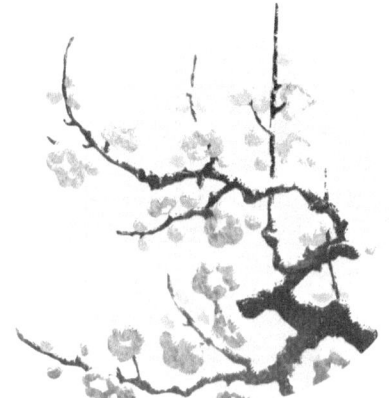

FLAMES LEAP FROM THE PRISON barracks. The sight of red and black dragon flames against the sky dizzies me. A plume of fire explodes. Bits of wood and smoldering iron fall as the fifth wing crumbles.

"No . . ."

Images of Yuki and Mother still trapped within the cell, huddled together while smoke creeps into their lungs, bombard my mind. Mochi's wool cap lies in the snow to my left on one trail, and the other—a deep ragged path—leads toward the fifth wing.

The snow slows my feet. I don't want to believe it's a real bear from the Winterwilds attacking, upsetting lanterns and setting the wooden prison to blaze. But the wound on that guard tells me otherwise. The look on the bear's face in the forest when the second shot rang out made it clear: that bear was cursed. A monster from the old myths and stories Mother had whispered. And my wayfinding must have led its kind right to us.

Magic attracts other magic, Mother had said.

An enormous shadow runs across the snow, startling me. It's the biggest, most horrible bear I've ever seen. I rub my eyes, thinking it a phantom of nightfall and ash, but it's still there—a terrible monster pacing outside the fifth wing. Waves of white powder toss in the air with each step. A jagged hunched back like a mountain sways as it knocks down an entire watchtower, gobbling up guards and fleeing prisoners. Its back is toward me, riddled with arrows and bullet holes scarcely denting the thick hide.

I hold my breath. Shivers like tiny spiders crawl over my skin as the massive grizzly bear—twice the size as the one in the forest—paws the snow and turns.

Ban. Ban.

More gunshots. I stop, frozen. Feverish, my eyes search for the source of the shooter, to warn him to flee, but the sky has turned to blizzard, whether from snow or falling ash, I can't tell. Then, behind the hulking monster, I spy the toothpick form of a starved girl holding a rifle. *Yuki.*

The gun trembles against her chest as she attempts to light the powder. Bruises mushroom across her pale face, a patch of torn skin at the brow. Why is she out here all alone?

"Yuki! I'm coming!" I run, plowing through the snow.

The bear roars, drowning out my voice. Then it charges.

My blood turns to ice. Not stagnant lake ice that freezes over in the winter like a cool mirror below my feet. No. This is glacial: a biting, grinding shard of ice that pierces the hulls of ships and scrapes the mountains until it claws its own path.

"Yuki!"

The bear lunges at her.

In one swipe of its paw, my sister's cry pierces the air and then she falls. Blood splatters the snow in crimson flowers and thorns. The bear bites, its teeth sinking into her arm. My head spins and the earth falls out from under me. A scream builds in my chest. A fury I've never known. My legs freeze, shaking violently.

The beast turns from his victim, black eyes with no end meeting my own. There's a wickedness beyond belief in its heartless gaze. It charges toward me, leaving my sister in a crumpled heap. When the bear is a stone's throw from me, it jolts to a stop. Great claws dig into the deep snowbanks, dripping with blood.

Yuki's blood.

Fear is a noose around my neck, stealing my breath.

The bear roars with a mouth big enough to swallow me whole. Shivering, I stare at the snow and the bear so close its rancid breath curdles over me. My heart hammers against my ribs, sick with anger and grief and fear. This creature attacked the guard, set the prison ablaze, and . . . and . . . *Yuki.*

I need to reach my sister.

I dash to the right, but the bear lunges, blocking my path. It snorts, a frigid blast of snow and stench. In the light of the fires, its teeth glisten, each one the length of my finger. Fathomless black eyes reach into me like claws. I tear my gaze from it and try to spot my sister again.

I'm too slow in the snow to get around him, but there must be a way. As if I'd spun that need into a spell, a thread of faint blue light appears in the snow. It whips around me like a blizzard. I straighten, latching onto the thin light encircling me. The bear snorts in surprise. Emboldened by the light, I take another step toward the beast and to Yuki beyond it.

Panic pricks at my mind, warning me to stop. But it's not as loud as the desperate voice inside shouting, *Yuki. Yuki. Yuki.* The light, the path . . . whatever it is, doesn't show me how to defeat the bear. Only that the way is straight through it. I gulp, forcing myself to look darkness in the eye.

The bear flinches. It rears to its full height with a horrendous roar before stomping the ground. I stagger at the impact, nearly knocked from my feet. Wicked eyes stare down at me. Then a flicker of something . . . not sadness, but pain, touches those awful, pitiless eyes.

A few more steps, and I'll be right under the beast, standing on its claws. I look up.

"L-leave!" I shout, my voice faltering. "G-get out of here!"

I raise my hands to ward the monster off, standing my ground with quaking legs.

Another building collapses in the fire with a crackling boom as guards and prisoners shout in the distance. The bear shakes its shoulders, shedding a downpour of broken arrows and snow from its back. With a frustrated snarl, its eyes narrow on me. My mind races back to the bear in the Winterwilds.

Did I lead this creature here by hunting one of its own?

Shivers rack my body, but a terrible pain in my heart forces me to stand for Yuki.

"Leave!" I shout again, holding the blue light close.

The bear's teeth gleam within arm's reach. Then, with a low moan like a dying beast, it turns and lopes toward the south side of the island, ground quaking as it goes. My breath spills out in a shaky fog. I launch myself over the slope where the bear had stood until I latch onto Yuki.

I cling to her, heart pounding like a thousand arctic butterfly wings trapped in a glass jar. I slide my arms under Yuki and haul her painstakingly to the top of the hill where the fire gives us light. Unruly brown hair sweeps her face and falls in a thousand strands around her shoulders, blurring into the snow like spring branches. I roll her onto her back and attempt to wipe the hair from her face, but it sticks to raw patches of exposed skin. I find my breath.

"Yuki, speak to me. It's Kira. I'm here."

Her face is pale with sweat and ash, eyes closed. She's breathing. I check for injuries and don't have to look far. Bite marks dig into her arm and sweeping cuts wrap from her shoulder to her stomach. Blood has caked into her clothes and seeps into the snow beneath us. A monster has done this.

And I fear that I brought it here.

I pull off my scarf and wrap it around her wounds, tying it tight, not sure how helpful it will be. She doesn't budge.

"No, no, no . . . Don't leave me, Yuki!"

Shouts echo from the barracks. There's no time to evaluate

more injuries here. I need to find Mother and get Yuki out of the cold before we freeze. The temperature drops at night are deadly.

"Don't die," I plead, touching my forehead to hers.

I put an arm under her neck and another beneath her knees, praying I don't break anything on my already fragile sister. She doesn't make a sound as I pull her to me and stand with her in my arms. There's barely a breath left in her body.

I promised I would keep her safe.

I trudge to the guardhouse in the middle of the courtyard, sinking knee-deep in snow with each step. Smoke puffs steadily from the house, but it's only the fireplace. The one place in the whole prison that has heating. When I open the door, a guard jumps to his feet. But upon seeing me, he relaxes and sinks into a chair to stare at the fire.

It's Beetle.

I lay Yuki in front of the fire and then tuck a nearby blanket tight around her. I check her breath again. *Hold on.*

Beetle laughs. "So, you survived?"

"What are you doing?" I ask. "Shouldn't you be helping put out the fire?"

He wipes his red nose with the back of his hand. "Too late for that. We stopped it from spreading to the other wings, but four and five are lost."

My heart drops. "My mother? Is she safe?"

Beetle shakes his head. "Doubt it. I'm surprised you and your sister found a different fortune. That is, if she's alive?"

He peers over at Yuki and cringes, but there's an odd twitch in his eyes, just a touch moist. A ghosting glimmer of compassion. If I didn't know any better, I'd say that Beetle cared. I don't trust him, but I have no other choice.

"Please, take care of Yuki." I point at my sister. "Treat her injuries."

"I'm a guard, not a doctor—"

"Keep her alive," I say it like an order, because it is. "There must be a medical kit around here or some alcohol."

Beetle glances at the half-empty bottle beside his chair and frowns. "Where are you going? Your cell isn't there anymore. Though I'm sure they'll be happy to throw you in another one."

"I'm going to find my mother. Keep Yuki alive."

"Your sister might not—"

I stare at Beetle. My gaze must be terrifying because his mouth clamps shut and he *flinches*. Fear no longer has a place in my heart. Not fear of him. My only fear is that I won't be fast enough. Or strong enough to save my family.

I dash out of the house, whispering a prayer for Yuki and trying to locate my mother by quieting my mind and listening to the path as I did in the forest.

But I can't feel her. I can't sense her. When I search for her in my mind, I'm met with silence. The faint blue light is gone.

Wing five was a long corridor with fifty cells and narrow skylights, too often covered with snow to give any light. Now, the wing is a blackened tooth in the snow, hollow with only wood and shattered pieces remaining. Fire falls from the last bit of roof still standing and gobbles up the remaining beams. I can almost hear her voice in the flames. A phantom scream from the unceasing hunger, a howl of winter winds.

Free, it seems to sing. *Be free.*

The pull of her voice blows a soft chill across my shoulders. Sparks of fire fall like rain. Mother's song hums in my mind. *Fire falls on me like rain, but I didn't care at all. When I ran the earth glowed blue, and your fine lips I saw were true.*

I walk faster.

Flames cling to the wood, crawling high into the framework and watching me with molten eyes through the cracks. Burning hot saliva drips, scorching the floor. I slide my feet across, barely missing a sizzle.

My heart aches. *Mother.*

Our cell is at the end, a small effort to give us privacy. But it was also the coldest cell with nothing to insulate it from the elements. My legs start running before I'm aware of it, and I've rounded the corner. The smell hits before anything else, and I gag. My body doubles over, wrenching my empty stomach. The sky is gray, a forest of snowing ash and fire-like rain. I can't . . .

A body remains, if it can be called that. I can't unsee. My eyes are glued to the spot, and my knees buckle. I don't even care when still-hot ash drops onto my worn coat, stitched by Mother's hand. I almost wish there was nothing left instead of the blistered blackened body, oh so human, curled on the floor.

I reel into a barely standing support beam, losing more of my stomach. Without my mother, who am I? She bore me, alone, as a prisoner, when everyone else had left her.

She taught me.

She fought for me.

She died for me.

And I can't even bury her. Not in the snow that would melt and the ground too hard with frost, even if I could dig through.

"Mama," I whisper her name like a prayer.

A voice creaks on the wind. My heart leaps, and I'm at her side in an instant. I bend down, choking on the smoke, listening for breath. I cannot take her hand for fear the skin will shrug off beneath my own.

"Mama," I gasp, tears falling. "Come back," I beg.

She doesn't, but her voice is a whisper in my head, speaking to me on the smoke-choked wind, an echo of memory. *Keep Yuki safe. Protect her above your own life. Find the rabbit in the talons.*

A gun cocks behind me.

Against the opposite wall, a shadow looms, black against the glowing embers. I glance over my shoulder, my body too dull from pain to care. The new inspector towers over me in full regalia with medals from the mainland and an iron face with pockmarked cheeks to match. Long fingers curl around the pistol, a ring on nearly every bone-white digit.

"What do you want?" I say.

"Back to your cell." He flashes the revolver.

"This *is* my cell."

I make a quick calculation that I could outrun him to the guardhouse, but the weapon makes me second-guess my odds.

"Move," he says in a dank, cool voice. A gloved hand jerks me back by the collar.

"No! I can't leave her." I claw forward, leaning over my mother—the light in my darkness. *You are not a prisoner.* Her words burn into my soul.

The inspector jerks me hard, and I'm dragged across the scorched floor until he pulls me upright, facing him.

I meet his gaze, glaring, feeling that somehow this man is responsible.

He shoves me outside the broken wing and gestures with his revolver for me to go ahead of him toward the guardhouse. I do so, moving quickly, keenly aware of his awkward gait in the snow, watching each step so he doesn't slip. The new inspector isn't used to the island yet.

But I was born here, among the cold-hearted and the ice.

CHAPTER 5

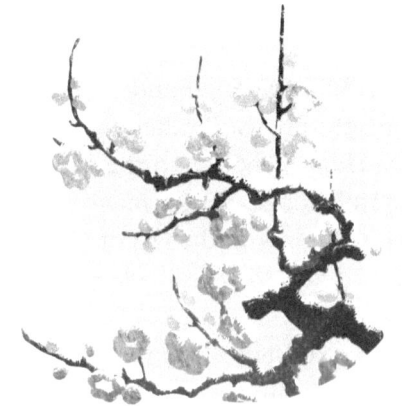

WITH A PISTOL TO MY BACK,

I step into the guardhouse. Echoes of mother—too fresh to be called memories—cling to the prison walls and slash at my heart.

A flame crackles in the hearth, Yuki's starved form sprawled near it, a navy guard's jacket resting over her shoulders and a fresh prison shift beneath. My heart catches with something dangerously close to hope.

But my sister doesn't budge. Beetle picks his nails over his rounded gut, a sullen expression on his hairy face.

With a shove to the back, I stagger into the room. The door slams behind me, and the fire in the hearth gutters at the snow-dusted wind. Yuki's eyes flash open. She scours the room with full moon eyes that shiver until she finds me.

"Yuki!" I run, knees crashing to her side. "You're alive."

"K-kira-rin."

"Guard, what is the meaning of this?" The inspector's voice booms with an air of injustice. "Why is a prisoner by the hearth?"

Beetle eyes him with amusement. "She's keeping my feet warm. What do you want, Inspector?"

My ears tune into the conversation as I survey Yuki, glad Beetle can be of use keeping the inspector off my back for a few precious minutes.

Yuki grips my hand, her hold near nonexistent. I check beneath the wool jacket and her prison shift. Her wounds are cleaned, stitched, and the blood flow stanched, although it's painfully obvious how much she lost. Beetle must have doused her wounds with the last of his imported rice ale. He *had* taken care of her. My eyes flicker toward the guard I'd hated for so many years.

A hard knot in my throat dislodges, and with it, a memory. I'd been a nine-year-old fool when Beetle caught me trying to escape on the ice. The frozen ocean broke beneath my feet, and I fell into the water. Yuki dove in after me. She's never been the same since. Dreadfully sick after the ice-fever left her. Her cracking bones and weak lungs are . . . because of me.

Beetle pulled us both from the ice. Then he grabbed my neck and his words hissed across my ear. "You're lucky to have an older sister. Don't forget it."

My eyes trailed over his bearded face, my body shaking with cold. Did Beetle have an older sister? Something in his eyes had flashed with guilt, with home. Only after that did he begin teasing me about escape, like rubbing salt in a wound.

The inspector slaps Beetle's face with a gloved hand. "Rank and duty?"

My shoulder jerks at the smack of leather on flesh.

Beetle shoves his chair back and stands. "With all due respect, Inspector, our prison is under attack. The cells have been destroyed in wings four and five, and this prisoner was injured. I don't know how you handle things in Taiga, but we're still putting out the fire."

"*You* aren't," the inspector says with a hint of a smile. "If anything, I'd say you're starting a fire. A prisoner, female at that, in the cabin with you, *alone*. An officer in the Taigan army would be debarred for less."

"It's the guardhouse, sir . . ." Beetle blunders. "It's not like that. Look, the girls were injured in the fire—"

"Not girls," the inspector sneers. "Prisoners." He slaps

Beetle again. "So long as they are within the empire's rule, they are nothing. The only way for them to regain their humanity is through hard work and suffering." He paces the room, boots thrashing the floor as he circles us. "You know why I was sent here, don't you?"

I crouch over Yuki, protecting her.

"It's my job to inform the emperor of the state of his reform centers. And yes, I report directly to him. The emperor doesn't tolerate failure, especially not from the most secure prison tasked with building his majesty's railroad. Not to mention housing dangerous criminals and *traitors* to the crown"—he pauses, his eyes cutting to me—"but I will clarify an important matter. I am Pontius Jade, the Imperial Inspector. When this is over, the warden and any guards slack in their duties will be arrested."

"For what crime?" I blurt out and quickly wish I hadn't.

Inspector Jade's narrow eyes pin me to the floor. "Compassion." He kicks Yuki in the side, and she lets out a groan. "It's a weakness that must be pruned."

I grind my teeth, every nerve poised and ready to attack. But Yuki's bleeding again. I press a cloth against the newly opened punctures on her arm. I know firsthand that caring only causes pain, but punishing someone for it?

"We've never had an Imperial Inspector," Beetle says, his voice a notch too high.

"Of course not. It's a royal position." He flashes a silver ring with dual dragons, the imperial crest. "The emperor decided that he needed more than low-ranking soldiers and mercenaries to fuel his programs in the northern province of Ezo. I'm endowed with all authority to bring unity to the empire, and you know the price for that. Do you think his majesty will care if this prison burns so long as all the prisoners burn with it? You forget who you are serving."

"Sir, we've hit our quarterly quotas, our funding always comes through, the railroad is almost done." Beetle stands straighter. "The emperor has never been displeased."

"I've been sent to say otherwise." Inspector Jade sneers. "The natives are becoming resistant to change. I won't hesitate to inform his majesty that he was correct in his assessment—rebellion brews in the North. I'm here to snuff out the embers. There's an Ainur on the prison docket."

My hand freezes over Yuki's shoulder, wishing we could disappear.

"She's dead."

I blink at Beetle's words, the way his voice turns to ice.

He's . . . protecting us.

"How convenient." The inspector's jaw clenches. "The Ainur resisted the emperor over a decade ago when we seized Ezo for its own good. Can you imagine what would've become of this country if we'd let a dragon rule it?"

"King Soran isn't a—"

"Of course, you think it all rumor," Inspector Jade snaps, his eyes narrowing. "You're from Ezo. I know a few Ainur escaped that rebellion. And now that I've finally tracked them here, you want me to believe that they're all dead?" The inspector's pale green eyes rove across the room before landing on me.

My hands tremble, even near the fire, as I apply pressure to Yuki's still-seeping wound. I don't understand. Why is the empire hunting the Ainur? The rebellion ended long ago. There's peace now in the outside world. Isn't there?

Merciless eyes burn into mine. "Protocol states that when a prison facility is in breach, all prisoners found outside their cells must be executed to prevent escape."

"Y-yes sir," Beetle stammers. "But these two are children. It was their mother who was convicted and—"

"They are on the prison docket," the inspector says. "And they do not look much like children to me. You have your orders."

"Yes, sir."

"Well?" Inspector Jade steps back and waits.

My eyes dart between the two men. One demanding our death and the other warring with his soul. A hungry gleam darkens the inspector's eyes. He's not ordering Beetle to execute us because he trusts him. He's using his own twisted law as a weapon—to punish him. Beetle grabs my arm, pulling me to my feet. His fingertips pry into the soft skin beneath my elbow, and I wince.

"I'll take them outside to finish the job," Beetle says. "No need to mop the floors in here."

A low growl comes from Yuki's throat as I'm torn away from her. I shove Beetle off and lift Yuki in my arms before the two men can stop me. She curls into me, as if her life depends on it.

"K-kira?" she breathes, eyes fluttering.

I've lost Mother. I won't lose my sister too. I clutch her tight and march toward the door, my heart tripping over itself. We're walking to our death. Inspector Jade holds the door open with a white-toothed smile. When I pause in the doorway, the cool steel of his pistol presses against my spine.

This can't be the end. A march through the snow with a pistol to my back. Yuki curled against my heart, fighting for breath . . .

A saying Mother always quoted comes to mind. *Paths are forged into the impossible. That's how every trail begins.*

I step outside, and Beetle follows us. I'm certainly walking into the impossible now.

A few paces from the guardhouse, Beetle grabs me by the shoulders. I startle, turning to him, the wind beating my face and my vision blurred by the remaining ash.

"I'll carry her," he says.

"No." My arms curl tighter around Yuki, and my gaze shifts to the rigid inspector standing in the doorway. He must be unfamiliar with snow, the way he hunkers away from the eaves and doesn't follow us.

"I'm sorry," Beetle whispers. "I have to do this."

There it is, again, that dangerous pinch of compassion. *Why?* I turn to face him, but his fist collides with my jaw.

I reel back from the punch. Yuki falls from my arms with

a soft poof in the snow. *Has Beetle lost his mind?* His apology echoes in my head—sorry—I've never heard a guard say that. It almost hurts more than the sore swelling on my lip. I push myself up and squint after Beetle who marches ahead, carrying my sister.

"Don't take them too far!" the inspector calls out, his voice tangled in the wind.

I run after my sister along the poorly cleared path.

There is no designated place for execution. But it would make sense to eliminate us somewhere away from the guards' residence, preferably near a fire to destroy the bodies.

Fire. Mother. Home.

Beetle trudges toward the remains of wing five, and panic claws my chest. As my suspicions are confirmed, I run faster. A sickening feeling swirls in my stomach. Are we to be buried in the same ruins that house our mother's bones?

Before he reaches the wing, he sets Yuki down on the path we had dug and tucks his wool hat over her matted hair. I stop, out of breath, hands fisting my knees. Beetle pulls out his ever-favored baton.

"My offer still stands," he says, eyes shifting watchfully. "Take your sister. Run."

I gape at him, but for the first time the possibility that it *isn't* a trick ripples through me. This guard beats other men for money. He gambles on how long we'll last in the winter. He wouldn't risk his neck to help us—but he is.

I heave Yuki onto my back, never breaking eye contact with Beetle. Warnings trill in my mind that he could shoot us, betray us. But his brown eyes stare back with a strange sadness and twinkling hope, like a lost man rocking back and forth at sea, wishing on a star to guide him home. To forgive him.

I turn my back and walk.

The impact of the first few trudging steps is heavy as I hurry to the gate. I don't look back. Perhaps Beetle is making up for whatever happened to his older sister. I had a feeling, a sense of path tracing back through time that she'd died very close to him. As close as I now hold Yuki to me. I've never seen Beetle as a human until now. What made him let us go? Perhaps he realized we were all in prison together, the strong and the weak, the cruel and the innocent, the guard and the convict.

"Stop them! Guards!" a cold voice knifes in the wind. The inspector's footsteps pound across the snow. A gunshot echoes behind me, followed by a powdery thud as a body hits the ground.

Beetle.

My heart stifles a cry, but I keep on—running as Beetle had told me.

No looking back.

CHAPTER 6

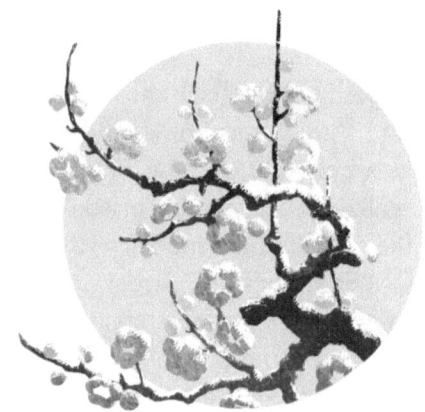

I'D ALWAYS WANTED TO ESCAPE, but not like this. My sister's body hangs limp over my back. Sweat breaks across my forehead, and my arms shake from exhaustion as I hurry to the gate. Inspector Jade's footsteps thump against the snow far behind. He's not used to the ice, not like me.

I duck into the shadow of the watchtowers for cover, edging toward the ice floes. Mother had taught me so little of her wayfinding magic. How the Ainur use the breath within their bodies to connect with the outside world, to find paths in the ever-moving ice and hunt the sleek-bodied deer. She could discern which plants to eat and how to find safe havens in the mountains, simply by listening to the path.

I have much left to learn. Unlike Mother, I can't use my skill to fight or defend myself. I can't see the future—not even a glimpse.

If only Mother had told me more. How to use the ancient magic. How she came to be in prison. How the war ended. Maybe then I'd know where to find shelter and medicine for Yuki, but I don't. The mystery of the outside world wraps around my shoulders—the terror, the wonder, the hope.

"Hold on, Yuki," I whisper.

My sister's breath is slow, erratic. I stumble, and her head rolls to the side. "Don't give up."

Ice groans beneath my salmon boots as I pause at the edge of the frozen strait that stretches to the mountains beyond. I cast a nervous glance at the watchtowers at my back. The guards must have left to put out the fire, not expecting prisoners to attempt the death-riddled path across the frozen sea.

Cold burns my lungs as I hoist Yuki higher. The prison 'moat,' as we call it, is a gap of frozen ocean. Were it safe to cross, it would only take fifteen minutes. But with the shifting ice floes, it'd taken Mother an hour when she attempted to escape while pregnant with me. Of course, she'd been caught not long after. I stare at the treacherous ice, testing it with my heel.

"Halt!" Inspector Jade's voice booms.

My spine stiffens, expecting a bullet in my back. But I anchor my gaze and step onto the ice. Mother told me there was a bridge to the mainland, an ever-changing path across the ice if you knew the right steps. But she's not here to show me.

I look down at the ice and my reflection stares back at me: unkempt raven hair tied back and sticking out every which way, angled cheekbones revealing just how emaciated I am, chapped skin, and large, angry eyes.

I look like a criminal. *Maybe I am one.*

The ice crunches beneath my feet as Yuki stirs on my back.

"Don't listen to him. We'll be okay."

I chew on my bottom lip. Together, we're too heavy for the ice. A few more steps, and water seeps into the torn seams of my salmon leather. There's no way to cross without a path. I still my mind, listening to thundering footsteps, the flutter of ash, and the hungry ice. But the loudest sound is Yuki's heart. I listen, feeling the solid parts of ice in sync with Yuki's heartbeat time and time again.

I focus on the ice as I step, going as quickly as I dare. One misstep, and we will be trapped underwater if the ice breaks. I've been there before and shudder at the memory.

"Stop!" Inspector Jade's voice is closer than I imagined.

The hair rises on the back of my neck. I turn, expecting to

find him at the gate, held back by his fear of winter. But he stands on the ice, shoulders hunched, the prison watchtowers to his back and a shiny pistol in hand. A guard rushes to the watchtower and trains a spotlight on the ice field between us. I wince at the blinding light.

Yuki growls and tries to pull herself off my shoulders. Unease pinches my chest. In all her childhood pains, she's never complained—certainly not growled. I grip tighter with one hand and smooth her hair with the other.

"Shush, it'll be okay," I say, but it feels like a lie.

"Turn yourself in!" Inspector Jade steps closer and aims his revolver. "It's your fault we're in this mess. The rest of the guards might buy your act, but I don't. Why run unless you started the fire? Traitor blood runs in your veins, Ainur. Your mother called the beast to the prison to sabotage me with her tainted magic. But I always get what I come for."

Is he insane? Why would Mother do that?

"You know nothing about my mother!" I yell.

In answer, the Inspector fires. The bullet zips at the ice beneath my feet and a watery fissure appears. Yuki growls.

"You were born here," Jade says, so close now that I notice his smug smile. "That's what the records show. I studied every criminal record before arriving on that blasted ship. The prison didn't list you as Ainur. I had to do a lot of digging."

He stops close enough that I can see the imperial dragons of Taiga embossed on his coat buttons. He aims the gun again.

Yuki squirms, her fingernails digging into the soft spots beneath my shoulders.

The gun chamber explodes.

I fall and land hard on my back. My fingers stretch across the ice, expecting a hole in my side and a fractal of broken ice beneath me, but I'm unharmed. Breathless, my eyes land on Yuki. She grapples with the inspector, Beetle's coat still over her shoulders. I gasp, steadying myself.

How? It's not possible. She was barely breathing.

"Yuki, don't—"

Yuki wrestles the gun out of his hand and throws it across the ice. I crawl feverishly back toward the fallen pistol as the ice cracks and a blue rift appears.

"Yuki, the ice!"

The inspector struggles like he isn't fighting a little girl but a warrior with the strength of five men. The two spin in a horrible dance, arms locked, and the occasional swift movement trying to break the other's hold. Suddenly, the inspector flips her.

Yuki lands on her feet, half-bent over, and the veins in her hands and face bulge as if trying to suck in more oxygen.

Surprise registers on the inspector's face, but he angles his feet, ready for an attack. Yuki growls and charges again. I gape, shocked at her agility and her wild fists.

How is she doing this?

My throat tightens with warning. "Yuki, run! Run to shore."

But it's too late. A baton crashes against the side of her skull, and she collapses. Inspector Jade grabs her by the back of her tunic, holding her out like a limp rag doll.

"Stop!" I scream. "Please."

With a flick of his wrist, the Inspector snaps a silver chain over each of my sister's hands. The cuffs almost look like bracelets if I didn't know any better.

Yuki sucks in a breath between clenched teeth.

I've never seen shackles like these before and catch a whiff of burning flesh. Whenever Yuki moves, she draws a tight breath, as if the chains burn, but they don't look hot. It's more like ice.

"Frozen chains," the inspector says, noting my interest. "They're new in Taiga. Completely unbreakable. They burn the skin, tattooing it. Marks criminals for life, so there's no escaping who you really are. Of course, they're only meant to be kept on for a day. Too long, and she could lose her hands entirely, frozen right through the bone."

I run at him, furious.

"Think before you act." He holds the baton, ready for a swipe to Yuki's neck.

But I don't stop. He doesn't have the gun anymore, and I've lost enough. I feel the ice beneath me, the waves trapped beneath them, a path on the tip of my fingers. I jump and land on the weakest point of ice.

A worried crease nests on the inspector's brow. I wait for the ice to break, but it doesn't.

Suddenly, Yuki awakes, clawing at the sky. His baton swoops down, but she grabs it—with her teeth.

I gawk. *That. Is. My. Sister.*

He curses and drops the baton.

Yuki breaks out of his hold, her elbow crashing into his ribcage. I pitch forward, and together Yuki and I slam our weight into the ice with a kick. A fissure spreads beneath the inspector like a spider's web. He reels away from it—away from us.

"Let's go." I grab Yuki's hand.

She turns on me with a half-human snarl. Her usually large eyes are pinched at the corners, pained. Blood soaks her bandages; she'd reopened her wounds during the fight.

"Yuki—"

She snarls again, the faintest of tears touching her eyes, and then she bolts toward freedom, the ice breaking in her wake. Nimble feet race toward the frozen, rocky shore and the mountains beyond.

Inspector Jade curses as the ice splits, and he falls into the freezing water. His hands cling to the edge of a block of ice, pulling himself halfway out with a ghostly shiver.

A huge sheet of ice breaks off, and I run to follow Yuki. Panting, I turn for a last glimpse at the only home I've ever known.

Abashi Prison is a black smudge against the sky. Flames feast on the remaining buildings, and my heart cracks open wide.

Mama, I didn't find the right path. We were supposed to leave together. I promise to take care of Yuki above my own life. I promise.

I bat at the tears streaking my face and run across the ice. When I reach the shore, a snowy trail of footprints leads through a candelabra of winter forest. Yuki runs ahead of me like a phantom made for these mountains. My sister with the weak lungs and fragile bones. *What happened to her?*

Whatever darkness is following us, the only answer is to face it.

I step into the wood.

Kira's elmwood coat was inspired by historical attush coats

teddy bears are kinda cute with fangs

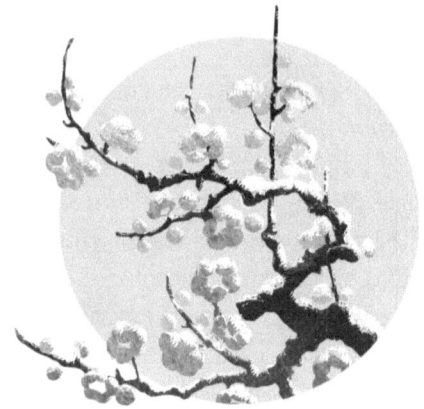

CHAPTER 7

BY THE TIME I CATCH UP TO Yuki, I'm exhausted. The winter whispers: *stop, rest a while, dream*. It's an ice-siren's call to death. We have to push on, no matter how cold or broken we feel. Without warmth and shelter, we won't last the night.

Yuki trails ahead with Beetle's wool hat tucked over her ears. I stop to catch my breath, the wind biting through my soot-ridden coat—the one Mother stitched by hand.

Mother. My heart breaks. *Why aren't you here?*

Her words drift back to me, *follow the rabbit in the talons.*

She'd spoken of the rabbit in the talons before, when she taught my sister and me how to build snow bunnies out of inedible berries and leaves. I thought she was just teaching us about survival and woodland creatures. What had she meant by it?

I scowl and squint at the moon glowing white through the trees. A shrill bark from a crow sends one of the pine trees rattling. Yuki dodges the falling needles, swift and alert, her body pushing past the limits of reason.

How is she not limping?

We stumble into a clearing between towering firs, and I notice a pinprick trail of red in Yuki's wake.

"Yuki, stop. Let me check your wounds."

My sister steps into the sliver of moonlight, the guard's coat wrapped tight against the wind. She glances down at her feet and the trail she'd left. Her side wound must have reopened.

"Yuki, stay near the forest edge. Away from the clearing," I say. "We don't want to attract any more monsters."

When she doesn't listen, I pull gently at her coat. "I need to bind your wounds."

She turns, and the clever, calm eyes I've always known vanish. Two dark, hungry slits latch onto me.

I stumble back.

Yuki's brow furrows as she studies me. The winter wind plays havoc with her grizzly-brown hair and the edges of the wool coat, now open and flapping in the snow. She smiles, as if reassuring me, but her teeth glint in the dark.

Yuki. She's always been strong in spirit, albeit weak in body, but this . . .

A chill licks my spine as I shake away thoughts of bears and ancient curses. Yuki blinks, batting away the dark slits in her eyes. A confused frown on her lips.

"Are you a-alright, Kirarin?" she asks, her voice hitched.

"I'm fine," I say too quickly.

I'm tired. I'm seeing things. I'm the daughter of a wayfinder—and I'm lost.

I open the coat to inspect the large cuts on her abdomen and arm. Beetle had cleaned them well, but the stitching was sloppy. It's nothing short of a miracle she's alive.

"Thank you," Yuki whispers as I secure the bandage and retie her shift. "I thought we were done for back there."

"We will be if we don't find shelter," I say through chattering teeth. "Your wounds will get infected without proper care."

I don't mention that they've scabbed over, far too quickly. It must be ice-fever and delusion. I swipe at the blur in my eyes.

Faint smoke rises from the other side of the mountain,

carried on the breeze with hints of warmth. Yuki sniffs and points westward.

"Someone's cooking." She turns her head and traces the scent. "Mountain burdock, sweet nettle . . . *meat*."

I follow her example and sniff the air. "Are you sure? It's probably smoke from the prison."

"Trust me, Kira. I can't explain it, but I know what I smell." Yuki starts toward the next snowcapped mountain, but I stop her.

"We'll never make it over the top. Not in this wind." I study the landscape, using the few skills Mother taught me. "We should curve along the side of the mountain. The wind is against us, so we'll have to move fast. The inspector will have our scent if he's using hounds."

"Our scent." Yuki laughs. "I feel sorry for the hounds."

Smiling makes my dry lips crack, but it's worth it. Laughter is the best medicine I have. "My scent is better than yours," I tease.

Yuki leads the way, and my mind drifts into dangerous territory. *Why aren't her wounds bothering her? Did she see Mother die? Why did the bear attack?*

With a shudder, I recall Mochi's fingers against mine and his startling whisper in my ear. *A bear*, he'd said. The monster from the Winterwilds had disappeared—fleeing the same direction we were now heading.

Around the leeward side, the wind softens and the trees thicken, their long skeletal limbs clawing at us as we pass. Twin lanterns glow faintly ahead. The shadow of a large thatched house juts into the midnight sky, lanterns hanging from the eaves and casting an elongated glow on the snow.

"You shouldn't be out here at night!" calls a wary voice.

I pull Yuki behind me out of instinct. An old woman bundled head to toe in blankets and a tartan coat stands at the entrance of the house. It's tucked in a hollow on the escarpment, bordered with shrubs and rocks. It would've been easy to miss in the dark if not for the lanterns.

"Don't just stand there. Come in," she beckons.

Cautiously, we step toward the house. I scan the woman for clues of whether she's friend or foe, but I can't see clearly.

Yuki nestles against my shoulder, her energy suddenly vanished like spilled soup lost between the cracks in the floor. After all we've been through, she's on the brink of collapse. My own body teeters from exhaustion.

I approach the old woman. "We need shelter," I call out, my voice hoarse. "But we have no coin."

"What happened to you, dears?" She holds up a lantern for a better view. "No one wanders this forest alone at night."

"A fire destroyed our . . . village. We have nowhere to go."

"A fire? You must be from the colliery down south," she says, a worried squint in her eye. "No other village near here. Those coal mines work women and children to the bone." She shakes her head in passionate disproval. "Come on in, dears. Anyone who knocks on this door is welcome to stay. This is the Château of Our Lady of the Light, a refuge for lost souls."

Lost souls—that certainly describes us. Lost. Orphaned. Broken.

The woman waves us inside, her hand fluttering like an agitated bird. "Hurry now. It's not safe after dark. You must be freezing. I'm surprised you haven't lost a nose in this weather." She gasps and covers her mouth. "You're covered in ash, poor dears!"

Warily, I step forward with Yuki until we stand on a wide wooden porch. I heave a sigh of relief that she hasn't noticed our prison shifts in the dark. Tattered and faded as they are, it's possible she might not recognize the faded orange or the slogan on the back, branding us as Abashi property.

The woman bows as I step inside the entryway, which I return, careful to keep my coat on when she offers to take it from me. Heat rushes my face as my salmon leather hit the stone *genkan*. My cheeks burn and my eyes water from the sudden warmth. I turn, devouring the cozy interior with its fogged-up windows and polished cedar stairs leading to a second story.

"Do you live here alone?" I ask, watching the woman closely.

She nods, wool nightcap bobbing on her silver head. "Not quite alone. The deer eat my cabbages, and travelers like yourselves or the Northern Watchmen sometimes seek shelter."

I slip off my shoes, completely soaked through despite the salmon skins, and turn back, expecting Yuki behind me. My sister pauses before the open door, staring at two pots of resilient crimson flowers on either side of the frame. She shudders against the cold and hunkers away from the blossoms.

"Yuki, come inside." I wave to her, reluctant to squelch into my wet shoes again.

Yuki tucks her hands beneath her coat, but not before I catch the thin red rings showing under her sleeves where the icy chains have seared her flesh. She shakes her head, jostling Beetle's wool hat.

"Your sister is unwell." The woman's voice cracks with worry as she drapes an extra blanket over my shoulders. I stiffen, grateful she can't see the prison garb beneath my elmwood coat. The old saint moves to stand beside the door, nudging it wider for Yuki.

"It's safe," I coax, moving to put my shoes back on.

"Don't." The old woman lays hold of my shoulder, her grip surprisingly tight. "Don't go after her." She points to the red flowers beside the door. "She will not cross the doorway. Only the pure of heart can enter this house. I fear she is not clean."

I slip on my boots, my jaw tightening. Ignorance. The woman doesn't understand what we've been through.

"Our mother died." The words fall from my lips for the first time. "My sister's in shock. It's freezing, and she needs to come in."

Voicing the pain is an arrow to my chest, one that I don't have time to bear if I want to survive. Only when we are safe, far away from the prison and the forest, can we mourn. I plead with my gaze for Yuki to come inside, but my sister's eyes are distant moons that do not see.

Yuki crouches away like a frightened beast on the snow-dusted porch. Her eyes droop from exhaustion and her thin shoulders shake. The cold mountain air sucks the warmth from the cottage like a wolf inhaling its first meal.

"I understand," the old woman murmurs, a warmth to her voice. "Still, this is the house of Our Lady, and only the pure can enter. The camellia blossom exposes the true nature of those who walk through this door. Its sweet fragrance wards off evil. That is why your sister cannot come. It can sense a dark heart."

"Dark heart?" I shake my head. "Yuki has the purest heart I know."

"She's cursed."

"That's ridiculous," I say. "She's scared is all."

"She is dangerous, especially to you." The woman steps in front of me, her voice steady.

"Yuki would never harm me."

"Your sister must prove that to you. Not the other way around." A look ghosts across the old woman's eyes, a painful memory she shuts away with a wince.

Yuki crouches, knees to her chest and hands fisted against the hollows of her eyes. Tears smudge silken rivers down her ash-strewn face. I clench my jaw, doubt nipping at me.

What *had* happened to Yuki after the bear attack? How did she get the strength of five men, and why had her eyes turned to slits in the clearing? I want to dismiss the woman's fears as nothing but old wives' tales, but what if it's not?

"Sister," Yuki calls, but it comes out in a hiss.

The old woman flinches. "Oh, Lady of the Light preserve us. Your sister's turning into a *yajuu*. I've seen it before. At first, the transformation can be slow and sporadic. She might be safe to be around now, but come morning, she could eat you alive. She won't know her sister from a rabbit outside. It's a disease of the heart, claiming both body and soul."

Yajuu. My stomach recoils at the word. I'd heard about the fearsome monsters in the prison, born of dark hearts and broken promises. One of the many monsters that allegedly plagues the Prisoners Road. Humans infected by a corrupted magic that turns their hunger to a murderous intent. They were a myth like the sea dragons and the Sarush, the mother bear who protected the mountains and gifted the Ainur with the first winter coats made of pure white to fool the snow. Fables my mother told to help us sleep at night. Because it was better than listening to the screaming hunger in our bellies.

"*Yajuu* aren't real," I say, my voice frayed. "We'll find somewhere else to stay."

"You mistake me. Your sister is welcome to stay, *if* she can come through the door. I have no wish to separate you. No ill will toward her. But she must do so by herself. I, too, hope she will. For the things that walk these mountains at night have no mercy, not even on their own kind."

"She needs help."

"No," the old saint says, chin quivering. "Call to her if you can. She must come on her own."

I shut out the woman's protests and step outside. In three quick paces, my arms find Yuki. She folds into my embrace, trembling. I run a hand over her cheek, finding tears. Shame creeps over me for waiting so long to help her. I smooth the tangled strands of thick brown hair out of her face.

"You're safe," I whisper. "We have shelter, maybe a meal, but you must come through the door. Please."

Yuki whimpers. "Kira . . . I'm . . . so tired."

"I cannot refuse those who enter," the woman says from within the doorframe. "But the monster—you risk too much."

I glare, sending a clear message that I will not tolerate my sister being called what she is not.

"The girl," she amends, "won't come through the door, even if you carry her. She will fight it, and it could do her harm. But there is an old prayer that might avail her some strength."

"A spell?"

"No. A prayer is not magic. It's the cry of a heart."

"Go ahead."

Silver hair pulled beneath a nightcap, the old saint begins a simple chant whispered through steepled fingertips. The lantern dangling from her hands casts a warm glow on the wrinkled face.

"Blessings come at night,
Walls of mercy and light
Adorn a veil, sharp and bright
Slay the dark, flame ignite
Let this small one come in tonight."

I scoop Yuki into my arms, finding her lighter than before, and step across the threshold.

A growl gathers at the back of Yuki's throat, but I step forward until I'm through the doorframe crowned with red blossoms. Yuki's shoulders heave, her hands drop limp, exhausted, and then her head lolls back—unconscious.

"Yuki?" I cradle my sister's limp form and pull her close. *What have I done?*

Chapter 8

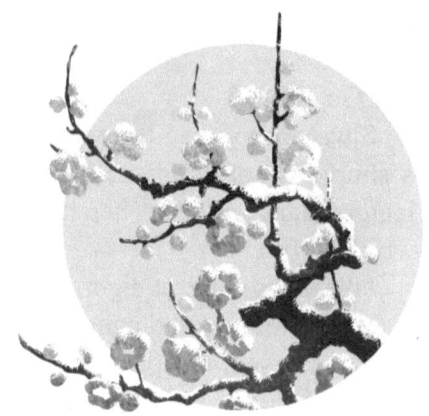

THE OLD SAINT GESTURES to a tall, wingback chair with rich embroidery. "Bring her here," she says with hushed urgency.

A low fire in the hearth sputters and hisses at the pelting snow blown through the doorway. I step into the room's warm glow and lower Yuki into the chair. At least we're safe.

For now.

The woman leans over her. "The cursed don't like camellia," she explains. "The flower is a poison to them. She is either very strong, or another power is at play. Either way, we have time before the transformation."

I frown, studying my sister's peaceful face for answers. "A curse? How long?"

"I'm not an expert," she says. "A few days or less, perhaps. Your sister is fighting it. Otherwise, she would have fared much worse coming through that door. I'd give her three days. After the transformation, the curse is irreversible."

I stare down at my sister. Yuki's limp body sinks into the plush fabric, her head rolled to the side. Thick lashes feather her cheeks like two butterflies landing on the snow. Even with her brow caked in ash and her clothes tattered, she still has a gentle countenance.

I want to tell the woman that she's crazy, that monsters and *yajuu* aren't real. I've heard the stories, but never have I heard of a normal person turning into one. But after what I've seen tonight . . .

The storm pelts the cottage windows as truth gnaws at my heart. Mother's stories come back to me, fables whispered at night, the ones I thought were fanciful tales. Maybe they were true. She'd tried to shield us from magic, but she never lied. I suck in a deep breath and sharpen my focus—on escaping, on keeping Yuki safe like I'd promised.

Yuki saved my life once, and now she needs me—and I her. She's all I have left.

The old woman drapes a soft blanket over Yuki. Woven threads form pictures on the fabric: a lamb nuzzled against a lion, winged beings overhead, and a tall spindled house with molten stars. I've never seen such dyes, thread, art . . .

Could people capture so many colors? I'm touching the fabric before I realize it, the threads softer than snow. Mother spent months making me a single elmwood coat. This must've taken years.

"A tapestry," the old saint says warmly. "It came from Silverwood, but in the Furan style. This picture is of a holy place that is very dear to me."

"Is that where you come from?"

"Yes, the weaving depicts a cathedral by the sea. Home of our order, the Ladies of the Light. It burned down before the war, but King Soran had it rebuilt." She straightens, her mouth pinched in a taut line of remembrance. "Come, dear, let's warm you up with tea and a bath. The two of you are more scroungy than coal miners."

"You have a bath? Here?"

The old woman gives a coarse laugh as she heats a kettle over the fire. "I might be a hermit, but I'm not *that* primitive, dear! Of course, it's nothing fancy as you'd find in Silverwood."

As I wait for the tea, curiosity tugs me to the fireplace mantle stuffed with old books and trinkets. My hand skims the leather-bound tomes, relishing the feel of so much paper. A pale blue pulse tickles my fingertips. I peer beneath my hovering hand to see a fat brown book, *Glimpses from the Marshland, a biography of life among the Ainur* by Sister Mari Vella.

"You know about the Ainur?" I ask, my voice suddenly thick.

The old saint's lips part in surprise, but she recovers quickly.

"My sister did." She extends a warm cloth to me. "Come now. Tea is ready."

I'm pulled away from the book and plunked into a soft chair across from Yuki. The warm cloth soothes my palms, but I've no idea what to do with it. Noticing, the saint gently takes the towel and begins to wipe my hands and face. I stiffen at the connection. The warmth, intimacy, like a mother cleaning her young.

Mother . . .

I catch the towel as it grazes my cheek. The saint's eyes jump to mine and I'm shook by the compassion I find in them. She bows and turns to clean Yuki's face instead.

Discomfort fills my throat. I swallow it down. *Will she be so kind if she knows we're criminals?*

I watch as the saint pulls the precious tapestry higher over Yuki's shoulders. Her fingers pause on a bruise, now stark against clean skin. "She's healing fast," she murmurs. "Still . . . I wish this world did not forge strength from suffering."

I resist sinking into the plush chair and lean forward with a question. "What's your story?"

Her smile returns, warmth lighting her eyes. "I was commissioned from the cathedral of Our Lady of the Light in Silverwood, the first of its kind in the empire. Perhaps you've heard of it?"

I shake my head, glad to shift her attention from Yuki. If she notices our prison uniforms beneath the coats, or the cuffs, we're done for.

"Ah, well, not many have these days," she continues with

a fond smile. "We built a cathedral in Silverwood, started a school for the ancient hearts, gardened, took in orphans, crafted beautiful stained glass, but I'm afraid what the people liked most was our homemade butter. I have some here."

She excuses herself to the kitchen, returning with a plate of what looks like a small golden brick. She cuts it easily, knifing a square onto a bowl of warmed rice. "It will give you strength," she says, passing it to me. "Though some say it has a strong flavor at first."

I devour the butter rice with little manner and little care except to fill my stomach. I moan into my last bite and lick the butter from my fingers. "Aren't you eating?"

"I already ate," she says, her stomach audibly rumbling. "But I set aside a bowl for your sister." Before I can protest, she pours me a cup of tea, swirling and golden.

I nod in thanks and sniff the cup—partially to check for poison—it's floral, earthy, and slightly sweet. Prison tea was always lukewarm, diluted barley tea with a hint of salt. This is paradise. A real home. I soak in the warmth of the fire. The storm pounds outside, but we're dry, safe, and fed. A glimpse of what I've always wanted for my family.

"I'm glad you made it inside before the storm." The old woman sits gingerly and stokes the fire in the hearth.

Wind howls from outside, and ice rings against the glass windows like bullets. Inspector Jade would be foolish to follow us in this, and if he did . . . hopefully he's dead.

I inhale deeply, easily—even if only for a moment.

The old saint sips her tea, her eyes shifting uneasily to my unconscious sister. "Tell me, have you noticed anything unusual about your sister lately?"

My muscles tense. I'm not giving her more reason to think my sister a monster. "Yuki wouldn't hurt a soul," I say.

"I don't mean to offend, dear. I just worry about the signs."

"What signs?"

"Rapid healing." She swirls her teacup dregs, eyes averted. "A surge of strength. A change in the eyes."

My hands tremble, and the teacup rattles as I set it down. "Hard to tell . . . We've been through a lot."

The woman nods sagely. "I didn't know much about the Winterwilds before I moved here. We thought the monsters were just rumors in Silverwood. They said that King Soran lost his mind when demons carried off his family piecemeal."

"What became of them?"

"First his sister-in-law and the little princess, then his wife, Queen Meera, and finally his own son. Of course, no one believed it. Taiga was to blame for the disappearances, not monsters. After all, the emperor *did* steal Queen Runa decades ago. But no one knows what really happened. Fables meant to keep us from sharing the light of salvation with the wild hordes that roam the mountains. I was naive when I first set out with my two sisters. But the tales were mostly true."

"Your sisters?"

"Yes, sisters not in blood, but spirit. The book you fancied was written by Sister Mari Vella, who started this mission with me. We learned too little, too late, from the Ainur. The Winterwilds are not safe, and the emperor's soldiers have not the interest or resources to protect the few who live here. Both my sisters were taken as they traveled the Road, offering fresh water to the convicts and caring for the poor farmers tasked with settling this region." Her eyes cut away, and she trembles with a nervous energy.

"Taken by what?"

She glances to where Yuki sleeps in the chair, a quiver in her tight jaw. "*Yajuu.* Monsters that were once human but have lost their soul while still possessing a powerful intellect. They take many forms, but the camellia *never* lies."

I pull my hands away from the warm cup. *Why would she offer us lodging and her own dinner if whatever my sister is becoming killed her friends?* Saint or not, my trust runs thin.

A protectiveness surges in me as I watch Yuki sleep. Beetle's hat rests lopsided on her head, reminding me that I'm not alone. That my path is woven with the faith and sacrifice of so many others who believe in me: Mother, Beetle, even Mochi.

I wish I'd learned his real name.

My sister shifts in the chair, upsetting the thick blanket, and a glint of silver catches my eye. The cuffs have cut deeper than I'd imagined. Yuki's hands ball into fists, her nails now longer—pointed. I hide them with the blanket and hush her, checking her temperature with the palm of my hand.

"Is she all right?"

"She'll be better in the morning," I say too quickly.

"Right then," the saint says, rising to her feet. "I'll get your room ready. I wish a good night's sleep could fix anything, but I'm afraid I'll have to send you off tomorrow. You understand, dear?"

"Of course." I bite back the fear and anger as my heart hammers with the icy storm outside. Neither the old saint nor I believe a rest will fix this. My sister is turning into a monster, and I don't know how to stop it.

Before bed, the old woman fashions a bath in a square, wooden tub. Steaming water pours into the barrel, pure and clear like melted ice. Drop by drop, she adds a vial of mountain lemon oil that soaks the whole room in citrus.

"Here are some fresh clothes and towels." Her wrinkled hands grip mine from beneath the cloth with a fierce warmth.

I startle and meet her gaze.

"If you want to know more of your people, you can find them in Ranzan. To the west, home of the bards and storytellers."

I glance at Yuki from the corner of my eye. *"My people?"*

"You can't have a gifting from the dragons in this house without my knowing." The old saint raises a brow. "The ancient hearts, the old magic, whatever you like to call it. Wayfinding is one of the few pure forms that can enter here, and distinct of the Ainur. If anyone can help your sister, they can." She smiles, a pinch of regret in her eye as she moves to the door. "Enjoy your bath, and have a good sleep, dear."

I grab the woman's arm to keep her from leaving. "How can they help? Is there a cure?"

She sucks in air between her teeth. "The Ainur have dealt with monsters for a long time, but not even they claim a cure."

"But there *is* a cure?" I press.

"In Ranzan, there is an apothecary by the name of Jey who claims to have one." She clears her throat. "I shouldn't have even told you that. Now, goodnight."

The old saint slips out of the room before I can thank her.

Her words traipse through my mind as I bathe and clean Yuki's wounds. *Could the Ainur help Yuki? Who is this apothecary?* Jey sounds like a Taigan name.

The bath water is a mess by the time we finish. I wrap Yuki's wounds with fresh bandages, whispering stories as I do so, like Mother would have done.

Usually, Yuki comments on her favorite parts, trickster princes with dark curls and pouty lips, but today she sits in rigid silence, fiddling with the cuffs around her wrists.

I stretch my legs as I sit on the floor mattress in new clothes. The white cotton garment is thick and soft. It's a far cry from the torn and grubby prison gown. I tug on my sleeve, a smooth wool with delicate lace trim on the end.

"Can you believe people have clothes just for sleep? *Pajamas*." I grin at the word. "I'd wear it always! It's perfectly decent."

"Sure, Kirarin." Yuki pulls her knees to her chest, her freshly combed hair falling on either side of her face. She winces as she inspects her cuffs in the room's lamplight.

"May I?" I reach out and offer a comforting smile.

Yuki jerks her arms down, out of sight.

"I can help if you'll let me try."

She growls. "I'm less free now than before. We should've stayed."

My world frosts at the edges. It's so easy to think another path would've been better. That anything would be better than facing this darkest day. I swallow hard.

"We can't erase our path," I say, "but we can make a new one. It's our choices that define us, that's what"—I gulp, and the words catch—"that's what she would say."

Yuki's eyes brim with unshed tears. She thrusts her arms out and pretends not to watch as I nudge the silver cuffs. The metal lets out a low hiss as it touches a new patch of skin. Yuki winces and bares her teeth.

"Sorry," I gasp. "I'll find a knife to break it once the old woman's asleep."

Yuki pulls her arms back, and I help arrange her sleeves so they cover the cuffs. Her brow furrows, her sharp little nose sniffling. I bite my lip, wondering if she's thinking about Mother too. About all the things we carry but can't speak. Not while the inspector is after us. Not while the wounds are fresh. But . . .

Had she seen what happened?

I shiver. I'm not ready for that talk either.

Yuki flops onto the feather mattress, hair splayed in a wet web. She fingers the plush blanket and bites at the corner.

"What are you doing?" I pinch back a nervous laugh.

She pulls out a feather and lets it flutter to the floor, head tilted in interest.

I force a smile while guilt nibbles at my heart. I'm studying my sister, looking for signs like the old woman said: growls, superior strength . . . healing. There's no way her wounds could have scabbed over already. But they have.

The signs are undeniable.

My eyes squeeze shut until tiny stars prick at my eyelids. It doesn't change anything. She's still my sister.

I crawl into bed, exhausted. I want to sleep and forget everything. Erase it from memory.

Yuki settles next to me on the mattress, stealing most of the covers.

I'm almost afraid to sleep here with so many things watching—the doll on the dresser, the pictures frozen like they're waiting for me to sleep so they can quit their pretending and roam about the room. But my eyes sting, and heavy eyelids pull downward. The inspector will find us when the storm stops, but we need sleep, even if just a little.

Yuki curls next to me, and before I can count to ten, she's snoring. I listen to the steady expansion of her breath, thankful we're alive.

I crawl onto the floor with a blanket. As soft as the mattress is, I want the familiar feeling of a hard, grainy floor. I push my face into the fabric, blotting out the tears that surface while no one is watching. The blanket smells faintly of lavender, or maybe it's just my mind losing touch with reality.

After all, it's the first night Mother isn't here.

I wanted to build a home together in Silverwood, to see Mother grow old and smile freely. To see the capital of Ezo and the emerald waters of the southern strait that separates us from the rest of the empire. But I've never seen a city. Never had to pay with coin to eat or sleep. All my life, it's been provided to me—stale, day-old rice with seaweed flakes or sardine.

How are Yuki and I supposed to live?

When I planned our escape, I'd always expected Mother to show us the ropes. To know the way—*the path*. My hands fist against the floor.

"Mama, why did you leave us?" I whisper. "I thought you could see the right path, but you didn't . . . now you're gone."

Tears fall, salty and warm against my skin. Pain blossoms beneath my eyes and in my chest like my heart wants freedom too, but it has nowhere to run. My head goes dizzy until sleep takes me like a bandit—swift and promising no harm.

Full of lies.

CHAPTER 9

THE NOCTURNE FOREST of the Winterwilds greets me in a platinum haze of fog and glittering ice. I have the strange premonition that I'm in a dream, but I'm too entranced to care. I hold my hands out in front of me. The hardened calluses and chalky white between my fingers from years of arctic exposure don't seem like a dream. But the blue path that glitters before me says otherwise.

A spider's web tangles across the forest floor. It's thin as a string and loose as a ball of magic twine unraveling in the wood. I pick my steps, bare feet careful not to trip on the web lest it turn into a snare. A strange sensation swirls inside me, a tightness from holding my breath too long. Someone is here to meet me.

Mother.

The thought ripples through my mind, pulling me deeper into the dream wood. The forest's undertow lures me into dark tunnels and deep tangles. I press on. Desperate hope calling me forward. I need to see her again.

"*Hurry. There's no time,*" Mother's voice calls. "*Follow the path.*"

I trip on the icy spiderweb. It doesn't break but plucks, striking an eerie musical chord. Vibrations rattle down the web, causing grass blades to loosen their dew and scavenging animals to dart up. A baby deer stares at me, wide-eyed and fuzzy brown. I feel the echoing of that string alerting something deep in the forest to my presence. A darkness is watching. I run, my feet plucking the web that is most certainly a hunter's snare.

It's just a dream. I'm not in danger.

I run to meet Mother. She is a light at the end of the string. What if it's her ghost come to tell me something? Finally, she'll say the words I've craved my whole childhood. "You were born into a prison because . . ."

Questions about my mother's past demand answers as I burst into a clearing dancing with sunlight. My mother lies on the ground, face down, her arms raised above her head like a dancer, covering something dear to her. She is younger, not weighed down by years of rough prison life.

I freeze, heart slamming against my chest.

Above Mother stands *the* bear. It's massive, hunch-backed, its body the size of a small whale I'd once seen in the harbor. The bear lifts its head, eyes like black mother-of-pearl meeting mine. Blood drips from its snout and down the stripe of white fur on its neck. It huffs, and the air explodes into a dozen hoarfrost moths scattering to the winds.

Mother turns her head from beneath her arms, her beautiful wayfinder's robe torn. Clear-blue eyes smile at me. She lifts her arms and beneath them is a little girl with muffled cries.

Is it my sister or me?

"Guard her above your own life." The wind brushes Mother's words like a whisper across my ear. "Find the rabbit in the talons."

My chest squeezes. Something dry and unwelcome scratches at my throat.

"Run, Kirarin," Mother yells. "He's coming."

"Who?"

"The one who came after me and your sister. The reason I was in Abashi—"

Her voice is cut off as the mountains rumble. The bear startles back on its haunches. The earth rolls. An avalanche plows into the forest valley. Violent waves of white slam into the bear and Mother, obliterating them.

The avalanche slams into my chest.

I jolt awake, sweat clinging to my brow. The room is far colder than when I fell asleep. Yuki must've slipped her head beneath the covers in the chill of night. I breathe deep and crawl onto the mattress, collapsing beside my cocooned sister.

A dream.

That's when I see it. The curtains billow as if stroked by the invisible hand of winter. Lace blows in and out of the room from an open window.

I pull back the covers expecting to find Yuki curled, arms tucked beneath her head and that dimpled smile when she sleeps. But the blanket folds in on itself, as if pushed back in a hurry.

Yuki isn't here.

I scramble upright, clutching the blanket as if she could still be hidden inside. Perhaps there are footprints in the snow, but I'm too frightened to approach the window. My hands scavenge the bed, absent-minded, frantic. *Where is she?*

I tiptoe to the open window and slowly pull it shut.

"S-stop," whispers a small, scared voice.

I turn, eyes locking onto the familiar shape of my sister and her large eyes glued to me. "Yuki?"

"I had a nightmare." Yuki sits on the floor, huddled against the wall like a second backbone, legs pulled to her chest.

I sit beside her and rest my back against the wall. "Why did you open the window?"

Yuki buries her cuffed hands in the folds of her too-big pajamas, moist eyes darting away from me. No answer.

I catch a glimpse of the purple tint in her fingers and nails, as pointed as the monster in my dreams. My throat goes dry, but

I scoot closer. She's just as scared as I am. And the old saint said we have three days to stop the curse.

Two days now.

"It'll be okay," I say.

"I don't remember opening the window," Yuki squeaks. "There are scratch marks on it."

The dream and Mother's stories come back to me, sketches from some of the prisoners of bears and wolves who were once human but had fallen under the influence of a dark heart. *Has she figured out that she's cursed?*

"The wind probably blew it open," I lie as I stroke her hair.

"I'm afraid." Yuki's words crack in a soft whisper as she curls into my side. "And that man—the inspector. He's coming for us, isn't he?" A visible chill racks her shoulders.

"I won't let anyone take you." I smooth her hair and kiss the top of her head. "Not ever."

"W-we can't s-stay." Yuki draws her hands to her lips.

I tuck a blanket around her and pull a pillow from the mattress.

"It's still dark. Rest another hour and then we'll leave before sunrise. I'll keep a lookout."

Yuki rests her head against my shoulder and soon falls asleep. A creak from the window jars me, but it's only the wind whistling through the cracks. *Be calm, heart.* I exhale, imagining that I'm sending my breath out to ride the wind and find a path for us.

"Mama, I need you," I whisper. "What would a wayfinder do?"

The answer comes to me, a whisper on the wind.

The rabbit in the talons.

I huff at the imagined voice.

I'll find the rabbit in the talons, whatever it is. But for now, Yuki's face is peaceful as she sleeps, her brow slightly pinched, warding off a bad dream. I try not to imagine what a real flesh and blood *yajuu* looks like. Or if she shapeshifts, what form she would take.

My sister is not a monster where it counts. But if the old woman's calculations are correct, she soon will be.

CHAPTER 10

MY FOOTSTEPS ARE SWIFT, moving in between the shadows, all too aware the old saint could wake soon. I swipe our boots from the entryway, then slip into the main room. The storm abated in the night, which means Inspector Jade won't be far behind.

In the kitchen, I find jars of sardines, dried persimmons, and drawers filled with strange silver, spoons, forks, and knives. My fingers swipe across the smooth inlaid handles, slippery as ice on my fingertips.

Mother wouldn't approve of stealing . . .

I've lived among thieves long enough to know that a crime is a crime—even if the cause is a good one. It doesn't stop me from haphazardly stuffing a sack with provisions and things to barter. I don't trust the old saint enough to ask for supplies.

She'd been kind to us, complete strangers, and let us stay under her roof, but it's because she doesn't know who we are. Why didn't she ask more about us? Two girls, alone in the wood. I'd be suspicious. A woman traveling alone in the frontier is either bent on trouble or deep into it already.

We are both.

A strong gust rattles a door at the end of the hall. I quickly toss our old prison clothes into the open hearth, burying them in a pile of ash. I'm about to rush back to the room when I catch sight of a map. I'd barely noticed it earlier when we first entered the house, not with the hunger in my belly and Yuki unconscious. Now I look at it.

The Isle of Ezo is the largest island ever conquered by the empire of Taiga. It's also the northernmost kingdom. I stare at our location, pinned with an ink seal: the Winterwilds along the side of Mt. Atan. And over the water is Abashi Island, a prison from end to end. Black lines mark the railroad from the port of Abashi across the large island of Ezo to the city Ranzan on the western coast. Along the path are illustrations of marshlands, forests, steaming geysers, sea dragons . . . and bears. I blink away and turn my gaze to the southernmost city, to Silverwood. A seaside castle is stitched into the fabric of the map, dotted with cherry trees.

Mother's home.

That's where we'll make a new home for ourselves. Once I find the apothecary and get a cure for Yuki. I stand on my tiptoes and, with a jump, yank the map from the wall.

I land with a clumsy thump and freeze, fearing the woman's appearance any second. But only the cold wind in the hall tugs at me.

An unsettling feeling roosts in my chest as I tiptoe down the hallway toward our room. Both our door and the old woman's are cracked open. A frigid breeze blows through the gap.

I peek inside. "Yuki?"

My sister sleeps against the wall where I'd last left her.

I turn to the old woman's room and my breath catches. The futon is a crumpled mess. A thin wisp of smoke wafts from a recently extinguished lamp. Outside the window, footprints pad the snow. A horse whinnies from beyond the frosted glass.

I gasp, hand flying over my mouth.

She turned us in. Why else would she be up this early? She must have taken a horse after we fell asleep and gone to the nearest police station or town.

"Yuki!" I spin out of the room. "We have to go. Now."

My sister's head slumps to her knees. She's in a deep sleep, real sleep for the first time in ages. Normally, I'd hesitate to wake her, but we can't wait. The inspector might be outside.

I shake Yuki's shoulders. "Wake up!"

Her eyes dart open.

I put a finger to my lips. "We have to go."

Yuki doesn't ask questions and pulls on the Beetle's coat over her wool pajamas. I check for locks on the bedroom window and push aside the curtains. The latch glides up smoothly, no bars to prevent our escape. I hesitate, the bag of provisions still slung over my shoulder.

"Can you run?" I whisper.

"Faster than you," Yuki quips, her lips curving.

I don't tell Yuki about the old woman's betrayal, if that's what it was. I shouldn't have trusted her, saint or not. Experience has always told me that kindness doesn't stand a chance against the law. Beetle's death proved that.

"Turn yourselves in!" Thick footsteps clunk in the hallway, followed by the voices of men.

With a push, the window creaks open. I drop the bag of provisions out into the snow before Yuki and I climb through, tucking sideways when our shoulders barely make it.

The cold nips my cheeks with a too-hard pinch and rushes beneath my elmwood coat to the wool pajamas. Together, we make a run for the woods across the saint's snowy garden and stone gate. A pale horse trots out from behind the house.

Yuki snarls, and I tug her hands to remind her to run.

"Over here!" the soldier astride the horse shouts. He spins the animal toward us at a gallop, ice clods flying from its hooves. More voices bellow from the house. Inspector Jade strides powerfully out the front door, a curse on his lips.

"You're as good as dead if you don't turn yourself in!" he shouts.

Does he think we're idiots? We're dead if he catches us.

I hunker beneath the stone wall, arms around Yuki. She shivers beside me. No, she growls. The sound chills more than the wind.

"Saint told me what's to become of your sister—a monster. Do you think she'll be kind to you? She'll destroy you like anyone else." Inspector Jade's boots crunch across snow, closer. "The saint has been merciful, given you another chance to surrender."

"Yuki," I whisper. "Run, now."

Together, we break from the stone wall sheltering us and dash across the snow to the forest. My lungs burn, and I forget to search for a path. We run, fear of the inspector's bullets hounding us farther into the forest. Yuki is faster than me and pulls me behind her into the dark wood just as the sun breaks over the cabin behind us.

The old saint stands upon her porch, lantern in hand, moving the warm light upward and sideways like a signal. I can't tell if it's a blessing or a curse. Mother never bothered to teach me about the saints. It's possible she didn't turn us in but tried to stall the soldiers. I'll never know.

Angry voices ring in the air, followed by the clomping of hooves. My heart slugs against my rib cage. I leap over snow-buried roots and tree trunks, dodging sharp spindly branches. It'll be too easy for them to follow us in the snow, except for the inspector. The winter is his one weakness.

I skid beneath a heavily skirted pine and release Yuki's hand. "Go!" I hiss, trying not to be too loud. "Trust me. I'll catch up."

Yuki eyes me questioningly before taking off deeper into the forest. She really is stronger than before.

I'm playing off a dangerous hunch. Time is against us. A horse snorts, loud and hollow, as if aware of my presence. The rider, too, must know I'm crouching close by. That is, unless he takes the bait of Yuki's fresh tracks in the snow.

Clop. Clop. The horse moves forward at a walk.

I ready my fists around a fallen branch and take a steady

breath, listening. There is only one horse. The soldiers must have split paths to snare us in the middle. *Perfect.*

Jumping out from beneath the pine, I swing my branch at the rider. He falls from the saddle with a thump. The horse rears, but I grab the flailing reins. The fallen soldier struggles to right himself in a snowbank. Quickly, I swing myself onto the horse, grabbing the saddle and mane with wild abandon like a drowning rat.

The beast charges into the forest, and my heart races along with it. Thin, icy branches lash at my face, which I tuck down along the horse's neck. I hold on for dear life, a victorious smile breaking across my lips. Fear fades with each pounding hoofbeat. Warmth tingles my skin where it touches the horse's thick coat. My fingers knit into its mane, unsure how to steer, and I crane my head for a glimpse of Yuki's trail. She isn't hard to find.

My sister had stopped a short pace away and climbed into a low tree, waiting for me. She hops down, eyes wide. The horse halts and shudders, snow dusting from its withers.

"Climb on," I say. "It might bolt if I get down. I don't know how these things work." A grin slips across my face, even while my legs tremble in the stirrups. I've never ridden a horse before, but I like it.

The horse whinnies and thrashes its head as Yuki approaches.

"Easy there." I pat its neck and hold out a hand for Yuki.

Carefully, she takes it and scrambles onto the back of the saddle. The horse shifts uneasily and gives a frightened hop. Muffled voices shout from either side of us in the woods.

"Let's go!" I don't need to knee the horse for it to bolt again.

We fly through the forest. I've little idea which direction we're heading, but the path seems to connect the horse's will with my own. Yuki's cuffed hands loop around my waist in a terrified hug.

I swallow a dry lump in my throat at the thought of her becoming a *yajuu*. Two days before the curse takes hold. I'm not sure what to expect—horns sprouting from her head or morphing into a wild beast. Perhaps the stay at the old woman's house, whatever magic or prayer she'd uttered, would stall the curse.

Or perhaps the saint thought I'd be safer with the inspector than with my sister when she turns into a monster.

An hour later, we release the horse, freeing it of its saddle and bridle in the hope that it'll find its way home—like us. There's no sign of the inspector. We rest at the crest of the next mountain pass. I pull out the map printed with roads and mountains, inked with place names, and smelling strongly of wild lemons.

I hold it open for Yuki. She leans in, shoulder pressed against mine, and points at the blue banners on the southern corner of the map and the sea dragon rising from the bay.

"Silverwood," I say. "That's where we'll go, eventually. But this . . ." I adjust my hold on the map and draw a path with my finger along the black dotted railroad. "This is how we'll find a cure. We travel along the railroad. It's the flattest ground between here and Ranzan. The saint mentioned an apothecary there who could help."

Yuki heaves a foggy breath into the cold. Shivering, she stares at her hands and the long, pointed nails seemingly grown overnight. Then her large brown eyes meet mine. "I don't want to be something I'm not," she whispers. "I heard what the inspector said. Don't let me become a monster. I can't hurt anyone, Kira."

"You won't." I grab her by the shoulders and pull her to me. "You could never be a monster, Yuki. That's not who you are."

"I don't know . . ." Her voice rasps, and she rubs her frost-nipped nose. "Not after all this."

"Mama said that hope is closer than the stars," I say. "If we have hope, we'll find a way. We've already survived our worst days. We'll survive this one, too."

Yuki leans into me, and the weight of that trust lies heavy on my shoulders. I stare at the mountains as my sister and I curl together for warmth. A great silver lake lies at the base of the snowcapped forest. Rumpled folds of white blanket the flat farmland beyond. How do the small towns and farming plots survive this far north? No doubt people lured by the Taigan Empire's promise of free land if they will come and tame Ezo.

But nothing is free.

My own freedom was costly. The young guard, Beetle, my mother, and now even my sister. *Will she remember me when the transformation is complete? Will she attack me like the bear attacked her?* A sharp ache pulls at my chest. I stand and stretch as if that will ease the pain away.

"Grab a bite to eat, and let's go. We need to keep moving."

Yuki sniffs at the bag of food and turns up her nose.

"Eat." I take a rice cake from the bag and demonstrate, shoving it into my mouth.

"I'm not hungry." Yuki shoves the cake back into the sack. She shields her eyes from the early afternoon sun and points down the mountain. The valley is exactly as I'd seen earlier. Only now I make out the thin, winding path of iron—the railroad.

"You found it." I grin. "Let's go."

I start walking. We should make it to the edge of the train tracks, the abhorrent Prisoners Road, by midday.

A hard shiver rolls down Yuki's shoulders. She rubs the cuffs on her wrist. With just the two of us in the woods, her low growls raise the hair on my neck. In two days, we should be in Ranzan. I only hope Yuki can hold out until then. She can't go without eating forever.

I'm not sure what *yajuu* eat, but I'm certain it's not rice cakes.

CHAPTER 11

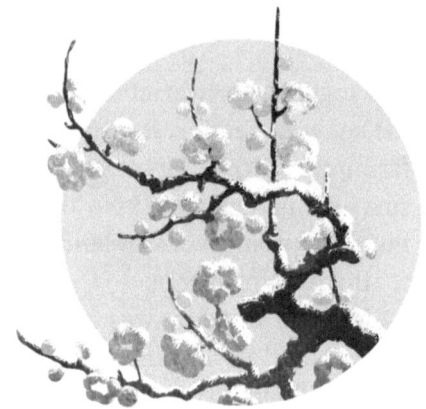

THE PRISONERS ROAD IS LIKE the scarred belly of a snake. Black iron tracks, each twice as long as a man, lie over the cold winter earth. My eyes follow the stretch of rail until it disappears in the distance—vanished, like the people who died building it.

"The Prisoners Road," I whisper, my breath spooling out in short puffs. "It could've been us building this. Men we know have died over it."

Yuki snarls and keeps her distance, clinging to the tree line, while I explore the barren railroad we'd nearly been sentenced to build.

I pull out the map. "This section looks finished, so we shouldn't worry about guards. We follow it to the Sorachi Mines and then a bit further to Ranzan. If we shadow it from the trees, then no one will spot us. The problem is staying warm."

"N-no." Yuki bites back a growl.

I turn. "Is something—?"

My sister crouches behind me, shivering and scratching at Beetle's wool hat. The hat slips off soundlessly into the snow, her long hair a tangled bird's nest. Yuki's eyes roll back, a flash of white. She bites at the cuffs on her wrists and then staggers, falling to her knees on the hard iron tracks.

In an instant, I'm by her side, placing a hand on her forehead. "You're burning up."

"N-no . . ." Her teeth chatter.

"We have to get you inside some place." I smooth her hair. *Blizzards, I need that cure now.* I can't bring myself to even think about what I'll do if I *don't* find the cure. My hands tremble from restraining her.

How am I going to make it to Ranzan with a monster at my side?

"We'll get help," I promise as she rocks back and forth between growls and hard shivers. "All we have to do is find that apothecary."

I scan the area for a natural shelter, a windbreak so I can build a fire. It doesn't matter that my sister is turning into a monster. She's sick and needs help. I used to always worry about her health, but since we left Abashi she's been stronger. She's managed a journey that she never would have survived otherwise.

Did Mother foresee this path?

After an hour of walking, I notice a broken-down shack on the other side of the tracks. Four hastily built walls prop up a tarp canopy that flaps like a crow caught in a snare. Cold air whistles through the open gap serving as a door. Probably where prisoners had slept while building the road.

"Come on." I hoist her upright. "There's shelter on the other side of the tracks."

She sags against my shoulder and shakes her head in protest. I hobble over the first black rail with Yuki still pinned to my side and thrashing with fever. "Almost there."

In the center of the tracks, the wind whistles fiercely. White mountains and wild forests rise on either side, the railroad a black spine between them. Yuki claws at her cuffs and growls.

Beneath the flapping canopy, she sinks against one of the wooden posts in the corner.

I drop the supply bag to the dirt floor, catching my breath.

"Here." I wrap a small blanket from the bag over her shoulders. "You need to rest."

Yuki growls, louder this time. Her eyes dart away from me.

I step back, torn between tending to my sister and afraid of what I don't understand. The second I move, she lunges. Teeth clip my coat sleeve with a snarl.

I jump, stumbling outside, my heart pounding.

She tried to bite me. She didn't mean to. Couldn't have . . .

My sister slinks beneath the canopy, pacing the back wall. The lights of her eyes follow me through the gaps of black canvas. I clutch the ripped hole in Mother's coat, too afraid—and shocked—to move.

"Y-yuki?"

The growls turn to snarls. Lower, more vicious, desperate, like a beast with its paw stuck in a trap.

I step back, knees wobbling. "It's okay," I say, unsure if I'm comforting myself or my sister. "We'll find help. I'm not going anywhere."

I have nowhere to go.

Yuki is my family, all I have left. I'm not giving up. I've dreamed of the impossible long enough to know that hope isn't about chances. It's stubborn. It burns. Like the moon behind the clouds, it's always there; I just need to remember.

My boots bump against something hard, and I glance down—iron tracks. When I look up again, Yuki is gone.

Snow swirls. Tracks rumble beneath my boots. A hum of distant thunder—train or footsteps, I can't tell. The hair on my neck rises with the familiar sense of being watched, and I turn.

Suddenly, hands slam into my spine.

My head hits the ground, just missing the iron tracks. Yuki towers over me, her hands at my throat, pushing with a weight she doesn't possess.

"Yuki," I choke, pulling at her arms to divert the pressure. "It's me. Please . . . stop. Something's coming."

Darkened eyes and pointed teeth bare down at me. I buck

and twist, but she's stronger than she should be. My arms shake, losing the little space they've carved out between us. Stars burst in my vision.

What would Mama do?

I stop fighting and look. Really look. The rail—just beside us. I shift my hips, hook a leg behind hers, and drive upward. We roll, and Yuki's head clips the metal rail with a crack. She jerks back, stunned.

I scramble up, glancing over my shoulder to make sure she's okay. *My mistake.* Yuki barrels into my chest and knocks me onto the tracks.

Sharp pain burns up my neck. Cold seeps into my bones. Above me, Yuki's face twists, her fury fading into something soft and human. Greif. Recognition. Tears.

The world tilts, then fades.

I drift into a river of memory, Yuki and me as little girls building snow bunnies and ice forts during Winterfest.

It was our favorite time of year. The guards let us out for several hours, and we'd play house like we imagined other girls played. A simple house made of compacted snow with a hollow space to fit two scrawny girls and occasionally our mother too. I never made a door. I liked the wide-open cut in the snow, the crusted feel of sun-hardened edges, and the caress of fresh air—however cold it may be.

That was freedom, the open door.

Coming and going as I pleased without fear of doing wrong. But not for Yuki. She always wanted a door. It wasn't a proper house if it didn't have a door. She gathered twigs and branches, bits of elm bark peeled back to reveal hibernating beetles. She'd spend a ridiculous amount of time weaving them to make a proper door, her fingers working magic in the numbing cold.

And then we'd set pretend candles in hollowed bamboo and imagine we were long-lost princesses.

"When they see the beacon, they'll come for us," Yuki would sing. "And whisk us away on the backs of noble silka to the hidden kingdom."

"I don't need anyone to whisk me away," I'd say. "I'll walk across the ice like the great Ainur wayfinders. They didn't need help. They only needed their heart to hear the path and eyes to see the icy blue threads. The wind instructed them, the branches whispered secrets, and the rocks spoke of ancient treasures. I will be one of those.

"The wayfinders discovered lands and medicines and doors into heavens. They found the places where myth and land merged. I'll be the greatest wayfinder to ever live! And when they hear of it, they'll make me their queen."

Yuki laughed, rolling on the floor of the snow house. "They don't have a queen. They only serve the dragons."

When I come to, Yuki is kneeling beside me. Her hands are off my throat, and she's shaking with an earthquake only she can feel. Grizzly-brown hair falls across her forehead, and scratch marks comb her face.

"Yuki . . ." I choke on my voice.

Her eyes jump to mine as she dives at me, hugging me with a growling sob. Cautiously, I reach up to stroke her hair, comb it as Mama would have. She trembles beneath my fingertips.

"It's okay," I repeat until I believe it too, my voice rough with emotion. "You came back."

A low, droning locomotion gathers in the distance. Could it be the train the prisoners had spoken of?

I prop myself on my elbows and attempt to stand, but the tiniest motion sends my head reeling. Gingerly, I touch the ring of bruises around my neck, and when my hand reaches the base of my skull, it comes away with blood.

The strange sound roars louder—closer.

Yuki crouches on the tracks as if to attack whatever is coming. Black clouds chuff toward the sky, dimming the sun.

I push up, but my right leg is wedged in the tracks. A loud roar rattles my bones. Whatever it is, will be here soon.

A jolt of purest blue shoots across my vision. A connection I've felt before. "Yuki, run."

Instead, she pulls on my trapped leg.

The ground trembles.

"Yuki, go!"

Out of the trees steps a guard, sword drawn and cloaked in a knee-length navy jacket trimmed in wolf fur. He walks fast, nearly flying over the ground toward us.

Yuki lunges at the guard. He twists, knocking her aside with a scabbard. Then he grabs me by the waist and yanks me free.

"Let me go," I yell, panic flooding my limbs as he hauls me backward across the snow.

The cold sting of a knife at my throat brings startling clarity to my mind. I still.

"I don't want to hurt you," a familiar voice says.

"Your knife says otherwise," I whisper.

The knife loosens at my throat but remains faithful to its purpose. A gloved hand checks my neck, coming away red from where Yuki bashed my head into the tracks. I turn my head slowly, catching the sharp profile of the young guard who had kept me safe in solitary confinement. *Mochi.* There's no mistaking someone I met so close to death.

Coldness radiates from him—nothing new to me—but that face. Even with my head throbbing and Yuki gone, I can't look away. There's something dangerously beautiful about him. And stupidly, infuriately, my heart skips for a beat longer than it should.

I shake my head and scowl. He's probably working for Inspector Jade.

My eyes dart for Yuki, but she's nowhere to be seen. I hope

she's escaped and not lingering nearby. "How did you survive? What have you done to my sister? Why are you—"

"Keeping you alive?" He tilts his head in confusion, a mess of dark hair beneath his wool cap.

"By holding me at knifepoint?" I push back.

"It's complicated," he says, lowering the blade. "And the monster?"

"Complicated." I rub my sore throat. "But—"

Before I can finish, a great black train rips along the railroad. The whoosh of its passing jerks my hair back, and wind pours into the corners of my eyes.

The train emits a tortured howl as it brakes, slowing but not stopping. Enormous wheels slice across the spot I'd stood only a few moments ago. Black boxes whirl past, steam hissing into the wintry forest. After a few breathless moments, the train finally stops.

On this side of the tracks, two horses emerge from the woods. Mochi releases his hold on me and sheaths the dagger inside his coat.

I stagger back, reclaiming space between us, and size up the guard. I estimate he's only had nineteen winters, odd given the twin insignia marking his jacket on either side—one a captain's rank and the other, a moon encircled by five plum blossoms. *The insignia of Silverwood.* Not the usual prison guard uniform like he'd worn earlier.

My eyes narrow at Mochi—a captain.

Horses paw the ground, tiny bells on their bridles swinging to a halt. One horse is riderless, presumably the captain's mount, while the other is a large snowy dapple carrying a rider with a similar uniform and friendlier face. The horse tosses its head as its rider slides from the saddle.

"Took you long enough," the captain calls out as the second man approaches. He's younger, built like a thin slab of tofu with light hair and a dimpled smile.

I judge the seconds as the second guard steps closer. If I

attempt escape now, there's a possibility I could make it to the forest, to Yuki.

I don't wait. I run.

But the captain is faster—inhumanly fast. His arm is around me before I take a second step. "You couldn't wait for introductions?"

His dark eyes slide to me with a blue sheen that reminds me of a flame. My breath hitches under his gaze, too close.

He straightens, as if aware of my discomfort. I'd always wanted to see how beautiful the world could be, but Mother hadn't told me about *this* kind of beautiful danger. He's different than in the prison storehouse, as if he was born for these woods, a shadow, at home in the snow and smoke.

"Apologies, Captain." The new guard offers a quick bow. "I should've caught them sooner. Took longer than I thought to set up the barricade on the tracks."

"Don't state the obvious, Zenri."

I follow the captain's dark gaze to Zenri. Pink scars crisscross one side of his face, half of the skin marred like troubled water and partially hidden beneath a thick, wool scarf. His soft brown eyes nestled in the scars feel warm and safe, so unlike the eyes of other men. Detecting my stare, he turns away and adjusts the horses' reins.

Did a monster give him those scars? He doesn't seem cursed like Yuki.

"Captain Ren, sir," he says, voice clipped. "It won't happen again. Shall I secure the prisoner? The other one must be nearby."

The captain lets go of my arm. He doesn't push me toward Zenri or hand me over. He simply releases me.

I brush my rumpled coat sleeve and glare at him. Black hair, almost blue, sweeps over his face like storm waves at night, the rest cropped short around his neck. He strikes me as too young to be a captain with his smooth jaw and grating confidence.

"This one's not going anywhere," he says to Zenri, his gaze

lingering on me. His dark eyes pin me to the spot like the cliffs watching the sea, unmovable and yet deeply changed by what they've seen. He leans in like a strong wind, pushing the breath from me. "Now, where is the demon?"

As if in answer, Yuki growls from within the badly constructed shelter, hidden behind the flapping canopy.

"Stand back." The captain gently pushes me behind him with one hand and unsheathes a sword with the other.

The silver blade cuts into the sunlight, and he takes one swift step toward my sister.

"No!" I dash forward. I'm not fast enough. A soft blue hums beneath my fingers as I reach out, missing the captain's cloak by inches. "Stop!"

He pauses mid-lunge and turns. His eyes widen and seemingly trace the invisible blue thread of path connecting me to . . . I step back in surprise. It's not Yuki the path is pointing at—it's the captain.

I drop my hands like they've burned me. A knot forms in my throat as I move in between them. Here, this is where I'm supposed to be, standing between my sister and the world. Just like I promised Mother.

"So . . . the rumors are true," the captain says, a slow smile touching his lips. "You *are* a wayfinder."

Does he sense the path too? Can he see it?

Mother had said to use magic sparingly, not to let anyone see. *Magic attracts other magic.* Apparently, I can do nothing right. I recall the bear in the woods, how I'd spun a word into a path. Had that happened again?

"Why do you want my sister?" I demand.

He snorts. "It's my job to kill her kind. I'm oathbound to slay every monster I meet."

"But she's still human! I can save her." When I don't budge, he raises a brow, his sword still angled for the kill.

"You looked like you had everything under control." His

eyes smile in jest. "I don't care about your sad story. Once a monster, they are no longer human. Let me end this."

"I don't believe that." I spread my arms to protect her. "Once a human, always a human. You can't take that away because someone is under a curse!"

"Listen," the captain drawls with silky impatience. "The Shadows, the Northern Watchmen, whatever you call us, have one purpose only—to rid the earth of monsters and protect innocent fools like you."

"The Shadows—you're the—" My jaw drops, and I cover my mouth.

"The Captain of the Northern Watchmen," he says and steps closer. If I were a ghost, he'd have walked through me already. "Out. Of. The. Way."

I shake my head forcefully.

"So be it." His voice is calm. With lightning reflexes, he produces two golden luprite stones.

"Where'd you get those?" I check my coat pockets in a frenzy for the glowing stones that had made up our prison island. The ones I'd taken from the Ice Crusher are gone . . . I'd put them in the supply bag.

"Same place as you." He pushes me aside with nothing more than two fingers.

Zenri takes me by the shoulders, as if steadying me. I glare after the captain as he dusts the stones in black powder before striking them together and flinging them inside the shelter.

The luprite explodes with the charge of lightning.

A cry freezes in my throat—*Yuki!*

Zenri covers my head and ducks at the blast. My body jerks toward the shack and the flames, hands clawing to reach my sister. I knew luprite stones were used to make weapons, but I'd never seen one explode. Tears blur my eyes.

"Yuki!"

"Stop, you'll get hurt!" Zenri wrestles me to the spot, his feet anchoring to the ground.

"Let me go!" I stomp his foot and jam an elbow to his ribs.

He holds me tighter, absorbing whatever punishment I throw at him, but his attention shifts toward the snowcapped forest. The walls of the winter forest on either side of the train tracks groan, followed by a not-so-distant rumble.

Zenri's grip loosens in his distraction. I break free and dash for the shelter to check on Yuki, scouring the remnants of splintered wood. Smudged footprints lead into the mountains. A shaky breath loosens from my chest—she escaped, but how whole?

The captain snags my arm and pulls me to his side. "Forget the monster. Caring will only hurt you."

I recoil. "You're the monster. How could you do this?"

His jaw tightens, but it's not with anger. A line forms between his brows as he studies me, his eyes rimmed in an unearthly blue. I stare back, forcing my chin to lift.

"I follow the law," he says, matter-of-factly. "Now, I'm taking you to Silverwood as a prisoner."

My heart flops like a fish pulled from water. "So you *are* working for Inspector Jade."

"You could say we're competing with him, though he doesn't deserve the comparison. The Shadows only serve King Soran of Ezo. We're probably the safest place for you given the circumstances. But you're a prisoner with a bounty now, remember that."

"Captain," Zenri calls out. "I don't think now is the time for chitchat—"

We both turn to the forest where a snowy mist rolls down the mountain, followed by a thundering roar. *Avalanche.*

"Time to catch our train," the captain says calmly. He squints at the cascade of snow and then at the train fuming smoke. "Zenri, secure the horses in the livestock cart."

The avalanche rips through the trees on the adjacent mountain, snapping them like twigs.

Captain Ren turns to me. "How fast can you run?"

CHAPTER 12

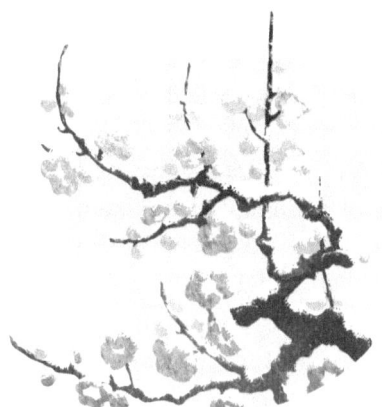

SHOVELS SCRAPE STEEL AND ICE as the last train car emerges from the avalanche. The captain works in silence, shoulders squared, every motion deliberate. Zenri banters with a few passengers, flashing an easy grin like this is just another winter inconvenience.

I edge back, my boots crunching snow. I should run. But Yuki's nails around my throat still throb in memory. She left behind Beetle's hat like a token calling me to follow her. She's still alive.

I press the fabric to my ribs. Hope alone isn't enough. I need a plan. If these men hunt monsters, they should know about the cure—or at least how to find Yuki. And the captain knows about the magic in my blood . . .

"You're not much help, are you?"

I turn. The captain's voice is low, almost amused. He throws down his shovel and wipes his brow with a sleeve.

"I've shoveled enough snow to last a lifetime," I say.

He studies me, as if gauging how much snow a toothpick girl could carry, then he nods. "When you're done enjoying the atmosphere, we're in car sixteen. You're coming with us."

My pulse stutters as he disappears into the train. *Was that an order?* If only I'd had something harder than mochi to throw at him when we first met.

A horn blares, signaling that the tracks are clear. Smog pours out of the metal pipes like dragon smoke. I jump at the sudden blast of heat. Passengers shuffle back into the train cars, guided by a haggard man in uniform brandishing a whistle.

"Nothing to see. Back to your seats," the man drones as if avalanche stops are completely day-to-day affairs. "We'll be off in no time, rest assured, ladies and gentlemen. The end of the line is Ranzan. Connections to Orsai and Silverwood."

Ranzan. The apothecary.

"Are you coming?" Zenri hops from one foot to the other and claps his gloved hands together. "It's freezing out here."

I hesitate. This wasn't the plan. It's the edge of something dangerous, new. I cast one last look over my shoulder. *Yuki...*

The snow-covered valley glimmers in endless pools of white. No trace of my sister. But I can almost feel her—alive—a heartbeat in the distance. The metal platform rocks beneath my boots as women in fur coats and men in fancy buttoned suits parade back to their seats.

"Come on. There's a heater inside," Zenri murmurs, suddenly beside me. "Pretend you're just another passenger. We don't want to draw attention."

I'm already climbing the steps. The train exhales heat like a living thing, the smell of coal and oil wrapping around me. Boarding this train is choosing a path without knowing where it will end. It's choosing risk, possibly prison again.

Inside, the corridor is narrow and dim, lined with flickering glass bulbs. Dollops of amber light fall on the upholstered benches and central heater. My eyes lock on the closed door at the end of the train car.

Walled off. Imprisoned. My breath shortens.

Instinctively, I search for an exit and spin into Zenri behind me.

"Don't worry. You aren't trapped." He smiles, a natural

kindness meant to disarm, but I'm already searching for another way out.

I don't trust tight spaces. I don't trust men in uniforms. I don't trust anything about this. Mother would tell me to search for a path, to observe those around me, to care. But every path has led to pain.

Caring, the captain had said, *will only hurt me.*

I fume inwardly at the words, but they remind me of something softer, older. Long ago, when I cried over the first rat I killed for food, Mama had said, "Caring makes the path harder. But without it, there is no path worth following."

Caring makes me stronger. I swallow the lump in my throat and push forward. Still, I scan each window and connecting door for escape routes just in case. I don't have to care about these soldiers planning to take me prisoner—only Yuki and our escape.

My fingers graze the Beetle's hat tucked inside my coat, and I wonder if the path I've chosen is truly mine, or if it's been marked by all the paths I never took—all the mistakes.

We pass through three cars before reaching a private cabin. Inside, benches face each other, separated by narrow tables between them. Warm air wafts over me from a black furnace, heating the cabin through a narrow shaft that directs the smoke outside. Spicy cedar and smoky coal tangle with the cool mountain air that seeps through the thin windowpanes.

The captain rests against an upholstered seat, his wolf fur jacket cradling his neck, one arm crooked in the fogged-over window, the other holding . . . *my* map!

The one I'd taken from the old saint.

I grit my teeth and take a deep breath that seems impossible to exhale. How had he even stolen it from me?

I storm up to the captain and rip it from his fingers. "What have you done to my sister?"

He lets go of it smoothly, and I nearly topple over. The

captain offers a quiet smile and pulls his wool cap lower over his eyes—as if I'm not worth waking up for.

"She's a *yajuu*," he says, too casually. "A little fire won't kill her. You know that too, or you would've punched me instead of interrupting my reading leisure."

My grip tightens on the map.

"He's right." Zenri gestures for me to take a seat. "Your sister healed incredibly fast after the prison attack. After a few days, she won't even have scars. She won't be human either, mind you. The explosion was just bait to get her to follow us. Captain knows his trade better than anyone."

"You make it sound like a legitimate profession. Killing monsters." I glance at Zenri, avoiding staring at his scars, then at the captain. He hasn't moved. Not a millimeter. Just that slouched, unbothered pose, like he could sleep through an earthquake.

"Why didn't the curse affect you?" I ask Zenri instead. "Your scar, it was from a *yajuu*, wasn't it?"

His smile dims momentarily, hand grazing the scar on his cheek. "Scratched, not bitten," he says. "You have to survive *a bite*. And while we can't heal like *yajuu*, apothecaries have found ways to speed the healing process. Like this powder that our associate in Ranzan concocted to heal scarring."

Apothecary. The word slices through my thoughts like a thread of light.

"Can you heal a *yajuu*?" I roll the map and stuff it into my coat pocket before sliding onto the bench opposite the captain. My eyes bore into the wool hat that conveniently hides his face. Is he really going to try to finish his nap?

Zenri glances away and lowers onto the bench opposite me. I wring my hands in my lap, fiddling with the edge of Mother's elmwood coat.

"Well?" I clear my throat. "Can you cure a monster?"

Zenri drops his gaze. "Only by ending its misery. Captain will tell you the same. There's no cure."

"Have you even *tried?*"

"Why do you think I have this scar?" Zenri's eyes meet mine and the resolve I find unsettles me. It's so much like the look Mother gave when refusing to answer my questions. "My journey began trying to save monsters, not kill them. I'm lucky to be alive."

"But the old saint said—"

"Rumors," Zenri interrupts, glancing out the window.

"But so were *yajuu* until yesterday."

I will him to meet my gaze so I can discern the truth. But he doesn't. I follow his gaze out the window. Outside, the forest whips past in a blur of snow and evergreen pine. Diamond dust and hoarfrost glitter in every direction. The sun paints colors on the snow and sky. So much unexplored land I've never seen whirling past like a vapor.

I hate this train, these walls. I hate that the one person who might help me refuses to even look my direction. What should I expect? They're planning to take me to Silverwood as a prisoner anyway. Still, they know more than they're letting on.

The captain knows about the path.

"You can find her, can't you?" I lean across the table, eyes wide, pleading with Zenri. My calculations say he's the one most likely to break under questioning.

"No," he says, "but the captain can." He flicks a glance toward the man still trying to finish his nap.

I cross my arms and tuck myself into the window corner. I'd rather work with Zenri.

The wind pricks at my eyes from the narrow crack in the glass pane, and the sting of coal dust makes them brim with water. I press my knuckles to my eyes. I can't imagine what I must look like right now, eyes bloodshot, face streaked with dirt and fine cuts, bruises . . . I stop when my mind flashes back to Yuki squeezing the life out of me.

That wasn't her. It was the curse.

Two very different things.

"The captain will find her," Zenri says, his voice soft, compassionate. "He's the best Shadow in the trade. And she's following us, no doubt."

"Why?" I ask. "Why her? You didn't come all this way from Silverwood to catch one prison escapee and my sister. Inspector Jade was searching for the Ainur. For my mother. Why?"

"Ask him," Zenri says, voice quieter now.

I roll my eyes at the captain. His breaths come slow and steady, his lips parted slightly as though he truly is asleep, and I find myself staring too long. I pinch a crumb of melting ice from my jacket and flick it at him. He doesn't budge. Doesn't blink.

"How do you know my sister will follow us?"

Zenri leans across the table, his voice low. "There're a few possibilities you'd best remember."

"I'm listening."

"One—" He lifts a finger to count. "*Yajuu* are vengeful. They mark those who've wronged them and track them down. Like the captain, for blasting her with luprite. Two, they track with smell like other beasts and sometimes with supernatural gifts if they have an ancient heart."

"What do you mean?"

"You should know." His voice drops to a whisper. "Your mother was Ainur. *May her path be eternally restful.* Wayfinding is the oldest of the hearts and the rarest, gifted from the heart of the very first sea dragon. Why do you think we arrived at the prison the same time it was attacked? Inspector Jade as well? There are a great many people interested in you—the last Ainur—and a great many who would have you dead."

"The . . . last?" I lean back against my seat for support.

The last Ainur.

Mother had talked of her family as if they were still alive. The saint had told me to find them. I've been locked away my whole life, unable to meet them, and now this boy tells me they're gone?

"I can't be the last."

Zenri reaches across the table, his expression soft, his hand inches from mine. It's strange since I've never been near boys my age who aren't criminals. I scoot away, not knowing what he's doing.

His soft fingers graze my balled-up fists, and I shrink away from the pity I find there. "Kira," his voice pleads. "This was the only way to save you."

"Save me? You expect me to believe that you're here to protect me after that man locked me in an isolation chamber, let my mother die, and tried to kill my sister!"

"That's correct," the captain shifts and yawns. "Our *job* was to get your mother and Yuki out of prison. To find the last Ainur. We didn't know about you until we arrived. Obviously, I failed."

"Obviously," I echo.

"He nearly became a bear sandwich because of you," Zenri interrupts, tension heating his voice for the first time. "It's no small feat to infiltrate a Taigan prison."

"You're right," the captain drawls, a slight smile crossing his lips. "I should've sent you, Zenri. We all would have preferred Zenri-the-bear-sandwich."

"Not fair!" Zenri slams a hand on the table. "I've already been mauled to within an inch of my life once. Don't joke about sandwiches—I make the best ones in the empire."

"I *never* joke about sandwiches." The captain stretches and removes his cap, his face framed in choppy dark hair. In the train's firelight, it really does look blue, like a cloud before a storm or an iron pot with a bluish tint in the flame. His stomach rumbles as he stretches. "Zenri, fetch the meal cart."

"I'm a soldier, not a waiting boy," Zenri grumbles but jumps to his feet at the captain's order. "Be nice while I'm gone," he warns, eyeing the captain, before slipping away into a separate train car, still grumbling.

Be nice. Ha! The captain doesn't seem interested in kindness. I return my gaze to the window. Heat spreads across my cheeks as I feel his gaze on me.

"There's nothing to see out there." His eyes burn a hole in the back of my skull, but I refuse to look at him.

"There's nothing to see in here either," I say. "And you were listening to us, weren't you?"

"I'm a good listener," he says. "But it's not a magical gift like yours. Only Ainur can be wayfinders. Though I'm assuming you were never properly instructed. Otherwise, you wouldn't be in this mess."

A not-so-subtle tick affects my jaw. I start to protest but decide against it. After all, he's right. Angry questions bubble to my mind.

What were the Shadows doing at the prison when it was attacked? Did he plan on killing my sister? Why take me as a prisoner if they came to rescue us?

But the only question I ask is in a whisper. "Am I really the last Ainur?"

"Yes." The captain's eyes meet mine, unwavering. "Unless you're still including the monster."

"She has a name."

"I'm aware." His eyes narrow briefly. Then he gestures for me to put my hands on the table.

Reluctantly, I do.

He drops a soft cotton satchel in my palms. "It'll help with the cuts and bruises."

I bend over the satchel. "Is it poison?"

"How'd you know?" He arches a brow, a glimmer of amusement in his eyes. "I always poison my prisoners. I'll have it back if you don't want it."

"No." I clench the small satchel and pull it close.

Bitter herbs, lavender, and peppermint waft over me, sending a warm sensation through my body. I dab it across the bruises and scratches on my face and throat. They tingle, the pain lessening.

I study him warily. "Why help me?"

"I take care of those under my watch—even criminals.

Besides, even if you were in good health, you're not the kind of person who runs," he says as if discussing the weather. "You're weak. You'll stay with me because you know I can find her."

"Blizzards." I choke on a laugh. "I'm the only person to have ever escaped Abashi—and I didn't need your help. I'm not going back to jail."

He crosses his arms. "Not right away, no. Would you be interested in stopping in Ranzan to find this so-called cure? We have a short mission in the city dealing with another monster before we can return to Silverwood. And I could use your . . . skills. The trip would be profitable for me and eye-opening for you. Unless you're in a rush to visit prison and your inspector friend? I have a bounty to collect."

I ignore his taunt. "How do you know I want to go to Ranzan?"

"I told you, I'm a good listener."

"Who told you?" I narrow my eyes.

"That doesn't concern you." He leans forward, a slight pluck to his lips and his dark blue eyes a flame of warning.

I glower. But the warm cabin air stings my face, forcing me to sniffle and wipe my nose with my sleeve. *Intimidating, I'm sure.* My situation sinks in like snow melting into the ground.

I may have escaped Abashi, but I'm still a prisoner.

My sister is turning into a monster.

The only chance at surviving on my own was taken from me when Mother died. There is no one to teach me wayfinding. The only path is sitting right in front of me with blue-black hair and a would-be handsome face.

If not for that irritating smirk.

"Cover those bruises before we reach Ranzan," he says, untying his scarf and tossing it to me.

My fingers trail to my neck where my wound still seeps. I don't want anything of his touching my skin, but the scarf is soft, and I don't want trouble. I wrap the silk-wool blend gently around my neck. It features a different insignia from his jacket, and I pause, smoothing it with calloused fingers.

"It suits you," he says, softer this time.

"Does this have a story?" I finger the embroidered threads.

The standard symbol of the capital city features a moon encircled by plum blossoms, but this is different—a rabbit caught in the sharp points of a crescent moon—*talons*. My heart quickens.

"It's one of the Silverwood crests," he says. "It belonged to my mother's family."

Silverwood—where my mother grew up as well, the southernmost tip of Ezo. Before the empire of Taiga had taken over and subjected the king as a vassal.

My fingers thread against the silver rabbit on the captain's scarf—Mother's lessons a beating drum in my skull, *"follow the rabbit in the talons."*

"Does it mean something to you?" The captain's rough voice imitates a softer tone.

I shake my head, tying the scarf around my bruised neck. "No. But I'd like to know what it means to you. What's your story?"

I lean against the table, staring at him like I'd stared at dozens of prisoners. His eyes flinch in surprise and, for a moment, he reminds me of a younger Sasa, my fellow cellmate and friend. Blue threads of path hum against my fingertips, surging at the question.

Had Mother known who the rabbit in the talons would lead me to? I pull my hands beneath the table, hoping the captain doesn't notice the blue hum as he did before.

"My story"—his eyes harden—"is a curse."

Zenri wheels inside with a cart full of seaweed-speckled rice balls, dried squid, and petite sandwiches wrapped in brown paper. He passes me a fish-stuffed rice ball, which I take gratefully.

"Did I miss anything?"

"Family business." The captain reaches over to grab a sandwich.

"You're not my family."

"Definitely not." He plucks another petite sandwich from the tray, thanking Zenri. "But catching the rest of your family *is* my business. Only, I'm on a deadline to snare a monster in Ranzan first, and you're going to help me."

Ren is definitely hiding mochi in his pocket...

CHAPTER 13

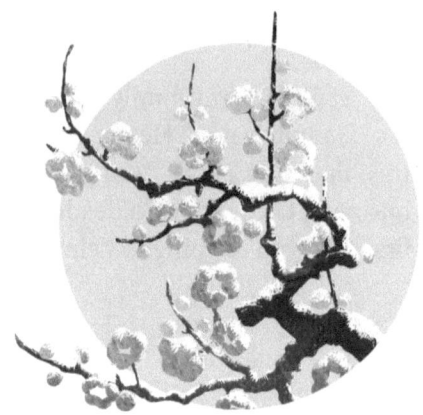

WE ARRIVE IN RANZAN the following day just before nightfall. Glass orbs like small moons glow from atop hundreds of lampposts on the city streets. My breath catches. Colorful banners drape across the brick-and-mortar shops, covering the street with a transparent sheen of moonlit color: red, gold, and aquamarine. It's the most beautiful city I've ever seen—the only city I've ever seen.

"Mama didn't do it justice," I whisper, stepping off the station platform and gawking at the buildings, spindles of brick and stone rising from the ground, copper-plated roofs mixed with wooden ones. Papers litter the train station walls, plastered with more words than I'd seen in a lifetime—and wanted posters. I ogle the reward money for each one, hundreds, thousands, millions of zeni.

"That's . . . me," I say, studying the likeness of my face inked on paper, angry and starved. The numbers, one hundred million zeni, jump out at me. "Do I really look like that?"

"It's a good likeness." A hat plunks upon my head, and I startle at the captain's gentle touch shielding my face from the crowd. "Except for the eyes."

I don't miss the way his gaze lingers with those words, like a sailor admiring iridescent ice floes—assessing the danger and the beauty.

Definitely not the latter.

A crowd jostles us on the station platform, pushing me into the captain. He loops my arm in his, guiding me away from the wanted board, but there's an iron sturdiness to his hold, reminding me that I'm a prisoner. He leans into me as we walk, his voice low. "Stick with us if you want to see your sister again. I'll find her."

I stiffen and tear my gaze away from the glowing city to this smooth-faced soldier with a voice like the sea and just as cruel. Any passerby would have thought he was remarking on the city lights or the color of the moon. Not holding my sister's life in front of me like a rice cake.

As if troubled by my stare, he turns to Zenri and whispers. I catch only crumbs: "coronation," "Gion," "Valcon," whatever those mean.

"Is he always this rude?" I say, glancing at the friendlier of my two Shadows.

"The grumpiest ray of sunshine you'll ever meet," Zenri says.

The captain's arm stiffens beneath mine. "I'm not grumpy."

"If only you could hear yourself," I say. "You're all clouds and no sun."

"Don't be too harsh," Zenri says as he bows in departure, presumably at the captain's orders. "All living beings have light, even Shadows."

I puzzle those words as Zenri saunters away, catching a glimpse of the faded pink scars that curve from his hairline to the tip of his jaw. What monster had he fought to earn those? He's not as tall or broad-shouldered as the captain. In fact, he's about as thin as a slab of fried tofu, but behind that friendly face is enough strength to slay demons. He's exactly the kind of prince Yuki would fawn over, even with the scars.

As Zenri disappears into the swarm of travelers exiting the station, the captain drops my arm. He cuts through the crowd, expecting me to simply follow. His confidence is chafing.

I could run.

Escape the Shadows and find my sister and the apothecary on my own. But I didn't survive seventeen years in prison by taking every chance that caught my eye. Paths must be carefully considered. There are no second chances.

I haven't the faintest clue how to survive in a city on my own, and not enough time to risk it. Tomorrow morning, Yuki will be unchangeable.

I need the captain, for now.

"You should unfurrow your brow," the captain says when I catch up. "People might think you're cross at me."

"Good. Because I am." My gaze shifts to the crowded streets. "Zenri said your orders were to save my family from Abashi. But now you're taking me to Silverwood as a prisoner. Why? Is it the bounty?"

"I follow the law," he says. "It's honest, unlike . . . feelings."

"You're hardly in danger of those," I say with a laugh.

"A relief to be sure." His eyes linger on mine, dropping to my lips until the laugh wilts and my cheeks bloom instead. Then he clears his throat. "Our orders *were* to get your mother and sister out. But you—you're a wanted fugitive and the law states you must go to the magistrate. And your sister is—"

"Lost," I finish for him. "Orphaned. Alone. There's no law against that."

"There are laws against dark magic and monsters."

Words of protest are on the tip of my tongue when the captain tugs me to the side of the road. A horse-drawn cart thunders past at devilish speed where I'd just stood. Strong arms anchor me against a stone wall as the crowd surges around us. Blood thrums in my ears, echoing with the carriage driver's much too late announcement: "Out of the way!"

So much for carriages being slow as snails. What else did I misjudge in the world? How does the captain react so fast?

I should've paid more attention to my surroundings. Heat rushes my cheeks as I register the captain's tall frame leaning over me. I force my gaze to his, suddenly aware of his hand warm against my waist and the other a protective shield hemming me away from the crowd. Eyes like gentle rain clouds brush over mine before tearing away.

"No harm done," he says, stepping back and adjusting his uniform with a crisp tug. "Keep to this side. Wouldn't want you under a carriage."

His words could be mistaken for concern, but the edge in his voice cuts clean.

My heart thunders like the carriage wheels that'd nearly trampled me. I peel myself off the wall, heat crawling up my neck, and hurry to keep up with the captain. I won't be taken off guard like that again. Still, I accept his advice and walk on his left side closer to the vendors. The streets are louder than icebergs crashing into the sea—a roar of voices and the squeaking of wheels.

How do I start looking for the apothecary and my sister?

A path seems impossible in this chaos. Powerful fragrances crowd my senses, half of them indiscernible. Everywhere men, women, and children flock to shop windows, stroll down the cobbled streets, and ride over the mayhem in horse-drawn carriages. I don't realize my hands are clasped to my ears until the captain pries them off.

He bends to my level, eyes searching mine with thinly veiled annoyance. "You can't hear danger if you close your ears to it."

I pause, wide-eyed and hands now fisted beneath his touch. He guides me to a quieter alcove, and I back into a paper lantern. Air winds tight in my chest. I don't tell him that the crowds are too much for me—the sights, sounds, smells—all of it. I gulp down air like a hot meal on a starving stomach.

The captain runs a hand along his jaw and sighs. "It's okay to admit when you need help."

I stare at him, dumbfounded. Asking for help is the same as losing your dinner or your family getting extra lashes. "Have *you* ever asked for it?"

A muscle twitches in his jaw. "Once."

He takes my hand and leads me down a cobblestone stair. We stumble out into a thinner crowd, the occasional vendor hawking octopus dumplings with dancing fish flakes. A child beams at his mother, pointing to a wooden spinning top with bright colors. I gape at the round cheeks and stubby hands. I forget that humans start off so small.

"It's a festival day," the captain says. "Blasted coronation week. Stick with me. We'll be there soon."

I follow after him. My heart hammers at the slightest thing that everyone else ignores—a paper ornament blowing in the wind, the chime of iron bells, the cry of a baby. All new. Exciting. Terrifying. Everything except the twilit sky and the tightness in my chest that worries for my sister.

"Captain . . ." I begin, toying with a plan to lead me to the apothecary. I touch his scarf at my neck, ignoring the faint scent of lavender and clean soap, and wince. "Any chance they sell that healing powder here?"

His pace slows to fall in step with mine. "If you need it," he says. "But it'd be in the back alleys, the Nehu district. Not a safe place. I can look at your wound tonight. The next ferry isn't until tomorrow, so we'll rest here before heading to Silverwood."

"No," I say too quickly. "I mean—I'd rather have a proper physician."

"You won't find that in Nehu. You'd be better off letting me clean it to reduce infection."

"I'd rather have medicine."

Dark blue eyes steal over me with caution, reading between the lines. He knows what I'm after—the cure, the apothecary. He glances down the street and sighs. "I'll see what I can do."

I resist the urge to raise a brow. Doubt is safe. Suspicion has kept me alive. He might help me find my sister—and then try to kill her—but something tells me he won't help me find a cure. And I can't find it on my own.

The old saint had spoken the apothecary's name—Jey—like a

curse. Not the kind of thing I should ask strangers if I'm trying to keep a low profile. I need more information.

"Can you at least tell me where we're going?"

Another shopping street intersects the alley and beyond with a decorative gate jutting on the horizon. In different circumstances, I would have loved to explore the city with unbridled curiosity. "What's that gate over there?"

"You have an appointment, my lady," Zenri cuts in, stepping up behind me so suddenly that I jump like a rabbit. "At Lu Gion Boutique. I called in a favor with an old friend."

"You're late." Captain clears his throat and levels Zenri with a look. "*The lady* is curious about the gate. Perhaps you would like to tell her about that too?"

"Oh, the Nehu gate." Zenri grimaces. "Nehu's the exact opposite of an oyster. Beautiful on the outside but hideous within."

"It's made from sea coral and pearls," the captain continues. "Natural things taken, exploited—now dead. Prisoners were forced to build it and paint it with rare metals that we later learned caused poisoning. I wouldn't go there if I were you."

If I were a criminal. He doesn't say it, but the unspoken words churn in my mind. Is that how he sees me? Or just how I see myself?

An insatiable curiosity pulls me toward that gate. Why warn me against it so strongly unless the apothecary lies hidden there? When I find my sister, I'll need that cure in my hands. And I've just been told where to find it.

"We're late for the appointment," Zenri says. "Madame Gion is very particular. It's honestly a miracle she agreed on such short notice."

"What appointment?" I ask.

The captain gestures to the whole of me with a look I can only describe as offended. "You need a bath and a dress."

"What? Why?" Dread and curiosity climb the back of my throat. I'd never even seen a dress until the ladies on the train.

Zenri laughs. "Have you looked in a mirror?"

"You're one to talk." I clench the tattered elmwood coat tight around my shoulders. "And I *have* looked in a mirror. Several times in fact. Besides, I hardly see how a bath and a dress fit into your plans to capture a monster tonight. Don't you just pounce on them unawares? Why do you need me?"

"We're not savages," Zenri says. "We're Shadows. And this monster happens to be attending the governor's ball tonight. Dignitaries from all over the empire will be present to honor the coronation happening at the end of the week. Of course, it's nothing but a puppet coronation, but if the Taigan Empire is good at one thing besides cruelty, it's parties."

"And wayfinders can find people," the captain says drily, "*if* they've been trained."

I ignore the jab. "Surely a monster won't be hard to find in a ballroom?"

"Not all monsters look the part," Zenri says. "*Yajuu* take many forms. Some look like normal humans and walk this very street." He shivers for effect. "Others take the form of animals, bears, wolves, even dragons. But this particular monster is—"

"Zenri," the captain cuts him off, his tone censuring.

"What will my sister turn into?" My throat goes dry, but I have to ask.

"You already know." Zenri turns away to look at a passing candy trolley. The pale scars on his face seem to burn beneath my eyes, and I know the answer.

The captain stops suddenly and pulls us to the side of the street. A carriage trundles by, carrying a bright orange banner with the words "Come One, Come All—The Nehu Circus" painted across it in glittering letters, followed by the stomping feet of a small woolly elephant. The crowd parts, and the strange menagerie rolls through.

"That's an elephant!" I point with a thrill of excitement. I'd seen one once in a picture drawn by another prisoner, but I thought it was a fable.

The captain pushes my hand down. "Don't draw attention."

I force my gaping mouth to close. Wonder burns my eyes to tears. It's so large, so different, so gentle, and it too is a prisoner.

"It's a woolly Neumann," Zenri adds. "Blasted circus traders and imperial hunters. They sell everything from Seshu dogs to *yajuu*. Those elephants are native to Ezo. Only a handful left now."

Another part of my homeland that's dying. Pain balloons in my chest at the list of marvels I'll never see or experience.

The small procession slows as it crosses beneath the coral gates and a crowd gathers. A fat metal pipe rolls out the back of the carriage and explodes over the cheering men, women, and children.

Thousands of tiny golden papers, like fireflies, take flight over the open courtyard. One twirls effortlessly over my head. I reach out to touch it and snag the paper from the air.

The menagerie is calling you, the golden ticket reads in inky black letters.

The captain snatches it from my hand and tears it.

"What was that for?" I ask, feeling a physical weight leave my hand in disproportion to the tiny slip of paper. "Is it magic?"

"Magic attracts other magic," he says, scanning the crowd. "Don't forget your wanted poster. They're looking for you."

"Who? The inspector?"

"Yes. And every bounty hunter and imperial spy this side of the border. Ranzan's crawling with them tonight. All looking for monsters to use for extra coin. It's the only city that would even think of taking advantage of cursed magic." His eyes flick to my hands. "Including your particular talents."

He nods to Zenri. "Keep her close. Don't let her leave your sight."

"Yes, Captain." He gives a quick bow.

"I'm not planning to run away," I say, lifting my chin.

"That's exactly why I don't trust you," the captain murmurs, gaze slicing through me, his voice almost gentle. "But I was asking Zenri for your protection, not as a jailor."

He doesn't wait for my response. In a second, he's gone, swallowed by the crowd.

I'd misjudged him. But just because he wants me safe doesn't mean he cares. He has a law to uphold, and likely a bounty too.

"Does he always disappear like that?" I ask.

"If he wasn't a Shadow, I'd call him a ghost." Zenri points down another cobblestone street. "But don't worry. The captain's not after your sister now. He has other quarry. Your sister's probably hiding nearby. If *yajuu* show themselves in Ranzan, they're either already owned by someone or soon will be."

"I thought you killed monsters, not captured them."

"The Shadows, yes. But the illegal trading of monsters is popular in Ranzan. We try to stay out of it unless it gets out of hand."

"And has it?"

Zenri nods. He takes me by the shoulder and spins me to face an enormous stone wall.

The lower portion of the wall is made up of houses stacked on top of each other with barred windows and hanging flowers. Parapets are stationed equidistant atop the walls with red ribbons flapping in the harsh wind.

"That's the wall separating the Winterwilds from the rest of Ezo. Ranzan's literally on the wall. No other city dares get this close. Everything on the other side belongs to the winter and to monsters."

"And my home." An odd feeling of affection and hatred washes over me.

Zenri frowns. "You mean Abashi Prison? Just because you grew up in a place doesn't make it your home."

"But isn't that the way of things? Prison was my normal."

"Just because something is normal doesn't make it right."

Those words should be soothing, but not coming from Zenri.

"Isn't that true of the law as well?" I say. "It's not always right. Sometimes there are more important things."

Zenri rubs the back of his neck and gives a nervous laugh. "The captain doesn't see it that way."

"And you?"

"I follow orders when they come from someone I trust," he says. "And right now that order is to keep you safe and not smelling like . . . this."

My jaw drops. Do I really smell that bad? I resist the urge to sniff my armpits.

I cast my gaze to the end of the street where steam puffs from a small hut. The captain ran off so Zenri could give me a bath! My feet start back-pedaling.

"No, no, no," Zenri chides, pushing me forward until we stand before a public bathing house. "You cannot go to Madam Gion's like this."

I need to find that cure for Yuki, fast. The prison bath is one thing, but in the middle of town with all these people . . .

Zenri drops the coins into the till and ushers me inside the enclosed space. Thankfully, he waits outside. After I've cleaned with a rented towel and donned my pajamas and coat again, we arrive at the dress shop.

"We're here!" Zenri says, pointing to the awning of a shop glowing with lanterns and a tiny horde of leopard spotted moths. *"Lu Gion Boutique."*

Twin statues—mannequins, Zenri informs me—stand in the window, hands posed unnaturally and dressed in what I presume to be mainland fashion with jeweled hats and tight sashes pulled around their ribs.

"I am *not* wearing that."

I've imagined myself in new clothes, a pair of warm pants and a collared shirt, but a dress? My face breaks into a flush. *Would I even be . . . pretty?*

Warm nerves color my cheeks, and I dig my heels into the

ground. "I can't go in there," I mutter. "I've never bought anything in my whole life. My pajamas are comfortable."

Zenri laughs. "I'm afraid fashion isn't about comfort. Though, that's a novel idea." He pulls out a bag of coins and grins. "Captain gave me *all* his money. You're going to wear something nice to the ball. Believe me, you don't want to show up in rumpled pajamas with a coat made from tree bark."

I fluff the lace edges of my white pajamas. "I think it's quite fashionable."

Zenri raises a brow.

"But I don't know how to wear a dress," I whisper harshly, turning my back to the store. "And don't say you'll show me how."

"I would if it'd convince you, but they have staff for that." Zenri winks and whisks the door open with a dimpled smile. "Go in. You don't want me to get in trouble with the captain, do you?"

I relent and step inside the store, but it's a tremendous effort. That is, until I see the kimono and dresses—smooth fabric like melted stars, colors that would shame a sunset, coils of heavenly silk, and warm lush furs.

I let out a long breath, fingers steepled over my mouth.

"I told you it's the best shop in town," Zenri whispers.

I reach out toward one of the silk rolls, and a familiar blue tug tingles on my fingertips. It loops out the store and over the walls—toward Nehu and the circus.

I take another look at the dresses, the softness of silk melting beneath my fingers. Yuki would've loved this place. Trying one on wouldn't hurt. My sister's close, I can feel it. And the cure is just on the other side of that wall. If a dress will help me blend in better, I might as well try.

CHAPTER 14

THE GOVERNOR'S BALL STARTS in an hour, but I'll be on the other side of town by then if all goes according to plan. I smile, imagining the captain's scowl when he realizes he's been bested by me. The path has grown stronger since I left prison behind. I won't be as easy to catch this time around.

My sister and I will trace our own way.

I turn in front of the dress shop mirror, modeling a pale blue silk with a bursting star pattern and a wide black sash pulled suffocatingly tight around the waist. "I can't move in this," I breathe, lifting a long draping sleeve and searching for my hand inside it. "Can I try another?"

Madame Gion purses her lips. She taps a long finger against her temple, and I'm drawn to the dozens of pearls embedded in her skin like a bejeweled tattoo. I can only imagine it's a fashion statement for high society in Ranzan.

"I have one last ensemble," she says in a haughty voice. "But I doubt you can afford it."

"Let's see it," Zenri says, slouching in a velvet chair.

Madame Gion raises a brow, eyes narrowing at his posture, but she slips out on soft-heeled shoes to fetch the next dress. I take another turn in the mirror, feeling exposed in the smooth fabric, like I don't belong. Like I've never belonged.

"I doubt the captain wants to waste more money on me than he has to," I say under my breath. "But it *is* the perfect disguise."

"You certainly don't look like your wanted poster." Zenri steps beside me, snagging a silk hat from a display shelf. "Don't worry about money. Captain gave me the purse, and I'm going to spend it. You deserve it after living in that . . . place." He plops the bewitching blue hat onto his curly lob and makes smug faces in the mirror.

I will my lips not to smile.

"Besides," he continues, "only the wealthiest and most famous people in all the eight kingdoms make it to the governor's ball. It pays to dress well to avoid the damages should we be found out."

Exactly. What damages is the captain avoiding?

Tearing my gaze from the mirror, I let my thoughts trail to the Shadow and his insufferable dedication to the law. What will he gain by turning me over to the authorities? Money, power, a position in the empire? He still hasn't told me why he was hired to extract my family from prison in the first place.

The shopkeeper returns with an armful of parchment cases. She raises a pearled brow at Zenri's hat and the crystal cufflink he's using as a spinning top on the dressing table. He grins and then sets the items back on the shelf with an affectionate pat. Satisfied, the shopkeeper unties the case and gently pulls out a cinnamon brown dress with a crisscrossed back and silver clasps on the shoulder made from shells and the whitest of claws.

"This isn't the one," she says with a sharp frown. "Rinka, what have I told you about order?"

A hunchback attendant bobs her head from between the curtains dividing the room.

"Wait, I like that dress," I say.

"It's for the circus, not the ball." The woman sneers and shoves the dress back into its case. "But this"—she opens the next case—"is perfection. Crafted from finely ground abalone by the best artisans in the Mariner Kingdom. It's like mermaid skin to the touch."

Mermaids, I'd heard of those. Women with tentacles and fins who drowned pirates like Sasa in the ocean. *Why would I want to look like one of them?*

Madame Gion holds an exquisite gown that glistens in a rainbow of colors. When I try it on, it spreads out behind me in a featherlight train made of pink pearl and glittering white.

"That's the one!" Zenri echoes and beckons the shopkeeper aside to discuss prices.

"I'll send my assistant to help you with the fitting," Madame says before slipping into the other room, separated by a beaded curtain that I'm certain must be made of real jewels.

My hands run across the smooth abalone fabric. How did they weave fabric from rocks and shells? It fits soft against my skin, revealing curves I didn't know I had. I finger the captain's silk scarf at my throat, thankful it conceals my bruised neck. When I look in the mirror, I gasp. I barely recognize the girl staring back at me with eyes like a warm autumn sky.

The pink coral adds a touch of fire to my eyes and warmth to my tawny skin. Even my long black hair slips across the gown with a violet sheen that brings out the soft purple in the abalone. The whole dress sparkles with life, and so do I.

The attendant appears from seemingly nowhere and brushes my hair before pinning it up with a pearl comb and sprigs of red coral fronds. The girl's hunched shoulders and bent knees move quickly around me as she retouches spots and pins the dress in areas that don't fit perfectly. Unlike her expert hands, mine shake against the fabric. All my life, wearing the same dingy, shapeless rags. I'd never known I could be . . . beautiful.

A sharp prick steals my attention. I glance down, and the attendant cowers from where she adjusts the dress. "Forgive me. It was an accident. If-if my mistress knew . . ."

"Don't worry." I smile to ease her fears. "No harm done. I won't say a word."

The attendant's shoulders buckle in an awkward bow and then she spreads her hands over the numerous dress pins as if working magic. She nudges me to turn with long fingers that pinch my skin.

I spin, watching her discreetly in the mirror. How did a girl my age come by such a bent and broken body? A brown cape covers an oddly shaped bulk on her back. And then, in one quick flash, the girl's eyes meet mine, two serpentine slivers of black covered by a milk gray film. *Yajuu.*

My breath comes in shallow—and it's not the tight wrappings around my ribs. The girl takes one last loop around me, quickening her pace, and then backs out of the room with a bow.

"Wait!" I reach out to beckon her back.

The girl narrows her eyes with a flash of barred, pointed teeth, then slips soundlessly behind the jeweled curtain. My arm shakes as I draw it back. This wasn't the fearsome creature everyone whispered about, not a hulking beast in the wood or a shapeshifting monster lurking in an alley. The girl was sensitive, broken . . . fearful. Surely she's not in the early stages of the curse like Yuki, but how is it that she still seems human?

I glance at the mirror, then the window and the bustling street beyond. Sharp voices rise from behind the curtain where the shopkeeper and Zenri continue to barter over prices.

"I tell you, the captain will pay the rest!" Zenri raises his voice from the adjacent room. "We're not leaving without it."

"It must be paid in full. I can't allow precious merchandise from my homeland out of the shop otherwise. But there are other ways to pay. Surely the Shadows have something of value? Are you tracking any beasts in the city? Any bounties?"

"None that would interest you." Zenri's voice turns cold. "Be careful. It's illegal to sell monsters, and some might get the wrong idea."

"Fine. You can pay seventy percent now."

I take a turn in the mirror. Every spot the girl had pinned is completely fixed. The pins gone—evaporated. She hadn't been sewing the dress as she inspected it. Was it magic? The back of the dress swoops down low around my neck, the captain's scarf tied in a bow and bringing out the blue in my eyes. He won't have a chance to see the dress his money purchased.

I'm not going to the ball. I don't have time to chase demons, not when Yuki is on the verge of becoming one.

My elmwood coat hangs in the entryway. Snatching it from the hook, I fling it over my shoulders and grab a pair of new boots from the rack.

Stealing a glance at the beaded curtain to make sure no one sees me, I slip out the door. I grit my teeth at not being able to question the shop attendant. Surely another monster would know where to find her own kind? Perhaps she'd received the cure, and that was the reason for her human appearance?

No, the cure *has* to do more than that.

The opal gown sparkles in the moonlight, and I quicken my pace. Even with my mother's elmwood coat covering the dress, I stand out. Like the moon fleeing the night sky, anyone could spot me. But I can't afford to be seen. I just need to slip into the coral gates—into Nehu—and ask around discreetly. The apothecary can't be that hard to find. Jey, I repeat the name to myself. Surely someone would point me to his shop.

A gentle hum of path slips between my fingers—not enough to grab hold of, but I'm on the right track. I slip into the shadows of the shop awnings and trail the crowd that meanders toward the coral gates. Two large white towers stand in the darkness. I'm close enough now that I can make out the sharp edges of the building, completely unscalable due to the rough coral coating.

A spark of blue flashes before me, followed by an instinct to dodge. I bend down and spin to the right. My breath comes up short. There's no time to think. After so many years of prison life, I do the one thing that comes naturally—protect myself. My arm swings up in a blocking maneuver and slams into solid muscle. A hooded figure snatches my wrist and pulls me deep into the nearest alley.

"Predictable," drawls a familiar voice. Captain Ren stands beneath the lanterns of the narrow alley, a hooded winter robe obscuring his face. He's dressed in a dark navy suit with a long jacket fringed in silver, his appearance more polished, cleaner—as if ready for a royal ball and not a brawl with demons.

My eyes narrow, and he releases my wrist.

"You said I wouldn't run." I jerk my hand back, soothing the smarting skin where my block had hit his arm.

"You call *that* running? About as clumsy as a moon bear. It's a wonder you ever escaped Abashi," he says, pushing back his hood.

"But I did escape. And I'll do it again." I square my shoulders and step into the lantern light.

The captain's dark blue eyes widen as he scans my now smooth raven hair, washed face, and the shimmer of my gown in the glowing light. His eyes jump to mine with an attentiveness I've not seen before, and warmth floods me. One minute he's cold as ice, the next he's the sun melting it. I can't understand him. Quickly, I turn my gaze away and survey the rest of the alley.

The captain leans closer, his shoulder brushing mine and his voice is soft in my ear. My cheeks flush, but the words are anything but warm, "Do you really think Zenri let you go so easily? What if I planned to let you run away? To test your wayfinding abilities. To use you to lead me to your sister."

I pull myself to full height, which only comes to his jaw, so it doesn't have quite the effect I'd hoped. "Stay away from Yuki."

The blue in his eyes flickers like flames trapped in a gas lamp. He smiles and lifts his chin as if musing. "Deflection, good. So you're after the apothecary first, not your sister. Maybe you *have* learned a little more wayfinding than I gave you credit for. But you won't find him in Nehu. Not tonight."

He's lying. I bristle and eye the alley exit behind him. Yuki's curse will be permanent come morning. I need to find that cure tonight.

"I'll take my chances." I make to step past him.

"Suit yourself." He slides out of the way with a polite nod. "But if you choose the wrong path, your sister will be the one to pay for it. She has what—a day or two—before the curse claims her?"

I pause mid-step, my back going stiff. He knows something about the apothecary that I don't—or he's bluffing.

"She has until tomorrow morning," I say, turning to face him. "You want me to join you at the ball so you can catch another *monster*. You're just milking my magic before turning me in to collect a reward."

"That's not—"

"What's in it for me?" I cut the distance between us.

The blue flame in his eyes shines brighter, wary and curious. "Occasionally a path is mutually beneficial. You need the apothecary, and I need to find a monster. At least, what I call I monster."

"Another *yajuu*?" I scoff.

He closes the last step between us, bending beside my ear with a whisper. "No. A man. But Valcon Jey is more monster than any demon I've killed—he's your apothecary."

I stifle a gasp and nearly grab his arm. "He's at the ball?"

"Shall we?" He holds out an arm to escort me, eyes twinkling in the lamplight.

I weigh my options. After we find the apothecary—if he's telling the truth—then maybe he'll be distracted enough for me to escape with the cure. That is, if he doesn't kill the apothecary first.

I breathe deep, every fiber of my being stiffening as I hold out my hand.

"You'll have to hold on tight," he warns.

Before I can protest, he reaches behind him, drawing a strange metal contraption like a bow. A three-sided hook launches from the tip of the bow as the captain catches me by the waist. In a flash, my feet fly off the ground, heart in my throat as we soar upward. I'm pinched and buffeted, my skin on needles, like unfreezing too fast. Then we reach the top of a building.

Frigid wind bites at my skin as the Captain swings me over the edge onto a roof and unties the rope. "What was that?" I stand, shivering. A cry catches in my throat as I look down. I'm on a flat rooftop high above the ground. The stars feel closer than the pinpricks of people on the cobblestone below. I step back from the dizzying height, but my boot slips.

"Careful." He snags my arm and pulls me back.

Cold wind screams against my ears. I gape at the many paths I sense—voices, feelings, and colors carried on the wind. The captain's hands soften and steady me, drawing me a safer distance from the edge.

"Where are we . . . ?"

He studies me. "The governor's ball is inside the Wall. Some of the best mansions in the empire were built into the Wall separating our world from yours. That's the Winterwilds and Mt. Atan, and over there"—he leans over my shoulder, pointing to a far speck of black in the ocean—"Abashi Island."

I gulp, and the shivers run deeper. My hands and toes are beginning to lose feeling, and the thin dress beneath my elmwood coat doesn't help. "Did you build that contraption?"

"Yes. Now save the questions. It's cold." The captain leads me to a rooftop door.

He pushes it open, and we step down a dark spiral staircase. I follow, eyes adjusting as he flings open the curtains, letting moonlight filter into a large room. He shakes off his coat, flicking a few stubborn specks of snow from the lapel. I steady myself against a nearby bookcase.

"Why are you trying to find the apothecary?" I ask. *It's certainly not to help me.* "It seems like the only business you conduct is either bounties or death."

"You're not far off." He smiles and begins rifling through a desk as if he's been here before and knows what to look for.

"Do the Shadows always sneak into parties?" I ask, edging closer.

"I hadn't planned on *sneaking*, but someone made me late." He casts me a pointed look and leans over a large mahogany desk littered with papers. "There are dozens of offices within these walls, but this is Jey's private study if I did my calculations correctly."

"I don't see what being late has to do with breaking into a ball." I peer over the desk as he combs through drawers with quiet precision.

"You can't get into the ball if you're late," he explains. "You could be the emperor himself, and they'd bar the gate. It was the only way."

He gives me a look that clearly says *thanks to you*.

"I'm beginning to think you weren't invited in the first place," I say.

He laughs and continues searching the desk. "Oh, I was invited."

I lift a fountain pen off the desk and inspect it between my fingers. What I would've given to have this in prison with my journal and all those empty pages needing to be filled.

"So why do you need me to find the apothecary? You already know Valcon Jey is at the party, and you seem to be looking for something very specific in that desk."

"It's Valcon I want," he says, still rifling through the desk. "I've been after him for years, but he's not easy to find, even when you know where to look. I need something to help you track him. Wayfinders can't work off names alone. You need an object that's tied to him, to his core. That's how you can find your sister—you have a connection."

"Oh?" I work my way back to the door, playing with a handful of path in my mind to escape once I've found the cure. "Since when did you become an expert in wayfinding?"

He shuts the desk drawer and looks at me, his voice dropping to an exasperated whisper. "You're the last Ainur. Have you wondered how I know that? How many I've met before and what happened to them?"

My breath stills, and my eyes search his. But his stare isn't cruel. His eyes seem to change color with his mood and are now dark blue, writhing like the sea beneath a storm. Remorse, pain, and anger toss those waves, secrets hidden in the dark.

"I'm sorry," he says, breaking the stare. He pushes back from the desk, and his hand trembles on a scrap of paper. "I've been after Valcon for a long time."

I gulp back my questions about the Ainur and focus on the task at hand. "So, what are we looking for . . . this core?"

He steps into the moonlight, producing a small black and white filmy paper. It holds a replica of a face, two of them to be exact, standing stiff and impassive with eyes hard as ice.

"How did the faces get there?" I ask.

"It's a photograph," he says, handing it to me. "An albumen print. Have you never seen one before?"

I shake my head, mesmerized by the replica of a living person imposed on paper.

"Can you tell which one is Valcon?" he asks, his voice softer.

Without hesitation, I point at the man with a rounded jaw and a wizened face, his youth hidden behind beady eyes like a vulture.

"I can find him," I say, surprising myself.

Those cold, beady eyes spark a thread of path into existence—a fat, frayed path with loose ends and tangled knots. It uncurls like ink spilled into the sea, and I'm not sure I'll like what I find at the end.

CHAPTER 15

VALCON JEY IS MADE OF BLOOD, bones, and skin like everybody else. The only part missing is perhaps a soul. My eyes scan his photograph, and I feel it—a disturbing evil staring back at me from the glossy piece of paper.

I memorize this face in order to draw a path to him, but I'm too curious about the albumen print itself. I've turned it over a dozen times trying to figure out how the picture got there. It's not drawn or inked onto the thin slip of paper. I've heard about hooded machines that render a person's likeness, but I've never actually seen one.

How does it work? Curiosity churns inside me.

I pass the photograph back to the captain with a short nod. I won't ask him for an explanation. Besides, we don't have time.

"Now, remember your breathing and feel the path before you see it," the captain instructs. "You won't find him if you don't focus. There are a million sights and sounds outside this door, and—"

"I won't find him with you rambling in my ear," I snap.

The captain smiles. "A good wayfinder knows her mind, but . . ." With one hand, he gently removes my elmwood coat.

"That's my mother's!"

"It's not ballroom attire," he says with an apologetic smile.

"Once the mission is complete, I'll come back for it. You have my word."

He tucks the coat into the bookcase with gentle care.

"Why do you want Valcon?" I ask, trying to sort him out.

His eyes drop to my mother's coat as he stows it. He turns to me and readjusts a loose strand of my hair into the coral hairpin, a distant look on his face. "At least you have something left of your mother's." His jaw clenches. "Valcon took everything from me."

A change sweeps over him with those words—desperate, warped, like a man's voice below the waves. *Why share something so personal? And why does it sound like a confession?*

He reaches past me, whisking the door open into an elaborate hallway of polished cedar floors and banisters. A sound like hail pelting a rooftop stings my ears. My eyes squeeze shut to focus, trying to find a path to the apothecary. The blue path had illuminated when I first saw him in the picture—it connected him to Yuki. That's what a path does, reveals the way to your deepest need or longing. It isn't just the captain who needs Valcon Jey—we both do.

The pinging sound settles into the background as my senses lock onto the frayed, inky trail that hums beneath my fingertips. A breeze blows in the atrium, a large open space surrounded by spiral hallways and numerous doors. With the soft breeze comes the warm scent of sweat and perfume and a glimpse of blue sweeping down several floors. The color weaves like a thread down the atrium and across a wide expanse littered with dancers.

My hands clench as if trying to hold the path, which is impossible. *Find the apothecary. Find Yuki.* I will the path to lead me to the cure, to Yuki, but the blue remains stuck, writhing anxiously several floors below, its color shifting from blue to inky black.

"I think he's downstairs," I say a little breathlessly. "On the first floor."

"What's he doing?" the captain asks, his voice low.

"I'm a wayfinder, not a seer," I say. "Honestly, I thought you knew more about wayfinding than I did."

A smile touches the captain's face, but he ignores the jab. Together, we descend the curved staircase to the main chamber. I square my shoulders and face the low rumble of excited voices.

A cavernous ballroom opens at the last staircase. The floor shines with polished swirls of rich mahogany, light birch, and amber bamboo. Chandeliers hang from a ceiling painted in stars. A crowd mingles about the room in elegant kimono, smart suits, and shiny dresses painted with exotic flowers, inky mountains, and golden scales, representing the power of Taiga.

"Stay close," the captain whispers. For once, I'm grateful for his strong arm beneath my own. "We're going to draw some attention to lure Valcon out."

"I don't belong here," I murmur, hesitating as we step onto the ballroom floor. I'm suddenly aware of my dull complexion and gaunt features, my inability to dance, to be normal. "We don't need to go out there. I-I can try to narrow down his location—"

"You belong anywhere you choose to step," the captain says, his eyes brightening to a cerulean blue. He offers a hand with an inviting smile and a deep bow. Slowly, I place my hand into his, and he leads me to the center of the grand room where the chandelier shines brightest.

A few heads turn our way as the captain's arm slips around my waist, pulling me closer. Dark hair frames his face like waves in a midnight sea, lending a wild air to an otherwise noble bearing. His fingers meet the hollowed curve of my spine, and my skin tingles with awareness.

Does he really think I belong?

"I can't dance," I say, my voice unbearably hitched.

"Nonsense. Anyone can dance. And wayfinders *should* be the best at it."

"They don't exactly have dances in prison," I whisper.

But before I can protest further, the captain gives me a gentle nudge, and we spin out into the other dancing couples, a tangle of feet and music.

"I really can't—" I say between breaths.

"You can," he says, his gentle nudge. "Make your heart stronger than your fear."

My hand spins within the captain's rough palm. It's no different from the hands of the men in Abashi Prison, except that it's gentle, warm, yielding. I quickly snatch my hand away on the next turn, hating the feverish effect his touch has on me. The man who wants to destroy my sister is evil, no matter how kind his hands seem. But inevitably, my hand returns to his as our spinning continues. I trip at the next turn, but he catches me as if it wasn't a mistake at all. His every step is gentle and effortless, designed to make me look like the better dancer.

"Not bad," he says as the dance slows and my bare arms rest against the softness of his shirt and the strength beneath.

I follow the subtle inflections in his hand and the tensing muscles as we move as one, swirling along the polished floor. A smile tugs at my lips as a new path graces my hands. One that dips and dives and dances. The threads of blue almost feel like laughter . . . joy. The path whirls between us, and then it vanishes, leaving only a pounding in my ears and a warmth in my body.

The captain spins me and then pulls me close with a rapid tug. I glance breathlessly at the other dancers, feeling their hot stares on my back and especially on the captain. He's undoubtedly the best dancer on the floor and, perhaps, the handsomest. He takes a graceful step back and bows as the dance ends, his eyes studying mine with a curious smile.

My heart thunders, like the cascade of pinging rain coming from the corners of the room. Strange boxes full of tiny wooden balls line the hall. The captain turns toward them as the dance shifts to a new melody. I notice there are machines with numbered balls inside that are spun or tossed by the players.

"What are those?" I struggle to keep up with the captain's moving feet again.

"Fortunes," he says, as if that explains everything. "Now that we've caught everyone's attention, let's focus. Where's Valcon?"

I let him lead me for a moment, but I can't concentrate with the music, the noise of the fortunes, and the way his smell reminds me of warm lavender and fresh soap.

"Tell me about Valcon," I say, nearly shouting to be heard over the din. "It's hard to find him without knowing more."

The captain's arms tense beneath my fingers. "He invented the cure. Promised it could heal death itself."

"Can it?"

"No." He whisks me into another turn, his gaze distant. "Valcon *is* death himself. He sells many potions besides, cures and half-cures, truths and lies, hope in one bottle and death in another."

"But it works. I saw a *yajuu* at the dress shop. She wasn't dangerous. How else do you explain it?"

"That's the half-cure, a tonic used to enslave monsters. Evil practice. It's illegal except here in Ranzan. The people here are almost as bad as the *yajuu* themselves. You wouldn't want such a life for your monster."

"My *sister*," I correct.

He grimaces as though I'd stepped on his toe.

"And the cure," I press. "It must be real too."

"Yes and no." His voice is barely audible over the noise of the fortune machines as we dance closer to them. "But if Valcon *can* cure your monster, there's a price, and it's not worth paying. Nothing worth having is free, Kira."

His eyes meet mine so intently that I wonder for a moment if he's talking about me.

The music stops, and with it whatever spell the captain's eyes have on me. He releases my hand with a formal bow. My breath calms with the distance between us. I try again to picture Valcon in my mind, and two different paths emerge.

Which leads to Yuki and which to Valcon? Could it be the same path? It has to be. The metal ping of the 'fortunes' crowds my senses.

"I don't know which way." I throw my hands over my ears, trying to concentrate. "It's too loud."

With a gentle touch, the captain guides my hands away from my ears. Our eyes meet. Cold determination replaces the kindness he'd shown on the dance floor. Something dark sparks in his eyes, and I can't help but wonder what exactly Valcon had taken from him.

"Try again, before the next song begins." He smiles as if to reassure me, but it doesn't quite reach his eyes.

But we both know that we're only on the same team right now because we're after the same thing—the apothecary.

I close my eyes, but the minute I do, my skin chills. Something is wrong. I can't sense the man in the photograph or my sister anymore. The blue light turns dark and vanishes like a startled rabbit, zigzagging in and out of the crowded dancers until it's gone. I shake my head, and my feet grind to a stop.

"Looking for someone?" A cool, dank voice creeps over my shoulder.

I startle, swinging around so that the captain and I are standing side by side. Blood drains from my face, and my knees begin to shake. I've heard that voice before—in the ashes that house my mother's bones.

"Pontius Jade." The captain greets the man in full regalia who leans over us with pockmarked cheeks and an iron jaw. "It's been a while. Rumor has it you've been inspecting the emperor's prisons lately. A demotion?"

I try to keep my legs from shaking, to not run and make a scene. The captain takes my hand and places it over his arm—a gesture meant to say I'm his guest. My fingers dig into his arm, no doubt squeezing too tight.

"Captain Renjiro," Inspector Jade croons, a playful smile on his thin lips. "What a surprise to find you celebrating the coronation this year. I thought you hated coronation parties. Though . . ." His eyes drop to me and flicker. "I suppose you're here on business?"

"As always." The captain—*Renjiro*—pulls me closer, and I don't resist, wishing I could hide behind him instead.

"I as well. I'm searching for an escaped prisoner." The inspector's greedy smile widens. "But apologies, I don't believe I've been formally introduced to your guest?"

I focus on where I am—the feeling of my toes cramped into the black boots beneath my dress, the gust of air brushing my bare back when someone passes by, the warmth of the captain's hand wrapped protectively around mine. Still, when I return the inspector's gaze, my stomach tightens. A wave of sickness washes over me.

The rings on his fingers look like polished bone, set with an assortment of crystals. One for every finger, except for his right forefinger, which is bare. As if noticing my gaze, he makes an elaborate sweep of his hand, bowing. White hair falls across his green eyes and weathered oak skin, as if the man had once lived inside a tree and crawled out.

Aged, bitter, and unrooted with a malice against all he'd seen in a thousand years.

"How rude of me." He laughs. "Let me be the first to introduce myself properly. I'm Pontius Jade. I inspect His Majesty's ports and keep the law in the vassal provinces. I'm also quite the collector."

"What do you collect?" I venture, my voice tight. If the inspector is going to play this game, I need to play along . . . long enough to keep him from arresting me on the spot.

"Treasures for His Majesty of Taiga. One from each of his vassal states to be exact. I'm in search of one now. Rumor has it that it's been found at last." A knowing glance passes between him and the captain, brewing with animosity.

"Should I expect to go home lonely?" the captain says. "You can't mean this beautiful lady?"

My cheeks go hot as his eyes turn to me—*beautiful*—did he really mean it?

Inspector Jade laughs, but it sounds off, as if he'd been caught doing something wrong. "Of course not, Captain Renjiro. Any guest of yours is above suspicion."

"Good. Excuse us. We've a dance to finish." The captain gives a stiff bow and then steers me away from Inspector Jade.

"No well wishes for His Majesty?" The inspector calls out, forcing him to turn. "Nothing to pass on, dear Ren? How you've changed."

"Blizzards, Pontius." The captain bristles, his jaw clenching and unclenching as if holding back a curse. "When I have a message for the emperor, I'll tell him to his face."

The inspector's smile widens as if he's won a fortune.

I don't miss that he'd used his first name. I glance at the captain for answers. Why didn't the inspector arrest me? Was it just to avoid a scene or something more?

Captain grabs my hand and storms through one of the fortune aisles, full of odd machines and games where women in silk kimono embroidered like dragon scales toss dice or pull levers for the fortunes. The hollow ting of wooden beads rattles my senses. Perfume, laughter, and strong wine mingle through the galley of fortune games. I cast a glance over my shoulder and notice Inspector Jade signaling three guards to follow us.

"I should've known he'd be here looking for you," the captain mutters as we run through aisles. "Jade won't dare attack in the open, not while you're with me."

"I have to find the apothecary." I raise my voice in a shrill whisper and slam my feet to a halt. "I can't leave without the cure. I need it. More than you need, whatever it is—revenge or some bounty. We find Valcon Jey tonight."

The captain throws me a measured look. "Can you find him again? There are passages within the walls that Valcon uses to travel between the elites living here, to collect information. It's possible he was in the atrium and fled when Jade arrived."

Weaving between the fortunes, I study the blur of machines, mingling players, and... "There!" I point to a wooden door that blends into a wall painted with the outline of a coiled sea beast. "Dragons are the symbol of the apothecaries. There was one in our prison, a poisoner, and he drew it for me once. The path showed Valcon was below us. He could be on a lower level."

"Good thinking." He takes my hand again, and I stiffen at the thread of connection between us.

We slip into the hidden door and hurry down two flights of stairs. Then we hit another door and shove it open. Our feet skid to a stop at a broken-off ledge. Cool, musty air gushes from a dark cavern below where the hallway simply ends. There must be a plank bridge to the other side.

The captain holds up a hand, signaling quiet as he shuts the door behind us, leaving only a tiny slab of stone for our feet.

"How do you know Inspector Jade?" I lay hold of the captain's arm for balance.

"Ezo and Taiga aren't on the best of terms," he says, eyeing the cavern for an escape. "Any chance you see a path out of this?"

"That man wants to kill me," I say, catching my breath.

His eyes drop to my hand on his arm, and I straighten, wiping my hands against my glittering dress.

"He wants to put you back in jail, which is the law," he says. "And I have to let him do so once we've completed our bargain."

"Which is what?"

"You help me find Valcon. I get your mother's coat. Then, you lead me to Yuki. I deliver you to the authorities, and our dealings are complete." He drops a coin from his pocket into the abyss and listens for it to stop falling.

I huff and peer over the ledge. "I'm not inclined to rot in jail."

"I won't let you." His voice is low, kind, even. "Until the right time."

"How comforting," I say. "You're lucky I don't push you off the ledge, being a hardened criminal and all."

The captain's eyes glimmer with amusement. "I don't expect to be falling for you anytime soon. Now, the path. Which way?"

"Oh, I'd like to see you fall," I snort.

He leans in closer, a clever gleam in his eye. "Are you sure?"

I tear my gaze away with a sudden need for fresh air. There has to be a way out of this cavern. The wall on the other side is about a deer's leap from us. I make out another serpent chipped into the rock, faded with time. Beneath it is a small ledge, identical to ours.

"I don't need a path for this." I point at the opposing wall. "There's a door."

The captain squints into the darkness, and his face lightens, eyes flaming blue like a dangerous fire. "Do you trust me?"

"Absolutely not."

He smiles wide, and his hand grips mine. "Now you're learning. We're going to jump."

"No, we aren't," I say, my feet too close to the cliff edge for comfort. "We don't know what's on the other side of that door!"

"Would you rather run into the inspector?" Footsteps pound on the stairs behind us, followed by the shouts of guards. "Will you jump?"

I eye the cavern and then my gaze slides to him. I nod.

"On my count. One . . . two . . . three."

We take a solid leap and clear the gap. But instead of barreling into the door, it opens, and we tumble into a den that reminds me strikingly of Abashi Prison. Only the cold, dark chamber houses a single gargantuan stone table laden with roasted silka and wine, surrounded by seven men fit enough to be prison guards, all staring at us.

The square man in the center is unmistakable from the photograph. Valcon Jey.

CHAPTER 16

VALCON SQUARES HIS SHOULDERS and watches us with an amused smirk, his watery eyes shifting between the captain and me with a hint of recognition. "Desperate to gamble with the big boys?"

He holds out a hand toward his companions at the table, one of them reluctantly lowering his pistol. "I can't remember the last time my private room was interrupted with such flair. But I'll accommodate you if the bets are large enough."

He tugs at his wool blazer, adept hands trying to hide his seal-shaped body beneath the tweed. Eyes narrowing, he turns toward the captain, as if sensing the greatest threat from him. His stare lingers there, trying to remember something. He's every bit the replica of his photograph, only thicker and of less substance, as if his soul had long since vacated and his body grown fat and tired.

"Your names and bets?" Valcon thrusts his arms in a wide gesture for us to join the game. He settles into the largest chair, exchanging a conspiratorial glance with one of the more dignified men.

From the large, polished wood pieces arranged across the checkered table, it seems like King's Crag—a strategy game.

"What's in the pot?" I ask, my voice too small in the cavernous room.

I'd only gambled bits of hoarded potatoes, dried fish, and scraps of paper with the other prisoners. Always a crude game of Blind Beggar or Dragon Snap with sticks and pebbles for chips. My fingers curl into a fist at the memory of smooth rock dice in my palms.

Yuki often bested the prisoners in King's Crag. She was so proficient at it that the guards even gave up betting with her after she scored an entire bottle of rice ale and a pair of leather mittens. Even the beating that followed the game was worth the warmth in our stomachs and rush of heat to our ice-chapped fingers. If only Yuki were here now.

"Names first," one of Valcon's cronies snaps. "Or we throw you out."

"You'll need more than that pistol hidden beneath the table," the captain says with a sardonic lilt. "Besides, I've heard the loser gets thrown out anyway—across the wall into the Winterwilds—to feed your experiments, Valcon."

A slow smile of recognition stretches across Valcon's greedy lips. "You've heard correctly." He tosses back a shot of rice ale, looking pleased. "You were only a boy last time we met. Ren, isn't it?"

He winces as though slapped, and his hand drifts to the sword at his side. "Only my friends call me that." His voice is low, measured. "And you're not among them."

My muscles tense. The captain isn't his usual collected self. Whatever grievance lays between these men grips the room in a chokehold.

Sweat sticks to my skin as I survey the men staring back at us, all of them richly dressed, clean, men of power. Valcon's smile falters, his hands slipping into his lined blazer pockets like reluctant wolves slinking into a den, and then, he laughs. A deep, bellyaching roar.

A few dignitaries around the table laugh with him, hesitant at first, revealing they haven't the faintest clue what Valcon is up to. Two of them reach slowly beneath the table, likely for a concealed weapon.

The captain's jaw is set, determined, his eyes a glint of midnight. He's here to kill Valcon. Deadly intent is written on his face. My gaze shifts to his feet, angled and ready. One move, one word, and there will be blood.

And I've had enough of that.

Ren. I want to say his name aloud, to ask him to stand down. I need that cure and, whatever his grievance, bloodshed isn't the answer. I'd learned that much in prison. One punch leads to another, and seldom does it end without consequence.

I breathe deep and focus, searching for a path in this darkness. I focus on one of the men at the table, hunched in a white fur stole. Like Mother said, I open my eyes to observe, to care. Suddenly, his arm tenses and two paths fork out like a serpent's tongue.

I sense the *shuriken* before I see them—two sharp-tipped blades of metal stars flung toward Ren. In an instant, I throw myself against the captain.

I meant to knock him aside, but the captain sidesteps effortlessly, and I land on my side in an embarrassing dive. A throwing star skitters across the floor.

The captain glances down, one brow lifted—but his eyes flick to where the blade landed. Too close.

He extends a hand, but I pull myself up. The man in the white stole stands at the table, his eyes narrowed at me. My hair tumbles to my back and strings in my face as I search for the red coral comb that must've fallen. So much for the noble lady disguise. All eyes in the room swivel toward me.

"You're the girl from the wanted posters," the man in the white stole says. Another throwing star peeks out from his closed hand.

The path was right about his intentions.

I lift my chin. "You've heard of me, which is more than I can say for you."

The captain coughs. "That's the prince of Thesia."

"Oh . . ." *A prince.* My luck landing in a pit of nobles that I can't name. *What are they doing here with Valcon?*

I swallow hard.

"We're here for the *yajuu* cure," I say, loud and determined as I'd learned to be when I needed something badly. Confidence is the key to dealing with bullies of any kind.

The captain throws me a disparaging look. At least *I'm* here for the cure.

Valcon steps toward me, his eyes taking in my sparkling gown and my raven hair now besotted with flyways. He's careful not to turn his back on the captain. "The cure? Really?" The laugh in his voice is unmistakable.

"It's for my sister," I say, and immediately chide myself for offering an explanation. To make up for it, I meet his step forward with one of my own.

This is a battle of confidence. It happened all the time in prison.

But I'm at a disadvantage. An entire armory glints on the far side of the den: swords, repeating rifles, knives, and pistols. My heart hammers. I can't fight my way out of this.

"Where's the cure? I've been told you're the only apothecary clever enough to figure it out. The only one who has succeeded." I wait to see if playing to his vanity is the right pitch.

Valcon turns his gaze solidly to mine. "You're correct. But has dear *Ren* told you about it? About the price?"

I falter, turning to the captain.

"She doesn't want it," he says, his face a mask of barely concealed rage. He'd murder Valcon if given the chance. Is he waiting for an opening when the princes and dignitaries are distracted, or is he waiting for . . . me?

I turn to Valcon and ask, "How much?"

I can bear almost any 'how' if it means saving Yuki from a shapeshifting curse that would eventually devour her soul.

"I'll make you a deal, girl." Valcon holds out a hand to the princes around the gambling table. His nimble fingers reach into his blazer and deftly pick out three vials. "You're Ainur, aren't you? I'm familiar with your wanted poster. I've heard the rumors about the prison escapees, and Ren"—he hoots with laughter—"wouldn't take a traveling companion unless it was for an impressive bounty."

"Stay out of it," Ren snaps, stepping forward. "It's none of your—"

"We're all gentlemen here, Captain Renjiro," the prince of Thesia counters, raising a pistol this time. "Let him finish his discussion with the young lady."

I don't miss how the prince uses the captain's full title. Or how he calls me a lady when he clearly sees me as a roach beneath his boot. To my surprise, Ren doesn't give the prince a second glance. He has eyes only for Valcon.

Valcon's greedy lips curl and he turns to me. "So, Kira is it? I'm betting you're one of those who just escaped, here to save your sister from the unfortunate curse. Did you know, they're blaming you and your sister for the prison burning? They say your sister's been a monster all along, controlling her shapeshifting powers until the right moment. And you're working with the new rebels in the North who still believe Ezo is its own nation."

"Rebels?" I give a dry laugh and shake my head. "I've been a prisoner in Ezo my entire life. Why would I fight for it?"

"It's Taiga that controls the prisons, my dear. You can't deny the rumors look to be true."

My heart races at the cruel injustice of his words. *How can someone so evil be the one to invent a cure? More likely he made poisons.* "My sister didn't burn down the prison," I say. "It was the bear—the *yajuu*, whatever it was!"

"Then explain how only you and your sister escaped. People in the cities, especially the Southern Empire of Taiga, scarcely believe in monsters anymore. They're just fairytales. And there are witnesses vouching for the whole affair. It's published it in the papers. The fear is making me thousands. So I tip my hat to you and your sister."

I stifle a sharp breath, trying to calm my pounding heart. I can't let him distract me. "Enough," I say, steadying my gaze. "Where's the cure?"

"Kira," Ren calls my name slowly, steadily. "Don't take anything he offers you."

Valcon displays the three vials, and I can't look away. "I'm willing to give you the cure out of my gratitude. No conditions. You simply have to pick which one it is." Valcon chuckles, pleased at his joke.

He's offering me a chance—or a bluff. I stare mesmerized by the glass vials that could save Yuki, could save me and my promise to Mother.

A swoosh of steel, followed by an explosion, jars me back to the situation at hand. I spin around. Captain Ren weaves across the room with his sword drawn, his footwork faster than I can trace with the shouts and smoking gun from the prince of Thesia. I guess he got tired of waiting for me to make a deal. But if Valcon is the only one who knows how to make the cure, we need him alive.

Suddenly, a lightning flash of silver steel cuts the air in front of Valcon and me.

The vials. The cure.

"Stop!" I yell, the path surging beneath my hand.

Ren's blade nips at Valcon's throat, creating a thin line of beading red across his neck. The captain growls, his hands gripped tight around the sword hilt. He tilts his head toward me, jaw tense as our eyes meet. Anger, betrayal, surprise stare back at me.

Then it hits me—he can't move his sword.

Everyone stands, weapons fisted tight, and eyes locked onto my own. The shock registered on Valcon's pale face drains slowly, and the once beady green eyes widen with greed.

Ren curses but doesn't lower his blade. It shakes in his hands as if fighting against him, refusing to sever that thick, fat neck. Blue fire scorches his eyes, and I understand.

The path.

I'd spoken a word that had reached out and become a path as I did with the bear in the woods . . . and everyone in this room had witnessed it.

I stopped Ren from killing Valcon.

"Now I know why you're traveling with the pretty little convict." Valcon chuckles, earning himself a few more drops of blood as Ren presses the blade more firmly. "A wayfinder would be worth a king's ransom."

"Kira, take all the vials, and let's go," the captain says, measuring each word.

I stare at his sword and his white knuckles, marveling that a path-spoken word had been the thing to stop him.

I reach forward to take the vials, but the prince of Thesia releases two more throwing stars. With a murderous whoosh, one sinks metal teeth into the hem of my dress, and I reel back at the blur of the second barreling toward me. A sharp breeze follows the sound of metal on metal as the throwing star clatters to the floor in two halves.

My mouth goes dry as Ren stands in front of me, his sword held in both hands.

"Thank you, Thesius." Valcon dabs at his now freed throat with a handkerchief. "This ought to make the game more entertaining. Now, Kira dear, how about you pick *one* pretty bottle and be on your way. Just ask Ren to stay for us on your way out. It seems he listens to you."

I hardly register the words as I stare at Ren's back, rising and falling with measured breaths. *Why did he save me? Was the bounty only good if I lived? He could've killed Valcon if I hadn't stood in his way.*

"Kira," Valcon's tone is sharp, drawing my attention back to the vials in his hand. "You know that Ren's only keeping you alive for the bounty. I *know* him, dear. He doesn't care about you. Once he takes you to Silverwood, you'll be delivered to the capital of Taiga for a public execution. That is law. It will once and for all quell the rebellion. Which, let's be frank, is dead already."

I step back from the captain, my eyes swiveling from Valcon to the dignitaries to Ren again.

"You said you'd turn me in to the authorities," I murmur, feeling lost and wanting the path's warmth and light to return. "To jail—not an execution."

His eyes meet mine, a debate shimmering in the blue.

"It's the law." Ren glances away, a tick in his jaw. "I can't control what happens after I do my job or what the authorities decide. I just do what's right, even if I don't understand it."

I gape at him, hating how Valcon laughs at my expense, and the princes watch me hungrily. Ren doesn't even deny it.

Do what's right? How can surrendering an orphan to an evil man like Inspector Jade be right?

"Is it true that the authorities will execute me?" Dread worms into my gut as Ren refuses to meet my gaze.

"Kira . . ." his voice is an exasperated plea. "Don't listen to them. Just because I follow the law—"

"Doesn't make you right," I snap, my heart hardening like ice. Cold sinks into my bones, the cold I was born in.

"Kira, you can't control it as well as you think," Ren warns, placing a hand on my shoulder.

I brush him off. Mother warned that men will use wayfinders to seek their fortunes. The warden used Mother to track wild game in the Winterwilds. The captain had used and tricked me to get his revenge on Valcon. I have to tread carefully.

A gentle breeze touches my cheek, warm like Mother's hand. *Compassion,* it seems to whisper, *hope.* But those had only hurt me.

I let those words freeze and turn from Ren to the gambling princes and the apothecary dangling the three colorful vials.

"Valcon, I'll take your offer."

CHAPTER 17

"ONE VIAL IS THE CURE. One is poison. One is a tonic, a half-cure I give to the circus for their monsters. Take your pick. It's a generous offer, a cheat for a wayfinder like yourself." Valcon's slippery voice drips with laughter.

The princes continue to stand, and I study them better. Each one has a different attire, presumably belonging to his homeland, thick robes of green, thin sashes of blue, gold and crimson of Taiga, the white furs of the north. My eyes turn to the captain, who watches me with a mixture of concern and anger. Both hands still on the hilt of his sword. He stands the farthest from the table and close to what may be an exterior door.

The vials lay before me within arm's reach. My fingers itch to grab all three and run for it, the captain battling for cover at my heels, but . . . we can't escape with seven armed men and a fat apothecary dripping poison.

And, as much as I hate to admit it, Ren's right—I don't know how to control the path. I would use it on Valcon if I knew how, but it doesn't always listen to me. There has to be a connection, an understanding of some kind.

I bite my lip, thinking of the bear and Ren, the common factor between them when my words carved a path into existence—*caring*. I had wanted both of them to live, but I can't say the same thing for Valcon.

Amber liquid in the vials sloshes against the glass containers. Could I pick the right one? It hadn't occurred to me that I could use wayfinding for objects. I'd only ever looked for animals and people before, and even finding Valcon had been a stretch. Without Ren, I wouldn't have known how to find him.

A pinch of regret causes me to look away. So what if he'd helped me get this far? It was only to serve himself and take me back to prison—for an execution. I exhale sharply, concentrating on the vials.

"What's in it for you?" I ask Valcon. "What do you want with the captain?"

The question slips out before I can bite it back, but it's been gnawing at me. If Ren's chasing revenge, is Valcon after the same thing? I don't want blood on my hands. I'm not that kind of criminal. But I'm done being a prisoner.

An involuntary shiver passes through me as a memory surges to mind. Mother's hand pinching my chin, holding it high while we huddled in our arctic cell. "You are not a prisoner," she'd said with authority. "No one can chain your soul. No one can take away your choices."

"Don't worry," Valcon croons, mistaking my shiver for fear. "No harm will befall the good captain. I just have some things to discuss with him. Pick your vial."

He splays the three vials across the long table, each no longer than my pinky finger and each a different earthen shade. The first is metallic amber, the second is a deep marine blue, and the third is a frothy moss green. I cast a furtive glance at Ren.

Blue-black hair sweeps across his brow; his face is a hard mask. Does he know which is the cure? I can't risk guessing, not when one is poison.

The captain shakes his head, mouthing the word '*don't.*' He's still battle-ready, eyeing the princes at the table and their weapons. If I say the word, he will try to take them all out.

I take a deep breath, find my center, and try to connect the object to what matters most to me: healing Yuki. *Which vial will save her?*

I stare at the vials from amber to moss, but nothing sparks. The path doesn't light up. Not even an inkling as to which I should pick. It could be that none of them are the cure, but the twitch in Valcon's eye makes me think he's not bluffing.

"Which will it be?" Valcon says, growing impatient. "Pick one already. Do you need a hint?"

"No."

"It's a trap, Kira," Ren says. "Think about it. Why is he letting you leave with a bounty on your head? I can get us both out of this."

I shut out his voice and lean over the vials. I can't trust either of these men, but the path isn't clear. The cure is so close. I steal another glance at the captain. He looks ready to call it off and just fight his way out, but he doesn't. He's letting me make this choice.

Why?

My heart flies to my throat as my fingers hover over the vials. A chance. A future. A guess. Is it worth the risk? I try to summon the path again, pouring my thoughts into that one need—saving my sister.

The blue light is absent, the path silent.

"This one." I snatch the amber vial from the table. Had it flickered blue for a moment? I smile to convince them I've chosen right.

Valcon's smile widens. "I hope it serves you well. Give your sister my good wishes. It's always in my best interest to help those in need."

A few of the princes incline their heads as if acknowledging the deal, but their eyes never leave Ren. I take a shaky breath. *Is it the right vial?*

Valcon pockets the other potions and then moves to the side of the room where he presses his hand against the stone door. "As for Ren, would you ask him to stay, my dear? Per our agreement?"

I step toward the door, the amber vial secure in my now sweating palm. I meet the captain's eyes. But instead of a loathing, dark stare, his eyes shine cerulean in the dark, a color I'd seen only once before, while we danced. My throat goes dry, and I'm not sure if the path will listen to me. I'm not sure if I want to do this.

Am I making the right choice?

"Go on," Valcon nudges, a worried bite to his voice.

I breathe deep and focus, letting the cold settle over me again. I imagine the captain attacking Yuki on the mountain, the explosion of luprite, his icy words, the way he showed no emotion and promised to send me to my death when all was done. When I look up and meet his eyes, I have no problem using the path against him.

To save Yuki.

To save yourself, a quiet voice whispers in my mind.

"Ren . . ." I bite my lips, wishing away the sweet taste of his name that should be bitter. He gave me a choice. Shouldn't I give him the same thing?

No, he doesn't care. It was all an act. My hands fist, nails digging into my palms as I find my voice. "Ren, don't follow me."

No one else can see the path, but I do. The vibrant blue light that hums between us snaps.

His eyes narrow, a tick in his jaw. "I thought better of you, Kira."

"What did you expect?" I say. "You said yourself that my journey ended in prison."

His sword whirls, a fiery silver that whips through the air like smoke. Valcon shoves me backward through the now open door. Shouts slip through the closing gap as I land hard on my back in the street. The door grinds shut with a loud thud, sealing the captain to an unknown fate.

"Ren . . ." I repeat his name, clambering to my feet. He's fast.

He'll be all right. I didn't bind him to the spot as Valcon had asked, I'd only asked him not to follow me.

Cold evening air brushes my back. I grip the vial tight before stashing it inside the lining of my dress and steel myself for the long night ahead.

I'm no longer a prisoner, not of Abashi, and not of the captain.

"Good luck," I whisper to the stone, willing my words to impart power to the Shadow beyond it. Then, leaving the door shut behind me, I follow the blue light to Yuki.

Makeshift tents line this part of the street, cluttering the sidewalk and pressing the crowd into a tight funnel, like a fisherman's net. I melt into the crowd as it's pushed through the coral gates to the Nehu district.

Three stalls direct foot traffic at the entrance, each coated in red and white stripes and manned by uniformed ticket masters.

"Ticket please," the gatekeepers drone.

One by one, cheerful denizens offer their tickets and watch with stunned wonder or fickle amusement as the ticket vanishes into thin air when taken by the officer, like magic.

"Step right up, ticket please," he says to me. A grin spreads across his face as he takes in my dress. "Ditching the governor's ball for the real party, huh?"

"I-I don't have a ticket. I mean, I had one, but—"

The keeper leans over the ticket stall and reaches behind my ear. I hold back a shudder as his fingers scrape the soft underside of my ear and then produce a golden ticket.

"Here you go, sumptuous." He hands me the ticket.

"Thank you," I stutter.

He doesn't take my ticket but gestures for me to move through the gates. Then the pinstriped man motions to the next guest with a wide smile. "Ticket please."

The crowd doesn't seem bothered by the gatekeeper's brazen magic. Could they be accustomed to it? Ranzan is an eccentric place. The dress shop had even employed a *yajuu*. Likely half-*yajuu*, partially cured, or the shapeshifting process blocked by one of Valcon's tonics. I place a hand absently over the amber vial, hoping it's the real cure.

I scamper away from the gate and into a circular courtyard that breaks off into eight streets, all lined with vendors advertising sweet foods and warm drinks. Music spills into the courtyard, and the crowd loosens. People break off to dance or simply sway with the music. Couples steal kisses in narrow alleyways or wander, hands intertwined, down the merchant streets. Down one street, a woman without an escort whistles to the men passing by. I had no idea Nehu was that kind of district.

A clock tower stands in the center courtyard, reminding me with every tick that Yuki's time is short. The hour hand strikes a large numeral eleven, and the clock face glows a brilliant gold as its melody rings across the square. A few passersby pause to glance at it before continuing their pleasure-seeking. I calm my mind and focus.

"Show me the path," I whisper, hoping no one hears save for the wind and the messengers of the hidden kingdom I'm only beginning to understand.

I splay my fingers at my sides, expecting some connection with the blue tide of magic. Within seconds, a vibration tickles across my palm. I open my eyes, and a thin blue line stretches from my hand to the leftmost alley.

I flex my fingers, and the magic thread stays, pulsing with a faint blue light. As I follow, the string remains taut. Couples press together as they walk, bumping clumsily into each other at the hip, but my string doesn't break when they glide through it. I gather my courage and pick up the pace into a shadowed alley with a low-hanging banner that reads: The Palace of Lost Souls.

CHAPTER 18

I CLUTCH THE THIN PROMISE that my sister is on the other side of the invisible blue string. The thread of connection Ren had taught me to find.

My gut twists and the blue light flickers. Can't think about him right now. Yuki's here. I know it.

I quicken my pace, aware of the eyes watching me from the shadows. I sorely wish my gown wasn't so thin and glittering.

Cedar shop-houses, blackened by soot and rain, shoulder me on either side. Their curved clay tiles stare down at me like so many disapproving frowns. Laughter bubbles from rooftop parties, and chimes tinkle on shop doors. I lift the torn hem of my dress and press on, nearly tripping over a pipe jutting from one of the houses, and step into a filthy puddle instead. I shake out my boot, knocking over an empty barrel.

"Get outta here," a busty shop woman shouts, swatting at me with a bamboo broom.

"Sorry," I squeak, clutching at the invisible path between my fingers. It's almost a physical weight in my hands, soft and ebbing.

Yuki, please be all right.

On the darkened street, only a few brave souls stroll the alley. Laundry wires crisscross the darkened sky above, and the rumble of voices overhead suggests a party in one of the many bars and shops. I read the names of the stores as I follow the flickering path toward the bay: Dragon Pearl Inn, Nehu Ramen, The Salty Tavern.

Suddenly, the string goes slack, and the blue light vanishes on the evening breeze. My gut tightens in worry, but could it be that it stopped because Yuki is here?

The alley forks, leaving me to choose the way. To the right, the street curves wider with frosted windows and savory smells of salted pork, garlic, and fresh seafood. To the left is a downward slope leading to the dark, flat line of ocean on the horizon. Voices come from the oceanside alley, climbing the hill.

A boisterous couple scrambles up the last step—a middle-aged woman with hair wrapped into multiple scarves that spill down her back and a boy dressed in a navy pantsuit with wild red hair who is preoccupied with something in the flap of his jacket. If I didn't know better, I'd say he was sharpening knives. He catches me staring and whispers to the woman in the profusion of headscarves. The two of them close the short distance.

"Good evening," the boy says, his teeth a flash of white in the dark.

I freeze. "Good . . . evening."

Every instinct screams to run. But this is where the blue light stopped. Yuki is close. I can't step away from the path now, not when I have the cure in my grasp.

I study the odd couple. Unlike Mother, I don't know how to find pathways *in* people. A way to work around difficult people or, more correctly, through them. Using my words on the bear and the captain was one thing because I had a connection to them. Even so, it didn't feel right, which is probably why Mother never taught me.

Prison had given me years to study people. Facial expressions and ticks, subtle movements that indicated a person's intentions. But something about this boy told me I'd need more than that.

It couldn't hurt to try.

My feet plant on the wet stone as I channel my focus on the rust-haired boy, summoning a path. The beat of his heart surprises me, calm and steady like a drum. A tickling of anticipation floats on the air, anger . . . warm and red and like a rhododendron. And then it's gone.

"Looking for something?" The boy tilts his head with a slight chuckle. "Maybe we can help?"

"The circus." I hold the ticket up to the warm glow of a lantern. "If you point me in the right direction, I'll be on my way."

The boy's eyes gleam at the golden ticket and then travel my iridescent gown.

"Trusting little thing," the woman crows. "She don't look like much to me. Look how thin it is, just bones." She draws out the 's' like a snake, and I wonder what lies behind her blanketed headscarves. "Poor dear must be cold. Takuma, make our guest a fire."

"That's very kind, but my sister is waiting. I'll just be going." I step back, searching for space in the narrow street to pass them.

They spread out, blocking the way. The boy's eyes flick up as he reaches into his pocket. A quick, silver blade with red rhododendron carved into its handle catches my eye, then another. Four daggers flip between his fingers, weaving in and out like feathers turned to steel but never once drawing so much as a scratch.

Rhododendron. It couldn't be coincidence. I felt that word when I searched him out, before I saw the knives. Had I seen a path? Something about this boy would lead me in the right direction—*to Yuki*—however dangerous. I must be careful.

He tosses the knives around my feet in a perfect circle, and the blades burst into feathered flames. I draw my feet in close, away from the ankle-high flames. A circus trick, no doubt.

"That ticket you're holding is to mark the night's contestants," the boy says, snatching the thin paper from my hand. "You might have wondered why they let you keep yours. We'll get a handsome prize for bringing you in tonight."

"Well done, Takuma!" squeals the woman. "Should fetch a good price at the circus. Now I can buy my ruby baubles!" She circles me as if sizing up a fish for the market.

"I think you're confused," I stammer, trying to hide the fear coiling in my gut. "I'm not alone. I have friends here, and they'll be missing me if I don't show up. Let me pass."

The woman crows, hands on hips. "Honey, the gatekeepers picked you for a reason. Your face was on a wanted poster, right? They profile everyone."

I blanch and force a weak smile. Ren was right. Valcon knew I would be caught if I entered Nehu. He never intended to let me go.

"It was a flattering poster," I say, stalling for time as I search for an exit.

Takuma raises a brow and tilts his head. "It could've been better."

The woman reaches across the low fire with a rope to tie my hands, but I jerk away. I will not be made a prisoner again.

"You like to fight?" Takuma asks, collecting his knives. The flames dissipate at his touch, making me wonder if it'd just been an illusion. "They'll like that at the circus."

As he sweeps up the last knife, I spin on my heels and run.

Behind me, the woman barks orders. My feet pound the dirt until a hand jerks me back.

"You walk with us," Takuma says, twisting my arm.

"You're hurting me!" I pull against him, but his grip is iron.

He glances down at his hand as if surprised. "I forget others have feelings."

My hands turn to fists as I thrash. "What does a circus want with criminals? You can't do this! I have somewhere I need to be."

"And where might that be? Or should I ask with whom?" Brow raised, his eyes linger on the abalone dress that feels altogether too tight now. He bends down to meet my gaze, his eyes dark slits in pools of ink.

I gasp. "You're a—"

His smile widens and the teeth are pointed. "Not from Ranzan, are you? And you're not afraid of me."

I wouldn't say that.

"My sister was infected with the *yajuu* curse," I say. *Had this boy had the half-tonic like the girl in the dress shop? Just how dangerous is he?*

"*Yajuu* don't have family," he says, his voice suddenly hard. "We eat them."

I gulp. That answers my question.

"Hurry up," the woman calls over her shoulder.

I'm pulled after them, held close to the boy's side to prevent escape. When I search for a path, it flickers a pale blue following in their footsteps. Perhaps it has a twisted sense of justice for what I'd done to Ren.

Or maybe Yuki is here too? Captured by these same people.

"Are you in the habit of selling people to the circus?" I ask, mulling my options.

"We aren't selling you, honey." The woman dances around to face us as she walks. "You've a *bounty* on your head. It's different. Besides, in Ranzan they don't care what we do with criminals, long as you're off the streets. The circus master likes to invite them to the midnight act. It's a fabulous show. You'll love it."

"I highly doubt that."

The rust-haired boy's jaw clenches as he drags me along. I search out details in his expression that might help me escape. He doesn't care for the woman—at all.

"Are you her servant?" I whisper, knowing it's a risk.

"Yes."

Anger bubbles beneath his words, ever-red rhododendron like the knives in his coat. This is my chance. This weakness—if wanting freedom could be called a weakness.

"I've heard there's a cure." I watch for his reaction.

He jerks my hand harder, forcing me to trip down the hill. I wince. But I shut out the pain and grasp at the chink in his emotional armor.

"It's here in Nehu," I continue. "I've been trying to find it for my sister, Yuki."

"Quiet," he barks and squeezes my hand so hard that I cry out in pain.

I won't let him win.

"What's your problem?" I ask. I learned this question led to a fight more often than not in prison, but it also shows I'm not afraid.

"He's a problem with everyone, sugar." The woman grins, her rot-stained teeth showing behind rosy lips. "Takuma, don't let her drag her feet. I want my ruby baubles before the night is over."

He casts a frustrated glance in my direction and then throws me over his shoulder. I pound at his back, but it's like rock. I feel every bump as we take the stair-laden hill down to the bay.

"Why don't you look like a *yajuu*?" I ask, resigning myself to this position and letting curiosity take over. "Is it the half-cure?"

"Ah, the tonic." He skips another step with his long-legged stride, jarring me on his shoulder.

"But the cure—" I oomph, as he takes another step. With one hand, I clutch the vial secured in my dress lining, hoping it doesn't break. "What if you could get the real cure, not just the tonic? I can help—"

He takes another hard step as the clock chimes, reminding me that I have half an hour before midnight. Possibly enough time. If I followed the right path. If Yuki is near.

Tomorrow the curse will be unstoppable.

Takuma halts at the bottom of the stairs and slides me off his shoulder. The woman hurries beneath a large banner made of luprite-coated shells that reads: *Circus on the Sea: Welcome to the Pearly Gates!*

The ocean breeze hits my face, feeling of home and salt and the freedom I'd always dreamed was on the other side—but isn't.

"You're a strange one," Takuma says as we wait for his master.

"If you mean being abducted by demons and fat old ladies makes me stand out, then yes." I take in the moonlit ocean and the circus. Colorful tents flap in the sea breeze, decorated with shells and sparkling jewels. The woolly elephant I'd seen earlier balances on a bamboo pole in front of a laughing audience.

"No." Takuma's gaze drifts toward the menagerie. "It's strange you aren't afraid."

His words seem funny to me. Of course, I'm afraid. But then I notice my heart isn't beating wildly. My mind rings with curiosity and calculations. Perhaps he can sense those things too. Do *yajuu* have different senses than most?

"The tonic seems to work," I tell him. "So, I've no reason to fear."

"It's foolish not to be afraid," he says. "If I didn't have the tonic coursing through my veins, you'd be dead. Every *yajuu* reacts differently to the tonic. For some, it's a sedative. For others, it keeps us from shifting or losing our minds . . . mostly."

My hand flies to the vial secured in my dress. *Cure. Tonic. Poison.* Which one is it? I'm suddenly not as confident as before. I'd thought the tonic lasted forever. All these *yajuu* on the verge of losing themselves, teased with a cure . . . it's cruel.

"What will they do with me?" I ask, nodding to the circus tents.

"Ask the circus master yourself."

"No," I plead. "Let me go. I can help you."

He spins me in front of him, the surf nipping at my heels. Now that I see him up close, his chest is too wide for a normal boy, his face narrow and drained of life, and his eyes are too hungry, lost, wanting. I shouldn't care. But I do.

"I'll help you," I repeat. "When I find my sister, I'll save some of the cure for you."

"No one has the real cure," he hisses. "It's a fool's dream."

I take a sharp breath, the vial chafing at my skin. "But—"

"You shouldn't care," he says. "It'll get you killed."

Where else had I heard those words? *Ren.*

I should've listened to him.

His master reappears beneath the tent curtains and motions us inside. A sharp tang of salt and sweat and unfamiliar spices choke the air as I'm shoved into the tent. Footsteps disappear behind me as I look up at a cushioned throne.

"Hello, pearl," says a thin, middle-aged woman sitting on a throne of blanched coral. Long light brown hair falls across her shoulder in a voluminous braid, trailing over the fur robe that reveals her toned arms, inked with tattoos. A roll of parchment snaps shut between her spry fingers as her eyes cut to mine. "So . . . Valcon did keep his word. Do you know how much your pretty face is worth?"

"Valcon." I grind my teeth, throat going dry. "How did he know I would come here—"

"He said you were naive." She smiles, tapping the parchment. "Sent me a message that you'd head this way. And he was right."

She throws the parchment at my feet. A gaunt face with large, angry eyes and sallow cheekbones stares back from my wanted poster.

Low growls accompany her laugh, coming from either side of the circus throne. Chained to the tent pegs are two wolves with ragged fur and bottomless black eyes. Only they're nothing like wolves at all—a hulking shadow of them. A wolf hide with something wild and darker underneath . . . like the bear that had attacked Yuki. Growls reverberate from their muscled throats as I'm greeted with a flash of teeth.

"My pets," she says, slouching on her throne. "Don't be afraid of them. These precious beasts are under my command, mostly, thanks to the tonic."

"What do you want with me?" I ask. "Are you going to send me to prison?"

"Oh no," she says through a crooked smile. "That would spoil the fun."

I gulp, hard. "Then what—"

"Patience, pearl. It'll be so much more fun to show you."

CHAPTER 19

THE WOMAN'S GRAY EYES watch me carefully from the back of the tent. "I'm not a cruel taskmaster. If you play your part in my little act tonight, I'll grant you a wish before collecting my reward for your capture."

"One hundred million zeni?" I ask, my eyes straying to her snarling wolves. "Or are you splitting it with Valcon?"

Her lips purse into a petulant grin, and she heaves a sigh. "Middlemen are so insufferable. But you're not here to talk money. I'll grant you a wish if you don't try anything foolish before I hand you over."

"A wish?" I scoff. "You look more like a criminal than a fairy godmother to me." I nod at the black marks inked across her arms, tattoos given by different prisons to mark crimes—usually for murder or arson.

She's probably committed both.

The woman's smile comes easily, but the squint in her eyes tells me I've hit a nerve.

"I'm called *Lady* Kumo now. And I pay for my crimes by catching others like me. Escaped convicts, arsonists, *yajuu*." She smiles, stroking the head of the dark gray wolf beside her. "It pays well. But I do have compassion for those like me. A few of the *yajuu* I've collected have special abilities. I can grant practically any wish with their talents—even finding a lost sister."

The path hums within my clenched palms, every fiber of my being wanting to follow it to Yuki. Tugging at me that she's here. In this circus.

"You already know where she is," I say. "Take me to her."

"After our little game," she says, a laugh playing on her lips.

I scan the room searching for a weakness, a way out. I'm a thousand percent sure she's going to hand me over to the inspector.

Question is, does she need me alive? Or is the bounty worth a fortune either way?

I swallow hard. "I'm not in the mood for games. My sister will become a *yajuu* if I don't find her tonight."

"Fabulous," she purrs, pulling a silver tassel next to her throne.

The tent curtains swoosh open to reveal a motley line of men and women who plod inside, hands tied with thick rope. A child stumbles from the group with big, scared eyes that latch onto mine, desperate for hope.

"Tonight's contestants." Lady Kumo opens her arms to welcome them, five in total. "You're all here because you won a golden ticket for the bounty on your head."

"That one is only a child!" I protest.

"He's a thief." Lady Kumo's eyes slice toward me in warning before turning back to the motley group. "If you perform in the circus, you'll be granted a wish. Ranzan can grant any wish—a chance at wealth, health . . . anything. But you must do exactly as you're told."

"I don't have time for this," the tallest prisoner spits and squares his shoulders.

"That's terribly ungrateful," Lady Kumo says with a feigned pout. "But you are free to do as you please."

Scowling, the tall man stomps toward the tent flap, arms flexing in an attempt to break his bonds. Lady Kumo snaps her fingers, and the wolves on her right and left lunge. An unearthly howl rips the air, and it takes a moment for me to realize it's the man screaming. In a second, the scream is torn from his throat as one of the savage beasts clamps its jaws around his neck. The man convulses and then goes still.

Cold fear slinks into my stomach as I tear my eyes away from the scene. The circus manager smiles, studying my face—my horror—while resting her head on a jeweled hand.

"Well, treasures," she says, facing the remaining group. "I hope you'll do your best tonight. If not, my pets will see you out."

I guess that answers my question about the bounties—Dead or Alive.

The little boy grabs my hand and squeezes. Hot, sweaty fingers tremble within my palm, mirroring the rest of him. Startled, I pull him close and wrap a protective arm around him. Tears prick the corners of his eyes and fall in fat dollops on my gown.

"Please," he blubbers into my dress. "I didn't mean to steal. I'm sorry. It was just a cup of rice. It was for my mother, she's starving. Please, I don't want her to die!"

"That's up to you." Lady Kumo pries the boy away from me. "And you," she says, eyeing my dress and lifting an unkempt strand of raven hair from my shoulder, "will be the princess in the circus arena. The last princess didn't last very long. But I have a feeling about you. Only, I'm sorry to part with you after the game is over. The inspector is paying Valcon and me quite handsomely." She raises her brows as if daring me to defy her.

I can't speak. Not with the wolves salivating in their corners and the man still lying on the floor. She steps over him and takes me by the arm with an eerily gentle touch.

"Valcon usually picks people the world won't miss." She drops her voice to a whisper and nods toward the bones. "Thieves, traitors, orphans . . . but you're worth a great deal to the inspector. One hundred million zeni," she says with a contented sigh. "You wouldn't happen to know why, would you?"

"I don't know," I say, my throat tight. "I was born in prison."

"Weren't we all?" She claps, and an attendant enters the tent. "Take them to the arena."

What kind of story does this woman have to think all of life a cage? Did Ren know about this place? Was he trying to protect me?

I shake the thought, the guilt, from my mind. He'd been after the bounty too. Right now, I need to escape. Mother was right to keep our wayfinding a secret.

The last Ainur.

I'm a sorry specimen for the last of my kind. I can't even find my own path. I try to still my mind and listen, but the wind doesn't speak. The blue light that had guided me toward the cure, toward Yuki, is gone.

I shield my eyes from the harsh spotlights trained on the fenced-in arena. Slatted bamboo walls and wooden planks surround me as I shiver in the cold, stripped of my warm boots—presumably so I don't run away.

Even if I *could* scale the wall, Lady Kumo's pet wolves prowl the other side of the fence. The little boy from the tent clings to my dress again. He's probably no older than six, though I'm not good with children's ages. I place a hand at his back, rubbing with a circular motion as Mama did whenever I was sick.

How did I lose my sister's trail and follow a path so terribly wrong?

Other prisoners from the tent wander the arena, tugging at the fence and shouting. One kneels in the dirt with desperate prayers on his lips. Their voices reach me on the wind as I survey the caged-in field: "We have to find a way out," "It's a bullfighting ring," "The city patrol would never allow it!"

My eyes follow the fence line to a row of sizable claw marks, and my mouth goes dry. "It's definitely not a bullfight," I murmur.

On closer examination, it looks like the elephant's holding yard. A curious brick building stands off to one end of the circular enclosure. A stall? It could house two elephants from its size.

I rub my arms for warmth and focus on the darkness sticking to the outer edges of the circus, where my eyes make out the shape of a crowd. Around fifty festival-goers huddle in warm fur coats, carrying hot rice wine and sticky mochi drenched in amber sauce as they wait for the performance to begin. My stomach growls.

A commentator's voice crackles in the evening air.

"Welcome to the Menagerie by the Sea! Now for the show you've all been waiting for"—drums pound—"the Tournament of Champions! Who will survive? The soldier, the thief, the spy, the princess?" A light shines on each of the supposed characters with the pronouncement. "Only one will be crowned winner! Let's hear a round of applause for our volunteers!"

The little boy tugs on my dress. "What's going to happen to us?"

"We're going to get out," I say, scanning the crowd for a path to escape, for a thread of hope. Blinding light blasts my face from the spotlights, and I shield my eyes. "Stay close."

Takuma enters the arena with a basket slung over his shoulder. He tosses it on the ground, spilling an assortment of javelins, rope, and a shield. His slitted eyes meet mine, and he gives a faint nod, as if wishing me luck. Then he opens the door to the brick stable and ducks out of the arena gate, locking it behind him.

A disjointed snarl comes from the stable, followed by a black snout and a shaggy black body. I push the boy behind me and remain completely still. A monster lurks into sight, nearly as tall as the fence—a wolf.

Unlike Takuma and the girl in the dress shop, its eyes aren't half-moons but full and blackest coal. It lunges at the nearest prisoner, tossing them across the arena before they can reach for a weapon. The crowd roars.

Path, listen to me! My thoughts turn desperate, palms sweating as I try to summon it. It had come so quickly back in Valcon's lair. Why won't it listen?

"Let's see what the inspector finds so valuable about you," comes a silky voice from behind the fence.

I spin around and glare at Lady Kumo. "Stop this now!"

"Don't worry, pearl. I won't let it get you. But I can't say the same for the boy. No one would tell me why you're worth so much, and I fear I'm being taken advantage of. I *hate* getting the bad end of a deal."

I grab the nearest javelin and hurl it at the fence where she stands. It clanks uselessly against the bars.

"You'd best start running, pearl."

A growl sounds behind me. I stiffen, grab the boy, and bolt for the stable across the arena. Perhaps I'll have a chance if I can barricade myself within. The monster leaps after me, its paw grazing my footsteps. I duck as the beast's claws tear a ragged line in the brick.

"Let us in!" I jerk on the door, the boy anchored to my side.

Inside the brick stable, two prisoners stare back at me from a barred window, their shoulders trembling. They won't open the door. My options are running out.

The wolf crouches for a pounce as I'm cornered against the wall.

Path, I need a way out of this. Help me. For the boy's sake.

A faint warmth buzzes against my palm. The blue path spins the lightest of threads straight toward the black beast. The wolf pounces, and I run toward it, sliding beneath the monster—following the path. I lose hold of the boy and he spins across the ground not far from me. The wolf slams into the wall with an angry howl.

Blue threads hum against my fingertips as I straighten. It lights the way across the arena, hinting at the monster's next movements. Hinting at someone edging nearer on the other side, a familiar tug.

I scour the crowd, hoping no one else can see the living thread of path, before grabbing a rope and javelin.

"Help!" the little boy cries, crouching against the fence.

My heart thunders, realizing the boy's mistake. Never make yourself small before a bully—or a wolf. Hurriedly, I tie a loop in the rope. Then, tracing the blue path, I dash forward and throw the snare. The monster turns toward the child and lunges.

I jerk the rope, and it snags the wolf's hind leg, throwing it off balance. The rope burns within my palms, and I let it go, stumbling forward.

"Kira!"

A shadow drops from the walled fence and lands soundless beside me. I catch the glint of moonlit steel before the blue fire of his eyes snaps to mine. A flash of cerulean in the dark.

"Ren?"

The Captain of the Shadows gives me a brief once-over before he has me by the arm. "Move."

"Not without the boy!"

How did he get here? What happened to Valcon?

The wolf rounds on us, a vicious snap of its jaws only feet away. "I thought we talked about this caring business," he says, slashing at the monster as the crowd cheers.

I grab the boy while Ren fends off the beast. I wish Mother had taught me to fight. I wish the Beetle had taught me to fight—surely someone at a prison for the most dangerous criminals in Ezo could have trained me. Instead, here I am facing off against a monster with a man who wants to kill my sister.

Ren's sword carves the air with unflinching certainty, forcing the wolf back.

I anchor the little boy to me, reminding myself to not lose heart. There is a way out of this. There is always a way.

Suddenly, Ren's sword slices through the wolf's leg. It reels back with a howl.

"Quick," Ren says, tethering me and the boy to his grappling bow. He tightens the belt at my waist, jerking hard, and our eyes meet.

"Why did you come for me?" I ask, voice strangled with guilt as I hold my head high. "Is it for the bounty?"

He shakes his head and tightens the belt, handing me the propulsion device he'd used earlier. "Something like that."

Before I can protest, he hits the lever, launching the arrow and pulling us over the wall.

We land safe atop the fence, Ren close behind, and we rappel down the other side. A mob crushes in around us, some pointing and laughing, others calling for the circus owner to make us pay for ruining their fun. I untie the boy and shove him toward the crowd. "Go!" I say. "Run! We'll distract them."

The boy gives a frightened nod before disappearing into the crowd.

Ren changes the hold on his sword as the crowd parts and a singular figure marches forward flanked by two smaller wolves.

"You didn't keep your bargain, pearl," Lady Kumo says. "I'm disappointed. And you!" She turns on Ren, close enough to swat his sword with her bare hand. "How dare you interfere with my business! *My* bounty."

Ren's eyes narrow at the two wolves prowling beside the woman. His sword glistens in the moonlight. "Captain Renjiro, here on official business for the Shadows," he says, arching a brow. "Would you like a demonstration?"

The wolves recoil with a low growl, fur hackled against their arched backs.

"That won't be necessary." Lady Kumo's eyes shift from the captain to me, raking over my torn dress and dark unkempt hair with visible scorn. She tilts her head. "I've never heard of a Shadow stealing a bounty, even one this high. What do you really want, Captain? It can't be *that*."

"Yes," he says. "It is."

Lady Kumo smirks. "Hmm, is it for the money or something

more . . . sentimental? I didn't know the Shadows let feelings come between them and their work."

"I don't."

Before I can blink, his sword comes down on the wolf at the woman's right side. I don't even see the blade touch it, but a gust of cool air whips past my face. The beast falls, its blood as red as mine, seeping into the cold earth. But its body turns to dust as if it had never been. A monster, once a human . . . My gut clenches. The second wolf meets the same fate.

"I'm here to slay a monster," Ren says. "Where is her sister? Where's Yuki?"

CHAPTER 20

LADY KUMO LEADS THE WAY through the circus tents to a cave on the coast. Bluish white water catches the moon's glow and crashes against the rocks.

"This is where we keep our more dangerous pets," she says. "The ocean catacombs. Take a look and see if the girl's sister is among them."

"It's a trap," I say.

As soon as we crawl into that cave, she'll close the gate, the tide will rise, and something terrible will happen. Gooseflesh pricks my arms in warning.

"Of course it's a trap," Kumo says silkily. "I always protect my investments. But you'll never know if your sister is here if you don't go inside."

Ren leans one foot against a rock and cleans his sword across his knee, listening. Even if we overcome the trap, I still have to keep him away from Yuki. He'll kill her if he goes into that cave.

Why did he come back for me? His dedication to the law? The bounty . . . ?

I eye him with suspicion, but the hard line of his jaw and pained expression remind me of myself. Of the wanted poster. That look when I'm protecting someone I care about.

No, I shake the thought away. He's only here to throw me in jail and slay a monster—my sister.

I clench my jaw, judging the height of the moon and the crash of the waves. My best chance is to approach it near high tide, which will be soon.

And without Ren.

I could try to climb the rocks and slip inside from the top, but I might lose my grip and fall. No doubt secrets lie hidden beneath the water, rocks and monsters, waiting to waylay intruders. My bare feet scuff against the rocky edge. I've scarce time before the curse fully consumes my sister—this is my last chance.

"I'll do it," I say.

"She stays," Ren says. His voice drops to a whisper, "You don't need to see this."

Lady Kumo's mouth twists into a mocking grin. "How touching. I don't care if you both go, but you have ten minutes before Inspector Jade arrives."

"Thirty minutes," Ren interjects coolly. "My second-in-command is detaining him as we speak."

Lady Kumo swats her hand in dismissal. "It hardly matters. If you don't leave the cave in time, you'll both be mine—or dead. When the tide rises, no one can get out."

Ren lays a hand on his sword. "Then don't waste our time. How do you get into the cave? No tricks. I don't care about your sanctuary status in Ranzan. I'd happily turn you in to the Silverwood authorities for arson—the emperor's summer house, I believe."

"How do you know that?" she hisses. "You can't prove it."

"Are you willing to test that?"

Kumo blanches. "Just remember, by Ranzan law, the *yajuu* are *mine*. You'll take her sister alone or go to court for destroying my property. It's punishable by death here."

"Like everything else." He pulls out a carefully wrapped mochi from his wool coat and chews on it thoughtfully. "But I'd just as well kill your beasts than steal them, and *that* is not illegal." He grins with a mouthful.

Lady Kumo's eyes narrow with a ghoulish effect and her

cheeks flare. "Don't you dare. I *will* make you regret this. I'm calling the inspector myself." She gathers her performer's cape around her, mouth contorted in fury. "I'll find out who you are, Shadow, and make you pay."

Ren straightens, twirling his sword and sheathing it in a swift motion. "I pay for my crimes every day. Add it to my tab."

With a quick glance between the captain and me, Lady Kumo turns on her heel and strides away. No doubt to hurry the arrival of Inspector Jade and reinforcements to spare her precious merchandise.

Ren turns on me. "I think that went well."

It's too dark to see his eyes, even in the moonlight, but there's something different about him, frayed. I want to apologize for leaving him in Valcon's lair, for using magic against him, ensnaring him with my words. Words that should be sacred.

"Yuki doesn't have time," I say. I hope he can hear my tone, the desperate plea to let me save her, to overlook my betrayal.

"She's gone, Kira," he says, voice tight. "Stay here. I'll put an end to this. It'll be quick and painless. There's no curing a monster. You've seen what they become."

I gulp, my fears clawing to the surface. This is why I left him in Valcon's lair. He doesn't understand.

"*No*," lodges in my throat.

Ren shrugs off his wool overcoat and drapes it over my unresponsive shoulders. His warmth and the soft scent of clean soap and lavender washes over me. His eyes search mine for a brief moment, his hand lingering on my left shoulder. For a moment I think he'll ask if I'm okay or . . .

He turns his back and then lays aside a number of knives, a half-eaten mochi, and a leather pouch.

"Are you going to dive off the cliff?" My eyes scan his strong arms, the taut muscles beneath a cotton dress shirt, and then the sword at his side.

"You'll thank me later." He secures his sword and reaches for his boots.

I'm sealing my fate, but I don't care. I promised to take care of Yuki. Keep her safe. And that's what I'm going to do. I shrug out of his warm coat.

"Ren," I say, and he stiffens at the sound of his name. "Don't hurt Yuki, please."

"I have to end this," he says softly. "It's the law."

I close my eyes, hating that answer. Hating what I'm about to do. I don't ask the path because something tells me it wouldn't agree.

Ren cocks his head in warning as if reading my thoughts. Blue-black hair falls into his eyes as he reaches over to cover my mouth, a flash of panic in his eyes.

Too late.

"Don't follow me," I say. The blue path leaps over my words, and he reels back. Then, gritting my teeth, I leap over the edge.

I fall, limbs flailing, into a pool of wind-tossed sea.

At the last second, I gather my arms in front of me and pin my direction, praying the rocks are far away. Ice cold shock registers in my nervous system. The dark water pushes up and then down, spinning me in a vicious circle. The cold tricks my senses, numbing me into submission. But I know what I must do.

I still my mind and summon the wind to my aid. *Help me find the path.* The cold in my own body responds. I feel the life gathering strength in my veins, clearing my mind. A wave slaps me from overhead, nearly pummeling me into the rocks.

And with the wave, a blue light glows in the water. It jumps like a fish made of stars and ice, springing from the foamy waves and then slipping into the mouth of the cave.

I don't dare glance at the Shadow watching from the cliff face. *I'm sorry, Ren.* I'm not even sure if the binding path worked, but I had to try. For Yuki. For my promise to Mother and the only thread I have left of home.

I crane my arms into the waves, struggling against the sea to stay afloat. Bless Mother's foresight to give us swimming lessons in the prison hot spring. A smile touches my lips as I follow the glimmering blue fish into the cave.

The path heard me.

Lungs burning, I crawl onto a dark and sandy shore. Inside the cave, luprite rocks glow with a warm butter sheen. The sea pours in, funneling into a creek on one side of the cave. A thin, treacherous path wends on the left side. Bells hanging from a rope overhead chime in the wind, a few whistling off-note.

"Kira! Stop," Ren calls from the cliff, his voice barely discernible among the waves.

I'd better hurry.

Slipping on the path, I trek quickly, using one hand for balance against the cave wall. I shudder, hoping my fingers don't snag a cave slug along the slimy surface. Luprite marks the way for my feet, its faint glow promising.

Around the bend, a stone dragon dripping with moisture blocks the entrance. Its open mouth frames the path, stalactites and stalagmites jutting like so many teeth from the ancient rock. Eyes glare down at me, obsidian stones that catch what little light the luprite emits in the tunnel.

Casting one look back at Ren, I step over the stone jaws and into the heart of the cavern. My bare feet slap against the cold wet floor as I round the corner. My heart sinks.

Black cages line the walls of the cavern, each one a freestanding unit shackled to the ground with a long chain to hold them in place when the tide comes in. How many had that awful woman tricked into becoming her slaves? Stalactites cling to the roofs of the cages, crusted over with salt and barnacles. There is no path, only a maze of the free-floating cages in ankle-high water, waiting for the next tide.

Yuki has to be here, but the cavern is vast, and there must be dozens of cages. The path is silent within the cave.

"Yuki!" I yell at the top of my voice. "Where are you?"

The cave walls rattle, and a stalactite crashes into the dark water.

A few growls and moans come from the cages that squeak and rock on the rising tide, each encrusted in white coral like twisted bones.

"You shouldn't be here, Ainur," comes a frail, scratchy voice.

I jump back as an old man steps out, human and weary. His gaunt features and long beard entangled with seaweed stand in stark contrast to his pinstriped suit—just like the circus workers.

"How do you know who I am?" I ask.

"I've seen many things in my time," the man says in a rusty, too-slow voice. "Before Taiga ruled, Ainur lived in these parts. But you cannot see out of this quagmire. Luprite is beautiful, but it also weakens the old dragon magic."

"What? But I've always . . ." *lived on an island of luprite.*

Whoever had thrown Mother into prison must have known about the Ainur's connection to wayfinding. It must have kept us—and our magic—hidden.

I study the man's shriveled face in the faint light. Curiosity pulls at me to ask his story, but time is running out. There's no clock to tell me how long I have before the next tide.

"Help me," I say. "I'm looking for my sister, Yuki. Where is she? Please."

The man shakes his head. "Turn back."

"No." I will the old man to look at me. His eyes seem vacant, like a prisoner about to die, all the hope bled out of him. "You can escape with us. Please, tell me where she is."

His eyes search for mine, and I realize that he's blind. Still, he points to the far end of the cavern. "I cannot go with you. My master wouldn't allow it. Go back. The monsters wake when the tide rises, and the gate shuts."

I step past him, compassion tugging at me as I leave the old man behind. What had led him to such a terrible position? What is his story?

Inside the large cave, mist-brined air swirls between the cages. I try to see the path to my sister, to find her cell and block out the growl of tonic-calmed *yajuu*, but it's useless.

"Yuki!" I call, checking every cage and sloshing through the ankle-high water.

Wet arms shoot through the bars at me, fingers writhing when they miss. Sharp hisses and rattling follow in my wake. Finally, at the end of a long row, tucked behind a massive stalagmite, is a cage encrusted with fresh coral that hasn't lost its color. Tiny coral animals tuck in as I approach. No sound or call for help comes from this cage.

My sister lies face down on the floor, sprawled out on her stomach with her arms tucked beneath her. Her long, tangled hair is a wild spray of brown, and her tattered nightgown screams to me of all those cold prison nights we spent curled together. Mama's loving hands combing our hair as she whispered of a future home in Silverwood. A place where we are safe and fed, where cozy streets are adorned with cherry trees in the spring.

"Yuki!" I clamp my hands over the bars, jerking them with all my might. Jagged coral cuts into my palms. "Yuki! Speak to me!"

I pull again, my knuckles going white. "I'm going to get you out," I say, not daring to accept that Yuki might not be alive.

The cell is damp from floor to ceiling, as if a wave had just gone through and left the prison like a wet sponge. "Hold on, Yuki."

The water rises to my knees as I hammer the cage with my fists. I gasp, seething as my hand comes away with a gash. Yuki stirs slowly, pulling herself up as the tide rises.

"Don't worry." I scour the dark cavern that will soon be flooded. Then I spy the soft yellow glow of luprite beneath the water that now reaches my thighs. I bend down, nearly gagging at the stench of rotten debris. My fingers scrape against the floor until I pry up a small piece of luprite.

I strike the cage door with the stone. Sparks flare, and part of the hinge melts. I hit it again and again until it cracks. And then the door breaks free.

I stumble back before righting myself against the bars. Yuki's cage floats on the waves, bobbing like a fishing cork. My sister clambers to her knees, swaying, head bent low. I scramble to her side, ignoring the rank filth on the cage floor and the gash on my hand.

How much has she progressed in her transformation? Was she given the tonic to calm her? Does she remember me? But my fears are nothing compared to the feel of my sister in my arms—alive—breathing. Here.

I wrap my arms around her as she sinks into me, nearly unconscious. She smells of salt and rotting crabs. No transformation mars her pale face except for the addition of fangs and general muscle tone. I lift her beneath the arms and drag her to the now open cage door. The tide gushes in, rising to my waist.

"I've got you," I cry, hugging her to my chest.

Yuki turns her head, her eyes sad, shining pools. "You . . . came . . . for me," she whispers, voice raw like a seashell scraped on the rocks.

"Of course I did. Can you walk? We have to get out, fast."

Yuki pushes her elbow against the wall to brace herself. That's when I see it. "Yuki—your hands."

My sister holds up two nubs of arm, blackened and scarred at the wrists. She chokes back a sob and shivers, lifting an arm to her heart as if to rub away the pain.

I glance back at the cage and notice the pair of frozen cuffs from Inspector Jade. My sister had been clinging to them at the bottom of her cell until she lost consciousness. Inspector Jade's frozen chains had finally burned through her wrists just as he'd promised.

My chest tightens with heat. I've no words. Only anger and pain and sadness.

"You came," Yuki repeats, her words a grated whisper. She hides her stubbed wrists beneath the tattered pajama sleeves.

"I was too late." A force colder than ice burns through me, a thirst for justice. I help my sister to her feet, leaving the cuffs where they belong—in the depths of this forsaken place.

I reach for the vial.

"Hurry, girls," a faint voice calls out, wheezing and barely discernible over the slapping waves. "Hurry!"

The old man. *How long had he been calling us?*

Metal creaks from the cave entrance. I hurry toward it, dragging Yuki through the surging water. The old man waves to us from the gate, bidding us haste. The walls shudder as an iron door with pointed teeth sinks over the cave opening. It closes with a sickening splash.

Trapped.

CHAPTER 21

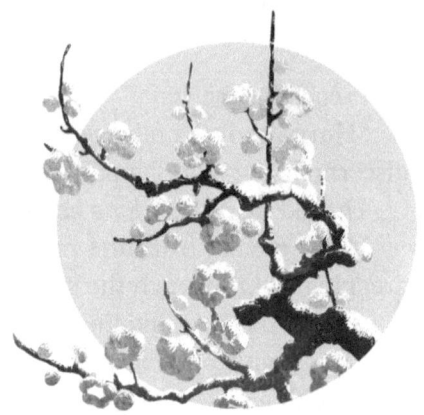

I WANT TO GRIP YUKI'S HAND, to tell her that everything will be all right, but there's nothing to hold. Yuki leans against me, her pale forehead pressed against my shoulder. Waves wash cold against my chest, pouring into the cave as the tide rises. It must be near midnight.

"I'm sorry," the old man says, shaking his head from the other side of the gate. "Back to the cage, both of you. Once the gate falls, the *yajuu* wake, and some can escape their cages."

The water continues to climb. I've no weapon to fight. No wayfinding to light the way. Only the amber vial, hidden beneath my dress.

"Kira." Yuki's head lolls against my shoulder, nudging me to go back.

"No." I hold her tight though my arms shake. "The path is forward, never back."

Another wave splashes against me and nearly washes Yuki away. It takes all my focus just to keep my sister close. Her knees buckle, and I struggle to hold her upright as exhaustion claims her.

The old man calls to us through the gate's bars, "Quick, back to the cage. The sedatives wear off at this time. You aren't safe. I'll go fetch my master."

A few loud clicks echo above the water.

With a splash, two *yajuu* crawl from their cages and swim toward us. They wade in the deep water like mermen, scales tarnished and licking pointed teeth.

"We have our master's permission to feast on any who escape," one of them hisses. "Join us for an eternity in the cage or in our bellies. The choice is yours."

Choice. There is always power in a choice.

I think back to my mother, the secrets she'd tried to share not in word but in action. There's no guiding blue light in this cave, but I have Mother's memories and a sharp mind.

The cave is vast, coated with a substance that dampens magic and wayfinding. Cages float in the water, but if we can climb higher, we might have an advantage. The top of the gate isn't protected, and moonlight illuminates a narrow gap between the mouth of the cave and the gate.

I fix my eyes on the *yajuu* and guide Yuki back toward the cages. Her eyes meet mine, questioning. Two monsters follow, swimming against the tide, their bulging yellow eyes trailing us in the dark.

"Trust me," I whisper to Yuki. "Can you climb?"

My sister looks at me, her face pale, and nods. Together, we sludge through the water icing our ribs until we are back at the cage that once kept her prisoner. But we don't climb in. We climb up. Coral scrapes my palms and the exposed skin on my feet. I haul myself to the top, then reach down and grab Yuki's arm.

She scrambles up, somehow untouched by the coral as if her skin is thicker than mine. Below, jaws snap. The creatures grapple with the floating cage, unable to climb the slick bars.

"We'll catch you at the gate," one of the *yajuu* says, licking his lips and then disappearing below the murky water.

I pull Yuki close and find her sturdier than before. She growls as more *yajuu* below attempt to climb after us. Their hands are too slippery, and they struggle to gain footing.

The prison cells float like wrecked freighter cargo. Yuki

jumps to another one, causing it to dip. I follow, thankful the cage tops are solid. Together, we leap from cage to cage until we're close to the cave entrance, only much higher.

The water *yajuu* follow, releasing others from their cages to join the chase. One creature has shapeshifted into a giant eel, its fin a silver blade curving in and out of the water. We don't have time to find out what other monsters dwell here now that the cages are open. I narrow my focus to the gap above the iron gate.

Suddenly, our cage jerks and dips. Yuki hugs me with her arms, her feet skidding off the slippery ledge as the cage tilts. The giant eel wraps around our floating sanctuary, squeezing the bars. Around him, the *yajuu* chant and hiss, waiting for the cage to collapse beneath the crushing strength of the eel.

"We need to jump," I say, eyeing the distance to the gate. "I'll hold onto you. Try to grab it with your arms, okay?"

Yuki nods, blinking to keep away the exhaustion that makes her sway unsteadily.

"Now!" I grip Yuki's arm and jump.

Together, we launch toward the gate and to a gap stretching across the top. Yuki thuds against the metal, a single arm looped over the top crevice, and pulls herself through the gap. A silent splash emits from the other side as my sister frees herself.

Can she swim without hands?

Ren is waiting on the shore for her. A half-dozen thoughts flood my mind—none of them good. I reach out for the metal gate, hoping I can climb to the top. But I fall into the water.

A wave catches me and slams me against the iron. Webbed hands grab me and plunge me beneath the waves. Strong, bony fingers pinch my throat, tightening.

I can't breathe.

I kick and claw at the sinewy arms to no avail. *Did Yuki make it out to the harbor? She could barely stand, much less swim. What if Ren finds her first?*

"No escape," a *yajuu* growls, jerking my head above the water.

Suddenly, another beast slams into him, and his grip falters. I tear free and lunge at the iron gate. My limbs are ice, but I climb fast up the metal bars. Claws swipe at my legs, and I kick back. Pain should be there, in my legs and feet, but all I feel is the cold wind calling me from beyond the bars.

I pull myself to the top, praying the crevice is too narrow for the creature following me. Then I drop over the other side of the gate—*free*. But the moment I hit the water, my leg cramps.

Pain lances down my thigh, sharp and sudden. The strength that had carried me this far vanishes, downed in exhaustion. I flail, waves slamming me under and back up—just long enough to see stars scattered across the sky.

I'm out of the cave.

A blue light beads through the dark water, close. An arm breaks through and reaches for me.

Yuki.

She locks arms around me. My lungs swell with pressure, but Yuki kicks frantically, pushing us until we burst to the surface. Her arms tighten beneath my shoulders, hauling me toward the jagged shoreline. The stars above blink in and out of focus like they're about to go dark.

Nothing else matters—Yuki is here.

I reach out for her, but she backs away. She clings to the rocks with the crook of an elbow, her breath ragged. I half feared Lady Kumo would return with Inspector Jade. Or Ren would be waiting with his sword, and in one piercing swipe, my sister would be gone. But all I see is my sister saved me again, her cheek nestled against a rock, and smiling with sharp, pointed teeth.

Then the stars go dark.

CHAPTER 22

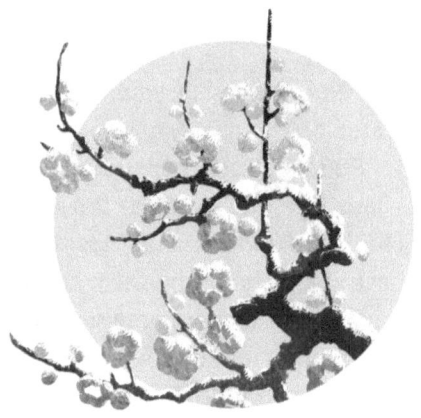

LIVING ON THE NORTHERNMOST island in the world, I'm used to the dark. But this darkness is different. My head spins as a dozen shimmering blue paths flash in my mind—trails of light racing through my past, illuminating every moment I failed. Then they converge. A single arrow of blue light flies toward me. It plunges into my chest, and I gasp awake.

My hands fly to my legs, my chest, my beating heart—*not dead*. Relief escapes in a breath. But it's short lived.

The amber vial is gone.

The floor lurches beneath me, threatening to loosen the contents of my already empty stomach. I'm not on the beach anymore. Darkness cloaks the room like a blanket, thick and drowsy, beckoning me to close my eyes and dream away the pain. Everything aches.

Where am I? Where is Yuki?

Cool air leaks through a crack in what I take to be a door. I inch upright on a plush bed covered in thick blankets and wide enough to fit Yuki, my mother, and me. A rough, familiar fabric brushes against my fingers as I search for the missing vial—my elmwood coat.

I pull it to me, balling it in my fists and inhaling deep, as if

I could find my family woven in its threads. This has to be a dream. I'd left Mother's coat at the ballroom.

Wings flap against my heart, violent palpitations that threaten to fly to my throat. *Ren was the last one to see this coat . . . Where is Yuki?*

Yesterday was the last day, the last chance to turn her back into a human.

I . . . failed.

Images of Yuki flash in my mind. Last night, she'd saved me, pulled me out of the dark water, just like she'd done when I'd fallen in the ice as a child.

Yuki's pale face grinning at me from the rocks flashes in my mind, her wet hair pasted to her skin, dark half-moons beneath her eyes. I wedge my fists into the hollows of my eyes, willing the images to stop. I have to find her.

I don't wait for my eyes to adjust to the darkness. Throwing off the covers, I swing my legs over the side.

A voice like brittle ice cracks the darkness. "You'll fall over if you stand."

Ren. I freeze, but my heart quickens. I beg my stomach to behave as the floor seems to tilt again.

"Where is Yuki? The cure?" I ask, my voice strained.

I draw the elmwood coat around me, fingers burrowing in the worn strands. *He brought the coat back as he'd promised, even after I abandoned him. Why?*

"What have you done with her?" My voice softens a smidge.

There's a scrape against stone that sets my teeth on edge, and then a flame appears. It gobbles up the wick of a narrow candle, illuminating the room and the hand that holds it—a strong fist lined with too many scars and calluses for the young man holding the flame.

Captain Ren sits in the shadows. The corners of the room are still drenched in darkness. He holds the candle at a distance, his elbow perched on the edge of the armchair. His handsome face is still eclipsed beneath his wool cap. I'm reminded that he's the youngest captain ever employed in the Northern Watchmen for a reason—he follows the law with an iron will.

"How are you feeling?" His voice is soft as he leans into the candlelight.

I rush to stand and demand what he's done to my sister, but cruel stars burst across my vision. The room shifts like melting ice. I collapse back onto the bed.

"Y-you drugged me," I stammer, the realization dawning. Definitely shouldn't have trusted him. "Is that why everything's swaying?"

I appraise my surroundings. My hair is dry and brushed, a smooth wool tunic covers me instead of the tattered ballgown, and clean bandages hug my arms and neck, covering a dozen patchwork scrapes. Heat rises to my cheeks. Someone undressed me.

My gaze snaps to Ren.

Please, not him.

"I suppose," he says, dragging out the word. "Kampo medicine, but it had quite the effect. That's common with dragon heart users. Concoctions with dragon bone don't sit well with them. As for the swaying, we're on a ferry. We'll reach Silverwood in a few days."

I gape at him, then clamp my jaw shut. "Well, you gave me too much *medicine*. At this rate, you'll have to carry me through the streets to reach the prison. Where's my sister?"

To my surprise, Ren stands and then sits on the end of the bed. His back is broad, glacial, but his slumped shoulders betrayed something else. A crack in the ice.

He sets the candle on the bedside table and offers me a cup that had been sitting there. His fingers brush mine. "Drink," he says quietly. "Then I'll answer everything."

"Is it drugged?" I lift a brow and smell it first.

Ren smiles. "It's water."

Cautiously, I lift the cup to my lips. After a few timid sips, I down the contents, water dribbling from my chin.

"Better?" Ren watches me from the corner of the bed, his expression tight, eyes shadowed with something like concern. "Your sister is safe for now."

"Truly?" I scoff. "That's hard to believe, coming from you."

"I try to speak the truth," he says evenly, voice like steel cooled in water.

"Then where is she?"

He runs a hand through his unkempt hair. "You still don't get it. *Yajuu* are *dangerous*. What you did on the cliffs was dangerous. Thankfully your path didn't work. I *chose* to stay back and hold off Inspector Jade. You're lucky I waited."

"I didn't ask you to . . . I—"

"Used magic against me?" His stare sharpens, cutting through me.

Shame heats my cheeks. He saved my life, yes. But I won't apologize. Not when he just wants the bounty.

"Abusing power makes you no different than them," he says, not unkindly. "Wayfinding illuminates and creates paths, but it doesn't tell you what is right. You alone bear the responsibility for your choices."

"Who can bear such a weight? Can you?"

A muscle twitches in his neck.

"Where is my sister?"

"In the hold with the supplies. Zenri's watching her. I gave her the vial, but it's only a tonic, the half-cure." He shakes his head. "She's still *yajuu*. The tonic's effects will wear off soon. You can't trust her just because she's your sister. Family loyalty doesn't go that deep."

"You don't know my family."

"I know *yajuu*." His jaw clenches like I struck a nerve.

"You're more dangerous than she is," I snap, remembering how his blade had sliced the wolves at the circus and nearly killed Valcon.

His shoulders tense as he turns to face me. "You're right." The ice in his voice melts on the next exhale. "I am."

I want to ask, to know the reason behind the heaviness in his shoulders and the pain flickering in his eyes. Again, I feel like a small girl watching the ocean cliffs when I look at him. Sympathy bubbles up from some forgotten place, and I want to swim out to those cliffs and ask what atrocities they've seen. *What's your story, Ren?* But swimming near cliffs in a storm is deadly. And so too is trusting this man.

"Take me to her," I say instead. "I want to see my sister."

"You must rest." It comes out as a command, albeit softly. "You'll need strength for the journey ahead. There are no *yajuu* in the capital—they're outlawed. Only found in the northern wilds and the border cities like Ranzan. The inspector will be waiting when we dock in Silverwood. I made a deal with him while you were in that cave. Bought us time."

Us? My gaze steals over his face for answers. *What is he hiding?*

"So you'll turn me in as soon as we dock?" I ask.

"I hope not," he says, then clears his throat. "You must be processed legally through Silverwood's criminal system first. The inspector can't take you on Taigan jurisdiction alone; Ezo has its own rules. We may be a province of Taiga now, but we're still proud."

"You speak with patriotism," I say, surprised. "I thought soldiers just followed orders—especially you."

Candlelight brushes the curve of his brow, catching on the troubled flicker in his eyes. Remorse. Maybe even regret.

Something inside me shifts. It's like a wave crashes through me, reaching for him in the dark. A flicker of path.

The captain breaks the silence. "Have you ever done something you regretted? Something so horrible no one could forgive you? You couldn't forgive yourself?"

I shudder like I've swallowed ice. The memory rises fast. The bear in the Winterwilds. The one I'd led the guards to. It had done nothing wrong, and yet I'd led it to its death. The path had shown me the bear, and I'd assumed that meant I was supposed to kill it—to survive.

I was wrong.

My mother and Yuki paid the price for my foolishness. That bear had been cursed, and I brought its curse into our lives. If anyone is responsible for Mother's death and Yuki's curse, I am.

"Yes," I whisper. "I know the feeling."

He nods. "I'm sure Zenri's told you about my past. He can't keep a secret."

"He said you rescued him a long time ago on Seshu. That's why he follows such a stubborn goat around the eight kingdoms." I throw him a pointed look. "And that someone in your family died from the curse. That's why you left and joined the Shadows."

"Yes," he says quietly, a crease pinching his brow. "That's why you need to stop chasing this foolishness. You don't know what it costs to break this curse. It's wicked, horrible. You'll never be able to go back."

I blink, pulling slightly away. He couldn't possibly mean that he'd seen the curse broken before. And it went wrong. Terribly wrong.

Did someone he loved die? Perhaps Valcon had tricked him and given him poison. Is that why Ren wants vengeance so badly?

He runs a hand through his blue-black hair. "I'm telling you this because the cure exacts a terrible price. I know you're still searching for it, even though your sister's time has passed. But Valcon Jey only ever had one vial. He sold it to my father."

He hesitates, his gaze shifting away. "For someone to use it, they had to . . . to make a choice."

"I don't understand."

He shakes his head and gives a hollow laugh. The candle flutters in the breath between us.

"Why do you think I hate them so much? Why leave my home to join the Shadows? I swore an oath to hunt monsters to the end of my days." His voice cracks, then hardens. "Because I couldn't bear to look my father in the eye. Couldn't thank him for the cure. I wish he'd let me die. There's no saving a life if it means taking another. I hate him for it."

The truth clicks into place. It seems impossible, but the answer is right in front of me. Who can sneak in the shadows and wield a blade faster than thought? Who outranked an entire legion of Shadows in less than a year? Who survived three months alone in the Winterwilds—longer than anyone in recorded history . . .

"You're a—"

"*Yajuu*," he finishes. "The only one ever fully 'cured,' and look at me. I'm less human now than I was as a monster."

He stares at his hands, normal hands, but I imagine he sees on them the claws that used to be there, the blood that never fully washed away, and the weight of what he did while the curse ruled him.

I'm torn between running out the door, smashing a lamp over his head, or . . . I move closer. Slowly. Cautiously. Until our fingers touch.

I thought he'd be like ice, but he isn't. He's snow—hands soft and even delicate as my fingers find his. His skin is warmer than mine. I wait for him to pull away, but he doesn't. He just sits there, still as a snared rabbit.

He was right. Caring is a kind of poison.

"I don't see a monster," I say, lifting the candle to read his face better. "Terrible things happened to you, but that doesn't make you bad. You're cured."

"Maybe. But I *did* terrible things." He pulls his hand back like it burns him. "Unspeakable things."

"For all your talk of not caring, I think you care a great deal," I say.

Ren stands slowly, each vertebrae straightening as he comes to his full height. Hands fist at his sides, and instead of turning away like I expect, he faces me.

"Caring is for the weak." His voice hardens. "Cold calculation and dedication to a single purpose—that's how to survive. Remember that when we reach Silverwood." His eyes meet mine, a finality in the steel gaze. "The authorities plan to execute your sister. I've stayed my hand long enough."

I catch a slight flinch in his jaw as he says it, but the words are strong and full. The captain doesn't lie.

"I won't let them," I say, matching his gaze.

He shakes his head, and his voice cracks. "That'll be hard to do when you're dead. Aiding or keeping company with monsters is a crime punishable by death. Valcon wasn't lying. I can't . . ."

His jaw tenses as if swallowing what he truly wants to say. "I can't go against the law," he finally manages. "It's the only moral code I have. The only thing I trust."

He nods toward the empty cup beside me. "Enjoy the extra sleeping draught. I thought prison might've taught you not to trust so easily."

I stare at him and then at the cup and back again. "Why?"

A flicker of guilt crosses his face. "Don't be a fool, Kira. I'm still a monster."

CHAPTER 23

SHARP MORNING LIGHT floods the port holes, accosting my eyes. My head throbs. *Yuki.* I jolt upright, groaning as I drag my hands down my face. She's in the cargo hold as a prisoner. *His* prisoner.

How much of last night was real?

Ren had once been a monster. He gave Yuki the half-tonic, but he's planning to turn us in the second we dock. My jaw clenches. *I never should've trusted him.*

A tantalizing smell wafts into the room: salted meat, umami seaweed, hot broth. My stomach growls. In Abashi Prison, I would've risked my life for a meal like that.

I swing my legs over the side of the bed. *How long have I been asleep?*

Circular windows line both sides of the room, looking out to an endless jade sea. Golden light carves up the wooden floor, slicing the room into bright, painful angles. My feet throb, puffy and scratched raw from the coral in the cave. Every muscle aches, and I wince. The captain will pay for this.

A rap at the door breaks the silence.

I hold a breath, hoping the sound will disappear if I stay still.

The door slides open with flair and Zenri peers inside, balancing a large tray. The tight breath in my lungs loosens.

"Where have you been?" I ask. I almost offer to help, but I don't trust my own balance yet.

He eases into the room and grins. "You'd be surprised how many errands the captain can think of." He sets the tray down with a flourish. "Here's your breakfast, my lady."

"Thank you." I lean over the tray. Steam rises in delicate curls, carrying the scent of pickled radish and salty broth. I seize the soup bowl with both hands and gulp it down. "Can I have seconds?"

Zenri chuckles and flops into the corner chair with an exaggerated slouch. "I thought you'd be hungry."

"Sorry." I give a sheepish grin, wiping my mouth with the back of my hand. "It's good to see you, by the way."

He scans my face like a mother hen. "You too. The bruising's almost gone. You took quite a thrashing in that cave. Captain was worried you wouldn't rest without the medicine."

"*Worried?* That's one word for it."

"It's true," Zenri says in his defense. "We had to stitch you up, and rest is recommended after harrowing events." He pauses, waving his hands as if to ward off my anger. "Don't look at me like that. The captain had one of the female passengers change you after treating your injuries."

"I don't need to rest. I need my sister and—" My stomach growls loudly. "More food. Where is that smell coming from?"

"That'd be the captain's breakfast on deck. First-class perks."

"Not anymore, it isn't." I start testing my legs beneath me. A little wobbly, but functional. "Will you take me to him, after I see my sister?"

"I'm not sure that's a good idea," Zenri says.

"Why not?"

"First, you need something to wear." He walks to a folding screen and pulls it aside, revealing a stack of folded clothes. "I brought these from Madame Gion's. Wool silk blend. It should keep you warm."

My fingers glide over the dove-gray kimono. A subtle lace

imprint glimmers like frost under the light. A haori lies next to it, the same dark gray as the captain's cloak and trimmed in white fur. "It's beautiful," I whisper. "Thank you."

"Don't thank me," Zenri says, waving it off. "Thank the captain. He picked it out himself. Do you know how to put it on?"

"I think so," I say, slipping behind the screen. "I tried so many of these at Madame Gion's, I think I've a grasp on it now. Is it true that my sister's below deck? Is she okay?"

"You were out for three days, Kira."

Three days!

I pull the kimono belt too tight. Where had we sailed in three days' time, or had we been on land for part of it? Ren claimed that Yuki's curse is permanent now, but I won't believe it until I see her.

When I finish dressing, I slip back into the room. "Has Yuki eaten anything?"

Zenri's gaze drops. "She doesn't exactly eat normal food, so . . . no." He folds his arms. "She's being kept in the hold. But she's okay, I promise you. The other passengers don't know about her, so we have to keep it quiet. That means you too."

"She's not an animal," I say, hurling a defiant look.

His soft brown eyes catch me off guard, warm and compassionate. I adjust my tone. He might just be my only friend in the entire world.

"Can you take me to her, please?"

"I'm sorry, Captain's orders. But you can ask him yourself." He offers a warm smile and opens the door. "Come on."

On deck, a spirited wind breathes life and clarity to my weary face. As if pulled by a magnetic force, I wobble to the railing and stare at the silver blue sea. In the distance, the silhouette of snowcapped mountains along the coast of Ezo greets me.

I've heard about the last mountain range that cuts Silverwood off from the rest of Ezo, blocking the winter winds and providing a warm, lush climate for the southern city. The warmth is new, rare, like a glowing ember without the bite. Here there is no snow. Only blue—a different blue than the coldness that ate at my bones. This blue is life-giving.

I wish I'd been born in it instead.

"Glad you find the sea refreshing." Zenri leans against the rail next to me, the scarred side of his face a pale pink in the morning sunlight. "I'm from Seshu, a tribe of seafarers, but the ocean makes me sick. I begged the captain to take the train, would've been faster, but no. With your sister's condition, a train's too risky."

"How is she, really?" I ask, inhaling the warm, salt-kissed air. "*What* is she?"

"A monster." Those two words drop from his mouth with such resignation that I imagine my last ounce of hope tumbling into the sea. Zenri takes a deep breath, allowing the wind and the waves to fill the silence.

"I thought I had the cure," I say, watching for a white puff of breath as I sigh, but it doesn't come. My gaze shifts to the racing clouds, here and then gone like winter hares.

Zenri doesn't reply, but the words lodged in his throat are obvious. *It's too late. Too late to save her.*

Tears sting my eyes, but I will my heart to be strong as ice. As long as Yuki's alive, there's hope.

We take a turn around the deck, meeting only a handful of passengers. All traders or businessmen hauling lucrative cargo. From the size of the boat and crew, I estimate nearly forty people on board. We head to the topside dining quarters, a sparse cabin next to the control booth. The door swings open easily, slamming against the inner wall as we enter.

Three long wooden tables sit low on the floor surrounded by embroidered cushions. A lavish spread of platters and steaming bowls dominate the nearest table, still warm and fresh. At the center of it all, Ren sits with his back to me. Completely at ease.

"Good morning," he says without turning, not even glancing up from his meal.

His posture is perfect, shoulders relaxed, chin slightly

tipped—as if I'm the one who's late. I bite back a sharp retort and scan the other tables, where a few men recline, trading notes on border tariffs and the last time they saw home. Zenri gestures for me to sit at the captain's table.

But I have a better idea.

I stride to the serving tray, grab a pitcher of water, and—ignoring every instinct for self-preservation or rationing—dump it on the captain's head.

Ren moves at the last second. The water splashes over his right shoulder, soaking his sleeve and the side of his tunic. He doesn't flinch, just straightens slowly and turns toward me. Blue eyes flash with surprise and a single droplet trails from his bangs to his cheek.

"It *was* a good morning," he says through gritted teeth. "Is there something on your mind, Mistress Kira?"

I nearly choke at his formality. Around us, a few onlookers chuckle behind their hands. Zenri stares at me, slack-jawed, before scrambling to fetch a towel.

"I couldn't throw you overboard," I say sweetly, "so this seemed like the next best option. That was for the last three mornings you stole from me."

"The fault was entirely your own." He returns to his plate, unbothered. "If you had stayed by my side and not run off to the circus, we would *all* be in a better situation. You sustained injuries. Rest was necessary."

Zenri hands him a towel, and while the captain is dabbing his wet shoulder and hair, I bend over the table. My mouth waters at the sprawling feast and an assortment of dishes I've never seen before. A few familiar things from the prison warehouse catch my eye, but never this beautiful or fresh—bonito flakes curl and sway atop hot rice cakes, sea bass roasted in miso glistens with crisp blackened scales, and bright fruits from the mainland—persimmons and wild mountain berries—are arranged in porcelain dishes.

My stomach howls, audibly to my chagrin.

I kneel alongside the table and reach for the candied persimmon. But I freeze when I spot a familiar sheet of parchment beneath the captain's hand.

"That's mine!" I point at the map from the old saint's cottage. He nods. "What I'm trying to figure out is where you got it. Was it your mother's?"

"No," I say, fingers tightening at my sides. I think of the old saint in the mountains. Her hospitality and care had probably meant the difference between life and death for Yuki and me. "A woman in the mountains gave it to me. Hand it back."

Ren chuckles and spears another piece of meat. "Gave? I'd bet my bacon that you stole it. From one of the sisters of the Lady of the Light. I'll have to return it."

I hesitate, but curiosity gets the better of me. "Do you know her? The old saint?"

"The sisters had a monastery in the heart of Silverwood. Only building large enough to compete with the castle in terms of stealing attention from its majesty. Except for the School of Ancient Hearts until it met an unsightly end. But the most spectacular thing about the Ladies was the delicious spread they made from cows' milk, the color of moonlight. They called it butter."

I want to ask about the Ladies of the Light, Silverwood, about what he's seen of the world beyond ravenous mountains and cursed forests. But I don't. Instead, I grab the edge of the map and jerk it toward me. His hand slaps down on it, eyes locked on mine.

I drop my voice so as not to be overheard by other passengers. "I need to see my sister. Now."

A bitter smile plays at his lips. "Yes, well. You may want to temper your hope. It's been over a week since you left *home*. She's not the same," he adds. "The part of her that you called sister is long gone." His hand moves over the map, close enough to brush my fingertip.

I study the words beneath our fingers. *The Winterwilds.*

"This is the only place she could live. But, as law requires, she'll meet her fate in Silverwood." His gaze darkens, a mixture of sorrow and resolve. "Or by my hand if that's kinder."

His words land like ice in my veins. The idea of anyone calling her fate a kindness makes my stomach turn. I lean in, my voice a hard whisper. "Why do you care so much about the law? You can't really want my sister and me to die. I know it's troubling you."

His jaw flexes. "The law keeps me grounded," he says. "Tells me what's right and wrong. Without it, I'm just a monster."

My stomach pinches at those words—though perhaps it's a result of the bacon I'm smelling. "You're afraid," I say. "Afraid of the wrong choice, the wrong path. But fear can't teach you what is right."

"Afraid?" he repeats. "You don't know what real fear is." He nudges the map in my direction and lifts his hands. "Take it. After all, it's Ainur made."

My throat goes dry, questions dying on my lips. *What did the cure do to him? How long was he a monster?*

I take the map, fingertips brushing the raised threads and deep ink valleys. A map made by my people.

Ren taps a calloused finger against the northern Atan mountains. "This erupted when we were children," he says. "The Taigan Empire conscripted the Silverwood Army to crush the Ainur here." He moves his hand north. "They pushed them back to the Winterwilds. This map has no wall separating our nations. That was built later."

My eyes rove the intricate ink—sea dragons clawing the coast, shadowy bears in the mountains, and the subtle pattern of swirling stars that reminds me of Mother.

"What is this?" I point to a winged dragon at the top of the map on the northernmost tip of Ezo, even farther than Abashi Prison.

Does such a place really exist?

"The Wraith," Ren says. "The first immortal dragon who

gave the Ainur his heart. He governed the creatures in the north, kept them from intervening in the lives of humans unless necessary."

"My mother told me the Ainurian legends," I say.

He raises a brow, turning back to the map. "You are one of few left who know them. Only someone who believes in a divine source to the ancients would make a map like this."

My skin tingles, a faint memory of something Mother had said. *Was it a song?* I shake it off and snatch a piece of bacon from his plate, popping it into my mouth.

"Was your breakfast not satisfactory?" he growls.

"It was second class."

"For a third-class passenger. Generous, I think." He scowls but pushes his plate toward me before standing.

I grab another piece and glance up. "And what of my sister? I won't eat another bite until I see her. What have you even fed her?"

He casts me an amused look. "First, I don't believe you. You'd eat an entire salted herring if I put it in front of you. Second,"–he folds his arms–"your sister isn't like most people. I'm not willing to put her preferred cuisine on the menu. Not sure how long she can survive as is."

"We have to try something," I whisper, glancing over my shoulder. The two other passengers in the cabin rise and slip out without a word. I'd nearly forgotten we weren't alone. "Perhaps she'll eat fish? Pickles. I don't know. I have to *try*."

Ren shakes his head. "Meat will only lead to a hunger for more. That's not a choice I'm willing to give her."

"There's no harm in trying," Zenri cuts in. He sits crosslegged on a cushion across from us, gnawing on a persimmon. "Lady Kumo gives her *yajuu* fish."

"They're fine specimens of morality," Ren says dryly. "Zenri, since you're so hopeful, why don't *you* escort Kira to visit the cargo hold?"

Zenri freezes mid-chew. "Go down there—again? I'll get seasick."

Ren shrugs, already moving to the door. "You're welcome to try if Zenri's willing to accompany you."

Clearly, he doesn't think I'll convince him.

I turn to Zenri, pleading with my eyes. The deep scars across his jaw catch in the morning light. He's already risked so much fighting monsters, can I really ask him to face another one? Even if it's to save her?

"Please."

Zenri's gentle brown eyes quaver with a look that's about to break. "Fine."

Relief pours through me. I pocket the map and start gathering food.

"You'll need something to carry that," Zenri says, tossing me a *furoshiki* to wrap it.

I roll two charred fish into the cloth napkin and stuff it into my pocket. Then I chug a too-hot bowl of delicious broth, nearly choking on a slab of tofu.

Zenri laughs. "You eat like a bear."

I wipe my mouth with the back of my hand. "You would too after three days without." I clench the knot on the cloth bundle. "Let's go see Yuki."

CHAPTER 24

MY SISTER IS IN CHAINS. AGAIN.

Only this time, it's a thick metal collar around her neck, bolted into the floor of the ship's hold. And the terrible thing is . . . she almost looks like she belongs here.

Yuki jerks and twists against the restraint, hair hanging in long, tangled knots, teeth bared and sharp. I don't miss that she's shivering, still clothed in the same ragged pajamas. What's left of a blanket lies strewn on the floor, rejected.

"*Hungry. Thirsty,*" Yuki snarls. She pulls at the chain so hard the veins in her neck bulge. If she had hands, she would've clawed at them.

"Quiet," Zenri says firmly. "More of that, and we'll give you more tonic."

Yuki slams her wrist-stumps against the chain, over and over, until she's bleeding. "I hate you!" she shrieks. "I'll cut your heart out. All of you! Cowards, face me without these chains!"

I can't breathe. The words are like icicles driven into my chest. Hope drips away. *How? Why?* My sweet, daydreaming, clever sister has never been so cruel. Never meant words like this. Is it really her?

A sharp cry catches in my throat. I clamp a hand over my mouth, but it's too late. Yuki's head swivels toward the sound. Her eyes lock onto mine.

"*Sister*," she purrs, voice honeyed and twisted. "You'll let me out, won't you? They're treating me like a beast. Like an animal."

My knees wobble. She's smiling now, too wide, too eager. Her eyes remain hungry slits.

Zenri watches me in silence, waiting for me to say I've had enough. I swallow my horror with a visible shudder.

"Fear's the real monster," I whisper, trying to be brave like Mother. I tremble anyway. I need a path, the warm blue light, to turn the darkness and questions into possibilities.

Yuki snarls and hurls herself at the chain again. It jerks taut with a metallic clang. "Give me food or get OUT!" she growls.

"Have you seen enough?" Ren's voice cuts into the darkness, his boots heavy on the stairs as he descends.

"I have." Zenri grips the stair rail.

"Wait . . ." I say, stepping forward. My eyes lock with Yuki's, searching.

She's still in there. Beneath the rage, beneath the curse. Would the real cure still work if I managed to find it? *If* there is one. Ren said he'd had the only cure ever made. That means it's possible.

I reach into my pocket and pull out the bundle of cloth. The fish is still warm, wrapped in napkin folds. Shaking, I place it gently on the ground and nudge it forward.

"Yuki." My voice cracks. "I'm sorry I didn't find you in time. I'm going to spend the rest of my life trying to get you back. I swear it. I'll find a cure."

For a moment, she's silent. Then, slowly, her lips curl. "Oh, pretty speech, little sister. But I like being a monster."

Then she lunges.

The chain creaks under the strain—then snaps with a sickening pop. One link goes flying, spinning across the hold. Yuki's eyes widen in gleeful shock and then she comes for me.

I'm watching my death in slow motion. My legs are heavy,

my heart a dizzying crescendo threatening to burst. Yuki slams into my shoulder, knocking me flat.

Ren moves in a blur. He throws Yuki off me, pinning her before I can even gasp. It's so quick that I barely make out what happened. He pulls a syringe from Yuki's shoulder and lays her head gently on the cargo hold floor. In a single exhale, her snarls fade and she goes still. My big sister lies crumpled, asleep on the floor.

"New irons," Ren says, holding out his hands. Zenri gives him a pair of long chains. He re-fastens them to Yuki's collar and bolts them to the wall, checking twice that it holds.

"Let's not do that again," Zenri mutters. "How much of the vial is left?"

Ren pulls the amber-toned flask from his pocket, the one I'd taken from Valcon. The wrong one. Just a tonic to keep her from shapeshifting and hinder her bloodlust for a time. *That part didn't work too well.*

Ren shakes the flask. Only a few drops cling to the bottom. "Not enough," he says, pocketing it again. "But we'll reach Silverwood today. She won't be our problem much longer."

"Our problem." My chest tightens. "That's my—"

"Your what?" He steps in, closer than he had in the ballroom. His face is too near. His steel gaze dares me to answer. "Zenri and I have risked our lives for you—and for your sister. I won't risk it again. You've seen how dangerous *yajuu* are. And those were only the ones with tonic in their veins." His voice cuts like glass. "Do you know how foolish that was?"

"It's not foolish to have a heart." I raise my voice, fighting back angry tears. *Why does caring have to hurt so much?* "She's dangerous. I see that now. But so are you . . . and so am I."

Ren searches my face, his dark eyes trailing over the cuts and scrapes until they meet mine. My heart is a cavern of hurts and bruises that never seem to heal. And still, I want to believe it matters to someone.

Ren takes a step back, no clever retort or dismal. I drop my gaze to my shoes. I'd wanted him to be the first to bend. So why does the distance make my heart feel emptier?

"I made a promise," I continue, offering him an explanation, "to my mother that I'd keep Yuki safe. She was the weakest one in our family. Her bones were always cracking, her joints sore, too tired to do chores and then beaten by the guards. But she was that way because she risked her life *for me*.

"When I was little, I tried to escape by myself—without them. I reasoned I'd come back when I was stronger, when I became a real wayfinder." I laugh, a brittle, humorless thing. "It was selfish. I fell in the ice. Yuki dove in after me. She'd been watching out for me because Mother made her promise"—my voice catches—"to keep me safe. I hadn't kept my promise, but Yuki . . . she caught fever and took my lashes. She never complained. *Never* blamed me. And she suffered for the rest of her life." I pause, my throat tight. "I won't let my sister drown for me again."

Ren exhales slowly. "At what cost?"

I lift my eyes, daring a glance. His stance is iron, all hard lines and shadow, but care is etched in his eyes—even if he doesn't want me to see it.

"I don't have an answer for that." I turn to Yuki, curled and silent on the floor.

"Well, I don't know about you two," Zenri says, breaking the tension as he opens the door, "but I could really use some fresh air."

I take the cue, brushing past Ren. I cast one last glance at Yuki before following Zenri out. The rest of the morning, I tie nautical knots with Zenri while he regales me with stories of his childhood on the far southern island of Seshu. The distraction is welcome; anything to keep my thoughts from spinning like a whirlpool.

What does Ren know about the real cure? Can it still save Yuki? And how will I escape with her once we land?

The tonic's gone, and my sister made it very clear—she'd rather eat me than have a friendly conversation.

I twist the rope, trying to follow Zenri's knot pattern, but I jerk too hard. The knot slips apart. Frustrated, I toss the rope with a thud and stare over the railing.

Sea spray mists my face. I try to remember Yuki as she was in prison—just a girl. But all I see is the snarl, the teeth, the monster. I clench my fists and glance at Zenri, his usually bronzed face pale with seasickness.

"No wonder you left Seshu," I say. "The seafaring life isn't for you, huh? Besides tying ropes."

"I can fish and swim as good as the rest of them," he says. "Just don't like boats. But let's talk about your plan, eh?"

"My plan?"

"You know." He drops his voice conspiratorially. "To not end up in jail?"

I laugh. "Why would I tell you? So you can run to the captain? I'm as good as dead when we get to Silverwood."

"He doesn't want you dead," Zenri says, turning his back to the sea, shoulders relaxing. The pink lines of his scar look softer in the light. "Our mission was to find your family. But you escaping prison and your sister turning into a monster . . . it complicates things. Captain's just following the law. Always has. It's the only moral compass he's got."

"A moral compass?" I scoff. "He's a bounty hunter dragging us across Ezo to hand us over to an executioner. And you're the same, going along with it. If I find a path out of this, I'm not telling a soul."

"That's the spirit." The smooth voice behind me sends a ripple of nerves to my gut.

I spin as Ren approaches the rail. He leans against it, casual, but there's nothing relaxed about the tension he carries. He takes a rope from the deck and loops it into a series of complex knots, then tosses it to me. "Practice untying these blindfolded. It might help dig up that magic of yours."

The rope lands heavy in my hands, a twisted path begging to be unraveled.

"I'll meet you in the cabin later," Zenri says. He pushes off the rail, casting a concerned glance back at me.

"I'm surprised you haven't found a way out yet," Ren says, as if talking about the weather.

"Hard to do on a boat I can't control."

"You know the old wielders of hearts didn't control them. They listened to them."

I spin to face him. "Why do you pretend to care?"

"Do I?" he asks, not looking at me. His eyes fix on a sliver of land in the distance.

I study the sharp angles of his face, searching for a crack in the mask. The way he suggests it's not an act. *But why bring us all this way just to turn us in? Does he care, or am I just a mission? A variable he didn't expect.*

"Why?" I ask, lowering my voice as a few passengers stroll nearby. "You've taken your time getting us back. You could've handed us over days ago. It seems like you don't *want* to go to Silverwood."

"I've been running from my home." His normally smooth voice turns sharp, glacial. "Like you."

I give a bitter laugh. "I wouldn't call escaping prison the same as running from home."

"Why haven't you used your gift to find a way to your mother's old home?" he shoots back, still not facing me. His gaze remains fixed on the horizon and the faint half-moon dissolving into daylight. "You're a *wayfinder*. If anyone has no excuse to be lost, it's you."

His words cut sharper than I expect. I bite them back, all the ones I want to hurl at him—the fear, the guilt, the magic that never made anything better. He has no idea what it's like to live in filth and silence so long that you start to believe you deserve it. Like you've done something wrong. Wayfinding is what got me into this mess. My gift is nothing but a curse. Or maybe I'm the curse.

"And you? What are you running from?" I take a plunge on a hunch. "Is it your father? The one who bought the cure from Valcon. He lives in Silverwood, doesn't he?"

Ren turns, his expression inscrutable. "I made my father a promise too."

"And?"

"He agreed to my outpost as a Shadow officer. He didn't like it. Too dangerous. But it would be advantageous later when I inherited the business. People admire the uniform. If it didn't hurt my resume—and I survived—my father said it might be good for me to disappear for a few years, after what happened with the cure." His hand scrapes down his jaw, then around the back of his neck. "A few turned into seven. I never planned to return."

"How old were you?" I ask quietly. "When you were sent away?"

"Twelve."

I blink. The wind snatches my breath. I remember twelve—in prison, shivering in the dark, too small to change my stars. But twelve as a soldier? When I look at Ren again, the strong, intimidating frame seems smaller, softer.

"So why go back now?" I ask, wary of getting lured into his story once more.

He turns his full attention to me, those dark eyes haunted. His story is the moon, pulling me closer with silver threads of pain, and sorrow, and something lost.

"I promised that if I found the rest of my mother's family, I'd bring them home." There's feeling beyond the ice lacing his words.

I want to reach out and break that ice, to thaw it with my warmth. But his words pull me back. "Your mother's family?"

He nods, staring at me so hard, I think time has frozen.

"I'm not . . . we're not . . . family," I stutter. I grab the slick edge of rail.

"It took me a while to figure out the truth," he says. "First, I found your mother, Serena. Not an easy task since she was in the one place no one would look for her—Abashi Prison. She was married to my Uncle Bastian, my mother's brother. They had a single child together before Ezo lost the war and the Taigan Empire ordered the removal of anyone with a dragon heart, particularly the Ainur."

"I don't believe—"

Ren holds a finger to his lips, his dark blue eyes silencing me with a gentle plea. "You and your sister are close in age, so it could have been either of you with the details I'd been given. I hoped it wasn't you."

He reaches out and adjusts the scarf around my collar, where a small scar from Beetle's knife stretches across my skin. It's never felt warm before, but it is now. We lock onto each other's eyes. A moment passes before he continues. "Yuki is my cousin, Bastian's daughter. All that's left of my mother's family."

I reel back. "Wait, your uncle and my mother—"

"They were married long ago, before Taiga meddled in our affairs. I don't remember meeting her. I would've been a toddler when she vanished."

"But . . ." I blink furiously, my eyes hot with unshed tears. Was it here, now, that I'd finally get the answer to my question? I almost yell the words, "Why was she in prison?"

His jaw tightens. "When Ezo lost the war, Emperor Casmir ordered the Ainur hunted down, wayfinders killed if they wouldn't serve him. From what I understand, your mother ran off and joined the rebels in the north. She was taken prisoner as the last survivor of her regiment."

"And Yuki?" My voice is barely more than air. "Why take her too?"

"I don't know," he admits. "I never knew my cousin until I met her as a *yajuu* on those train tracks."

"The battle of Mt. Atan," I murmur, remembering the prisoners' stories. "So, it's true. Mother was thrown in prison for taking part in the rebellion against Taiga?" My shoulders slump, as if I'd expected this much, but it still doesn't explain everything. Why Inspector Jade came looking for her at the same time as Ren.

"Yuki's your cousin," I repeat. "But we're not related by blood."

Ren nods, a flicker of a smile crossing his face, almost unwilling. "I would've liked to meet your mother. I'm sorry I didn't get there in time."

Something cracks within my carefully guarded heart. "Did you just say *sorry*?"

The poison of caring seeps in, slow and warm. My face flushes.

He glances away and clears his throat. "There's another rumor. About why your mother ran away." He hesitates, like he's unsure if this is a kindness or cruelty. "My father says she attacked Uncle Bastian before she fled. That he tried to turn her in to the emperor."

"She would never—"

"I know," he says quickly. "It doesn't track. People did terrible things in those days and the emperor is about as cunning as they come. But I think there's more to it."

"The warden might have known she was a wayfinder," I say. "Maybe they had a deal?"

Ren nods, admiration softening his gaze. "I think they did. Your mother and Uncle Bastian. He was the head of the Shadows before me. He must've known the empire wouldn't spare his newborn daughter, even if he betrayed his wife. Yuki's half Ainur. And any wayfinder could pose a threat to the empire. I bet Bastian arranged for her to be hidden in Abashi and made sure someone on the inside would protect her."

"The warden? But he was so cold."

He nods again. "He'd have to be, to keep up the ruse. One of the guards too. Both from old Ezo families. They would relish the idea of keeping a wayfinder from the emperor. It was their way of keeping the rebellion going."

I step closer. "Did your uncle tell you this? How *did* you find us?"

"Bastian's gone." Ren looks away, his jaw tightening. "No one's seen him since it happened. My father sent word, warning me that the emperor had dispatched Inspector Jade to Abashi. Jade only hunts two things: the ancient hearts and royalty. I suspected he was after your mother, and so I followed. I'd planned to scout ahead, to confirm your family was alive. But you . . . you were a surprise."

I lean over the railing, feeling sick. "No one knew I existed outside the prison walls until you found me. I don't even know who my father is. Don't *want* to know. Yuki's my only family. Can't you see why I have to save her?"

Ren's expression falters.

I tilt my chin, studying him, willing him to look at me. "Would you . . . can you . . . let go of the law, just this once?"

Ren stares out to sea before turning to me, his eyes searching mine like a blue flame that wants to offer warmth but can only burn. "Not a chance."

CHAPTER 25

THERE'S A DRAGON IN EZO BAY.
A real sea creature with slick iron scales and feather green moss fringing its muzzle. The old steamer's deck creaks underfoot, its weather planks slick with salt. I've lingered here to escape the claustrophobic cabins below. I feel trapped enough. But not even the dragon sighting soothes the chaos warring within me.

Yuki is Ren's cousin.

And he'll let the authorities execute her for a curse that's not her fault.

At least he won't finish her off himself. It hardly consoles me. If only I could change the laws—his obedience to them is infuriating. The law isn't the only moral compass. What of compassion? Love?

I swallow hard and clutch the deck's chipped railing. Ren's the only one standing between me and freedom. That, and Inspector Jade waiting at the docks.

A cold shiver snakes down my neck despite the warm breeze. I shrug against it, squeezing the hem of my elmwood coat.

Mother's secrets haven't aged well. They churn in me like poison. Of all the magic and chaos in the eight kingdoms, why hadn't she told me the truth? I was in prison because of a war my mother had fought and lost. Because of Yuki. Because of love.

My eyes squeeze shut, forcing away the thoughts. The ship docks in an hour. I need to focus on a plan—a path.

A tingle of energy shivers beneath my palms, and I get a strange feeling the path is trying to speak to me. "I want Yuki to be whole again," I whisper to it. "I want to see Ren without the law forcing his hand. I want to be free."

Mother always said that freedom isn't a place. But what is it?

I stretch my fingers across the water's surface far below, beckoning a thread of path to connect me to something Mother knew of this place—of her home. Fine threads of light zing across the ocean waves. A smile brushes my lips as I touch one of the threads. Suddenly, images pop into my mind. One thread slips into Silverwood, down dirt roads smelling of candied plums and charcoal stoves, into a shop with a wooden crest—a wolf with wings. The path lingers, a vision flashing of something ghosting through the walls like a frightened rabbit.

I pull back, surprised, and then move on to the next thread and the next, each one showing me some place in the city, perhaps where Mother used to walk. There are so many. Could one of these lead me to safety? To a different future than prison?

Mother, I wish you were here.

I test another path. It slithers up the sea dragon's scales, dripping with brine, and plunges into its fanged jaws. I jerk back, the thread snapping like frayed rope. What fate leads to a beast's maw?

The dragon shifts in the harbor, claws raking the silver sand. Golden eyes lock onto our ship—onto me. Does it sense my wayfinding? If the dragon were loose in the bay, it could sink our entire ship.

"Your face." Ren's mouth twitches with laughter, rejoining me on deck. "You look like a kid who just saw her first dragon."

I startle at his voice but move aside to make room for him at the rail. *Why did he come back? What more does he possibly have to say?*

My nerves tighten as Ren leans over the rail beside me, his

arm brushing mine. Hot splinters whirl in my stomach at the contact—*no*, it's just the sea jarring the boat.

"It *is* the first dragon I've seen," I say. "No one ever told me they still exist, or that your king keeps them in his harbor." I level him with a questioning look.

I've accepted that he believes he has to turn Yuki and me in to the port authorities—because he's terrified of his past and bound to the law—but I refuse to accept that he doesn't have a *choice*.

That's the part I can't forgive.

"You don't seem too surprised by the dragon," Ren says, watching me closely. "Awed, perhaps. The world is a lot bigger than most people think. Bigger than the eight kingdoms. Beyond that . . . who knows? But there are rumors."

He smiles, wistful, but his brow furrows. "Silverwood was once a hub of commerce and culture. You can still find old souls willing to spill tales of the beyond for a price. If it hadn't been for my curse, I might have become one of those explorers."

"Or a pirate," I tease, trying to relieve the tension curling between us.

His presence is both welcome and unwelcome. I can't think straight with all the problems he presents. I wish we could admire the shoreline together. I wish he could show me the city and where Yuki would have grown up if not for the war. I wish . . .

But an impassable wall separates us. Yuki's life—and mine—depend on staying on the other side of it.

"Silverwood is my home." Ren scans the coastline, searching for something, or remembering.

I step back, eyes catching on his wide shoulders, his dark hair tangling in the wind with an indigo gloss in the afternoon light. I tear my gaze away.

Along the pier, workers in midnight-blue tunics weave between cranes and ladders, swarming around the dragon like ants. It's the same scene embroidered on my map—one elaborate boat dock, built to hold one gigantic creature. Suddenly, the dragon's tail slashes through the water, upsetting the dock workers and smaller boats along the coast.

A wave surges toward us. The ship lurches as the dragon whips his tail again. I grip the railing, but too late. A wave crashes over the deck. I'm pitched forward, feet lost beneath me, as the boat tips. Then arms catch me. Ren's.

For one breathless moment, I'm weightless—nothing tethering me to the world except him. The ship rights itself, and my feet find solid wood. A boatsman shouts orders and instructs the passengers to go below, but no one listens.

My heart's a frenzy. The thought of getting swept overboard terrifies me. Sea spray drips from my hair and plinks onto the wood deck. I don't realize that I'm clutching Ren's arms and staring at his ever-changing blue eyes until my feet steady themselves. I drop my hands and look away, cheeks burning.

I turn back to Silverwood Bay and the sea dragon. Workers sling ropes across the beast's long snout and force it down onto the silver sand. It snarls, writhing against the constraints, and then goes still. Its head tilts toward our boat, eyes searching.

A pinch tightens in my chest. I know that look. I know what it's like to be trapped. The desire to fight, to flee, and the final attempt that surfaces—to freeze. That desperate stillness born of pain and wild hope that whispers, *maybe I'll survive this.*

The captain stands close to me, protective, or maybe just pretending. I need someone to lean on—but not him.

Mother used to be that person, but now I chart my course. Ren has chosen his path too. He made that much clear.

"How many dragons does Ezo have?" I ask, shifting the conversation.

It's not hard to do. Curiosity about Silverwood hums in the back of my mind. In a few minutes, I'll be stepping onto land I've dreamed of since childhood: the School of Ancient Hearts, the silver sand beaches, the star fortress. Excitement prickles my skin until reality drags it back. I'm arriving with a monster and a Shadow who thinks I belong in prison.

I grip the rail so hard my knuckles turn white.

"Only two dragons," he says, either oblivious to my discomfort or ignoring it. "That dock is for Rahmia, and that one over there is for Tyri. Extremely rare creatures, almost extinct now. Only a king or emperor can afford to keep them. These two have been royal guests for a decade. A gift from the Emperor of Taiga when Ezo became a vassal state. About the only good thing to ever come from that alliance." His voice sharpens, just for a breath. "The dragons are a central part of the electric tide festival. That's why they've been summoned."

"Summoned?" I know about the electric tide, just not the festival. Abashi also receives the glowing plankton that lights our shores with blue fluorescence below the ice.

"From the depths," he says, stretching a hand over the wide shimmer of sea. "They hibernate deep under the ocean, farther than anyone can dive. They only arise when called, or when summer stirs their playful side."

"Does everyone in Silverwood know so much about the daily life of sea dragons?" A rueful smile tugs at my lips.

"Everyone sees them during the festival," he says. "It's tradition to mark the coming of spring. I used to play jump rope with the beasts' whiskers."

"Really?" I lean closer, amused. "I can't picture you playing. It didn't hurt the creature, did it?"

What else does he know about this city? His family must be very influential to have so much knowledge. I suppose military captains, especially in the Shadows, are well received and generally in good standing.

"Course not. They're very patient beasts, dragons. At least, Rahmia and Tyri are. They've been trained, but they're still wild at heart."

A horn sounds, alerting the passengers to prepare for landing. Ren turns from the rail and calls for Zenri. The two speak in whispers, arguing about something. I make out a few details but not enough to piece together their plan.

"Ten minutes until we dock," Ren says, lifting his voice for my benefit. He presses the small glass vial into Zenri's palm.

The last drops of tonic.

"Right, I'll get the baggage." Zenri's voice wobbles as he pockets the vial. He offers me a phony salute and ducks around the topside kitchen galleys toward the lower decks and the hold.

I bristle as I intercept Ren. "My sister's not baggage."

"Of course not." He lowers a warning gaze, his eyes dark blue. "But the other passengers can't know that. And neither can anyone in Silverwood. Keep your voice down."

My spine stiffens, but I step closer, dropping my voice. "Our paths part at the docks, Ren."

He cocks his head, unruly hair falling across his brow. Somehow it makes him look less like a cold-hearted soldier and more like a homebound sailor. "I'm counting on it," he says. "Have you found a way out?"

The way he asks—*hopes for it*—gives me pause. But I'm no fool. Ren follows his head, not whatever is left of his heart.

"There's always a way," I say.

He motions for me to follow him. "Walk with me, Kira."

I hesitate, but whatever he's about to say might reveal his plans for turning us in. Our coats rustle together as he guides me toward the observation deck where a crowd has gathered to watch the glistening coast.

"What is it?" I cross my arms, holding them tight against my chest.

"I want to make a deal with you." His whisper is so close, his breath grazes my ear.

A swarm of butterflies stirs in my stomach—agitated, frantic. *A deal?*

His gaze is steady, challenging. I meet it, my lips set in a firm line. When his eyes lock onto mine, a dozen impossible paths hum beneath my skin.

"I can't break the law." It almost sounds like an apology. "It would be the end of me. But I can arrange for you to be pardoned. The law has a claim on you—you broke out of Abashi and abetted a monster. But I'll testify that I helped you escape. It's not a lie. Without me, you might not have survived."

I bristle, studying his cold blue eyes and trying to read the angles. It's obvious he's been working on this scheme for a while. But why? And I don't like him taking credit for my escape. "Won't they just sentence you for helping me?"

"They might." He tilts his head with a smile that dares the world to cross him. "But the Shadows have sway. We also follow orders, and if they knew who I worked for I doubt they'd want a scandal."

"What about Inspector Jade? He won't let you off easy. What's the cost?"

"Smart girl." He draws me close, arm warm at my waist, pressing us close within the crowd. All around us, people murmur and laugh, admiring the sunlight reflecting silver on the sand. His voice drops, "I need you to steal something for me."

I gape. "You want me to break the law for you? That's the same as stealing yourself! What's so important that you would sidestep your precious morals? Why me?"

"Do you expect me to answer all of those?"

I lift a brow. As if it would take him all day to answer three questions. "Fine," I relent, knowing too well that secrets come at a price. "Why me?"

"I don't want you in jail, Kira, or whatever punishment Jade comes up with." His eyes search mine, hoping for something—softness, maybe—but I don't give it to him.

"Then arrange a pardon without strings attached." I move to leave, tired of his half-help and half-truths.

"Kira, wait—"

I glance over my shoulder. I'll find another way. Without his help.

"I'll get you the pardon," he says, voice earnest, a warmth

to his face that has nothing to do with the weather. "Without anything in return. I'm sorry. I'm not used to—"

"Being kind?" I say, turning back to him. "Feeling?"

He lets out a trapped breath. "Dealing with girls . . . or extremely stubborn wayfinders."

"I can't tell which frightens you more, Captain Renjiro—wayfinders or girls." I return the smile, but a flicker of doubt still stirs. "What were you going to ask me to steal? I may have been born a prisoner, but I won't become a criminal to earn my freedom."

"It's not that kind of theft." A shrewd look in his eye. "But it takes a wayfinder to steal from the King of Ezo."

I blanch as the crowd presses in around us, a few couples gazing at the lustrous beaches. "Stealing would definitely make me a criminal," I whisper through clenched teeth. "I already see where this goes. I steal for you, and then I get thrown in jail. There's no guarantee you'll actually keep your word."

"It'll work if you don't get caught—"

I press a finger to his lips to silence him.

Instantly, I regret it. His lips are warm, and the startled flicker in his eyes twists my stomach into knots. I pull away.

"I have a deal for you, Ren," I say. "Can you get a pardon for Yuki?"

He jerks away, the answer written in the stiff lines of his shoulders. "No."

"But you have the power to," I press. "You found a way to spare me. What about your cousin? Free her, and I'll do it. Otherwise, find another wayfinder."

And we both know there isn't one.

He works his jaw, anger sweeping his eyes. "It would be a death sentence," he says. "For all of us. We've been over this, Kira. There's no cure. A pardon would just mean your sister is chained for the rest of her life. Do you want that?"

"I want her to *live!*"

I meet his gaze, unflinching, like I used to do in Abashi. "Yuki's life for the perfect theft. Do we have a deal?"

Ren closes his eyes, and when he opens them there is no warmth. Only ice.

"Deal," he says. "One demon in exchange for a crown."

My heart sinks to my toes. *Did he just say crown?*

CHAPTER 26

REN LEFT ME WITH A BRITTLE heart made of ice. One more disaster, one more secret, and it was bound to break me into a hundred tiny shards.

Steal the crown from the King of Ezo? What did I agree to? Why does he want it?

"Kira, you still up here?" Zenri calls from the stairwell.

"Just grabbing my things," I say as he reaches the top.

Zenri stops short, eyeing me with concern. "Are you all right? You and the captain arguing again?"

"No, just talking about dragons." My heart thuds at the half-truth, but I force myself to stay focused on the present.

I breathe deep, mulling my options. Ren will spare Yuki if I steal for him, but it could be a trap. The way he'd agreed to it felt like he'd bartered his soul. He'd been willing to pardon me, take the blame, ask for nothing. But freeing Yuki—a monster—is different.

It has a cost—one wrapped in blue threads and broken hearts.

Hopefully he keeps his word. If he needs a wayfinder for the job, then he has to keep his end of the bargain until the last moment, which means letting us escape Jade at the docks . . . Only, we didn't discuss that part.

Zenri waves a hand in front of my face. "He really bored

you stiff, huh? Captain can talk dragons *for hours*. Dangerous subject unless you need a nap." He pauses, then adds, "Thought you'd want to know Yuki's on deck. Captain brought her up."

"On deck? With him?" I gasp. Tension knots at the nape of my neck. I turn toward the lower deck, but Zenri steps in front of me, palms out.

"She'll be fine," he says. "Just get your things so we can leave this saints-forsaken ship. Captain gave her the last of the tonic. It'll calm her long enough—I hope—so we can get her somewhere safe. You trust me, don't you?"

I sigh. "Actually, I do."

My arms drop to my sides. I can't help surveying the pink scars carved across his bronze skin. He never told me how he got them.

"I'll get my things," I say. "Please keep an eye on Yuki."

"Of course," he says, holding the stairwell door open for me.

Below deck, I move quickly. If Yuki's already out in the crowd with Ren, I don't have much time. I'm grateful he allowed me a moment to put her into fresh clothes earlier, while she was out from the sedative.

A gong sounds—once, twice—followed by the sharp bark of a messenger.

"All passengers to the deck! Papers ready!"

It doesn't take long for me to pack. I finger Mother's elmwood coat, hidden beneath a warm fur-lined haori, as I step back on deck with a single bag slung over my shoulder.

There's a flurry of activity as passengers rummage through bags and cluster near the exit ramp. Towering above the ship, the Silverwood mountains frame the city and steal my attention. They rise above the bay, speckled with oak trees, bright green zelkova, and the soft blush of plum blossoms.

I'd only ever seen spring in my dreams.

A tingle runs over my arms, the hair rising with anticipation. What would it feel like to stand in Mother's homeland for the first time? Every taste, touch, and smell filled with meaning and purpose. Clusters of sunlit houses and winding cobblestone streets stretch for miles. The port unfolds like a scroll: long piers and a wide circular harbor. Footsteps thud across the deck behind me.

I catch sight of Ren and Zenri. A groggy, irritated Yuki wobbles between them as they make slow progress toward the exit ramp. I push through a few startled passengers to reach her.

"Yuki," I say, my heart ticking up a notch.

She doesn't make eye contact. A long, thin navy robe covers her shoulders, lined in white fur like mine, her pale face hidden in the shadows of a deep hood. Long sleeves cover her missing hands. She lists slightly to the left, dragging one leg as she hobbles between the two men who, in another life, might have been friends.

Her posture slumps with resignation. To anyone else, she probably looks drunk.

"How long will the tonic last?" I ask, sliding in beside her.

Ren's sharp gaze flicks toward me. Without a word, he transfers Yuki's weight to me with a graceful movement. The ice in his eyes needles me. Is it that bad that our deal obliges him to help her? She's his cousin.

"Less than thirty minutes." Zenri speaks up, shifting Yuki's weight on his shoulders. "We need to make quick work of it and get out of here."

He's right. We don't have much time to get through the next checkpoint before my sister erupts again. And this time there won't be chains to hold her.

Yuki's head jerks toward the exit ramp. What catches her eye along the harbor? Is it the redbrick warehouse strung up with lights, the people in their fancy kimono and wool suits, the warm air tasting of burnt charcoal, sweet plums, and spicy salt? Or is it something more elemental, a deeper scent we'd learned to recognize in prison—blood.

"More like ten minutes," Ren grumbles before strolling ahead like he just wants this to be over. He pulls a stack of papers from his coat and thrusts it at the nearest guard on the ramp.

Yuki sags against me, her head lolling to my shoulder with a low growl. I cast Zenri a worried glance.

"Keep going," he whispers. "Act normal. We don't want to draw attention."

"Riiiight." I say, plastering on a smile.

"So," he adds lightly, "is it what you dreamed of? Silverwood? Seshu is far better in my opinion. Warmer."

"I don't know." I scan the choppy water, the guarded ramp, the noisy crowd. "I haven't exactly seen much of it yet."

I adjust my grip around Yuki, her weight leaning heavily into me. She doesn't flinch or bare her teeth. The tonic's working—for now—but it won't last long.

As we step off the ramp, Yuki's long hair whips out from her hood, blowing haphazardly against her face. She straightens, as if sensing she is home. Stands tall, regal even. How Mother would've wanted us to come home.

My boots sink into soft sand. Home. It doesn't feel any different, but I want it to. I belong here. *We belong.*

"We made it," I whisper, hoping the real Yuki hears me.

"Are we . . . home?" She leans her head against my shoulder for a fleeting second, and I have a feeling she's thinking about Mother.

It should have been the three of us standing here. I'd brought Yuki this far, kept my promise in only the barest, scrappiest form. Now I have to do the rest—keep her safe. Even if it means becoming a thief.

A crown, he'd said.

At the first checkpoint, Ren waves the forged documents with all the casual irritation of a man used to command. He mutters a few words, his tone clipped, posture sharp, like the Shadow captain I'd first met. The papers must be fake, at least the ones for Yuki and me.

Ren gestures toward us, and I freeze.

The guard squints, eyes shifting from Zenri to me and Yuki slumped between us like a drunken girl.

"What's he saying?" I whisper.

"No time," Zenri says, pulling Yuki's hood down further. "Help me, will you? She's heavier than she looks."

We hoist my sister up by the shoulders and haul her between the guards. The sand gives way beneath my feet, making it difficult to walk. Ren strides up the beach, toward what looks like a second checkpoint.

I need a backup plan, one that includes Ren for the time being but gives me leverage if he changes his mind about Yuki. A tingling current hovers over my skin, the path nudging me. I close my eyes and reach for it: an alley tavern, at the end of the lane, cider apples, crest of a winged wolf.

The tavern appears in my mind with its faded crest, a blue hum around it, a place Mother once tread. That could be the answer. My best bet. I'll keep my deal with the captain, but I didn't tell him *when* I'd steal the crown. I'm buying time for Yuki and me. I only hope the tavern has something to help my sister. I can't fend off a full-grown *yajuu* alone.

Zenri trudges forward with ease. "There's the last customs checkpoint," he says over Yuki's low growls. Other passengers glance at us, whispering.

Ahead, the warehouse looms, redbrick and sealed tight. Guards in black robes line the cobblestone, hands resting on sword hilts. Each one wears the blue crest of a dragon encircled by plum blossoms—the city emblem.

"The only way into the city is through here," Zenri explains. "It's the customs house that once processed international trade. The only one in Ezo."

"What does it do now?" I ask.

"They screen banned goods, magic, and criminals. Force quarantine on weary travelers. The usual," Zenri explains, his eyes sliding meaningfully to Yuki.

My breath tightens. "Does the captain have a plan to get us through?"

"He's never without a plan."

Yuki growls and thrashes her head, walloping Zenri on the shoulder. He sucks in a breath.

"Yuki!" I scold.

The hood slips, and my sister's dark eyes turn on me. There's a widening, a flicker of recognition, and then her eyes roll back, drunk on the tonic coursing through her veins.

"Sorry about that," I whisper to Zenri.

"When you're done chatting, perhaps you'd both like to stop for tea," Ren drawls, stopping alongside us with an irritated quirk in his brow.

"Jasmine oolong please," Zenri says longingly.

"Oolong can wait." Ren nods to the singular one-man stations positioned across the harbor. Next to each station, the black-robed warriors turn, watching us. Five of them stride in our direction, black capes and rifles pinned to their broad shoulders, a sword at each of their sides.

"Those aren't the usual guards," Zenri points out. "They're from the castle." He steps in front of Yuki and me, shielding us as he stands beside the captain.

"Change of plans. Inspector Jade's already been here." Ren eyes the approaching guards.

"Are you going to turn me in?" My eyes narrow on him, reminding him of the plan to request a pardon.

"I always keep my word," he says, a flash of dark blue in his eyes. "And I hope you will too. We need to split up. They already know who you are."

"You mean . . . we're going to run?" I ask.

"Kira, I wanted to—" He hesitates, glancing down, a flush to his face that I hope has to do with the cold wind and not what he's about to say. "I know I don't have a right to ask, but . . . trust me. Stay safe. I'll find you."

Trust him?

Before I can reply, Ren turns toward the approaching guards. They halt, suspicion clouding their hardened faces.

"I must've been gone a very long time for you to approach me this way," Ren says in a calm voice, bearing all the icy indifference of the Shadow Officer. "Or perhaps I showed you the wrong papers."

"Sir." One of the guards steps forward and bows stiffly. "Your vessel was two days overdue. The Imperial Inspector ordered full inspections of delayed ships. In case of . . . pirating."

Ren arches a brow. "Do I look like a pirate?"

In unison, the soldiers draw their swords a few inches from the scabbard. He must have the countenance of a pirate after all.

But the lead guard raises a hand, motioning the others back. "Stand down. We've been ordered to inspect your possessions and company. If you resist, we'll—"

Ren turns back to me and winks.

Winks. Of all the signals he could give.

Yuki shifts uncomfortably at my side. I brace, rehearsing my plan to escape to the Winged-Wolf Tavern after the captain initiates the pardon process with the guards.

"Go," Zenri whispers. "If anyone comes after you, I'll hold them off."

Thank you. I mouth the words, wishing I could tell him that I won't be meeting them right away, that I have a plan of my own.

I turn and run, pulling Yuki along. Her hood slips as we dart toward the backside of the warehouse. *Please don't let anyone notice. Please.*

But everyone's attention is drawn to something else. After rounding the corner, I glance over my shoulder.

A flash of silver. Ren stands tall, sword unsheathed, the blade catching the sun like a signal flare across the ice. Every guard and passerby turns. Metal clinks as one by one the soldiers slide their swords back into their scabbards.

"I-I'm sorry . . . sir, my lord," the lead guard stammers.

I squint from where Yuki and I hunker behind the warehouse

barrels. Ren lifts the sword higher, chin angled, eyes shadowed beneath furrowed brows. Calm. Unmovable. Why is everyone so captivated?

"Sir? Is that all?" Ren levels the guards with a look that could freeze even my blood.

I grip Yuki's arm tightly, holding her behind me.

It's the same sword that had cut through the *yajuu* at the circus, the same ice-cracked sheath inlaid with mother-of-pearl. But now I see what I'd missed before. My gaze drifts to the pommel and the crest engraved into the handle: a rabbit in the talons of a half-moon.

His mother's crest.

The crowd bows, dropping to their knees in unison with the guards.

"My p-p-prince," the guard stammers.

CHAPTER 27

THE SOLDIERS DOUBLE OVER in fearful, rigid bows. A hush ripples across the warehouse center as carriages creak to a halt and heads crane toward the man they just called *prince*.

Zenri blows a stray hair off his brow, completely unfazed. Whispers take flight on the wind.

"Is that the prince?" a woman hisses to my right. "The one banished seven years ago."

"But he died in the Winterwilds," another mutters.

"He came back for the coronation!"

Yuki nudges my side. "Kira . . . let's go."

It's the clearest she's sounded all day. My feet turn to follow her, to run. But curiosity pulls me in another surprising direction. One cool and ethereal and so full of ice.

Ren's gaze meets mine for a brief second. Our paths connect as his eyes shiver over mine, freezing me in place. He turns the black pommel in his hand, like a signal. What is he trying to tell me? That's when I notice that Zenri is no longer by his side. What are they up to?

The captain flashes a dangerous grin at the guards. "Last one to notify the king of my return will be fed to the dragons. And you"—he points at the soldier bowing before him—"take some guards and tell Inspector Jade I wish to see him. There's a *yajuu* loose on the docks."

I fling myself behind the warehouse, out of sight, and bang the back of my head against the wall. How could I have been so stupid?

"He tricked me." My fists clench as the docks erupt into chaos.

"Your boyfriend's a rat," Yuki growls. "But at least he's a prince."

I blink at her lucid words, snarky even. The tonic must be fading. Shouts ring out past us as the crowd on the dock panics. Maybe Ren isn't trying to turn us in but give us a window of escape. Buying us time. *Trust me,* he'd said.

Never trust a guard.

Or a captain. Or Ren. Or . . . a prince.

Then that means Yuki is . . . royalty.

Paths jumble in my mind, too painful to hold. *Why couldn't I be the princess in my own story? Is her life more precious than mine? Is that why Mother made me promise to keep her safe?*

No, she made Yuki promise to protect me too. I study my sister, but am met with only a confused stare. She doesn't know who she is. *Royalty.*

"We need to go," I say, gripping her arm.

I turn and nearly slam into the rough hands of a guard. Three of them, in matching midnight-blue uniforms, glare down at us. The same guards who'd tried to intercept Captain Ren. Only standing taller, more confident. And with rifles aimed at our hearts.

Fear tugs at my chest. But that's never gotten me anywhere. A wayfinder always moves forward, always finds a way.

"Don't shoot." I step in front of Yuki, using my body as a shield, no matter how small or ineffectual it may be.

I stare down the end of one rifle and then the other, until I notice the middle guard with sandy hair and eyes full of disdain.

The guard smirks. "Prince said there'd be a demon on the

docks. 'Keep 'em alive,' he said. What kind of order is that coming from the Demon Prince of Ezo?"

The guard next to him pokes his rifle into Yuki's shoulder.

"Careful what you look for," Yuki snarls.

Two of the guards stagger back, but not the tall one. "Look at that, boys—a flesh and blood *yajuu*. Inspector Jade is looking for her too. Even has a bounty."

"Don't touch her," I say. Calm breaths, focus on the life around me.

It's hard to see life when the three lives before me are nothing but dirt in my eyes. But I know Mother's words are true. To find the right path, I must first see the life around me, listen to it. I look past the proud and angry faces into their lifeblood. The same as my own.

The guard to my left shifts his feet, nervous to be so close to a monster. Yuki growls and rubs shoulders with me. I'm not sure which I'm most afraid of, the guns or my sister breathing against my neck.

"Let me take them," she whispers hoarsely.

"Wait," I say, fearing the wrong move may cost our lives.

Where is the path forward? What if it's not one I would condone? My throat goes tight. *How far will I go to keep my promise to Mother?*

"There's no time to wait, little girl." The tall guard whips out a pair of chains as the one to the right keeps his rifle leveled at Yuki's heart.

My jaw goes tight. "People aren't meant for chains."

Then, with desperation on the verge of stupidity, I knock the barrel of the gun upright and shove my sister back against the warehouse wall.

"The window!" I shout. I grab Yuki and hoist her up.

She's one step ahead and bounds without my assistance, pulling herself through the window by her elbows. The guards rush forward. I scurry to pull myself through the open window, but the blond-haired guard grabs my legs. I'm caught halfway through the windowsill, kicking and biting my lip at the pain in my side.

Yuki tries to grab me under the arms, but she can only anchor me with the crook of her elbow. My stomach scrapes against the brick ledge. I kick at the guard. Once. Twice. Finally, I land a solid heel to his nose and roll inside.

I scramble to my feet with a wince. "This way!"

We run, hurtling past startled warehouse employees, over crates, and under hanging baskets of squawking chickens. Shouts call out behind us.

"Which way?"

"My job be hanged if we don't catch 'em!"

Leaning on years of survival instinct, I follow my gut. Left then right, over this crate, and now through the loft window onto the swinging hook. I hold Yuki and make the jump, my sister hugging me as tight as she's able without hands. The hook sways and sends us flying into the back of a delivery wagon full of damp seaweed.

"Gross." My arms tangle in the wet mass, practically swimming. *Squelch, squish.*

The heavy warehouse doors swing open, releasing a swarm of angry guards and dock workers. Ren and Zenri are nowhere to be seen, almost as though they'd expected this. Expected us to run in the chaos and get away.

He was clever, I'd give him that, using extraneous circumstances to prevent him from carrying out the law. It still satisfied his ludicrous moral code. But he wouldn't let us run forever. Not when I have a deal to finish.

The crunch of heavy boots sounds close.

"Hide," I whisper, gesturing to the seaweed.

Yuki rubs a wet frond from her hair. "I didn't hide before, darling, and I won't hide now." A wicked gleam cuts across her eyes as she stares hungrily at the guards. She crouches, one arm on the wagon rim, ready to pounce.

"No!" I place a hand on her arm.

Yuki stiffens. Her serpentine eyes slice to mine. "I'll give you two seconds to think of a better word than 'no.'"

Panic takes over. *How much of the tonic has worn off? Can we get to the tavern without being seen?*

"The horse," I cry, pointing to the dull brown creature at the front of the wagon.

"To eat?" Yuki wrinkles her nose.

"No! To get out of here."

"That's a relief." Yuki wiggles out of the seaweed like an eel and then slips over the back of the horse pulling the wagon. With one quick bite, the leather snaps. She tilts her head, motioning for me to follow.

The horse shivers beneath us, stamping with a nervous snort.

I sit at the front, Yuki behind me with her nubbed wrists wrenched around my middle. I press my knees into the horse, but it doesn't budge. Ears twisted back, the horse neighs and shuffles sideways.

Soldiers shout behind us, and a shot rings out.

"Anytime now," Yuki hisses.

I throw a frantic kick into the horse's soft flank. It bolts out from the delivery wagon. Bullets ring, followed by puffs of smoke. The horse runs faster, and my jaw goes tight, teeth clanking, as we fly over cobblestone.

Yuki clings to me as we weave through the dockside streets and into a narrow residential area. I grip the horse's mane, lowering myself on its neck and feeling which direction it will take as if it's a part of me. Blue threads of path form around the horse's muzzle and over its ears, telling it which way to go.

The horse slows to a jarring trot as the stone turns to dirt. Tall, paint-faded houses dot a pedestrian walkway lined with old trees. Here, copper gas lamps perch on every corner and plum trees cast long shadows in the late afternoon light. Yuki loosens her hold on me as the horse slows to a slouchy walk.

"These are stores," I say, pointing at the nearest house with muted yellow paint and a striped awning protruding from the first floor. "The owners must live on the upper floors."

Just like the tavern I'd seen in the path.

"We're close."

"Close to what?" Yuki's stomach rumbles. "Food?"

"Somewhere safe," I say.

A familiar tug pulls at me . . . wending deeper down the street. I can't explain it. The old horse pulls to a stop at the next crossroad to nibble at a patch of garden. It tears at a prickly bush, trying to reach the sweet grass beneath it. A sign creaks from the nearest townhome: Winged-Wolf Tavern. I lean over and sweep myself off the horse's back. Yuki lands beside me with a soft thud, crouching.

"Here?" she hisses.

Our eyes connect, and she jerks away, but not before I catch the flicker of curiosity. Like she's wondering how long I'll stay by her side. How long she'll retain control over her sanity.

"Let's find it together," I say. Then, slowly, I place my arm around her and gently pull her up. Her long brown hair falls across her back in grizzly tangles. Suddenly, she slumps against me. I gulp at the rank smell of week-old cargo ale wafting from her and force my eyes past her pointed teeth and knobby wrists. Her eyes slide to me, the narrow slits widening for one lucid moment.

"Kira," she says as her lips curve into the briefest of smiles. "You brought us home."

My heart swells. My sister is still in there. And there's something beautiful about her, even as a monster.

CHAPTER 28

"YOU LOOKIN' FOR TROUBLE?" A deep voice purrs from the bar. "Because we only take the worst."

The Winged Wolf Tavern is near-empty save for the woman behind the bar and a few cloaked strangers gathered near the fire. We step inside, greeted only by spice-scented flames in the open hearth and smoke in our eyes. The door clanks behind us.

"Pull up a chair," the woman orders, leaning over the bar with narrowed pewter eyes.

The men at the fire stop their game of Dragon Snap to study us.

"I need to speak to the owner." My voice catches on the smoke.

One of the men sticks out a muddy boot to block our path. "Not 'til you spill your worst. Costs a secret to enter this establishment."

I blanch. *Costs a secret?*

What could I tell them to get information, or were they just toying with me for sport? Suddenly, the man gives a high-pitched scream.

I jump and stare as the man howls and then clamps his lips shut, squeezing his outstretched leg. Yuki's bitten into it and spits out a wad of torn fabric, blood dribbling down her chin.

"Yuki!" I drag her back.

She wipes her mouth with the back of her long sleeve and shrugs. "He said to give him our worst."

I exhale, deep. The other men have all jumped to their feet, daggers and fists at the ready.

"Enough," the bartender shouts. She slides over the counter, a flash of black robes and metal cuffs, and strides toward us. "Out of the way, Rogin."

She jabs a small clay jar at the man nursing his wounded leg. "Pour this over it—not the whole jar, you idiot."

"I'm doomed!" Rogin wails, holding his leg.

"You'll only turn into one if it's shifted when it bites you." The bartender squeezes the man's shoulder, then her eyes slide to us. "Welcome to the Winged-Wolf." She extends open palms to Yuki and me. "I'm Sorachi, the owner of this fine establishment. And your secret is safe with me."

"What . . . is this place?" I ask, keeping one eye on Yuki. "Are you one of the soothsayers who sells secrets for gold?"

"It's a bar." Sorachi grins. "And not gold. I only take silver. Or better secrets."

"And how—"

"Oh no, it's my turn to ask a question," the wiry woman interrupts. Her pewter eyes spark with interest beneath her sweaty brow. "How did you find me?"

I struggle to find words. Under no circumstance would I tell anyone about wayfinding. Why hadn't the bartender asked about Yuki instead? Biting someone isn't exactly a normal welcome.

"I saw the sign outside."

"You're a brilliant liar." Sorachi laughs and runs her finger down a ring-studded ear. "And you . . . you are worth one hundred million zeni—to anyone dumb enough to think Inspector Jade would actually pay them."

I shiver, thinking of the frigid man who'd so callously stood over my mother's dying moments. The cool way Jade's eyes had raked over me in Ranzan, as if I were a collectible for his shelf. He too had known about my wayfinding. *Is my secret safe from no one?*

I force away the thought, homing in on what had drawn me to the tavern in the first place. Something was hidden here that I needed. I'd seen it in the path.

Yuki licks the blood from her lips and eyes the three men by the fire hungrily. She cracks her jaw with a wide yawn, making a show of her pointed teeth. One of the men releases a knife.

"Stop," Sorachi snaps.

But the blade sings through the air. It pierces the spot where Yuki had just stood. I spin around, searching for my sister between the papered walls and cramped tables.

Yuki stands behind the man who threw the knife, his neck wedged tightly in the crook of her elbow, his face purpling.

"Yuki," I begin calmly.

Our eyes meet, but they're not Yuki's half-sedated eyes. These are round, moonlike orbs pulsing with hate.

"Yuki, put him down," I say, forcefully.

Sorachi turns. "Now you've done it."

"Done what?" I snap, irritation getting the better of me.

"You let her bite someone. Now she's going to shift and ruin my shop." The bartender slides back over the counter and rummages carelessly through bottles. "You didn't give her enough tonic before bringing her into the city."

"We ran out . . ."

"H-help me," the man in Yuki's grasp sputters. He claws at her arm until his hands begin to twitch. I swallow hard.

Sorachi breaks a bottle against the counter and then shakes her head, muttering. "He doesn't pay me enough for this . . . cleaning up other people's messes. What's he think I am, a babysitter?"

I dash to the bar and search the bottles next to Sorachi. "You have *yajuu* tonic here, don't you?"

A deep line forms on her brow as she continues her search

without so much as a glance at me. "Look over there. It's in a silver bottle with a—"

"A silver rabbit," I whisper and instantly wish I'd kept my mouth shut.

Sorachi's eyes narrow, but she nods. Another bottle breaks as she rummages through the shelves.

Yuki sniffs at the man and then drops him with a dissatisfied expression before her eyes slide to the next. The remaining two men press their backs against the wall and scoot toward the door. I'm torn between confronting my sister and searching for the vial. The latter is our only hope but . . .

I sprint to Yuki and place a hand on her shoulder, willing her to remember herself. Ren was healed once. I have to believe there is still reason in her.

A low growl vibrates from her throat. She turns on me with a vicious swipe, and I jump back. Something jerks, hard, at my sleeve, and when I look down, Mother's elmwood robe is in tatters. Torn fragments hang from Yuki's fangs as she tears the coat from me.

My sister's eyes waver, a deep crease forming on her brow as she shakes off the elmwood scraps—memories of Mother stitched into every strand.

Ignoring the pain, I seize the moment and run to the counter where Sorachi searches for the tonic. Yuki steps on the elmwood scraps, momentarily distracted. I take a deep breath and spread my hands over the shelves of half-empty bottles. A path of light shimmers beneath my fingers.

Up three shelves and twice over to the right. One glance at the broken glass shards on the floor tells me Sorachi won't mind what I'm about to do. I jump onto the counter, pulling myself up, and climb the shelf. It wobbles beneath my weight, tilting. I freeze, waiting for the swaying to stop.

A man screams.

"Forget it," Sorachi sighs, and pulls a gun from under the

counter. She fires one shot into the air, blasting a hole into the apartment above. Then she aims at my sister.

"Wait! I found the bottle!" A tiny silver stoppered cup with a rabbit in the moon sits on the highest shelf. I stretch my hand, extending it until my fingers shake.

Ban!

Smoke wisps from the gunshot. Yuki turns, her mouth gaping in shock. Her eyes whip to Sorachi with outrage and then to me. Something dies inside of me.

I promised to keep her safe.

Yuki staggers, a dark circle oozing from a hole in her cloak. She presses an arm to her wounded side, hissing with rage.

Sorachi's finger curls around the trigger, her lips smirking with confident precision as she aims again. "Just try me. That was a warning shot."

Yuki growls, her matted hair hanging limp over her face. Then a shudder ripples across her skin as it begins to shift, dark fur covering her pale skin, back arching, claws appearing where she had no hands. She hobbles one step forward, then another, toward the counter. A low, angry roar rattles the tavern.

It's no longer my sister standing there but a great black bear with bottomless eyes—just like the bear at Abashi, only much smaller. My sister has changed into a monster.

Time has run out.

Eyeing the silver bottle, I jump. The shelves below me crumble. My fingers latch onto the tonic. And I fall. Flasks, bottles, and pitchers crash around me, breaking over my head as I land on my back. I groan, writhing on the floor.

Ban!

Sorachi pulls the trigger again, this time hitting Yuki in the leg. She howls in pain, dark animal eyes locked on the bartender like hot coals.

"Stop!" I shout, though my fall has winded me. "I've got it."

I crawl forward and pull myself up next to Sorachi. I have no idea how to administer the tonic. I'm hoping it will return her to human form and to a lucid state. Fisting the bottle, I thrust it out for Sorachi.

She unclips a canister from her waist belt and slaps the potion into it with rapid precision. Before I can even ask how she plans to administer the solution, she loads it into a narrow pipe and fires.

Yuki roars, her bear teeth snapping the air. A dart sticks out of the black fur, right over where the heart should be. She sways, once, twice, and then collapses to the floor with a heavy thud.

I shoot a reproachful look at the bartender before vaulting over the bar and kneeling beside the bear. "Yuki? Can you hear me?"

Slowly, my sister-turned-bear returns to her human form, shrinking until her thin body lies flat against the floor. Arms sprawled at her sides, her mouth twists in a look of pain.

"You didn't have to shoot her!" I snap, checking Yuki's vitals miserably.

She's alive.

I check the original bullet wounds, the ones leaking crimson over Yuki's thin coat now turned to rags. The skin is healing, shrinking the size of the wounds that made clean shots through her back and arm. Sorachi hands me a blanket to wrap over her.

"*Yajuu* heal themselves pretty well so long as it's not the brain or heart." Sorachi wipes down her gun and reholsters it beneath the counter. "Still, can't say that I like having one here."

"What about that man?" I nod toward the unconscious man near the fire. "Is he . . ."

"He'll be fine." She shrugs. "Rogin and Harlow will come back for him. The cowards. Good thing you found this place. It may be the last safe place for you."

"Safe?"

This tavern is anything but safe.

I salvage what's left of my mother's robe and then make a surreptitious search of the shelves again. Blue threads of path tug at me, warm and familiar. Whatever had called me to this place was still hidden behind these walls. It wasn't the tonic.

"Come on," she drawls, as if we'd just had tea and rice cakes. "Bring her upstairs. I want to introduce you to someone."

"Who?"

"You'll see." Sorachi draws back a hanging partition for a spiral staircase behind the counter. "But first, welcome to what's left of the School of Ancient Hearts."

CHAPTER 29

HOME. THE PLACE WHERE Mother grew up—these floors she walked on, this tavern she may have spent the night in. Every step was leading me here. Hope flutters to my throat, begging for a chance to see a piece of my mother's past. Shouldering Yuki, I climb up the spiral staircase.

The School of Ancient Hearts was destroyed during the war, the voice of reason cruelly reminds me. I pause on the top step with an audible creak. Mother had spun that story a dozen times when we were little, a tale of flame, death, betrayal. How the school was destroyed in the war, the magic of dragon hearts lost.

So what am I walking into?

Sorachi turns on the second-floor landing, long shadows obscuring her pewter eyes, but I swear a hardened flash of suspicion crosses her face. I squeeze into the tiny hallway, barely wide enough for two people. Is she worried about Yuki turning against us again? Or does she have doubts about me too?

"Where is this school?" I ask, meeting her suspicion with my own.

"It's more a sanctuary now," Sorachi says. "You'll see."

Instead of leading me down the hall, she turns to the nearest wall, facing a large portrait of a young man. I nearly jump out of my skin.

Captain Ren stares back at me from the inky brush strokes. His dark blue eyes smile, and the lips my hand once brushed curve into the faintest mischievous grin. His blue-black hair glows like an iron kettle pulled from the flame. Even in a painting, Ren is like fire to my icy heart, both welcoming and tormenting.

"Handsome, isn't he?" Sorachi teases. "The Demon Prince of Ezo."

"Is that what they call him?" I say, horribly aware of the heat crawling up my face.

"Do *you* call him by a different name?" Sorachi raises a brow.

My cheeks burn hotter. But before I can answer, she lifts the painted scroll, revealing a sliding door behind Ren's face.

"This way," she calls, already stepping through. "Watch your head."

I duck beneath the low frame. Yuki sags against my back as I turn and carefully descend a narrow staircase. The natural light above fades, and cold, stale air presses against my lungs. My thoughts linger on the portrait, the smooth brushstrokes of ink and vibrant colors pulled from the earth: cinnabar, tourmaline, charcoal, even flecks of gold.

What is a painting like that doing in a dying tavern? And of Ren no less—the prince.

"Who runs this place?" I ask, reaching the final step.

"I do," Sorachi says. "Though there's not much left to manage. It's a home of sorts, for the last masters of dragon magic, like Prince Renjiro."

"Captain Ren?" I stagger, caught off guard by the uneven ground beneath my feet.

Yuki nearly tumbles off my back.

Sorachi jumps the last two steps with a dull thud. "Interesting. I thought you'd be on better terms with him by now. *Captain.*" She imitates a stiff voice, laughing. "He was born with a gift, an abnormality much like wayfinding. He can sense it, the magic in others. Probably what drew him to you, if it's true that you're a wayfinder."

"How do you know so much? Who *are* you?" A familiar, untrusting cold wraps around me.

She doesn't answer right away. Instead, she unclips a velvet case from her belt and opens it, revealing a handful of luprite stones. "You're not the only one left with an ancient heart," she says. "The emperor didn't catch everyone."

Soft golden light glows in the palm of her hand, illuminating a cavernous room.

My breath catches, and I reach out to touch one of the cold limestone walls. "It's a cave in the middle of the city."

"Yes, but it wasn't always here." Sorachi strides forward, slotting the luprite pieces into waiting lanterns, which flare to life with yellow-green flames.

The chamber alights like the sun shimmering across a pond. I tilt my head up at the domed ceiling, wondering what part of the city lies above.

"Pull up a chair." She points at the far end of the cavern, where mismatched furniture lies scattered like a crow's nest.

I ease Yuki down into the least moth-eaten armchair and check her wounds. Her face is peaceful now—the tonic doing its work. I tuck a matted strand of hair behind her ear and glance around. Glowing lanterns anchor into the wall every few feet along with weapons, shields, and crates of rolled-up parchment.

"The cave splits into six shafts," Sorachi says, swinging a torch toward a branching tunnel. "This one goes to the castle, this to the harbor, and this to our rooms. The history of this place and the ancient hearts is written on the wall."

She raises the torch to a series of names and symbols etched in stone. I squint, wondering if Mother's name is written here.

"The school was near the palace ages ago, before it was burned to the ground." Her lips curl in disgust. "We were forced into hiding, those of us who escaped. Your mother was among them. She was like an auntie to me."

She clears her throat and paces the wall of names. "My family's been in the mining business for generations. Sorachi Steel, Sorachi Silver, we ran it all, even the coal mines in the North."

"You've lived in the North?" I lean forward.

"Yes." Her smoke-gray eyes soften in understanding, but there's pain behind them hard as steel. She swallows and continues. "When I was gifted a heart by a dragon, my grandparents decided to move the family to Silverwood so I could train under a master. Most children possessing a heart lived at the boarding school, but my grandparents insisted we stay together. The ore smelting business is a tough one, and after so many years of extracting and dividing metals, we knew that what stays together is strongest."

"Sounds familiar," I say. "My mother would have done the same."

Sorachi nods. "We relocated here and started a new silver mine for the king. It was very lucrative, not just for silver but lead, copper, and sulfide ore. It caved in during the war, taking my grandparents with it." Sorachi runs a hand over two names carved in the wall. "I had no interest in mining after that. I convinced the king that it was impossible to reclaim the mine and that most of the silver had already been stripped. A sunk cost.

"The king permitted me to build on the land for donating the last of the silver. And now . . ." She fans her arms out, indicating the vast walls of the glittering cave. "Now I have the Winged-Wolf Tavern and this, all we could save from the school. Mostly parchments, a few old relics, and training instruments."

"I'm sorry," I say. "About your family. It must be hard living in the same place that they—"

"Thank you." Sorachi smiles softly. "But it's an important reminder of what we're fighting for."

Fighting for?

The war ended ages ago. Questions pelt my mind like snow

in a flurry, all clumped together and confusing. But the urgency of Yuki's condition tugs at me. And Sorachi did know my mother . . .

"Is there any way you can help my sister? That's why I'm here. I made a promise to my mother to keep her safe. Perhaps if you told me your magic—"

"That," Sorachi says. "Should be your biggest secret. But it seems your mother and Prince Ren didn't warn you enough about that. People will do terrible things to control the hearts. And wayfinding is the one that feeds them all."

I press my lips together, suppressing the questions bubbling to the surface and focus on only one. "Can you help her?"

Sorachi eyes my sister. "I can't make her human again if that's what you're asking. I've enough tonic to last the week but . . ." Her voice trails off as she circles Yuki, lifting her hood, checking her pulse, her wounds. She pulls up a sleeve and dangles Yuki's limp arm in the air.

"What can you do?" I ask.

"I can give her hands." Her full lips spread into a smile. "But only while she's under the tonic, mind you. I'm a metallurgist. The art of bending alloys. A useful daughter to a silver miner."

"Hands," I breathe, scarcely believing it. "How long will it take?"

"A week at the most. I can extract and bend the metals, but I still need fire for the smelting. It'll also take time to cool."

"It'll be more like gloves than hands, won't it?" I ask, my excitement cooling. Yuki still wouldn't be able to use them if they were metal.

Sorachi purses her lips. "You don't know much about the ancient hearts, do you? A true master's magic is infused with a piece of their soul. We are talking about heart magic after all. *If* I make them right, the metal should respond to your sister's thoughts and move like a normal hand."

"Thank you." I struggle to contain my surging hope. "My mother never spoke of the other hearts. It's fascinating."

"Wayfinding works the same way," Sorachi says. "When you see a path, it connects to your soul for better or worse. I don't know all the details, but the hearts change you. It's part of you."

I wonder at her words and how the path has affected me. Does it have a cost? It's clear that hers does, and I've already wagered more than I can afford with Ren. What does Sorachi want? My jaw tightens. "How can I repay you?"

"Ah, well . . . you are the last wayfinder. And we need one if we're going to restore Ezo."

"You mean, free it from the empire?"

"Yes," she says. "The Emperor of Taiga is cruel, but those who stand by him are worse. Inspector Jade gathers a child from every vassal ruler and keeps them hostage in the capital of Taiga. None of the kingdoms dare defy the emperor because their children will die."

"That's awful," I say, casting a glance at Yuki. She too would've been part of the royal family then.

Had Jade tried to take her or Ren? Is that why Mother ran away with Yuki as a baby? To protect her from Inspector Jade?

"He collects those skilled in the ancient hearts as well. If anyone finds out that we have one, we'll be contracted into his services and then into the Imperial Army. Everyone thinks we just want to join the Emperor of Taiga, that it's an honor." She laughs. "Lies. We want our freedom back, and the only way to do that is to destroy the hostage system. Those rings on Jade's fingers stand for every hostage he's taken."

"I don't see how I can help." I comb out knots in my sister's hair with my fingers.

"Just follow through on your bargain with Prince Ren. I'll teach you what you need to know to accomplish the task."

"You know about that? He wants me to steal a crown. Is he still going to pardon Yuki and me?" My voice hardens, wary of betrayal. "It's not exactly a safe plan."

I have no guarantee either Sorachi or Ren will keep their end of the bargain. But if Ren did pardon Yuki—and Sorachi could give her hands—my sister would be safe, a little more whole. I need only to find more tonic, and eventually the cure. It *has* to exist, despite what Ren says. There's no future without it.

"The right path never guarantees a safe ending," Sorachi says, "but is that what you're living for, safe? Your mom certainly didn't. She took every path no matter the cost. She lived for hope, adventure, and love. And I guarantee she died satisfied that her integrity came before being safe."

I don't need to search for the right path. It's standing in front of me with a sooty outstretched hand and a smile that I just might dare to trust.

"A crown in exchange for a pair of hands," I say. "Once my sister has what you promised—a pair of working, metal hands on her flesh—we begin." I've dealt with enough prisoners to know the importance of being specific with my bargains.

Sorachi offers a sharp bow. "It's a deal."

CHAPTER 30

THE NEXT DAY, SORACHI TASKS me with training while I wait for her to make my sister's hands.

"Find a cluster of sulfide ore," Sorachi instructs. "Blindfolded. I'll need more of it to finish the mold for Yuki's hands. You might as well train while you do it. Remember the path goes three ways: past, present, and future."

"Course it does," I say.

I blow a wayward strand of hair from my mouth, wiping my brow with the back of my hand. I'd already scouted the tunnels for traces of other metals, and when Sorachi wasn't hounding me, I practiced with the long spear and read tomes about ancient hearts like *Deciphering Ancient Paths* and *A History of Waymaking*. I'd learned that the path works through the present in the blue threads I see, and also in the past and future through visions.

Sweat trickles down my neck as I listen for a path in the tangle of tunnels. A familiar tickle, like a spiderweb in the forest, brushes my skin. I wrap my gift around me, growing confidence guiding my feet through the limestone tunnel. The air grows cool and moist the farther I get from the tavern.

I pick up the pace, Yuki sticking by my side like a second shadow. I can't see the path with the blindfold, but I'm sure it's leading me to sulfide ore. Suddenly, the path darts up and over. I stop, breathing hard from exertion. There's a hollow dip at the edge of my foot. I peel off the blindfold and look down at a cavity in the cave floor.

"You weren't going to warn me?" I call over my shoulder.

Yuki snorts. "That would defeat the point of the exercise."

The tonic had brought Yuki's mind back to reason, but her body and voice still teetered on the edge of human. "But do hurry. I want to see the—" She gulps, swallowing the word she hadn't once mentioned since Ranzan. *Hands.*

"Almost done," I huff, sensing the end of the path is near. I climb the side of the wall using nooks in the limestone and jump to the other side of the pit. "I think we're right beneath the ore. The sooner we bring it to Sorachi, the faster we can take a break and eat something."

Yuki grimaces, like she'd rather avoid lunch. Sorachi is decidedly not the best cook, and that's saying something for a former Abashi prisoner.

I squint at the cave ceiling, which funnels upward in a short shaft supported by wooden beams. We scale the beams carefully lest they're aged and break under our weight. What Yuki lacks in hands, she makes up for in balance and tenacious strength. In a few short seconds, I'm at the top. I anchor my feet on either side of the earthen walls and push at the wooden slats above. A narrow trapdoor opens. I wave at Yuki to follow and pull myself out of the tunnel.

I slip into a large room beaming with sunlight. Not what I expected for a cluster of sulfide ore. Warm, heavily scented pine tingles my nose as I scan the empty sitting room. Woven bamboo mats bend beneath my feet, each one trimmed in faded silk. Paths fill this place, saturate the air, and spill into the open veranda.

"Yuki, you can come up now," I call, bending over the floor trapdoor.

From the outside, it looks just like another bamboo mat.

I grasp Yuki's arm and pull her out of the hole. My sister's awkward frame slinks across the room toward the paper walls. Her long, trailing sleeves trace over faint drawings inked into the walls centuries ago, family crests and seasonal motifs: dragons, cranes, hawks, and arrows. Yuki stiffens and points unceremoniously at a stone lantern in the garden.

A warm breeze combs through the house, carrying with it the humming of an age-worn voice. Someone else is here.

I startle and scan the perimeter. The blue path floats on the wind, brushing my skin with a playful breeze. I frown and step onto the slatted veranda. My eyes water from the afternoon brilliance and the shades of verdant green so close.

Why did the path led me here? This is not what I asked of it.

I'm not a servant, the breeze seems to say.

A shiver entirely unrelated to the cold bristles my skin. *Can the path . . . talk?* Mother had spoken of it as if she had a relationship with it, like a friend. But was she just familiar with it, affectionate toward the power that'd saved her life so many times?

I tear my gaze from the elaborate garden blooming over with chrysanthemums and peonies, and a shallow pond swirling with rainbow-colored carp. The humming I'd heard earlier pauses.

Does the intruder know we're here?

I hold up a hand for Yuki to remain where she is and keep quiet. My other hand curls into a fist as the left veranda door slides open on its track. I spring in front of the door, hands raised to ward off attack.

Teacups and saucers go flying as an elderly man stumbles back and falls on his bottom. Yuki rushes to catch the breakfast tray rocketing to the floor and is rewarded with a sploosh of tea. I gawk at the old man and then bow profusely.

"I'm so sorry," I stammer, dropping my hands. "I didn't mean to make you fall."

"You!" the old man shouts, his voice full of grave indignation. "You are in *my* house. I brought you tea." He flounders on the floor, collecting his broken things and dabbing the tea-stained mats. "Ungrateful. Degenerate. Unmannered." He shakes his bearded chin and snatches the unscathed teapot out of Yuki's arms.

Yuki growls but releases it.

I bow again. "I'm sorry, sir. We thought this place was abandoned. It didn't seem like anyone lived here."

"Hmph! Just because no one lives here doesn't mean it doesn't belong to anyone." The old man squints beneath bushy white brows. "What are you doing here? Where are your parents?"

I gulp, too surprised by the incident to answer. Had he noticed Yuki's growls, her pointed teeth, her nubby wrists?

I bite my lip and say the first thing that comes to mind, anything to keep his eyes on me instead of Yuki. "Dead. We're trying to find what's left of our family, distant relatives."

"But why are you here?" He gestures to the whole of the old house. "There are protections around this place. Only those truly in need can find it. That's why I brought you lunch." He glowers and then shakes his head.

"Protections? You mean magic?" Yuki asks.

"Yes." He draws out the word, his gaze shifting to Yuki's dark eyes and pointed teeth. "Magic."

"Please don't tell anyone we're here," I say. "We'll leave right away."

"That won't be necessary." His eyes remain fixed on Yuki. "You're supposed to be here."

The path circles the room in a faint blue glow, and my shoulders relax. I help pick up the last of the fallen cups. "You know Sorachi, don't you?"

A smile lifts his bearded chin. "I visit her sometimes through the hallways." He nods toward the now-closed secret door.

"This is Yuki, and I'm Kira," I say.

"Do you have a last name, a family crest?" The man rises from his knees while holding the tray of damaged things.

"A family crest?" I nearly laugh. "Only royalty or those brought by good fortune into such families have a crest. Do we look like royalty?" I let out a laugh as I run a hand through my hair, still smelling of damp cave.

Yuki crosses her legs unceremoniously, as if further proving my point. We are anything but royalty—except Yuki as the prince's cousin—but he can't know that.

The old man smiles and turns to Yuki. "Daughter." He addresses her with a familiar title reserved for people bound to the same family crest.

Yuki startles and drops her long sleeves to her sides.

"What are you tracing on the wall?"

I glance over at the paper screen. Ancient ink stains the parchment in skilled strokes. A smoky veil rises from the east, a raging fire from the west. The lines are perfectly drawn, thick and proud, without fear. Seven family crests mark the middle of the wall, all laid where the eye falls on them naturally. I recognize a few: the moon encircled with plum blossoms, the twin dragons of Taiga, and three spinning raindrops of Seshu. Yuki had smudged the last crest on the wall with her wet, tea-soaked sleeve.

"The oak tree." The man nods in approval at Yuki's preferred motif. It's the same pattern mother embroidered into our coats. She would put the design on our sleeves or on the back of the coat and said it was a symbol of protection, a symbol of love and family.

"The strongest tree in the forest isn't always the biggest, or the most beautiful, but the one that gives the most life." How I miss Mother's sayings. I don't tell the old man these things but watch him a bit more keenly.

"It is the last of the eight great family crests." He observes me as well. "The one belonging to the Ainur and the last of the dragon hearts."

"I thought it was forbidden, erased?" I stammer, piecing together why Sorachi had sent us on this errand in the first place.

It wasn't for more sulfide ore. "This is part of the sanctuary, isn't it?"

The old man smiles. "Well done, daughter. This is the House of the Wayfinder. Your mother's old house. And I am its caretaker, Todoroki, at your service."

CHAPTER 31

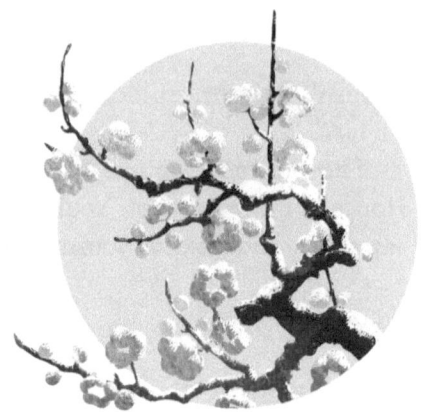

TODOROKI GESTURES TO TWO floor cushions, and we kneel upon them as he takes another on the opposite side of the open hearth. He starts a fire with a small flint box. The coals burn with a peaceful chatter in the square pit, heat rising to a large iron pot that hangs from the ceiling. Todoroki scoops out two bowls of fresh radish broth and hands them to us.

I cup the warm bowl between my hands. "Thank you."

Yuki scarfs hers down, slurping at the bowl between her wrists. Then she curls up on the cushion like an ill-mannered cat.

"Excuse my sister," I say. "She's not quite herself."

"Neither are you." Todoroki brandishes a ladle at me.

I raise a brow between loud slurps.

"You aren't what I thought you'd be." He nibbles thoughtfully on a radish, broth dribbling down his beard.

"What's that supposed to mean?" I feign offense. "I made it here across the Winterwilds. That takes courage and a good mind."

"A good mind? You're just as proud and stubborn as your mother." He knocks his head back and lets the soup run down his throat.

"Am I that much like her?"

He slurps, finishing off the rest of his soup. "The spitting image. But your sister there looks like her father, Prince Bastian."

At the mention of father, I wince. Of course I was like my mother; I've no father to compare myself to. I take another slurp of warm broth and study the room. The Wayfinding House, Mother's home in Silverwood, connected to a sanctuary for the ancient hearts and underground tunnels covering the city. This is what Mother wanted us to find, but why? It's more of a rebel base than the home we'd dreamed of together.

Perhaps she'd wanted me to train as a wayfinder, or perhaps she thought it was abandoned? I wish she were here now. Would she steal from the king to spare Yuki's life?

An icy blue path hums within me. Yes, she wouldn't even stop to ask the price. I set down my empty soup bowl and fist my hands in my lap.

"So, you knew my mother?" I level Todoroki with a pointed look, wrapping myself in the blue light that flows so freely here.

Todoroki tilts his head as if amused. "Serena? She was a general among her people. Perhaps not a great teacher, though. What did she teach you? Took you far too long to get here. You're late."

"Late for what?" I say, while feeling that I certainly am too late for Yuki by most anyone's standards. But giving up isn't in my makeup.

Those who gave up in prison died.

And whoever locked Mother away in that prison put her there for a reason—a reason that I bet is worth its weight in gold and blood. Perhaps it was to protect the last wayfinder, as Ren said. Or to stop the Inspector from taking Yuki as a hostage for the emperor. Maybe both. But it had cost *me* a lifetime of chains.

I don't care about kings and emperors. I only want to keep my family safe.

Todoroki shakes with a deep belly laugh. Dust flies as he slaps the ground. "Late for your training, late to stop the southern invaders, late to help your sister. Late."

"I get it," I say through gritted teeth. "But we showed up, and that counts for something. When did you meet our mother? What was she like?"

The question hits me hard as it falls from my lips. I don't really know Mother. The thought plummets me. I knew her in prison—as a warrior, a protector, a mother—but what was she like living free? Did she have hopes and dreams? What did she do for fun? These things I'd never known.

"I want to know what she was really like, before . . ."

"Pain and suffering don't make us any less real." The light in his eyes turns soft. "Your mother was real before the prison, and she was real inside it too."

"You know what I mean." Exasperation tugs at me. "In prison, you don't . . . don't have the same choices as someone else. Suffering changes you so you can't really be who you want to be."

Todoroki waves at the smoke rising from the open hearth. "You are real no matter your circumstances, but sometimes that realness is hidden deep down. Like those silkworms." He points to a shaded box nestled beneath a mulberry tree in the garden.

"It looks different in each stage of life. A cocoon should not compare itself to a butterfly. It's knowing who you are through it all that matters. Holding onto hope that whatever life throws at you, it cannot change who you are fundamentally. It might take away your smile. You might not look free and happy like others, but you always have a capacity for joy, love, and hope. Your mother knew that."

I stare into my empty soup bowl, a memory of Mother stirring—her smiling face, her chafed lips, her eyes dancing when they lighted on Yuki and me.

"Thank you for sharing what you knew of her," I say.

Todoroki inclines his head. "My work today is done. Remembering who you are is the key to finding the right path. You are ready now."

"Ready?" I nearly laugh. "Do you know what Captain Ren is asking of me? What Sorachi is asking?"

Todoroki gestures to the garden and stands with difficulty. "Asking is different than forcing. You have a choice," he says. "But what are you asking of yourself?"

I scowl, following him into the garden. I'm challenging myself to save Yuki and redeem Mother's memory, even if it means stealing a crown. He's right. "You know, you're pretty annoying for an old man."

Todoroki chuckles. He passes the shaded boxes of silkworms beneath the mulberry tree and loops around the pond. A soft chittering comes from the tree. I glance up into the large leaves and catch a fleeting shadow. Something soft leaps onto my shoulder. I startle, nearly clutching the stone lantern for balance. A tiny gray rodent with prickling claws nuzzles against my neck.

I cringe. "What is it?"

"It would appear you've been sent a momo message."

"A momo-what?" I pinch the tiny creature by the lumpy scruff of its neck.

Two large black eyes stare at me from the fluffy white face of a squirrel small enough to fit into my hand. It chirps as I plop it into my palm and then crawls up my arm with a contented purr.

"A flying squirrel messenger," Todoroki says. "They're all the rage in Silverwood. Careful! They bite." He plucks the fuzzy squirrel from my shoulder as it nips at my ear, and removes a cylindrical leather case from its back.

A miniature scroll falls into his palm. I lean over to read the message in perfectly practiced script:

Dragon Bay 1600 sharp
It's time for your part of the deal.
Leave the demon behind.
                                          Ren

My eyes gravitate toward those three letters. *Ren.* Now that I know he's a prince, it seems odd to call him by his first name. I gulp, scrunching the tiny scroll, and then throw it into the pond.

A mass of rainbow-colored carp mouth the water's surface, swallowing the scroll. I'd sensed the path to Dragon Bay, a winding tunnel smelling of salt and damp clay. I was fairly certain it led to wherever they kept the dragons when they weren't out at sea. My gaze shifts to Yuki, still curled asleep on one of the large floor pillows.

"Will you look after my sister?" I ask.

"Of course," Todoroki says. "But please be quick. The inspector's guards are searching every corner of the city. While there are protections around this place, there will be nothing I can do if the inspector himself appears. Go now, daughter."

I turn back toward the trapdoor, my gaze dropping to Yuki one last time.

"When I come back, we'll make this place our home," I whisper, tucking a strand of grizzly hair out of her sleeping face. "Home."

Dragon Bay is so cozy for the dragons.

CHAPTER 32

I CLIMB DOWN THE ROCKY cliffside that slopes into the bay. The dragon stables are built into a natural cave, expanded with iron and wood into a wide cylindrical tunnel lit by skylights. Hot springs from the mountains meet the ocean here, sending tendrils of steam where fresh and saltwater meet.

I summon my courage. *This is for Yuki.*

Inside, a fine warm mist wraps around me. Bowls of floating flowers line the paved path going deeper into the cave, each swarmed with insects attracted to the strong-smelling tincture. I hesitate to call the captain's name—*the prince's name*—as if the beasts resting beneath the water on either side of the path will awaken and devour me.

I'd seen a sea dragon from a distance aboard the ship, but this is different. Now, I feel their presence, their nearness. Do they sense the vibrations of my footsteps? I clench my hands and recall the brief training Sorachi crammed into the past week.

A path hums around me, warm and faint, like the mist heating my skin. Why had Ren chosen to meet here? Perhaps the city is on heightened alert with the coronation scheduled for tonight.

The coronation for a prince—for Ren.

Inspector Jade and his guards must be furious Yuki and I've evaded them for so long. Despite the warmth, a shiver runs down my spine. Dragon eyes watch me from beneath the water. Creatures without any thought for the future, who live perpetually in the now—survival. Like me.

Where is Ren? I can't detect him, except for a faint presence below my feet.

I step across one of the small planks extended over the shimmering water. A ring of bubbles rises from the nearest pool, and the surrounding water ripples with a force that could take down a small boat. I anchor my stance on the plank beneath me as it bobs. The water swirls faster.

A flash of silver breaks the surface. Scales glint like molten coins as a wingless dragon rises from the depths. Algae clings to its whiskered face. Dark fathomless eyes fix on me as its serpentine body unfurls like a silver thread.

Behind the dragon's neck sits Ren.

He smiles, gripping a leather saddle of sorts, and slicking wet hair from his brow.

The dragon arches its neck along the nearest plank, offering a bridge. Ren slides easily over the dragon's neck, dismounting as if it were no different from a horse. He lands beside me and the plank wobbles.

I pitch forward—and catch myself against his chest. "I-I'm sorry," I stammer, my throat going dry.

His breath is steady, calm. "Don't break eye contact with dragons," he whispers, gently turning me to face the beast. "It's an insult. You must offer it a gift."

"Oh," I manage, thickly.

The dragon watches me unblinking, intelligent eyes boring into me. It's breath reeks of dead fish.

Ren moves to place something in my hand, but I've pulled a thread of path to me, sensing the next step. I pluck a camellia blossom from one of the floating bowls and hold it out to the sea dragon, my eyes never leaving its face.

The beast swims closer, raising its head fully from the water and snorting at me. A warm, pungent mist speckles my skin. Its whiskered muzzle dips toward my hands. I freeze as it sniffs me, goosebumps prickling my arms. Then its mouth parts, revealing rows of curved white teeth, and I drop the tinctured flower onto its tongue.

The dragon slowly closes its jaws, blinks—a glimmer of gold dust in the dark—and then dives beneath the surface. The planks sway under my feet, and I instinctively grip Ren's sleeve to steady myself.

"You're not as bad at wayfinding as I thought," he says. "Which bodes well for our adventure tonight."

"Why do you say that?" I notice my hand fisted on his sleeve and pull away, wiping my palms on my damp coat. But it's more than water that clings to me. That dragon, did it understand the path?

Ren peels off his soaked shirt and pulls a dry one from the luggage pile at the end of the cave. "How did you know the flower would calm him down?"

"Him?"

He nods at the swirling water. "That's Tyri. The other dragon is a female, Rahmia. I've known them since I was a boy. The emperor gave them as gifts for each of the descendants of the moon."

"You mean the royal family?" I recall the crest of Silverwood, the full moon encircled by five plum blossoms.

"Yes," he says. "While Taiga's rulers claim their divine right from the sun, the kingdom of Ezo claims to have descended from the moon. My mother's family specifically, which makes your sister a princess. The next in line for the throne after me."

He tosses another flower into the water. "Tyri was gifted to me, and Rahmia belongs to Yuki."

The water stirs. A second dragon appears, obsidian black and sleek, coiling through the pool to claim the offering. I crouch beside the flower basin, brushing my fingers along a red camellia—the same flowers the *yajuu* hate.

Suddenly, an image ghosts across my mind in threads of blue: the roar of a dragon, black covering the water, and blood running from my hands.

I reel back and shake my head. Ren's at my side, steadying me.

"Dragons have that effect on some," he says, as if making a note about the weather. "It's a pity Yuki never met Rahmia. Dragons imprint best with children, the more innocent, the stronger the bond. It's difficult to connect with them otherwise."

His eyes catch mine. "Unless you're a wayfinder and have a piece of their heart."

"That's the first time you've used Yuki's name." I straighten my shoulders. "So you *do* see that she isn't a monster."

"She'll always be a monster." He turns away, facing the thick wooden door at the end of the cave. "Follow me. We don't have much time."

"Why didn't you tell me before that you're a prince?" I call after him.

"I joined the Shadows to disappear," he says, swinging open the door. "Haven't you heard my title? *The Demon Prince*—not exactly endearing."

I follow him into the room, taken aback by the sharp scent of wet leather, salt, and cedar. Before I can get my bearings, Zenri rushes at me and claps me on the back. "Kira! I half-doubted you'd show. How's your sister?"

"Thanks for asking." I throw Ren a pointed look. "She's doing well. Had another dose of the tonic. Seems Sorachi has the largest stash in town—or had. She only has a few doses left now."

I perch on top of a wooden stool, tilting my head at Ren. "So, want to explain how I'm supposed to steal this crown? And maybe, *why*?"

Zenri pulls a wicker basket from under a counter and plops it beside me. "You'll need these." He lifts the white towel covering the basket to reveal folds of fine silk.

"What's this? I agreed to be a thief," I say, brows knitting. "Not a princess."

"You hit the rabbit on the nose," Zenri says. "You're attending the coronation tonight. The prince will give you the rest of the details. We have to follow them to the letter. The emperor sent a delegation and soldiers for the ceremony. If anything goes wrong, it's not just our necks on the line—he could retaliate by attacking Silverwood. We could start a war." Zenri blanches, but his voice doesn't shake. He's seen war before. I'm sure of it.

"The coronation?" I turn toward Ren as he pulls a navy jerkin over his shirt. It's still hard to picture him as a prince. "Will you be given the crown?"

Ren wipes his face with a towel and slings it over his shoulders. He lifts a dragon saddle onto a storage rack and begins wiping it down. "My father won't let anyone near his crown. The ceremony is mostly symbolic, a formality to crown the next prince or princess on their seventeenth birthday. I missed mine."

"On purpose," Zenri interrupts.

Ren smiles faintly. "No one wanted a demon prince anyway."

"So why now?" I ask.

"It's complicated," he says, pausing. "But when the emperor found your sister, we had to act. If he'd gotten to her first, he would've used her as leverage against Ezo. I may not want to return home, but I won't let my country be taken hostage. I agreed to find her, to bring her home, and to present her to the royal court. That was the deal."

He sighs. "My father announced the coronation as soon as he knew I was here. Trapped me in it before I could slip away."

"Did you tell him Yuki's a *yajuu*?" I grab a cloth to clean the next saddle, anything to keep my hands busy. "You can't seriously plan to take her into the castle with all those people."

"Exactly." He meets my gaze. "That's why you'll pretend to be my long-lost cousin, Princess Yukiko."

I blink, the pile of silk suddenly making sense.

"I've arranged all the details," Ren continues. "My father only knew Yuki as a baby, so the chances that he'll see through the deception are remote. Use your position to get close to him and take his crown."

"Why do you need his crown?" My gaze narrows. "Can't you just ask for it? It's not like I can pluck it off his head without him noticing."

"The crown won't pass down to me until he passes away . . . which will be a very long time. And it's not the crown I want." His jaw clenches. "It's what's inside it."

"I don't understand."

"A wayfinder can use an object to trace any path it's touched—past, present, and future. *Memory pathways.*" He looks directly at me. "You can see what an extraordinary gift this is. And why a crown is particularly valuable to someone with your gift. You'll be able see anything it's witnessed, in the past *or the future.*"

I scrub hard at a smudge on the saddle, my eyes focused on Ren. "Why can't you just take it?"

"My father wears my mother's crown. Has ever since she passed. He won't let *anyone* touch it." Ren steps aside to wash the oil and soap from his hands. "He loved my mother more than life itself."

"But I've never used memory pathways. Could my mother?"

"I'm not sure," he says. "I've read the old scrolls, but I never knew your mother. *May her path be eternally restful.*"

"Your father will suspect that Yuki could be a wayfinder," I say, glancing from Ren to Zenri. "He won't trust her with the crown."

Ren shakes his head. "My father isn't fascinated by magic or threatened by it. He didn't ask me to find your mother and sister because they're Ainur. He asked because he's drowning in regret. He let the emperor blackmail him. He stood by while the Ainur and heart bearers were pushed to the brink of existence—including his niece."

I take a breath. "Why do you want to know the future, Ren?"

"Just get the crown and use it to find anything you can—what happens to Ezo a year from now, what my mother knew about the *yajuu* cure, who will become the next king."

"But surely that's you," I interrupt. "Why waste a path on that question?"

He holds a finger to his lips. "Because there might not be a throne if the emperor has his way. And then—most importantly for you—look to the past, to the moment I was cured. You might find how Valcon made the real cure, though it won't be pretty."

I whirl around, wicker basket in hand. "You mean . . . I might be able to recreate it? Will the cure still work for Yuki?"

Ren places a hand over mine. "Kira . . ."

I dare him with my eyes to stop me. He's just told me I can find a cure in the memory pathways. What is he so afraid of? Even if the cure is imperfect, even if it hurts—nothing will stop me. It had worked for him.

"I will try it," I say.

"I won't help you recreate it," he says, voice firm. "I don't want to hide it from you anymore, but I hope you'll decide against—"

I tug my hand away. "It's my decision."

"*If* you decide not to cure her," he presses, "then I'll have to put the monster down. Or keep her under tonic in prison, but that's not living. *I've been there before.* I know." He breathes deep, frustration lining his brow. "For you . . . I can ask for a pardon. Zenri has the resources to smuggle you out if it comes to that. I've asked him not to discuss the details with me, so it's not against the law."

"A kind offer from a Shadow." I make a show of rolling my eyes. "But it won't be necessary."

"Think about it," Zenri cuts in. "And now, Prince Ren, I think you'd better get to the castle before you're missed. I'll bring Kira up when she's ready."

"Don't be late," Ren warns, his tone light. "You'll miss the best hors d'oeuvres."

CHAPTER 33

I'VE NEVER SEEN CAMELLIAS in bloom. Vivid crimson shrubs soften the black-roofed castle—a cloud of softest red fringing its stone base and white walls. Our carriage rattles across the plank bridge, setting my teeth on edge with each jolt. I glance outside, gathering my courage to face the hundred or so guests that will congratulate me.

The lost princess.

It should be Yuki sitting here. My nails dig into the flesh of my palms as I think of my sister. If our plan fails, she'll be a monster forever. But deep in my soul, I know that even if the sun sets and I've not found the cure, I'll still search for one.

"There's always a way." Mother's words float back to me and bring a smile to my lips. Had she known which path was right? Which one would set us both free?

Zenri reins in the horses and passes them off to a castle servant for safekeeping before opening the carriage door.

"You were made for this," he whispers with an encouraging smile.

I take his hand and step gently from the carriage, keeping my chin up to strike a confident pose. But my forehead smashes against the top of the carriage, and I stagger onto the lantern-lit path, grace entirely forgotten.

"Perhaps I spoke too soon." Zenri laughs awkwardly. He helps me up, a look of mock severity on his face.

I rub my forehead, but the pain does something opposite of what it should. It hardens into resolve. "No," I say sharply. "I'm ready for this."

I square my shoulders and quickly inspect my hair. A few wayward strands spring from the elaborate top knot like rampant weeds. At least the dress is immaculate. I smooth nonexistent wrinkles, grounding myself in the silk's weight, its strength. Only a friend could pick an outfit so perfect.

The dress clings to me in the style of my people. Warm, knotted silk matching the vibrant hue of red camellia and flecked with silver swirls that represent *the way*—the path that moves us all forward and into the hidden kingdom. It's as if Mother's robe was woven from moonlight into a perfect gown, matching my raven hair polished to an elegant shine.

I straighten as a voice calls out to me, heat prickling my skin.

"Am I bewitched, or are you actually early?" The demon prince himself leans against a balustrade, wineglass in hand and sword at his side, partially concealed beneath thick cerulean robes. His eyes fix on me with a glimmer of admiration. He's about to betray his father, but he isn't even a tad concerned. He pushes off the stone wall and reaches over the garden to pluck a camellia from the nearest branch.

"You shouldn't do that," I scold.

"Why not?" he asks, plucking it anyway.

"Because it'll die." I touch the trunk's smooth bark. "If you leave it on the tree, everyone can enjoy it."

"But I don't want everyone to enjoy this particular flower." He hands it to me with a flourish.

Reluctantly, I take it because of the look on his face—tender, caring, almost like a gardener instead of a cold-hearted prince. I turn the red blossom in my hand, rubbing its soft petals between my fingertips. I move to toss it into the peaceful moat that wraps around the castle, illuminated by a hundred gas lamps, but he catches my hand gently. His fingers deftly remove a silver pin from his coat as he tucks the flower into my hair, fixing the largest flyaway.

"Enjoy this one." His gaze lingers on mine, steady and unreadable, like he's memorizing me. "It would be a waste to throw it away. It truly is . . . beautiful. A symbol of grace in adversity."

My throat goes tight, unsure if he's referring to me or the flower. He turns toward the main castle gate, waiting for me to follow. Nerves slip into my stomach like eels as we stride up the long stone steps toward open doors three times my height.

Zenri stalks behind us as Ren's personal guard, alertness shimmering over him as we pass beneath the gates. Rows of statuesque sentinels mark the path to the reception hall where the king is soon to announce me. Warm air wafts through a dark room, steeped in cypress and incense, with lavender curling at the edges like breath held too long.

A grand melody plays on bone-white keys and a symphony of strings floods the entrance like nature announcing the dawn. As I take my first step into the room, I swear the music skips a beat. Or perhaps it's my own heart, balking at this crowd, so many eyes glued to me. Do they see my clear-blue eyes—the eyes of the Ainur? They shout who I am, the daughter of the Ainur general who'd been thrown into prison and left to die. Amid their stares, I think of Mother and keep my head high.

A warm hand catches mine, and I let loose the breath that had constricted my ribs. Ren leads me down the stairs, stilling the whispering voices.

"We haven't had an Ainur grace this palace in over a decade," he says. "It's an *honor*."

My skin tingles where it touches Ren's gloved hand, startling in its tenderness. "And the return of the banished prince?"

"I don't think they missed me." A hint of bitterness frosts his voice. "The princess, on the other hand, has been a source of rumor and intrigue since the day she was born. And now she's reappeared after nineteen years. It's like a fairy tale. Nobles have come from every part of Ezo to witness your return."

"You mean Yuki's return," I whisper.

How long will he go along with the charade? I have to tread carefully. He promised to spare Yuki's life in exchange for the crown, even told me that the *memory pathways* hold the secret to the cure. The warmth in his eyes tells me that it's not just about the bargain anymore.

Drums sound to my left and right, rattling off a deep throaty pace as we descend into the open hall. I hold my chin high, a difficult feat after years of bending low, humbling myself in prison. I want to run, to avoid the curious eyes and whispering lips. The crowd is a swarm of color: riders of Thesia cloaked in rhododendron red, Seshu nobles in tide pool jade sashes, black silks of Koal artisans, and the gold dragon insignia of the Imperial City.

The music reaches a crescendo and stops.

"Prince Renjiro, Captain of His Majesty's Shadows, Crown Prince of the Northern Isles, and his cousin, Princess Yukiko, Light of the Northern Isles." An announcer shouts, stepping into the center of the room with an exaggerated bow. The voice fills the void left by the drums, reverberating through the arched wooden hall with its high windows barred by thick damask tapestries.

"That's quite the title," I whisper, arching a brow at Ren. How long is everyone going to stare at me? It'll be impossible to steal the crown with all these witnesses.

"That's the short version," Ren murmurs. His grip tightens as we cross the long room toward the throne. My treacherous heart pounds with each step. I scour the crowd pressed against the walls for any weak spots should my courage fail.

I tear my gaze from the whispering crowd and look toward the end of the hall. Three immense silver thrones shimmer atop an elevated platform, gleaming like ice under the star-strewn ceiling. Above them, the painted heavens swirl with constellations and clouds. And seated at the center—on the largest throne—is a man impossible to ignore.

His eyes are flecked in gold, as if a forge once burned behind them. They meet mine with a knowing calm, and I feel as though my secrets are laid bare. His hair is silvered with age, but not with weakness. He wears his years like armor, broad shoulders and upright, though in his bearing is something akin to grief—not as a weight surrendered to, but one he's learned to carry.

He leans forward, opulent blue robes trimmed in white cascading like waterfalls around his bare feet and pink pants. Somehow, the color makes him feel more human.

"Is that—?"

"My father," Ren finishes. "King Soran."

I'd expected a bitter tyrant who'd chased off his only son. But this man, this king, is not that. His eyes sparkle like gold dust in a lonely mine.

I want to pull aside the heavy tapestries, let the sunlight in, and chase the sadness from his face. He seems to have lived a thousand lifetimes and carried every one of them with dignity. Using the cure on his son had not made him cruel.

It had made him weary, lost even.

And yet, his presence fills the hall like an unfinished song, refusing to fade.

As if reading my thoughts, a servant with a long wooden staff opens the towering curtains. Fading sunlight, diffused through the high glass windows, spills into the dark chamber—dusky rays woven with every shade of color. I freeze mid-step, the cavernous room swallowing me in its swirling light.

"It's stained glass," Ren says, noticing my awe. "Your friend, the saint in the woods, designed them when my mother and father were married. It was the biggest wedding of the century, as he tells it."

"It's like being beneath the ice," I murmur, "but warm and safe."

A shimmer of memory runs through me: falling through

the ice as a child and then light breaking through—Yuki's hand reaching into the dark water. *Her hand.*

She'll have hands again soon.

But another glimmer pulls my focus—the crown. It glistens atop the king's brow. I step forward, an invisible string pulling me toward the white crown with its sharp points and its promise of answers.

Ren's hand stops me. A warning flickers in his gaze. He bows to the king, and I follow his example.

"My cousin." Ren waves a graceful hand in my direction. "I've spent the last three years searching for the missing princess and have at long last returned with her. Father, may I present Princess Yukiko."

I bow again, lower this time, and dare a glance at the king seated on his throne. His bare feet tap either in impatience or to a song only he knows. Then he rises, and the crowd falls to a fervent hush.

Two warm brown eyes search my face, shimmering with hope and sorrow. He grabs the edge of his throne, knuckles whitening under his weight. It's hard to believe his strong frame needs the extra support, but I'll wager his heart does. How long has it been since he's seen his son?

His eyes remind me of the sea dragons, eyes that have lived a hundred lifetimes in this one short breath.

What does he see in me? A commoner? A criminal? A niece?

"My brother-in-law's daughter was lost," he says, voice a low rumble, "but now she has been found." A slow smile softens his face, brightening the aged lines. "Let the celebrations begin. Today, all of Ezo rejoices. Lady Yukiko, your princess, has returned."

The crowd erupts in applause. Strings and bells rise from the outer halls in jubilant harmony. The king holds out a hand to me, a flicker of doubt in his gaze, as though afraid I might be a ghost and disappear.

With a deep breath, I take his hand—warm, accepting, solid.

But I am not his family.

The feeling stabs at me with a heart-sickening dread. Would this man be heartbroken if he knew the truth? Would he want to destroy Yuki like her cousin does? Would my father look at me with so much love in his eyes?

I take a seat on the silver throne on the king's right-hand side. Ren slouches into the one on the left, his posture crooked, restless, as if he can't wait for the festivities to end. He doesn't want to be here.

King Soran turns to me. "You look like Serena, your mother."

"I have her eyes," I say, forcing a smile, though his words cut deep.

"Much more than that." His eyes, flecked in gold, seem to peel back my secrets, prodding with unspoken questions. "But there will be time to talk later. This is yours."

He holds out a small diadem and gently places it on my head. It's clear as scorched ice shaped by fire and fitted with white pearls the size of my fingertips.

"Thank you," I mouth, touching the crown with wonder.

But my gaze shifts to his crown—the one I need to steal. No, *borrow*. How long would it take to trace the memory pathways? My fingers twitch with urgency, and my eyes linger longer than they should.

"A crown is a heavy burden," he says, mistaking the hunger in my eyes. "But you need not fear the responsibility. You are honest, like your mother. I see it in your gaze. The hard winters did not break you. They made you strong."

My jaw clenches. Something in me wars against those words. What good is resilience if it comes with loss? If it only teaches you to live without the things you love?

Heat prickles beneath my skin at the idea that prison helped me, made me stronger. I wish I were like Mother—brave, kind, whole. I wish I could keep Yuki safe, make her a home. But I've failed so many times.

My promise is all I have left.

Not all. A warm blue shimmers around me like a thread. The path.

I glance up. The thread twists toward the corridor beyond the throne room. Ren's gaze is already there, studying the mingling crowd. His fingers drum on the armrest, slow and deliberate. Is he waiting for me to make my move?

King Soran's voice interrupts my thoughts. "Ren told me about your mother." His lips pinch in a firm line. "I'm sorry. No child should endure what you have. I still remember the day you came into this world. They say we all come into this world crying, but you brought smiles to all around you. Your father was so proud. Bastian used to carry you in an elmwood sling with silver stars and winter hares. He always put fresh lavender in your crib. Your eyes were brown then. Tawny, like his."

"It's funny how eyes can . . . change," I say, the lie pitiful in my throat.

Eyes don't go from brown to blue, do they? My heart stutters. He's going to see right through me!

I swallow my fear and the pain that lodges in my throat. Yuki should be here. This is her family, not mine.

What do I have left? I want to yell at the path. Everything I care about is either broken or a monster: Yuki, Mother . . . Ren.

No, not him.

Is it because I'm a monster too? Is that why pain always finds me?

I found you, the path says as clear as if the words were spoken aloud. *Am I a monster?*

No, I think. *But you seem to follow trouble like a weasel.*

The shimmering blue nudges me again, insistent. I want to swat it away like a troublesome pest. But I still, realizing I'm not alone. The same path that guided Mother, the one she sang to, is here with me. My courage returns, and with it, a spark of determination.

"Your Majesty—"

"Please, that title has always been too stuffy for me. Call me Soran." His words crack just slightly behind the smile.

"May I see you without your crown . . . as family? Forgive me if it's too bold to ask."

"Never," Soran says as he reaches a protective hand to his crown. His body tenses, gaze drifting across the court and then back to me.

I lean back against the throne, wishing I could melt into it unseen. I was a fool to think it'd be so simple.

But then, slowly, Soran lifts the crown from his head. He sets it on the armrest between us, as if laying down a sword. "Never is a question too bold for family, my dear."

I swallow hard.

The king's heart beats entirely for his niece's return, and he's holding it out to me—silently asking me not to break it.

"Did your mother ever tell you about your family?" he asks.

"She told stories," I say, my voice shaking as I think about my father, long dead and unknown to me, and my mother . . .

What family do I have anymore? Only Yuki.

Ren glances from me to the crown resting near my fingertips. He shakes his head, almost imperceptible. A warning. But I didn't come all this way to stop now.

"Might I suggest we move this reunion to the gardens?" Ren interjects. "Too many ears of uncertain loyalty in here."

Soran chuckles, wry and warm. "Ever the Shadow, Ren, but you're right." He signals to the guards to follow and rises from his throne.

His jeweled hand reaches for the crown to replace it on his head, but I seize the opportunity.

"Please," I say. "Let me see you for a little longer without it."

My fingers wrap around the cold metal that points into seven silver spikes. I pour all my intention into the glittering crown, calling for its memories and the paths that led us here. *Show me. Show me the path.*

Jolting sparks like fire erupt beneath my skin. Flashes of

memory strike like lightning, a bolt of pain shooting through my mind. My knees smack the floor, and the cold metal beneath my fingers begins to burn.

Ren bolts toward me. Panicked voices shout. Hands reach . . . and then the world goes white.

CHAPTER 34

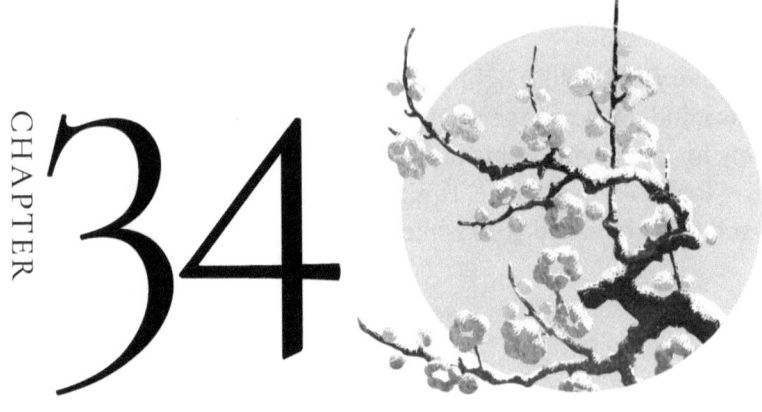

"ARE YOU ALL RIGHT?"
The voice is rushing water masked in blue threads.

I turn to face the source of that unmistakable voice. Mother stands next to me. Her long black hair spills like inky waves over her shoulders, and her mouth curves in a familiar smile that makes my stomach flip.

"Mama," I gasp, diving into her arms and drinking in the rich smell of summer birch and wildflowers. Strong arms fold around me, soaking me in warmth. "Are you—am I—dead?"

Mother pulls back, bracing my arms firmly and looking me square in the eyes. "They say the Ainur live a thousand lives, but what they really mean is that death isn't the end. It's not as final as you think."

I furrow my brow, still clinging to her hands, afraid that if I let go, she'll vanish. She jerks her head to the side. I follow her gaze to the surrounding room. Silver birch coats the walls and floor, leading my eyes to a lavish four-poster bed bearing the crest of Silverwood. A bay window looks out across a harbor flecked in snow.

"This isn't real," I say, touching the smooth walls.

"It was at one time." Mother's voice is reminiscent as she moves to the window. "You're inside the world of memory, Kira.

It's easy to get lost in here, reliving memories over and over again, trying to solve them, to riddle if you could've changed them with a different path. If you could've chosen better."

"So, you're a memory?" My throat feels dry, as if I'd swallowed bitter ash.

Mother nods as I hold her warm blue gaze.

"But this room . . . I've never been here before. How could it be from my memory?"

My hands sting like frozen flesh plunged into steam. The burning pulse spreads beneath my skin, and the crown materializes, gripped between my fingers as if it'd been there all along. "The memory pathways," I breathe. "These are the queen's memories, aren't they? Ren's mother?"

"Yes." Mother places her hands firmly over mine. "When you let go of the crown, this vision will cease. It's a portal tethering you to the world of memory."

"Have you been here before? The memory pathways? You never told me about them." I search her eyes. There are so many things she never told me. So many things I want to know.

She breathes deep, leaning her forehead against mine. "We weren't made to live in memories. They are like dreams, changing and fading, promising a future they have no power to give. Those who stay too long become like memories, fading. You must hurry, Kira. Leave me to the past and look for the cure."

I pull Mother into an embrace, clinging to her. "How can I? I want to be with you."

Her warm scent and the rough embroidery of stars across Mother's scarf make me feel safe, free, hopeful.

"I wish we were back in prison," I mumble into her shoulder. "Even if it was living in a filthy cage and starving, we were *together*. Yuki was still human. It's all my fault this happened to us—to you."

Mother heaves a deep sigh. "Shame is a destroyer of souls. And it is not yours to carry. The path led me to this end. I chose it. I called the cursed bear to the prison while we were still in the hot spring. I knew that the only way Yuki would survive was if she had the strength of a bear. I asked the curse to come, not you."

"But . . . the bear I killed in the woods. Wasn't it cursed? The creature was avenging its death."

"No, that was just a bear. Don't blame yourself, dear heart. You've carried enough burdens, but no one is made to carry them alone. Your path is ahead of you. I know you can find the cure. I took the path I did because I believe in you, Kira. I love you. Now go. There's little time."

"No! I don't believe it. It was *my* fault. You would've never—"

"Shame is one of the hardest things to let go of, even when there is no fault." Mother's tender hand touches my cheek, her gaze a warm embrace. "It was the only path, Kira. I want you to *live*."

"I-I'm not leaving you." I glance at the crown in my hands and imagine never letting go, staying here forever.

"Go," Mother whispers, a sad smile lifting the corners of her mouth. "Find the cure. And when you can't find a path, Kira—make a way. Before we were called wayfinders, we were waymakers." Then she disappears into the castle walls like a ghost.

The memory shimmers and jolts around me. I'm in the same room, but now I'm with a woman I've never seen. She stands beside me, starlight dancing from her soft, blue hair. As if the sky had wrapped its color around her and the sea wove depth into her long cerulean strands.

Her slender hands stir a green powder with thoughtful precision, her back curved to the side as she works, bent and deformed. Steaming water pours into the earthen bowl, blending the tea and crushed scarlet petals into a thick sludge. She carries the mixture down three flights of stairs, walking carefully, into the dungeons.

A wild boy in chains jumps to his feet as the blue-haired

woman enters. His small frame shakes with emotion, and a feral snarl gathers in the back of his throat as he bares sharp white teeth. The woman combs her hair to the side as if preparing for a tea ceremony and sets the bowl on a pedestal.

"I've found the cure, Ren," she whispers, her voice smooth as silk and tears. "My sweet boy, you're going to be okay again. I take this choice on myself, as a queen must. But the cost is more than either of us can bear. Drink this potion, made by the healers in Taiga. Princess Narcissa, the emperor's daughter, made it herself under the tutelage of the Head Apothecary. And Casmir wouldn't lead me wrong, he wouldn't." The queen bites her lip and braces herself against the small table as though her back pains her greatly. Or perhaps it's the thoughts I can't see that trouble her.

The child behind bars rushes at the cage with a snarl. I gasp as I recognize the dark indigo hair and the stubborn lines of his face—*Ren*. The queen doesn't shy away from him and rights herself.

"Meera!" The king's deep voice rushes the stairs as the door leading into the dungeon opens. Soran is younger, broad-shouldered, and his skin is a handsome summer's warmth. But his face is set in hard lines, colored with scarcely concealed anger—no, *fear*.

He stumbles on a step in his haste and grips the rail. "Meera, step away from the cage. This is not the way. We *will* find a way. But. Not. This."

Meera smiles at him, a sad crease forming on her pale brow. Tears stream down her face, but she doesn't attempt to wipe them away. "I've made my choice. Love is always the way."

"Meera, don't!"

A nearly unrecognizable Ren lunges against his chains, reaching for the bars of the cage with an angry howl. "Kill, slice, crush," he hisses in a raspy voice that can scarcely be called human save for the anguish in his eyes.

"Meera, don't move any closer." Soran says, his words a

lilting song as though trying to coax a bird to remain still. "I should've never hired Jey, and I can't trust whatever Casmir has sent you. I swear, even he would tell you to stop. It's not worth the risk. It might not even work—Look at him."

The wild boy shrieks, scratching at his skin as he howls in pain. Bruises blossom along his throat and wrists. Dark blue eyes forced into slits watch the king and queen hungrily.

"Ren, stop. Stop!" The queen pleads, nearly reaching into the cage. "You still have a choice, darling. Look at me." She steps up to the cage, key in hand. "I love you, and no curse can change that. Jey says that if a willing soul sacrifices itself, and you drink this potion, the curse will leave. You will be healed, dear one." A tear slips down her smooth cheek.

Ren mutters something murderous from behind the bars, an anguish hanging heavy on his scrappy shoulders. I want to reach out to the queen, to shake some sense into her. But she turns a key in the lock, opens the door, and locks herself inside.

"Meera, NO!" The king shouts, rushing at the bars and trying to pry them open, as if he could free her with strength alone.

"I am the ruler of Silverwood," the queen says, not turning to look at him. "I refuse to rule without my son at my side. Our son, Soran."

She holds out the earthen vessel like an offering. Her eyes shimmer with fervent emotion. Hands shaking, she pours the bowl over her head.

Sticky green liquid covers her sky-blue tresses. The potion runs rivulets down her face and shoulders, dripping to her sandaled feet.

Ren whimpers. Not a growl, but raw and childlike as the curse takes over him. "No . . . no . . . stay back."

Meera steps toward her son, casting a glance over her shoulder at the king. "I love you, Soran. Always. Forgiv–"

In less than a second, the boy Ren is shifting into a monstrous wolf and lunges. Blood pools along the floor to the king's bare feet. Soran staggers with a heart-rending sob and reaches through the iron bars.

My eyes shut, and I drop the crown. I can't unsee. Words curdle in my throat, begging the queen to stop. Soran's voice echoes in my mind, howling, cursing the apothecary, the curse, and Ren.

"I never want to see you again!" the king shouts.

My eyes burst open. I'm back in the ballroom.

The crown rolls onto an ornate carpet level with my eyes. Feet gather around me, a crowd of leather slippers. I gulp, my heart pounding in my ears. Ren bends down on his knees and draws me up until I'm pressed against his chest and staring into the face that had just committed unspeakable evil. Ren didn't kill her. The curse did. Still, I shiver from head to foot, memory still blanketing the world in sticky crimson.

Eyes like a deep winter sea search my own, desperate, drowning in remorse. His dark brow flinches, and his jaw clenches as though he knows I'll never see him the same way again. *But still he wanted me to see.* He's known all along what I'd find if I looked into the crown's memory pathways. I found the cure. And now I know why he didn't want me to find it.

The only way to cure Yuki is for me to die.

CHAPTER 35

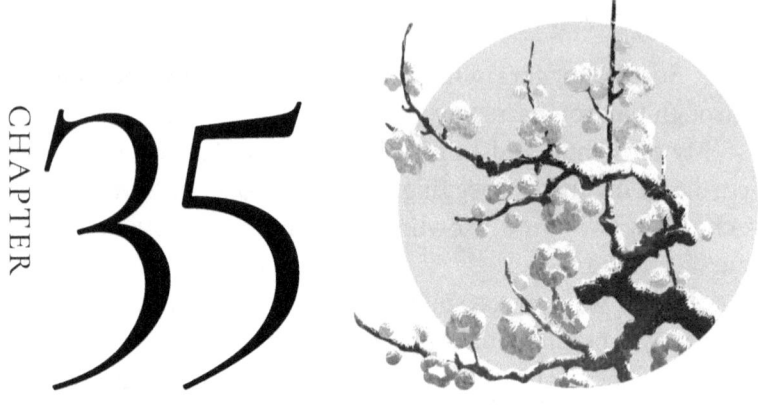

THE QUEEN'S DEATH REPLAYS in my mind as I stare at Ren. Blue light cuts across his face from the stained-glass window and fragments of who he was—who he still might be—flash through me: the monster, the boy, the man afraid of his own shadow. Ribbons of indigo hair weave into softest blue, shifting like the depths and shallows of the sea.

Everyone else must see a caring prince, but I . . .

His brow furrows as he pulls me gently to my feet, and flashes of memory dance before me: glittering teeth, a bloodied hand dragged across his lips, and eyes like dead stars.

"Can you walk?" His voice is a scarce whisper, but I reel back as if bitten.

Pain flashes in his eyes, and I want to take back my reaction. I don't mean him any harm, but I can't unsee.

Ren's eyes burn with questions. *What did you see? Do you know what I did? What I am?*

I shrink from his touch, tripping over a nearby guard. Zenri is at my side, shooing the crowd away and keeping a protective stance should anyone approach. My heart pounds as I scan the curious crowd of titled lords and prying servants, all speculating about my condition. The silver thrones sit like empty shells beneath a hapless blue sky.

"Where's the king?" I whisper, tugging on Zenri's sleeve.

Zenri's eyes narrow in thought. The crowd reluctantly disperses thanks to the guards. Shrewd glances cast in my direction as the onlookers drift into the banquet hall and surrounding corridors. My eyes drift to the crown abandoned on the carpet.

Ren scoops it up and nestles it beneath an arm. He swallows hard and steps toward me. "Did you see the next person to sit on the throne?"

No. Only blood. The queen's long hair shredded on stone. And Ren. She loved him.

My heart thunders. He's not a monster anymore.

I force my eyes to meet his as if hoping I'll read a different past in his gaze. Why had the light led me down a path that ended in pain? Mother followed the path to her death to free her daughters—to save me. I hesitate, the path shimmering over my skin, waiting for me to call on it for answers. But I can't.

Spinning on my heels, I flee the throne room. I need air, open sky, and wind—freedom. Panting, I dash out the giant door and into the gardens, throwing myself against the nearest gas lamp overlooking the moat. The sun is nearly gone, a pool of melted yolk against a purple sky. A cool breeze licks at the sweat dripping from my neck, forcing a shiver.

Ren appears behind me, keeping his distance. "I need to know what you saw."

He holds out the crown, an involuntary tic in his jaw. But it's the tone in his voice that makes me pause—soft, regretful, resigned. "I need to know what you saw," he repeats gently. "If you saw what I think you did . . . then maybe you also saw why I *need* to stop it. I don't care what it makes you think of me. I just want to make sure it never happens again—to anyone."

He grips the crown loosely, like it burns to touch, like he wishes he could throw it away. "I know it's cruel to ask, after what you just saw, but . . . It's all here in my mother's crown. She spoke with Valcon. She might know how to stop him—and this curse—forever. Help me end this."

I recoil a step, the air between us suddenly chilled. He's offering for me to look into the pathways again, but I can't.

"I'm sorry." I shake my head and turn, hiding a choked sob. I'm not sure who I'm mourning more—her or him. My voice drops to a whisper. "I understand now why you hate *yajuu*. Why you couldn't spare Yuki. But you lied to me."

Ren rubs his jaw and looks away. "I never lied to you," he says in a weary voice. "I told you I'm a monster. You wanted to believe otherwise. I warned you. Pleaded with you."

"You knew I had to die. That Yuki would have to do the same . . . same thing you did. She'd never be able to live with herself afterward." *Like you.*

He had tried to warn me, but I didn't listen. I couldn't.

I lean across the moat railing, watching the last ray of sunlight skim across the water's surface. How does he live every day with that guilt? He'd been under a curse, without consciousness, but it didn't change what had happened. I turn to Ren, seeing him for the first time—a boy who just wants to live without fear and regret.

"Perhaps now you understand." He steps closer, his eyes cautious, pained. "There is no cure worth the cost. We can only get rid of the source and any so-called cures. I need you to find Valcon. If anyone knows the source, he does. I need you to see what the future holds. I need to stop this."

I glance down at the crown in his hands, just within reach. The path shimmers over my skin, promising answers. Would stopping Valcon end the *yajuu* curse? Or is this just about revenge? I fist my hands at my sides and step away toward the bridge.

"I'm not using the memory pathways again. Find your own path, Ren. I know what I have to do to save my sister now."

Ren flies to my side. "Kira, no—"

Shouts erupt from within the castle's main gate. No guards

line the entrance, and the couples meandering the gardens have vanished. Ren darts a look back at the castle, his body tensing. My eyes narrow as scenes and memories connect into a familiar path. The king wasn't at the scene when I awoke because someone else had arrived at the castle.

"You told Inspector Jade where Yuki was." I don't ask. The answer is written across his face. "In case I didn't keep my part of the bargain?"

"No." Ren shakes his head. "I didn't tell Inspector Jade. But he's followed you since the docks, and I didn't stop him either." He looks away. "If you failed to keep the bargain, I was going to turn your sister in. I can't live without keeping the law."

I scowl at him. "Why?"

"It's how I know I'm not a monster anymore." A hopeless shadow flits across his face.

"The law can't save you from being a monster," I say, softer than I mean to. "But maybe caring—compassion—could."

A sudden gust of wind and rain showers pink-red petals across my face, plastering them to my sweating skin. The path whispers in my ear, *Hurry. This way.*

An invisible string unravels, tugging me toward the castle.

"He's here." I turn on Ren in a blizzard of pent-up coldness. "Inspector Jade is here with my sister. I don't need your help anymore. Not when it's coming from a place of fear. You're so afraid of the monster you used to be that you've forgotten the prince you were made to be. Now leave me alone."

Ren doesn't try to stop me as I run back to the castle. The whispering path leads me to the throne room and into a narrow corridor. Voices drum from the far side of the castle facing the ocean port. I run down a maze of passages designed to keep out intruders, following the path as I go, and nearly slam into the last door. It slides open with a loud rattle.

Faces turn toward me as I lean in between the doorframe, panting. A vast banquet hall stretches open before me, built onto a veranda overlooking the sea. Guests turn to stare from long tables festooned with steaming plates, silver bowls, and tiered cakes. But their attention is reclaimed by a tall figure leaning against the balustrades.

Soran.

His back is to me as he squares off with a man in uniform, one with an iron face and ring-studded fingers. Guards flank the king, armed with pistols and swords, their armor catching in the lantern light. Guests cower around the furthest tables, clutching the backs of their chairs and buzzing rumors. The brave ones reach for their weapons, stances ready should a fight break out.

"You have no business here, Inspector Jade," Soran says, his voice glacial and carrying across the room with a thunderous crack. He's discarded his blue robe, revealing a black tunic, his broad shoulders more like a soldier's than I'd imagined. "Your magistrate has authority in the city but not within these walls."

"A shame I wasn't invited to the coronation," Jade says with a sneer. "Afraid I'd collect something precious?" He steps forward, tugging a hooded figure beside him.

My heart slams against my ribs. *Yuki.*

I melt into the crowd, edging along the wall. Yuki sways, hands hidden in her sleeves, hip bent at an awkward angle. Her feet are scratched and bare.

Jade jerks her forward like a stray dog. "Princess Yukiko wasn't lost," he says. "Her father sent her away to hide her from me. Because *you* had promised to give her to me and then went back on your word."

Whispers ripple through the room.

"You know the law, Soran," Jade says in a haughty tone. "The emperor can claim one of your kin on their first birthday and raise them as his own. You refused to give up your son, so you offered the princess instead. When Bastian found out, he smuggled the girl and her mother away. Did you think a prison was better than the emperor's palace?" His smile sharpens. "I'm relieved your kingdom finally knows the truth."

Soran doesn't deny it, and the guards shift uncomfortably.

"Leave." Soran's voice is still strong, calm, though I detect a slight tremor in his hand. "If the emperor wants my niece, he'll have to come in person. I'll gladly face him. Guards, remove this man."

The guards step forward, but Inspector Jade pulls back Yuki's hood and thrusts her in front of the crowd. "Here is your lost princess," he shouts in triumph. "A demon, just like her cousin. The whole family is cursed."

Yuki glares out from under tangled hair, a silver muzzle curved tight around her mouth. Her body jerks, guttural snarls reverberating from her throat—just like Ren in the memory pathways.

I slink to the closest table, urging Yuki to see me.

"*Demon*," the crowd mutters, "Monster. That's not Princess Yukiko! We saw her earlier at the coronation." Chairs scrape as several people make for the back door.

I notice a shadow in the background, the soft hum of path beneath my skin. Ren glides along the back wall, unnoticed, his eyes focused on the inspector.

"No one leaves!" Inspector Jade bellows. And then he points straight at me. "The girl you crowned today is an impostor. The princess's half sister, born and raised in prison, a common criminal. Not a drop of royal blood in her veins."

Gazes turn to me like a consuming fire—judgment, disgust, confusion. But I stare daggers at Inspector Jade. A man beside me scrambles over a chair to get out of the way. Soran draws a sword from one of his guards and steps forward.

"I consider myself a pacifist," he says, voice hard with resolve. "But no one comes after my family. I knew the girl wasn't my niece, but that doesn't make her any less family. She and her sister belong to the house of Ezo."

He lunges at the inspector, but Jade jerks Yuki in front of him as a shield. The king twists to avoid her, his momentum falters, and he staggers.

"What's become of the great Dragon King?" Jade sneers. "Love has weakened you."

"It's not a weakness to have a heart," Soran says, "or to give one away."

Ren is lucky to have such a father. Care emanates from him, a loyalty similar to how Mother watched over us in prison, a fierce determined love—stubborn, in the best way. He didn't need to stand up for me, but he did.

Whispers rush through the crowd. Guards come to the king's aid, and I spy Zenri among them. The king holds out a hand toward my sister, pain and regret etched onto his once sun-kissed face. "Forgive me, Yukiko. I'll find a way to get you back."

Yuki snarls in response, writhing beneath Jade's hold against her neck. Jade laughs. "The Emperor of Taiga still requires one guest from the king's household. Who will it be? Your long-lost niece or your son?"

The king's face burns with anger, his eyes searching for a way forward. He never expected both his son and his niece to turn into monsters. My heart breaks for him. Maybe Ren was right. We need to find Valcon to stop this curse from destroying any more lives. It's taken too many, too soon.

Ren strides to his father's side, throwing back his hood, a sword gripped in one hand. "Ezo doesn't negotiate with madmen," he says, his voice sharp.

Jade jerks Yuki's chain, kicking her in the back so that she stumbles to her knees. She snarls and chokes, her savage eyes glaring at Ren as if he'd caused her pain.

Soran lays a heavy hand on Ren's shoulder. "I won't make the mistake of choosing between two lives ever again," he says. "Jade, if you must return with someone, take me. My son will rule in my place. He has royal blood in his veins, not I. It comes from his mother's noble lineage."

Jade laughs. "An honorable sentiment, but old men make terrible hostages. I'd rather let the house of Silverwood tear itself apart as a punishment for hiding the princess for so long. I'll take whoever's left standing."

Jade unclasps Yuki's chain with a swift movement. The silver muzzle falls from her mouth, clattering to the floor. Yuki licks her pointed teeth and smiles. She crouches, her muscles tensing for attack, and her eyes narrowed slits. With one bound, she leaps up on the nearest table, sending dishes scuttling to the floor. Glass shatters against the walls, splashing plum-colored wine.

Jade draws his pistol as Ren dashes forward with his katana. The two miss each other by a breath of wind. Zenri jumps into the fray, leading the guards to help the crowd escape. But Yuki flies across the tabletops, reaching the door before them. A wide smile stretches across her pointed teeth, hungry eyes scouring the guests as if picking the juiciest one.

"Yuki!" I shout, pushing my way through the crowd. The metallic ring of swords clashes behind me. "Yuki, stop! This is not who you are!"

Images of the gentle queen with cerulean hair flood my mind. Her kind eyes and delicate touch as she prepared the cure, the determination lining her brow as she opened the cage and locked herself inside. Yuki lunges at Zenri. He thrusts two quick parries to her attack, but it nearly knocks him over. There's no time. But I don't have the potion.

Will the sacrifice work without it?

Zenri blocks another powerful swipe with his sword. But not the second one. A sickening crack sends him reeling backward, sword flying from his grasp.

Jade and Ren dance around each other, one trying to keep distance and the other to close the gap. I scour the tables for the green tea powder I'd seen in the pathways. Surely they served it here. It probably wasn't the same as in the vision, but I have to try. Swiping Ren's pin from my hair, the camellia tumbles into my palm. I grab the nearest tea bowl and mix the blossom inside it. A loud clatter sounds behind me, followed by a howl of pain. Yuki pins Zenri against the wall, sharp claws at his throat.

If I don't act now, more blood will spill.

"Give me strength," I whisper to the path.

I leap upon the table and pour the bowl over my head. Definitely not as graceful as the cerulean queen. But if it means saving my friends, saving the king whose heart had broken one too many times, and . . . Ren. Even if it doesn't work, I can buy them time.

"Yuki!" I shout, my voice wrenched with emotion.

She turns, her eyes widening for a brief moment. She slams her arm into the wall next to Zenri's head, breaking through the wood with a glimmer of silver—Sorachi's metal hands.

Blizzards, had Jade stolen them and given them to Yuki early—without the tonic?

Zenri slides down the wall with a groan. Yuki's eyes shift into moonlit slits. She holds up her metal hands, the fingers bending. She lunges at me.

I keep my eyes open. Every nerve in my body tenses, knees threatening to collapse before Yuki hits me. I imagine Mother's embrace, warm and affirming, her calm as she chose the path to save us. I found the cure to save Yuki. I kept my promise. Thick green sludge from the tea concoction drips down my face, tasting bitter as it hits my lips. It might not work, but I care too much about the lives around me to do nothing.

A shuddering crack splits the air as someone jumps in front of me. I teeter, collapsing with a hard shiver. My hand flies to my throat, expecting blood and teeth and snarls. Instead, the table quakes beneath me as Yuki slams into Ren.

A cry freezes in my throat.

He doesn't fight her, just stands like a shield, as Yuki's metal hand tears through his heart.

Ren thuds across the table. He faces the ceiling with unblinking eyes and a horrid gash plunging straight through his chest. I clutch at the tablecloth beneath me, the room tilting as my heart gives a painful lurch.

"Ren!" My cry is a visceral howl that scrapes against my skull. Words fly from my throat, but I can't hear them. I can't hear anything except the ragged breath coming from his lips.

Yuki jerks back, chest heaving as she inspects her metal hands. Her eyes meet mine, and she frowns, shaking her head as if doused with scalding water. She slinks off the table like a whipped dog—wincing, head shaking—and bolts toward the balcony overlooking the sea.

I'm too shocked to think. My knees sink beside Ren onto the broken dishes and spilled food staining the once white linens. Ren blinks, his eyes searching but not seeing.

"Ren," I whisper, leaning close to feel his breath upon my cheek. "Ren, what have you done? Why did you save me?"

His eyes dart, trying to find me. Then he gasps as if no breath can fill his lungs deep enough, and the air doesn't stay. It leaks into the chaotic, starless night.

I smooth the indigo strands from his pale, sweating brow. He had jumped in front of me and taken the blow to save me, to save Yuki. To save all of us. I wish I could take back my last words to him.

I wish we had all taken a different path than this one.

"You're not a monster," I whisper, leaning over him until our foreheads touch. "You were never a monster."

Scraping chairs, clattering swords, and throaty yells fill the air of the banquet, but I drown them all out. I should go after Yuki. I should check on Zenri and Soran. But my hands lock onto Ren's face, onto his chest that scarcely moves.

"Live," I breathe, daring the word to become a path. *"Live, Ren!"* I wad table napkins and press them to the gaping wound in his chest, blood—life—pouring over my fingers.

No, no, no . . .

Path listen to me, please! He needs to live!

"Help! Someone help!" I scream, my inability to save him swallowing me whole.

Soran rushes toward us, his eyes darting between his son and the girl who'd pretended to be his kin. A heart-wrenching cry escapes his throat as he folds himself over his son. I pull myself away from Ren with a monumental effort, forcing my eyes to survey the banquet hall.

The path shimmers over my skin, warning me that the battle isn't finished. I glance toward the open courtyard, searching for Yuki, but she's vanished. I have to find her now or I could lose her forever. Two figures disappear over the ocean balustrade.

Yuki and Inspector Jade.

CHAPTER 36

THE KING'S CRIES ECHO through the banquet hall, louder than the clatter of broken dishes and the hurry of frightened footsteps as the crowd flees. A shoulder jostles me, then another. I'm shoved backward by the tide of terrified guests. In the chaos, I glimpse a man stealing silver from the table before leaping over the fallen sliding doors. A lone woman remains at her seat, tears marring her powdered face and kohl-rimmed eyes, too afraid to run.

The king holds Ren's body, trying to stop the bleeding with his hands. His lips quaver, uttering nonsense between the tears. "Someone help! Get a doctor, someone!"

He sings between the crying, as if wishing his song could raise the dead. If only songs could heal. Why couldn't there be a dragon heart like that?

"Sorachi might be able to help," Zenri says, limping toward the table. "I'll send a message but . . ." His eyes trail from the red-soaked robe to Ren's rattling breath.

"Your Majesty." I lay a hand on the king's shoulder, at once feeling it isn't proper and that it's the most proper thing in the world. "The inspector has Yuki."

The king stiffens, his back to me as he stares at his son. I can't help but look at Ren's pale face. The caring breaks me. I swallow hard. It's more than caring.

"I spent my life trying to find her, to pay recompense," Soran mumbles, his eyes unfocused. "And I lost the son right before me. Now I've lost her too." His voice breaks, but he squares his shoulders, one hand still on Ren's motionless body.

"Yuki's not lost. Not yet," I say, cementing my gaze on the king, forcing myself to ignore the gaping hole that is Ren.

Is he . . . gone?

I force the thoughts aside, squaring the king with a determined gaze.

"Take the soldiers to the South Star," Soran says. "It leads to the harbor where the inspector docked his ships. Jade will try to take her to the Taigan capital as one of his hostages for the emperor." His voice is strong despite the tremor in his jaw. He slips a moon-shaped ring from his finger and hands it to me. "Show the guards this, and they will follow you."

I take the ring, too big for my own scrawny hand, and fist it tight. "Yes, Your Majesty. About Yuki, I'm sorr—"

"We've all made mistakes." Soran clasps my shoulder with a blood-stained hand. "I know why you remind me so clearly of your mother. You're a wayfinder too. Make a way to save my niece and this kingdom. True wayfinders make the impossible possible. Can you do that?"

My shoulders duck into a deep bow, the king's ring fisted in my palm. "I'll bring her back."

As I turn to leave, I snag a knife from one of the tables and tuck it into my boot. My eyes cut to Ren, lingering on a thin thread of hope. His body lies motionless across the dining table, a terrible gash in his chest, his eyes like vacant stars. I resist the urge to touch him, to see if he's still there.

The boy who'd done the unforgivable under a curse and never trusted himself. The boy who hated evil, pain, and death but couldn't see clearly that he'd purged those things from his heart. He'd repented a thousand times over. And he'd never know how his father mourned him, how he'd loved him but hadn't brought himself to say the words.

He was not a demon prince. He was a broken prince. And he'd burned more brightly than all of us. His last wick extinguishing for a single cause—love.

He had laid down the law, his kingdom, his own life—for me. He risked everything.

And I will too.

I dash from the banquet hall, my eyes burning from tears and my heart afire. I gather all the guards I can find, flashing the signet ring at them and beckoning them to the docks. Because I can't forge a path alone and that's okay.

Zenri joins me after summoning all the doctors in the kingdom, even though we both know no one can heal a shattered heart. But like a true leader, Zenri delegates duties with acute precision and defiant hope. With a group of eight guards at our command, we hurry to the South Star port.

I only hope we're not too late.

Moonlight replaces the day as Zenri leads the charge, positioning guards at the entrance to the port. I follow behind him with two guards, dispersing along the rocky coast that juts into the strait separating Ezo from Taiga. A black iron ship stains the bay with puffs of smoke and whirring engines.

"That's the one," Zenri pants, his back against a large pillar used to tie smaller vessels.

I join him, crouched against it, the sea spray whipping our faces. Fallen plum blossoms pelt the ground in a storm of color brought on by the fierce wind.

"Yuki and Jade are on board," I say, listening to the path that connects me to other living beings. "How much time before the ship pulls anchor?"

"Maybe fifteen minutes," Zenri says. "But they'll have a plan and reinforcements. The Imperial army isn't one to go against. Especially not with busted ribs." He cracks a grin, wincing at the pain in his side.

I tilt my head against the pillar, a headache churning. "There has to be a way."

"Over there!" Taigan soldiers yell from the iron ship, flinging a volley of bullets in our direction.

"There's too many of them!" Zenri signals for the guards to take cover and return fire. The king's guards crouch along the port, hidden behind other vessels, ramps, and crates. Our bullets pelt the iron ship, a few landing their mark, but eight men against an army doesn't seem like good odds.

"The king told me to find a way," I say.

"We can't win this match, Kira." Zenri holds his wounded ribs and squints at the ship from our hiding place. "Ren wouldn't want us to do anything foolish. We make a plan, and we strike back on the inspector's soil, in Taiga."

I spin toward Zenri, a new idea forming, and an excited chill creeps over my skin. "I know why Ren wanted to meet me in the caves. He's brilliant." I rocket to my feet, making a run for the caves on this side of the harbor.

Zenri curses under his breath and follows me at a run, dodging wayward bullets.

The guards cover our steps, and shouts ring from the ship. "They're retreating! Ezo scum."

I ignore it and keep running until I reach the dragon stables.

"Ren told me how to tame them." I say, rounding breathlessly as a bullet dents the rocks outside. "We have our army right here."

Zenri doubles over behind me, wincing as he holds his side. "Dragons? Are you mad?"

I lift a flower from one of the tincture bowls and step across the ramp for Tyri, the dragon gifted to Ren as a child, the one who had eaten from my hand and seen me with its master.

No, with his friend.

"You take the guards to the dock and prepare a loading ramp. I'm going to start a little distraction." I drop the flower into the dark water. It swirls counterclockwise, bubbles rising to the surface along with two large eyes armored in silver scales.

Imperial flags pop in the wind, the Taigan crest a black mark on our skies. My knees hug the dragon, and my hands grip fast onto his curved horns as we break the water's surface just beside the large iron ship. It's nothing like riding a horse, which bends and moves according to my wishes. The dragon seems to sense, intuitively, my end goal, and I'm along for the ride, holding fast to the most powerful beast on earth.

Path, where are you?

I calm my breath, quieting my mind and heart to listen. The dragon snorts water from its nostrils and slinks close to the ship. Its serpentine body is large enough to wrap around the hull and sink it, but the weight of this particular ship and its make—iron—might be too much for it.

As we near the ship, the dragon shudders beneath me. A path leaps to my fingertips, cascading images from the dragon's mind: a crown in golden scales, blood filling the sea, and the weight of agony. My eyes snap shut and the images end. I run my hand against the dragon's scales. It, too, has a grievance with the kingdom of Taiga.

On the port, the king's guards hunker against the wind, waiting for my order. But moving without the path would be foolish. I'd done that enough already and look where it led me. Cold waves chop against my ribs and chest as I listen, hunched over the dragon's neck.

Ren would've had a plan, known what to do. I shake away the image of him dancing with me at the ball, the way he kept his promises—bringing back my mother's coat even after I betrayed him, how quickly he stepped in to save me. *Ren. Live.*

A path opens before me, a vibrant blue ribbon of wind that dips into the dark sea and then wends through the ship like a perfect map. I lift a hand, touching the wind. It glows brighter than before, fueled by my hope. The dragon flicks its tail, motioning for Zenri to besiege the ship.

Shouts sound from the deck. The ship's hull creaks as it pulls from the dock, but Zenri and the Silverwood guards level a ramp against the bow. The guards fire volleys for cover as Zenri races across the wooden ramp. Two guards and Zenri make it across before the emperor's soldiers push the ramp into the sea.

"Now it's our turn, Tyri." I pat the dragon's smooth scales, each one plated like armor, the width of my hand.

He rises from the ocean, a strange rumble reverberating in his throat, and hoists me to the ship's railing. I swing myself overboard, wishing the dragon speed on his next task.

Blue light hums beneath my fingers, leading the way to Yuki. I hunch against the iron surface, careful to avoid being seen. Hopefully, Zenri's not drawing too much fire in his direction. Speed is my ally. I pick my way across the ship, dodging the Imperial soldiers and following the path into a narrow chamber below.

Everything is metal, from the clanking walkway to the rounded doors. We should've brought Sorachi. I feel the path flicker, straining to find its way in the maze of lifeless ore. Voices come from the left. A dank, cool voice followed by a clatter. I gulp. This is the part where I have no plan. Zenri was right. Perhaps I *am* running into a trap.

But I'm not alone. I grip the warm blue thread against my fingers and reach for the door.

It swings open, and I startle, throwing my back against the wall. I tuck behind the door and hold my breath.

"We'll stop the intruders, sir." A soldier marches out of the room, his boots clanking down the hall.

Seizing the opportunity, I slip into the room. The inspector stands alone in a small cabin, his face illuminated on one side by a round glass window. A broken cup lies in pieces on the floor, transparent rice ale pooling into the cracks along the tile.

Inspector Jade stares at me with barely concealed shock. He

scowls, anger and exasperation ticking at his pockmarked jaw. "You don't give up easy, do you? Guards!"

I shut the door behind me and lock it, never once taking my eyes off him.

"Where's my sister?"

"Can't find her? I thought you were a wayfinder," he sneers. "You would make a great addition for the emperor. And with your mother and the prince gone, no one will miss you. I, for one, think the world is better off without *any* of the ancient hearts."

I gulp, my hands tightening. The hole left by my mother and Ren wrenches open, threatening to swallow me. "I belong in Silverwood, and so does Yuki. Where is she?"

"You're welcome to look for her. But we'll be far out at sea before you find the monster. How sweet of Ren to die for her . . . or was it you he died for? I wondered if he had a soft spot for you at the ball."

A wicked smile slinks across the inspector's face, drinking in my pain. He paces the short room, one hand lingering on the pistol tucked into his belt. I'm keenly aware of my lack of weaponry—only the path at my fingertips and a kitchen knife tucked in my boot.

Flashes of my mother in the scorched prison cell flood my mind, the inspector at my heels, his cold words on my back.

"You're the monster," I say. "You have no compassion, no sense of true justice. I'm going to find my sister and sink this ship."

He laughs, tilting his head back, his beady eyes glinting with mirth. "How? Wayfinding won't save you here. It's all but dead, just like the Ainur. And soon, you."

I make a rush for his pistol, but he's faster. He jerks it from its holster and cocks it in one swift movement. I latch onto his arm, shoving my weight into him, which isn't much. He slams both our hands into the wall, face twisting in scorn.

"Get off me." He pounds his hand against the wall again, shoving me along with it.

But prison made me tough. I wrench my teeth into his forearm, and the gun clatters to the floor. I swipe it into my hands and aim at Inspector Jade's chest.

His hands fly up even as he steps backward. "Do it. Show me the criminal that's been inside you all along. Go ahead, prove I was right."

I will my hands not to shake. I've never fired a gun before. *I'm not a criminal. I'm not a prisoner. I'm not...* My eyes burn where I focus on the target, two stiff inches of uniform covering Inspector Jade's cruel heart.

Justice for Mother, for Beetle, for Yuki...

But if I fire the weapon, I'll be no different than him.

Jade's smile widens, sensing he's won. He begins to slowly lower his hands and steps toward me. "Guards!" he yells, louder this time, alerting the entire hall to my presence.

"I won't live as the emperor's hostage," I say, keeping my arms taut. My palms sweat against the pistol. "You won't hurt anyone ever again, Inspector."

I pull the trigger. The glass window shatters behind his head as he ducks down with a pathetic sob.

"You missed," he gasps, unable to believe his good luck. "A yard away, and you miss." His lips curl.

"I didn't miss." I let out a low whistle.

The ship creaks and groans. Metal bolts shoot from the riggings as a high-pitched whine issues from the sealed gaps keeping the iron plates together. The boat tilts, and I anchor my feet against it. "Go ahead. Look outside." I throw the pistol through the broken porthole and into the waves.

Inspector Jade runs to the window, jeweled fingers clutching the rim. "Dragons," he whispers, sinking against the metal. "No, it's not possible. They only listen to the king and the prince."

I shrug, stepping backward toward the door. "Apparently, dragons speak with wayfinders too."

I bolt for the door, unlocking it as water begins to pool inside the iron ship. Jade lunges for me, his jeweled hand grazing my arm.

"You'll never find your sister in time."

Zenri skids around the corner, sword in hand. Our eyes meet and I motion to the door. Jade grabs at me again, but together Zenri and I shove him back and force the door closed.

"It won't lock," I shout, my back pushed against the door.

Zenri nods and wedges his sword into the handle, locking it from without. Jade pounds against the door, swearing at the small window, his face distorted in rage.

"You'll die for this, wayfinder! The emperor will come for you after the chaos you've caused. And you'll never find your sister—"

I turn away from the door and Jade's powerless threats.

"Did you find her?" Zenri pants, grimacing at the water lapping his ankles.

"Not yet," I say.

The ship groans with a deep rattle and shifts beneath my footing. Perhaps I should've found Yuki first, but the blue path tugs at my fingers. I know where she is. I slog through the water and reach the last door just as the water seeps to my calves.

"Yuki," I gasp.

My sister curls against the porthole on a metal cot. Her keen brown eyes turn to me, brimming with tears. She reaches out with open arms, metal fingers beckoning me to come. I sweep into the room and dive into her embrace. Yuki sobs against my neck, her body shaking and shoulders cracking again. I never thought I'd miss that sound.

I pull back for a moment, my hand cupping her cheek, damp with hot tears and sticky flyaways. The smile that breaks on her face is soft, her teeth smooth pebbles—no more fangs.

"You're alive," I say, scarcely believing it. "The curse is gone. But how?"

"Ren," she whispers, wiping her cheeks with her arm. "After

I . . . the curse . . . attacked Ren, I started changing. The pain was so horrible. But I-I can think again, Kira. And then the inspector brought me here. Is he . . . ? Is Ren okay? I didn't mean to—"

Yuki's breath comes in short, tearful waves. I kiss her forehead, thinking of Ren's sacrifice. Whatever he'd done, he paid the price to free her. *He cured her somehow.* But she couldn't know, not now.

"We have to go," I say. Cold water slaps at my knees and Zenri grunts in agreement behind me. "The ship is sinking. Can you walk?"

"Don't treat me like an invalid." Yuki sniffles and smiles through the tears. "I can do better than walk, darling."

"Good," Zenri cuts in, "because we need to run."

The entire ship groans with a violent shudder. Metal bolts zing from the floor and walls as the water rises, then tilts with the ship. Zenri pushes through and scoops Yuki up in his arms.

"I can walk," she protests but tightens her hold against his neck, cheeks flushing. Maybe my sister will get her knight in shining armor after all.

"This way!" I yell, focusing on the blue hum of path that leads to the outside.

Slogging through the water and tilting our bodies with the now angled floor, we take the stairs up. Zenri goes first, gritting his teeth as the water slams at his waist. I follow behind in case he falls, anchoring myself with the stair rail.

Early moonlight cuts across the bow of the black ship. Even a dim light seems bright in the darkness. Imperial soldiers dot the upper deck, looking over into the churning sea, judging when they should jump.

Zenri sets Yuki down as the ship shudders again. She leans against him for balance, her eyes red-rimmed as she stares at Silverwood Castle. White walls stand tall above the ocean caves and southern docks, untouched by the battle raging around it. Is she thinking the same thing as me?

Ren—is he still on the banquet table? Did they find a doctor to save him? Or . . .

I take Yuki's metal hand in mine, squeezing tight. My eyes turn to the sea and a path of silver scales cutting across the water. *Tyri.* In moments, we'll be on the back of the powerful sea dragon and sailing to the castle where answers—however good or bad—await. I'll send boats back for the Imperial soldiers. They won't drown on my watch.

Caring—that's what makes the path worth following. It's what Ren chose, in the end.

Yuki touches my face, and I startle against the coldness of her metal fingers. Her sharp brown eyes narrow gently as if trying to draw something out of me. "You did it, Kira. Mama would be so proud. We're free at last."

Free. Not just in location, without chains or walls, but in mind and heart.

I grip Yuki tight, supporting her as she stands.

"You're right," I say, feeling all at once like that girl from Abashi island and yet profoundly different. Stronger. Like a fire was planted inside me and the fear and pain can no longer trap me. "The whole world longs to be free, every inch of it, and we found it, Yuki. We chose our path. That's our freedom. Choosing this."

I hug my sister, willing the earth to never part us again. But even if it does, I know that I'll always find a way.

CHAPTER 37

REN
Three months later

SHADOWS STILL CLING

to Ren's vision. He leans against the propped-up pillow in his old bed, in a room he's not touched in . . . Seven. Long. Years.

Bandages squeeze tight against his ribs and shoulders. Stiff, insufferable, scratchy. He wriggles in the harsh white wrappings and stifles a seething groan when the pain hits.

"Good, you're awake." The palace doctor leans over him, a familiar face from the lucid moments between sleep and pain.

"Your bones have healed, but you need to take it easy for another month," he says. "There's no telling how much of the regenerative effects of the, umm, curse, are still at work. You were quite fortunate, my prince."

"A month?" Ren gags on the words in disbelief.

"The wayfinder said you'd be difficult," the doctor huffs.

Kira. Ren pushes himself to sit upright, his ribs protesting like hot splinters in his chest.

A slender girl enters from the back of the room with sharp brown eyes and long hair pulled into a thick braid over her shoulder. She hands the doctor a heavy bag stuffed to the brim with wrappings and mechanical tools. Silver glistens as her fingers release the handle.

Yuki. So *this* is his cousin? She has the sharp, defiant chin of the Silverwood family and Uncle Bastian's eyes—the same eyes that had trained him as a Shadow. And the hands responsible for his almost dying.

A flustered blush rises to Yuki's cheeks, and she flicks her long sleeves over the metal hands. She gives the doctor a gentle nod. "Thank you. My cousin is most grateful for your attention."

The doctor bows and strides out the open door manned by two guards.

Ren reaches for a shirt on the bedside table. It probably won't fit over this cotton prison. *A month.* Doctor's orders are nothing but suggestions.

Yuki rounds on him, her metal fingers carefully covered beneath her sleeves. "I'm glad you're finally awake. Sorry about . . . your heart."

The words lack feeling, but her eyes are kind.

"The doctor says the remaining effects of the *yajuu* cure in your body saved you. That, and Sorachi made a metal piece to fix what didn't regenerate. It doesn't all come back." Her eyes drop to her concealed hands. "Even so, it's a miracle you're still alive."

Ren's jaw clenches. He remembers fragments: the pain, flashes of light and shadow, the acrid stench, mumbled words breaking into brief lucid moments. That word—*live*—that grabbed him like a thread refusing to break. Had Kira used her words to speak life? Had a path saved him?

Ren breathes deep, his ribs punishing him again. An unfamiliar fear scratches at his mind.

Where is Kira?

He turns to his cousin. "Why are *you* cured?"

Yuki cocks her head. "You don't know?"

"I wouldn't ask if I did."

Yuki steps up to the window and adjusts the curtains, letting in more sunlight. "The cure flows in your veins, Ren. When you sacrificed yourself, with the cure still inside you, I was healed. I'm forever grateful."

"It wasn't for you." Ren's eyes snap to the ceiling, hiding his relief: *Kira is alive.*

Yuki smiles. "I know. But I hope we can become friends."

Ren laughs and immediately regrets it. Pain rips across his chest and forces him to double over. Yuki startles, but he holds out a hand to stop her from helping. She doesn't listen and rearranges the pillows behind him.

"I'll think about it." Ren eyes the wispy girl with indestructible metal hands. Then he straightens and smooths his face to a detached mask, the one he used as a captain. "Where's the wayfinder?"

Yuki pulls up a chair by the window and sinks into it. "She's in a meeting with Soran about the ancient hearts. We might have a chance against Taiga if we recruit whoever's left of the ancient masters to our cause. The emperor's preparing for war. It won't be long now. Kira looked into the crown again—at the memory pathways."

Her mouth sets into a firm line, unreadable.

"Tell me what she saw instead of making me ask." Ren gives Yuki a pointed look. One that she meets head on.

"Why don't *you* ask her?"

Ren looks out the window, his jaw tightening. Kira was part of the job, a valuable asset to the kingdom. Of course, now that she saved the princess, he was going to have to see her. And with bruised ribs and a broken heart—quite literally—the Shadows won't accept him back yet. He and the girl would have to work together, but he hadn't prepared for a future where they both . . . lived.

"Send Zenri in here," he commands, willing his voice to appear polite. A rattling cough follows, but he bites it back. It's insufferable being unable to move at will. "Zenri!" he bellows when Yuki doesn't leave to fetch him. "I'm starving. Where is he?"

A thin girl made of sharp corners, skin like a wild chestnut, and gray-blue eyes steps from the nightingale hall outside the door. No sound preceded her, defeating the purpose of a hallway designed to chirp when intruders walk across it. The guards cast her a glance, respect bowing their features as they allow her to enter.

Ren's faulty heart speeds up as she steps into the room. Kira rests one hand on her hip, the other holding a heavy silk napkin.

"You should treat Zenri with respect," she says, her mouth quirked in a half-smile. "He's taken your place as Shadow Captain. Doing a better job of it too."

Ren smiles at the jab. Zenri would readily hand the title over as soon as he recovered; it doesn't worry him. But somehow, this girl does.

The last time he saw her was at the banquet hall. The day he stepped in front of a monster without a second thought. Because it was right. Because the pain didn't matter. Because it meant that she would live.

Had she visited him while he recovered? Or had only family been allowed?

Ren sits a little straighter, wrapping the shadows around him for protection. His treacherous heart beats a little too fast as the girl strides into the room.

"Mochi." She thrusts the snack bag toward his face and then smiles.

He never thought of himself as lucky until now. To wake up to something so beautiful.

"You should say 'thank you.' " Kira plunks the array of mochi onto the bedside table. "But I owe you those words too."

Ren shifts his gaze from the girl to the carefully wrapped package and back again. A low, mechanical click breaks the silence. Once. Twice. Ren clenches his jaw as the rattle in his chest finishes its cycle, reminding everyone that he's no longer made of blood and bone—but also steel.

Kira's eyes widen, but to her credit, she doesn't back away.

What's running through her mind? Does she still see him as a monster, a prince, or . . . He shoves the thought away. Kira had seen everything in the memory pathways and again when her own sister nearly killed him. Those images, memories, they cement with time, not lessen.

Kira's clever eyes find his, searching, but for what?

He clears his throat. "Thank you."

"For the mochi or sinking the *Iron Clad*?" she quips.

She sunk the Iron Clad?

He shakes his head. "With Tyri's help no doubt. And I believe you owe me for taking Tyri out of the stables without my permission."

"You were dead," she snaps back, both hands on her hips.

He leans forward with a wince and studies her. Letting those words sink in with all their strangeness. *You were dead.* But now alive. A second chance, or maybe this is a third. It's impossible to reconcile these wants that he doesn't deserve—to be a Shadow again. To protect his homeland. To know this girl . . . to have a friend.

Ren slides from the bed, forcing himself to stand as pain lances his ribs. He sucks in air, examining the far double-door leading into the hallway. The guards step forward and Yuki jumps from her chair.

"Are you trying to kill yourself?" Yuki reaches out, offering a hand.

Ren staggers and braces himself against the nearest windowpane. The doctor said take it easy; walking *should* be easy. Short breaths scrape his lungs.

"Let him be," Kira says, moving to his side, the mochi forgotten. "Where do you want to go?"

"I have something for you."

She raises a brow. "How is that possible? You've been asleep for months."

"I'm calculated. This was done before the ball," he says, smiling and holding out an arm.

Kira rolls her eyes and loops his arm over her shoulders to help him walk.

Yuki glances between them and then snatches the bag of mochi. She rifles through it, helping herself.

"Over there." Ren motions to a long cedar chest at the end of the bed.

"Yes, my prince." Kira nods in a subtle bow, her words light, friendly even.

"Prince?" His steps fall in pace with hers. "You're not that scrappy girl I found in the Winterwilds. What've you done with her?"

"Scrappy? That's probably the nicest thing you've ever said to me." Kira waits for him to shift his weight and then gently shrugs him off her shoulder.

"I thought a wayfinder was supposed to be truthful," Ren says, leaning against the chest for support.

Kira looks up. "I *am* being truthful. You've called me a criminal, dirty, and ignorant—but never scrappy."

Ren's blood grows hot as their gazes lock. His eyes betray him, shifting to a brighter blue. She stands a mere arm's reach away, the dark sweep of her hair, the reckless light in her eyes . . . His hands go sweaty against the cedar chest even as his heart sinks. Had he been so cruel? She deserved none of those words. More synonymous choices lodge in his throat: *brave, caring, beautiful.*

Ren waves a hand, signaling for the guards to leave, and opens the chest. He lifts a long box neatly tied with a colorful blue ribbon and pushes the package into Kira's hands before sinking onto the edge of the bed in exhaustion.

"What is it?" Kira hesitates, her thin fingers wavering over the lid.

"A gift from the Demon Prince of Ezo."

She raises a brow and unties the package. Gasping, her hands fly to the smooth handwoven fabric embroidered with stars and swirls. "My mother's elmwood coat. But it was in tatters. How did you . . . ?"

She leans over and seizes his hand, covering the calluses and scars with warmth. The mechanical chamber in his heart whirrs. Ren stiffens, resisting the urge to return the gesture, to hold her hands—to keep them safe.

To keep her safe.

Shadows never lose their hearts. To do so forfeits them from service. The route Bastian had chosen when he married Kira's mother. Something Ren will never do.

"You can stay here, in Silverwood," he says, his voice distant. "The old house on the bluff that Todoroki manages is your mother's and by default, yours, if you want it. My father will rectify the wrongs of the last decade. Pardon the prisoners employed on the emperor's railroad, all of it. We'd spoken of it before I agreed to come back for the coronation, and my father is loyal to his word."

"I saw the memory pathways, Ren." Her voice is firm and gritty and perfect. "I can't stay."

"You say it like you don't have a choice." Ren straightens, ribs cursing him. "Build your home in Silverwood, while you can."

Her hand slips from his, the warm blue hum he'd sensed from her evaporating. "My path isn't one of comfort," she says. "Not yet. What I saw . . . Ren, if we don't take this to the emperor's shores first, there won't be a Silverwood. My mother's home will be ashes. And Valcon—you were right. He is the key to stopping this. He knows how the *yajuu* curse started. Soran's asked me to go to Taiga and find the other masters of the ancient hearts to help us. Together we can find a way to stop the curse and the war."

"Kira." Ren takes a deep breath, exasperation getting the better of him. *When will she stop chasing the impossible?* "You've never been to Taiga or fought in battle. We have soldiers for that."

"I saw a path," she says, a sad crease on her brow. "We have a chance to save Ezo. But it's so fragile. A thousand things could change it, from a fleeting feeling to a wasted second, but just chasing the right thing is worth it."

She smiles as if to reassure him. "There's nothing too broken that it can't be fixed. And that goes for empires and curses and hearts too. You showed me that."

"You sound like a monk in the foothills of Thesia," he says. "Finding the masters of the ancient hearts won't be easy. You'll need help. It's dangerous."

"The only danger is in not acting." She wags her brows. "How was that for a monkish quote?"

Ren winces from the laughter that sears his ribs. "At least wait until I can go with you."

"There's not enough time." Her gaze softens before she turns to Yuki. "When does the festival begin tonight?"

"The Electric Tide?" Yuki chimes in between mouthfuls of sticky-sweet mochi.

Kira nods. "I'd hoped to see it before I leave."

"Let's go together," Yuki says. She picks at a piece of mochi in one of the metal grooves of her fingers. "Ren can use that wheel-cart Sorachi made."

Ren's gaze shifts to a dark shade of blue. Yuki shrugs and takes another bite.

"Or you two go, and I'll catch up later. I've got to find Sorachi and get these joints greased." She waves a metal hand and winks at Kira.

Ren glares after his cousin as she leaves the room.

"Don't mind Yuki," Kira laughs. "She likes teasing and likes having a cousin even more."

"I liked being the only child in the family."

Kira swings on the elmwood coat. Her eyes flutter shut, taking in the familiar threads as she pulls the fabric tight. She extends a hand to him. "Come on, I'll help you to the balcony."

Ren loops an arm around her neck as she pulls him up. They step out onto the balcony, hobbling to the very edge for a view of the harbor and the dragon stables.

Fireworks erupt in the distance like stars in battle. Kira lowers him onto an empty chair, her smooth hair falling across his cheek. His arm twinges in pain where it wraps around her neck, but he doesn't say a word. Ribs be cursed. He'd endure it for this.

"Thank you," he says, his voice like gravel. He stares at the darkening sky, smoothing over his emotions. "When do you leave?"

She pulls a chair up, crossing her arms over the balcony railing with a sigh. Her chin nestles into the soft spot below her wrist. "Tonight, after the festival. I wanted to see you before I go."

His heart gives an annoying mechanical whir, like he'd hiked Mt. Atan and not hobbled ten paces to the balcony. He studies the small girl who'd lived her entire life on a block of ice, save for the few short months he'd known her. Their gazes meet.

"Keep my mother's home safe," she says. "And be nice to Yuki. She's not as tough as she thinks."

"I'm not a caretaker," he says. "Todoroki will do that."

"I don't know what you are." Kira turns her head so that she's facing him, her brow pinched in thought.

He swallows hard, resisting the urge to reach up and smooth the crease from her face.

"You saved my life, Ren. Because of you, I have a home, a family again," she says.

He turns, shifting his gaze to ocean waves speckled with electric blue froth. Small, glowing creatures dance in the dark water. "Not everyone needs to see a path to know the right one," he says.

Kira purses her lips and stands to leave. "I hope you keep leaning into those instincts of yours. They were right."

Protests rise to his throat, but he bites them back. She's too inexperienced. Taiga is full of wild animals, Moebi warriors, and the emperor's spies. But he won't warn her. She doesn't need more caution. She'd spent her whole life in a prison and now has an opportunity to explore the world, to serve the king, and stop a war. It'd be wrong to take that from her.

"Take Tyri." His voice comes out gruffer than anticipated. "He'll keep you safe, and you'll travel twice as fast."

"Ren." She steps in front of him, forcing his gaze up. "If I take Tyri, I'll have to bring him back. Are you worried I won't return?"

Admitting worry feels like admitting weakness, that he cares. "I paid dearly to keep you alive—so you could stay alive—not throw it away," he says, willing the cold words to hide his concern.

Kira's face softens. She takes his hand, threading her fingers through his. He forces himself to stand, though his ribs ache and he staggers. Kira nearly tumbles over as she catches him, her hands clutching at his shirt where the mechanical heart struggles to keep up. She straightens her arms for distance, but her warm hands remain, anchoring them.

"Be safe," he says, hating it when her hands finally pull away.

"I can't guarantee that it'll be safe." Kira's eyes search his as if she'd seen something he hadn't. A path? A future? "But I can promise that it'll be worth it. And Ren . . ." She bites her lip, debating on her next words. "Don't follow me to Taiga."

"Is this because of the memory pathways?"

Her eyes flash as she pulls her elmwood robe around her shoulders. "Just trust me."

He'd asked the same thing of her once. His head tilts in confusion.

"Ren, caring isn't a poison. It's a cure. But I don't want to see you die again." Kira turns away, and he wonders if it's more than the path she's hiding. If the cure isn't simply compassion, but . . . something deeper.

Kira strides toward the door without a goodbye, her hurried footsteps drumming in his ears.

"Wait." He hobbles after her before she reaches the door. He braces himself against the wall, ribs blazing in agony. "I watched you die that day too. I was afraid. But I think I've found the antidote to fear. I'm not afraid to make my own path."

She holds her breath, pink frosting her cheeks. "And what path is that, Ren?"

"The one where I find you." He leans in, wincing from the pain in his chest.

Kira meets him halfway, slipping under his arm with a hug that's at once careful and warm. "I'm right here, Ren. Don't go to Taiga, please."

Don't follow her and keep her safe when she's walking into a war zone? She might as well have asked him to die again. The mechanical valve in his heart whirs, reminding him that he's not the warrior he used to be. Not as whole. Not as heartless.

When he looks down at the brave girl in the elmwood coat, a disturbing truth settles over him: He'd die for her all over again—against his better judgment and against the rules.

Not only would he die for her.

He'd live for her.

And for the hope of a better world. Together.

THE END

THANK YOU FOR READING

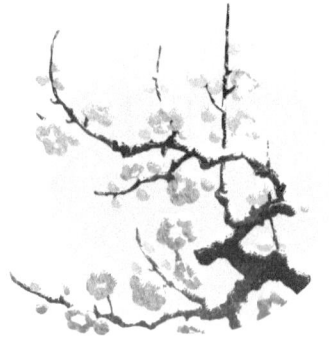

Dear Reader, if you enjoyed this story may I ask you to leave a rating or review on Goodreads or Amazon, or your review platform of choice? As an independent author, this means the world to me. Thank you!

Ellen

If you enjoyed **THE LAST WAYFINDER**, try the first interconnected standalone in the Hearts of Ezo Series:

SAINTS & MONSTERS

A YA fantasy perfect for fans of **SIX CRIMSON CRANES** and **HOWLS MOVING CASTLE**. An autoimmune-compromised princess must claim a powerful sea dragon's magic heart at the risk of being devoured by the shapeshifter and losing her kingdom.

HISTORICAL NOTES

While strictly a fantasy novel, *The Last Wayfinder* pulls inspiration from historical and cultural elements of Japan. The world is largely a fantastical reimagining of the Meiji Restoration (1868-1912).

I've always loved this time period as it's imprinted deeply on my city from the street names to the historic buildings repurposed as shopping malls and museums. That Japan is more than green tea and samurai goes without saying, but this rich time period helps illustrate the beautiful fusion of culture and creativity that Japan is famous for today.

When I first started this story, I was in Hokkaido and found myself fascinated by the Boshin War, Abashiri Prison, the Prisoners Road (which is now a highway), and the accounts of chilling attacks by Ussuri brown bears in the early 1900s. I wove small details into Wayfinder, like the use of butter and cookies made popular by the nuns at the first monastery in Hakodate, the ironclad ship, even the advent of the circus.

In previous books, I tried not to use many Japanese words to avoid confusion, but several readers have requested them, so you'll find:

- shuriken (throwing star)
- yajuu (beast)
- genkan (entryway)
- haori (outer kimono jacket)
- futon (floor mattress)
- ban (sound effect for gun)

I also wanted to emphasize seasons throughout the Hearts of Ezo Series, so I needed a winter flower. The camellia, or *tsubaki,* blooms in the depth of winter and has rich symbolism for both healing and hardship. The entire flower falls instead of the petals. It was used to show grace in adversity, perseverance, and as a symbol for the persecuted church. It's also a common ingredient in many beauty and medicinal products.

ACKNOWLEDGMENTS

Dear Reader, you are a wayfinder. We all are. Life is full of impossible paths, dark forests, and hungry bears, but there is always a way forward.

This story came about when facing my own bears. I couldn't find a way. But with the help of family, friends, and faith, I discovered that we can all be waymakers. I wanted to write a story about hope closer than stars and stronger than ice. Hope with action.

Thank you to those who believed in me, who held the light when I was lost, and who told me to finish this book. So grateful for you all!

To Nova McBee, for your friendship and for demanding more of Ren's story.

To Megan Gerig, for your support and enthusiasm.

To Victoria McCombs, for fun brainstorming sessions.

To Melissa Poett, Caitlin Miller, Laura Frances, and Candace Kade, for reading all those early drafts and cheering me on!

To beta readers, Bekah Stegner, Constance Lopez, Amanda Auler, and Moriah Chavis for all your feedback and support.

To the Reader, for taking a chance on this story.

To the incredible artists who made this book even better, Sonia for her exceptional case laminate art and chibi design, and Jamie Foley for her typesetting wizardry.

Huge thanks to my biggest supporters, my husband and my three boys. And last: I thank Jesus Christ for being my hope above all.

And my heartfelt thanks to ALL the Kickstarter backers who helped bring this story to life! Thank you for supporting this creative endeavor and truly giving life to this book. The Last Wayfinder was my first Kickstarter and your excitement and support meant the world. Thank you! ありがとうございます！

Gabrielle Landi, Mandee N., Josiah DeGraaf, K Hendrick, Liza Clarke, MadiJoy, Eric Gossett, Louise Rigali, Kinuruin, Chelsea, Michelle Noel Terrebonne, MacKenzie Moore, Anna Vranopoulou, Elisabeth Brown, Angela Morse, Victoria McCombs, Laura Frances, C. F. E. Black, Kimberly Dunham, Melisse, Samantha Rae Ortiz, Larissa Green, Charlotte Hickman, Helena Š. George, April Choate, Merrie Destefano, Anne Elizabeth, Ashton Reynwood, Hannah Rissler, Catherine Roberts, Nicole Wright, Allie Woodland, Suz Rodgers, R. Dugan, David K. Leighton, Autumn Jackson, Rachel Bellerose, Morgan Stawski, Anne J. Hill, Kelsey Christofis, Tara Lundmark, Sadie Fivas, Annarose Willhite, Amanda Auler, LJF, Z.R. McCormick, Kristin Morgan, Samantha Mendell, @becksreadingbooks, AP Snell, Victoria P, Cortney Babcock, Kristy Brendle, Ana Lewis, Dorothy Jennings Tecumseh, NanashiNova, Jules Dyrud, Jessi, Kysa, Karyne Norton, Larisa I., Jes Drew, Sheldon Albertson, Sara Ulibarri, Megan Gerig, Jessica A. Tanner, William Michael, Rebecca J. Thompson, Ronie Kendig, Tabitha Orr, Moriah, Faith Drake, EL, Lena, AndieRae, Gianna Christopher, M, Hannah Rose, Stephanie Price, Malin, Ash D., Tarri L. Williams, Cooper, Erin Davis, Kelsie Carlson, The galleon guy, Kithara, Tirzah Rae, Mason Arron Rogers, Katelyn Fowler, Giselle, Naomi Sowell, Victoria Clemm, Emily G, Jack, Rachel F., Trisha Sparrow, Heather Clark, Marley Hammond, Connie Hendryx, Jebraun Clifford, Richard Grosschedl, Natalie Jolin, Cathryn deVries, Christina Medina, Stephanie & Kacie Hill, Pamela Hart, Ian Ashworth, Nirkatze, Taska Jukes, Lindsay Phillips, Polinchka, Moni, Franchesca Caram, Navith Segaram, Catherine Holmes, Celeste, Jessica Meuth, Liz Hutchings,

Anthony Son, R.J. Setser, Isabel L., Carrie O'Rourke, Sunny Ryan, Caitlin Eha, Gabi Tesauro, Kristen Schleif, Whitney H., Adriana Loughridge, Holly Coffell, Brittany Mack, Kyla Stone, Merie Shen, Abigail Hawthorne, Alex Harlequin, Halee, Rebekah Doose, Beka G., Clarissa Kelso, Jon Hopkins Jr., Emma Shirley, Kayla Bouren, Eris, Christopher D. Shramko, Jane Maree, Rachel Ann Michael Harris, Zek, Ariel G. Wach, Morgan G., Amanda Balter, Julia Libby, Rachel, Lloyd Tong, Alexa Muntean, Chelsea Rogers, Isabel Schumann, Josie Pozo, Tiara Song, Vicki Hsu, Joseph Leskey, Lauren Thurston, H. Shupe, Casey Custer, Ethan P., Jared Guinn, Angie O'Reilly, Ryan Alford, Ana Kennedy, Kayla Banyas, Daniel Ayala, Axel KNG, Gloria Gardenia, Irene, Brooke J. Katz, Rachel J, Kel Peterson, Katherine Malloy, Sarah Z, Rose Hales, Ven, Shanon M. Brown, Samantha Keil, Carol MacLennan-Gonzales, Alexandra Corrsin, E. Leet, Kati, Madelyn S., Kristin Flanagan, Claire, Bekah Stegner, Stefanie Chu, Florentina, Matthew Phillips, Kim, Mireya, Kelly S. Castañeda Corona, Jessica Manuel, Ashley Galliano, R.S. Kellogg, Tyrean Martinson, Anna Beth Harrison, Ryan F, Meagan Masik, Ashley, Lindsay F., Rosa Thill, Alexandra, Patty Mooney, Lexie C., Katie Briggs, Casey Loehrke, Meghan Dzurichko, Marissa Childs, Amber, Ariane Beauparlant, Abigail B., Ashley Tsuji, Amy Trent, Christina Baehr, Ashley, Lisa Stoneburner, Bridget Duros, Nicki Chapelway, Devon Hood, Mike Dubost, CharityDL, Cyann Ava, Emerald Bruce, M-H Ayotte, Ron Wood Jr, Emily S., Jen H., Anna Crockett, Nathsan-san Sky, Ashley Bustamante, Ready, Kamryn Rackley, Sarah Nightingale, Joshua Gerdes, HC, Aisha Froese, AuroraTheDragon174, Jeanna Mason Stay, Marybeth Davis, Makani Mason, Angela Kern, Vanessa W., Olivia Perkins, Emmah Gill, Amber Smagge, Risa, Hanna Dalgety, Karen Ferrario, Jada Hernandez, Timothy C. Linusson, K.Q. Kimler, Rachel Strehlow, Lena, Moriah Kramer, Eileen-Marie, Rebecca P, Mya Peterson, Milly Peterson, Theresa Nicole Ortiz, Haven Woody, Anna, Anna Doro, Karli Klemm, Katherine G.,

Stas Szumowski, Anna Mykkeltvedt, Chance Hightower, Lorien Cord, Amsel, Celia Hartmann, Abagail, Justin W. Brannon, Susan Laspe, Faye Quinn, J.L. Hendricks, Tetiana Kocherhan, Melissa J Massey, Ashley Vinson, Prescila Ares, Natalie Claire, Rebecca P. Minor, Carrie Loofbourrow, Tracy Lee, Lauren E. Hughes, Kyle Luke, Nick, Olivia Winslow, Judy Liu, Ivo Ziskra, Phoenix, Elaina J, Liz Kiley, Hope Jian, Alivia Johnson, Elise, Jaime Gross, Ticia Messing, Leah Marie, Juliet Elizze, Natasha Hill, Zachary Zayas, Rackabone, Sarolta, KSEE, Matthew Kitajo, MAE, Lou Sanchez, Craig Zecca, Robert Torbitt, Manu, Denisse, Liana, Kendra, Janine B, Jens Helvig Dahl

ABOUT THE AUTHOR

ELLEN MCGINTY is an author and editor of Young Adult fantasy and historical fiction. She lives in the Tokyo metropolis with her husband, three boys, and a hypoallergenic cat. When not writing or editing, you can find her exploring the wilds of Japan with an abundance of espresso and the occasional kimono.

For more books, updates, & giveaways join the newsletter:
https://ellenmcginty.substack.com

www.ingramcontent.com/pod-product-compliance
Lightning Source LLC
LaVergne TN
LVHW041645070526
838199LV00053B/3565